AT MIDNIGHT

ALSO EDITED BY

DAHLIA ADLER

That Way Madness Lies:
Fifteen of Shakespeare's Most Notable Works Reimagined

His Hideous Heart:
Thirteen of Edgar Allan Poe's Most Unsettling Tales Reimagined

AT MIDNIGHT

Fifteen
Beloved Fairy Tales Reimagined

EDITED BY

DAHLIA ADLER

FLATIRON
BOOKS
NEW YORK

AT MIDNIGHT. Copyright © 2022 by Dahlia Adler. All rights reserved. Printed in the United States of America. For information, address Flatiron Books, 120 Broadway, New York, NY 10271.

"Sugarplum" © 2022 by Anna-Marie McLemore. "In the Forests of the Night" © 2022 by Gita Trelease. "Say My Name" © 2022 by Dahlia Adler. "Fire and Rhinestone" © 2022 by Stacey Lee. "Mother's Mirror" © 2022 by H. E. Edgmon. "Sharp as Any Thorn" © 2022 by Rory Power. "Coyote in High-Top Sneakers" © 2022 by Darcie Little Badger. "The Sister Switch" © 2022 by Melissa Albert. "Once Bitten, Twice Shy" © 2022 by Hafsah Faizal. "A Flame So Bright" © 2022 by Malinda Lo. "The Emperor and the Eversong" © 2022 by Tracy Deonn. "HEA" © 2022 by Alex London. "The Littlest Mermaid" © 2022 by Meredith Russo. "Just a Little Bite" © 2022 by Roselle Lim. "A Story About a Girl" © 2022 by Rebecca Podos.

www.flatironbooks.com

Designed by Devan Norman

Library of Congress Cataloging-in-Publication Data

Names: Adler, Dahlia, editor.
Title: At midnight : fifteen beloved fairy tales reimagined / edited by Dahlia Adler.
Description: First edition. | New York : Flatiron Books, 2022. | Audience: Ages 12-18.
Identifiers: LCCN 2022013356 | ISBN 9781250806024 (hardcover) | ISBN 9781250806031 (ebook)
Subjects: CYAC: Fairy tales. | LCGFT: Fairy tales.
Classification: LCC PZ8 .A92236 2022 | DDC [Fic]–dc23
LC record available at https://lccn.loc.gov/2022013356

Our books may be purchased in bulk for promotional, educational, or business use. Please contact your local bookseller or the Macmillan Corporate and Premium Sales Department at 1-800-221-7945, extension 5442, or by email at MacmillanSpecialMarkets@macmillan.com.

First Edition: 2022

10 9 8 7 6 5 4 3 2 1

To Caleb, the brightest star in the darkest sky

CONTENTS

THE ORIGINAL TALES

INTRODUCTION

*f*airy tales are often our earliest exposure to complex stories. So many of us were raised on narratives of princes and princesses, talking animals, powerful witches, and dreams coming true. But the more we read the stories, and the older we are as we read them, the more we come to understand all the different elements that formulate these foundational texts, including not just sparkling romance and rising from rags to riches but uglier themes like abusive parenting and manipulative trickery.

Are these stories meant to teach us morality? Are they meant to entertain? Are they cautionary, or are they aspirational? Is the intent for us to plumb their depths, or to sit back and simply embrace the magic? However you view fairy tales, there are certainly conversations to be had about their place in both literature and history, perhaps best exemplified by examining the way each story's narrative changes over time and place. While the contributions in *At Midnight* were primarily inspired by the Brothers Grimm, Hans Christian Andersen, and Charles Perrault, there are countless versions of these tales stemming from cultures all over the world, varied in every detail from character names to whether they end in laughter, tears, or bloodshed. And then, of course, there's always the Disney effect.

In this anthology, some of YA's most innovative authors take their turns breathing new life into the stories we know so well, remolding a hood into a hijab, a puss in boots into a coyote in high-tops, and a fatal fire into the flames of passion. The stories range from horror in the frigid reaches of Canada to historical fantasy in colonial India to a thoroughly modern tale of a social media Cinderella, with one thing in common: teens at the helm.

While the hearts of the originals have been preserved, prevalent themes of the original tales, such as transformation, toxic relationships, sibling rivalry, and the pursuit of the forbidden, are closely examined and spun on their heads to reflect their places (or lack thereof) in a more diverse world.

So polish that apple, double-check your roses for thorns, and settle in for a collection of absolutely inspired magic.

–DAHLIA ADLER

THE
TALES
RETOLD

SUGARPLUM

Anna-Marie McLemore

Inspired by "The Nutcracker"

RECIPE FOR THE SILBERHAUS ANNUAL CHRISTMAS PARTY

YOU WILL NEED:

- One intimidatingly enormous house (complete with actual columns)
- Your father's boss and his wife
- Roughly thirty adults
- Approximately five hundred million bottles of imported wine and top-shelf hard liquor
- Enough fancy hors d'oeuvres to sandbag against five hundred million bottles of wine and liquor
- A Betty White impersonator
- Organic chicken tenders
- Dye-free soda
- ~~A powder-puff tutu~~ (No fucking way, not this year)
- ~~A pair of split-sole ballet shoes you don't mind anyone spilling grenadine on~~ (See above)
- Substitute for above: the most annoying girl in five zip codes

Begin by arriving at the enormous house. Feel exceedingly small compared to the white pillars in front of the brick facade. It will be just as you remember it, so cloyingly and ridiculously nice that the cream drapes might wrinkle if you get too close. (*But really*, says Mrs. Silberhaus, *make yourself at home*.)

Observe the adults, all of them employees and their spouses who each want to make an impression at their boss's Christmas party, one that suggests they are fun and relaxed and definitely not nervous about performance reviews in three months.

Say a prayer of gratitude as these adults deposit their children in the plush-carpeted finished basement. There, they will be fed the organic chicken tenders and dye-free soda by the nanny who used to take care of the Silberhauses' now too-old-for-nannies children. She's a Betty White type who is retired but comes out of retirement whenever the Silberhauses have a party. About five different parents will bring her plates from upstairs—*Knock, knock, I thought you might want some grown-up food*—as an excuse to make sure their children haven't destroyed anything priceless.

It is good that the children are down here. No kid should see what's going on upstairs.

Upstairs, witness the opening of the five hundred million bottles of imported wine and top-shelf liquor, or at least enough so that by the end of the night, most of the adults present have revealed themselves to be either hard drinkers or willing to just play one on TV for the night. Witness the artful arrangement of hors d'oeuvres on gilt-edged plates, directed by a chef who demands absolute silence for the sake of her artistry (and really, you have to admire the woman for being able to shut up the rich people who hire her).

Cringe at how few people are here. Your mother and father are always determined to be among the first to arrive, proving to your father's very white boss and his very white wife that just because you're Mexican doesn't mean you can't show up on time. While Mr. Silberhaus leads your father to the wine fridge so your father can praise his choice of vintages for tonight, your mother will help Mrs. Silberhaus arrange overpriced cookies on pewter serving trays. No, the catering team will not do this part, because lifting the cookies from their glossed white bakery boxes makes Mrs. Silberhaus feel as thrillingly domestic as if she'd baked them herself, and inviting a brown woman to do it with her makes her feel like a good person.

Meanwhile, take this opportunity to warm up your muscles, stretch out, work on that stubborn spot on your left calf that always feels tight. Because partway through the party—when she's had her third or fourth glass of sémillon—Mrs. Silberhaus will ask if you could show her guests *just a little of your ballet, it always makes me feel so festive, won't you indulge us, just this once?* And all the other drunk people will clap their hands like you are Tinker Bell and they can make you light up by applauding.

But Mrs. Silberhaus is your father's boss's wife. And when Mrs. Silberhaus gets what she wants, and when she gets to show off to her friends, she's happy. And when you have done something to make Mrs. Silberhaus happy, Mr. Silberhaus is happy with your father.

So you indulge them. Just this once.

Repeat.

Just this once.

Every fucking year.

But not this time. This year, you will not dance. This year, omit the tutu and the ballet shoes, both of which you have left at home, and please note the following alterations to the previous directions:

This year, there is something else Mrs. Silberhaus wants from you. And that is to go cheer up her sullen daughter. Petey Silberhaus is always a little sullen, but in addition to being sullen she's also currently a little sad. She screwed up her arm playing hockey or frozen crew or whatever it is she does at the school she goes to.

Having to interact with Petey more than usual is not ideal, but it is far better than dancing for a bunch of drunk people like a figurine on a music box, so you will gladly do it.

Smile as Mrs. Silberhaus leads you from the marble foyer up the stairs. Try not to stare at her hand on the banister, the nails impossibly shiny, like the inside of a shell. If you stare, you will feel compelled to hide your own nails, which are bitten down. Yesterday you applied sparkly fuchsia polish, which is already chipping.

Smile again as Mrs. Silberhaus says, "Petey's going to be so glad to see you. She's always liked you."

Refrain from telling Mrs. Silberhaus that no, Petey has not *always liked you*. There was just a stretch of years where you and Petey were the only kids around the same age at these parties, cowering away from the older ones and staying out of the way of the younger ones, who were so sugar-infused they were bouncing off the holiday decor.

Do not roll your eyes when Mrs. Silberhaus's delicate knock and song of "Your friend is here" is met with a grunt of acknowledgment from the other side of the door.

Gain an unexpected modicum of respect for Mrs. Silberhaus when she gives you a tight-lipped smile and a "Good luck," because Mrs. Silberhaus apparently knows just how much of a delight her daughter is not, and you were not aware of this.

Open Petey Silberhaus's bedroom door.

Observe Petey sprawled on her bed with a book (has she gotten taller since the Siberhauses' Fourth of July party? Really? Again? While you're still waiting for Madame Arnaut to decide you've reached a suitable height to audition for Aurora and Cinderella?).

Observe how your dress, which you loved until this moment, looks ridiculous in the same room with Petey's T-shirt and sweatpants.

Observe how Petey sees you, eyes the full length of your dress—with its pink-mauve satin, its tea-length tulle, its trailing ribbons and lace detailing that you and your mother both decided were adorable—and bursts out laughing.

Say, "Shut up."

"You look like a sugarplum."

"And you look like an asshole. No special outfit required." Sit on Petey's bed with the full force of your Mexican ass, wrinkling the duvet as much as possible.

Ask Petey: "How did you get out of this?"

When Petey lifts the cast on her arm, say, "Yeah, I don't believe it for a second. If your mother wanted you down there, you and your cast would be in your best blazer."

"I'm a moody bitch these days," Petey will say. "She doesn't want me ruining her party. This is just a good excuse. She gets to tell me to rest and feels like a caring mother. I get out of smiling at everyone's vodka breath. We all win."

Look at the cast and ask, "Hockey?"

"Curling."

"You are *not* on a curling team."

"Oh yes I am."

This will annoy you, because you watch curling whenever it's on TV, and you think it's kind of hot, and you refuse to let Petey Silberhaus be hot or even hot-adjacent.

Try not to glare when Petey smirks and says, "Oh, you're into that?"

"You wish."

"You want to see my rocks?"

"Eww."

"The ones we slide over the ice. You're the one making this dirty."

Spread your sugarplum skirt so it covers as much of Petey's duvet as possible. Gold and silver embroidery and the pink underskirt everywhere. Take up the whole fucking bed.

Ask Petey: "What are you reading?"

"'The Nutcracker.'"

"Wow. I didn't think you were the holiday-spirit type."

"Holiday spirit, my ass. This is the original. This shit is weird."

"How?"

"Look."

Do not hesitate when Petey scoots a little closer on the bed and holds the book between you. If you hesitate, Petey will know that the fine hairs on her arm brushing against yours just made you freeze for a second. Do not think too hard about this. Remember that Petey is the Most Annoying Girl in the World. Petey has made fun of every frilly holiday dress you've ever worn.

When Petey asks, "What?" just shake your head like you're shrugging something off.

When Petey asks, "Are you okay?" just nod.

Skim the words in Petey's book. The part about Maria bandaging the broken nutcracker with a ribbon from her dress. The grandfather clock. The dolls coming to life. Maria rescuing the nutcracker prince from being taken prisoner by throwing her slipper at the mouse king (really? That works? Should you try this at school?).

Agree with Petey that this shit is indeed weird.

Alert when your mother calls your name from downstairs. Sigh.

Get off Petey Silberhaus's bed.

Stop just before the door when Petey says, "Good luck. I'll be here if you want to know what happens next."

Make a round at the party. Let your mother show you off while your father pretends to care about the conversation he's having alongside the giant Christmas tree with its giant glass ornaments.

When Mrs. Silberhaus asks if you're "going to do your little dance for us this year," like you're a toddler in a sequin-edged tutu, say nicely, "Not this year."

When Mrs. Silberhaus lets out an exaggerated *awwww* of disappointment and says, "What a shame. Our guests always look forward to it," smile and say, "Maybe next year."

Hope that the sugary smell of white wine on her breath means she will not remember you saying this.

You will not put on your split-sole ballet shoes and dance on the fluffy carpet in their living room. You will not be their Christmas doll. You will not be their Marzipan, or their Sugar Plum Fairy, or their Spanish Dancer.

Wait until both your parents are absorbed in conversation and go back upstairs. You are being nice, after all. You are keeping Petey company. You may be denying Mrs. Silberhaus the show she wants, but you are lifting the Christmas spirits of her youngest child.

Ask Petey and her open book, "What's happening now?"

"There's a court astrologer. And a ridiculously convoluted prophecy. The usual."

When Petey eyes your dress again, sit on Petey's bed and throw your skirt even wider, so Petey can't even move without brushing it.

When Petey flicks away a corner of tulle and asks, "Is that for this year's performance?" tell her, "No, I'm not doing that this year. I told my mother."

"So she punished you with that dress?"

Throw the fluff of your skirt at Petey Silberhaus. "I picked this out, you jerk."

Try to see it coming.

You won't. Try anyway.

Try to see it coming that when you and Petey Silberhaus bat the layers of your skirt back and forth like you're having a pillow fight, a film of heat brushes against your legs like another layer of tulle. When ribbons trailing off your skirt stroke Petey's arms, do not notice that she's blushing.

Tense your legs until that invisible layer of tulle vanishes.

When it doesn't vanish, when Petey goes still, with her mouth slightly parted and her eyes half-closed, like she's looking at you for the first time, do not come closer.

Do not kiss Petey Silberhaus. Your father's boss's daughter.

Seriously. Do not kiss Petey Silberhaus, no matter how much you like how she smells right now or how her hair is getting in your face. Kissing Petey Silberhaus will fuck up your perfect chignon and probably your heart.

Both love and hate your mother for calling your name from downstairs again at exactly this moment.

When you and Petey look at each other, startled out of what was just about to happen, break the tension by saying, "If they're relying on me to be the life of the party, this is gonna be a disappointing party."

Do not notice how cute Petey's half smile is.

Do not look back as you leave the room.

Try not to jump fifteen feet when, downstairs, Mrs. Silberhaus comes up behind you, puts her hands on your upper arms, and chirps, "I just heard the good news."

Wonder for a second who's pregnant, until Mrs. Silberhaus says, "Your mother says I *might* be able to persuade you to dance for us after all."

Notice how your next breath feels like it takes two minutes.

Notice how the whole party goes still, reduced to this woman's hands on your arms.

Look for your mother.

Say, stammer, "I didn't bring my stuff."

Locate your mother. Who is holding out your ballet shoes with a pained, apologetic look.

Imagine what polite, delicate pressure Mrs. Silberhaus put on your mother while they refreshed the trays of holiday cookies.

We've just all gotten to expect it. It's sort of a holiday tradition, isn't it? We've always considered your daughter part of our family. We just love seeing her.

Look back at Mrs. Silberhaus and say, "I didn't bring a costume."

Look forward again, at your mother, as Mrs. Silberhaus says, "Oh, you can dance in that dress, it'll be perfect. You look darling."

Know that, in this moment, you hate your mother for the betrayal held in those satin shoes, but that you hate her more for letting you think you might get to say no to this.

Watch your hands take the slippers.

Try not to flinch as Mrs. Silberhaus's golden, perfectly barrel-curled hair brushes your shoulder and as you realize that everyone at this party is watching and waiting.

Do not look at your father, who looks at a glass ornament, as though he is ashamed that his daughter must please not just his boss but his boss's wife.

Slip on the ballet shoes.

As Mrs. Silberhaus gives sheet music to the man she hired to play the piano for the evening, do a half-assed job of warming up your muscles and stretching. Everyone is watching, and stretching does not interest them.

Then dance.

Dance for everyone in the Silberhauses' enormous, richly upholstered living room.

Dance as the Christmas tree seems to grow toward the vaulted ceiling, the ornaments swelling to the size of gazing globes.

Dance with bourreés as delicate as the Marzipans.

Give them the confident port de bras of the Spanish Dancer.

Arabesque as gracefully as the Sugar Plum Fairy, with the tulle of your party dress spilling across your legs.

Leap high with each pas de chat. Spin in a coupé jeté, secretly hoping you will break something expensive. Spin in piqué turns so fast the party guests must move back toward the walls.

With one of your turns, lose your spotting just enough to

notice Petey at the railing at the top of the stairs. Try not to see the pain in her face, like she wants to tell you that you can get off the music box, that you don't have to stay there. Do not fault her for realizing that you don't get to stop spinning until the music box winds down.

Dance, and ignore the tiny tears in your muscles from not being properly warm. Dance, and feel the hard edges of the split soles digging into the bottoms of your feet each time you point your toes. Dance, and let them all watch, like a brown music box ballerina is the strangest marvel they have ever seen.

When the music stops, hold your arms in the perfect pose.

Wait the half second before they applaud and roar their approval.

Curtsy with the shy humility of a snow princess. Stand back up with a fake smile so big it will leave your jaw tight until tomorrow morning.

Stand there, in the middle of the living room, as Mrs. Silberhaus laughs and applauds her thanks. Stand on the plush carpet as wine-breathed adults in sparkling party clothes tell you what a graceful young lady you are.

Stand there, as your mother and father are swept into new conversations that begin with what a lovely and talented daughter they have and then quickly move to how even more lovely and talented their own children are.

Keep smiling, so big that everyone could still see it if you were onstage.

Keep smiling, especially when you realize that the Betty White impersonator brought her charges upstairs for the performance. Smile at the ones who pull on the tulle of your skirt and ask if you're a princess. Will the tears on your cheeks to turn into dewdrops or sugarplums or snowflakes or marzipan so that they will not see them.

When Betty White tells these children that it's time to let the princess get her beauty sleep, when she claps her hands and says she has cupcakes for all of them, give her as much of a silent thank-you as your frozen-in-place expression will let you.

Keep your arms in demi-seconde, as though you are still onstage, even though no one is watching you now.

When a hand appears in front of you—open, a little tilted down—you wonder if you are imagining the Sugar Plum's Cavalier in this sparkling living room. Brush your fingers over the hand to see if it's really there. When you do this, Petey will clasp your hand and lead you upstairs.

Feel each stair in the thin satin of your slippers.

Sit on Petey's bed and stare out the window, your own tears blurring each star into a silver ornament.

When Petey asks, "Are you okay?" try to unknot your throat. Fail.

Barely hear Petey as she says, "Wait here."

Laugh, dabbing away a mascara-dyed tear, when she comes back with a cake and two forks. She will not bring plates, except the decorative frilled-edged one underneath the cake. "My mom ordered a bunch of them. They'll never notice one's gone."

When Petey sits on the edge of the bed next to you, join her in tearing the cake apart with the forks. Tear open the shell of swirled meringue frosting to reveal the Christmas-red cake underneath. Let the sugar and meringue dissolve on your tongue.

When Petey asks, "Are you sure you're okay?" lie back on her bed, your skirt fluffing out.

Hand Petey the book and say, "Just tell me what happens next."

Shut your eyes as Petey Silberhaus tells you what happens next.

Feel a glittering cold on your face. Wonder if the tears on your cheeks are in fact turning to sugarplums or marzipan. Then open your eyes and realize that as Petey reads, snow is falling from the ceiling of her room. With each word she reads, a few more snowflakes drift down over the bed, gilding the satin and tulle of your skirt, glittering in Petey's hair. Watch the walls around you vanish, revealing a pine forest.

Take your cavalier's hand and lead her into the snow-silvered trees. Pull a ribbon off your dress and gently tie it around her cast. Throw one slipper, then the next, at anyone who tries to follow you.

Kiss the snowflakes catching on Petey's eyelashes. Lick the tiny meringue snowdrift off her lower lip.

Know that you will have to dance for them all again next year, and the year after that, and every year that your father works for Mr. Silberhaus and that his wife is amused by your dancing.

Know that you will have to leap onto the thin velvet stage of their music box whenever they turn the windup key.

But for now, dance under the silver winter of this night, for no one but your cavalier, and you.

IN THE FORESTS
OF THE NIGHT

Gita Trelease

Inspired by "Fitcher's Bird"

That spring, the girls began to disappear.

The first girl, picking tea in the white heat of midday. In those long rows of emerald-green bushes, vipers sometimes sunned themselves, threaded through the branches like deadly streamers. But if it'd been a snake that killed her, where was her body?

The second girl, herding goats through the cool of a pine forest. On the other side bloomed a wildflower meadow perfect for picnics where, by a stream, blue butterflies danced. Two days later (most of) the goats found their way back. The girl did not.

The third girl—the skin on the back of my neck prickled when my sister Maya told me—sitting in the shade of her own doorway, mending a rip in her sari. Her brothers heard her scream. In the space of a breath the enormous cat vanished in the elephant grass. Throwing rocks, they gave chase, but the tiger was inhumanly fast. They shouted her name until their throats ached, but all that came back were echoes.

The third girl was the daughter of my grandmama's driver.

Incandescent with rage, Granny swept off the veranda of Orchid House, into her car, and down the hill into town. There she stormed the British club, where no Indians, not even Granny, were allowed. In her deadliest voice she demanded the chief of police send for Captain Colin Fitcher. An army veteran, he'd once killed a man-eating tiger that had taken 210 lives. And though normally the deaths of three Indian girls wouldn't have raised a single English eyebrow, Granny was the widow of a Rajput prince, and that was the kind of thing the British understood.

Captain Fitcher was summoned. As it turned out, he'd been nearby the whole time. He'd arrived last year from the west; no one knew where. No one had seen him; none of us knew what he looked like. He didn't socialize with the British, and he definitely didn't socialize with us, but lived alone on the outskirts of town, in an old bungalow overrun by jungle. Without knowing it was his, I'd seen his place on my way to school. Five red points of roof above the treetops, a chimney snarled in vines.

Our lives changed after that. While Fitcher with his men and guns stalked the tiger (many against one), we girls were trapped indoors. Except for school, but there the nuns were more eagle-eyed and suspicious than ever. Finger in the air, Sister Thomas warned, "Your very lives depend on being obedient!" Which only made me want to race out of assembly and smoke bidis behind the refectory with Ash and stay out all night, doing wild, unpredictable things.

Our parents and everyone else who should have come up from Delhi (like living in an oven) didn't, because of the tiger. A telegram, though, arrived for me: Ash's ship had docked in Bombay. After almost a year away at Oxford, there was only one long train ride left between us. In the muggy afternoons, I listened for the steam engine's distant whistle and wondered: After all this time, had Ash changed? *Had I?*

I used to be a fairly good student (*Lili's work is exemplary, if at times too imaginative*), but since the killings it'd become impossible to concentrate.

The air in our biology classroom was always thick and warm, like something you could touch. Next to me, Savita doodled hearts in her notebook; dust motes drifted in the syrupy sunlight. As Sister Agnes endlessly explained cell division, I stared out the window—and saw the curtains twitch. When they trembled again, longer this time, I knew: something was trapped behind them.

Carefully I lifted the fabric. Caught between it and the window was a silvery moth. Its wire-thin legs tapped at the glass that must have looked like sky but was only a dead end. Exhausted, it beat its scalloped wings, slow as death, and then went still.

I stood and shoved up the window's heavy sash. It made a terrible cracking sound.

Sister Agnes spun around. "You, Lili! Where do you think you're going?"

I dropped into my chair. "Nowhere, Sister! I was just—"

The moth crawled onto the windowsill. The other girls tittered.

"Just what?"

She was the biology teacher. If anyone would understand, she would. "A moth was trapped behind the curtain—"

Sister Agnes frowned, wrinkles knotting above her glasses. "What a story! Don't think for a minute I've forgotten your escapade at the lake. Didn't you go out the window then as well? And lead so many others into your misbehavior? You are a rash and irresponsible girl, Lili Blake."

It *had* been my idea to go down to the lake.

Last spring, Ash and I had planned to sneak out of school and rent a boat. To row out onto the jade-colored water with the hills rising lush around us, and beyond them the silvery peaks of the Himalayas. To lounge on tasseled cushions and stare up at the clouds—or at each other. To feel the sweet air on our skin, the dazzle of him next to me: one boat ride, just us, before he left for England. Was it too much to ask?

Apparently it was, because Edith Vane saw me climbing over the school wall and followed (no imagination), as did three of her friends. They rented one boat, Ash and I another. But so many English girls on the lake set an alarm ringing in the boat wallah's mind, and he sent a boy up to the school. We'd barely left the dock when the headmistress stepped out of a rickshaw, her face murderous.

Ash had tried to take the blame—one-eighth Indian being more credible to the headmistress than one-half—but it didn't work. Instead my parents came up from Delhi to consult with the headmistress (everyone was *very concerned*). At the train station, before they left again, my English father said fondly, "Do try and be careful, darling, won't you? We can't always be here to get you out of scrapes." And my Indian mother said, "You mustn't draw attention to yourself, Lili. We only want to protect you."

From what? But I think I knew, even then.

Normally Sister Agnes would have kept me after school, writing on the chalkboard *I will not open the window* or *I will not save a moth*. But these weren't normal days. That morning a farmer had spotted a tiger on the winding road to school.

When the nuns learned of it we were sent home with our books and extra assignments.

It got hotter.

Late in the afternoons, thunder murmured promises of rain. The monsoon was coming. While Maya scribbled secret letters she paid the sweeper to deliver, I sat on the veranda, kicking my heels against the wicker rocker, tormented by whatever adventures Ash was having without me.

The walls of Orchard House crept nearer and nearer until I felt like Alice in the storybook we had, grown so big in Wonderland she no longer fit indoors. In the black-and-white illustration she looked angry enough to kick the whole house down. Everything felt too close, even the jagged teeth of the far-off mountains.

At night a tiger roamed the hills behind the house, growling and huffing. In the pitch black I slipped into Maya's room and lay next to her as the ceiling fan clicked round and round.

Against the window, the oleander tapped nervous branches.

Had the girls who'd been killed heard a warning—a monkey's call, a snapped twig? Or hadn't they known the End was coming closer, making no more sound than a shadow? Did they turn and fight, or run?

Once, I heard the tiger breathing, hot and restless and close. As if it were on the other side of the wall, whispering in my ear. I made a dark wish then, the kind you're not supposed to make: I wished the tiger would slip through Fitcher's snares, past the beaters and shooters that roamed the hills. Free, and away from here.

My wish didn't come true—not all of it.

Because three days later, Captain Fitcher announced that he'd killed *two* man-eating (girl-eating) tigers.

Granny threw a party to celebrate.

It was nearing dusk when the first guests arrived. Drinks fizzed on silver platters; jazz poured out of the gramophone's trumpet-shaped horn. On the terraces, people were laughing and gossiping as if they'd been released from a long siege. Which I suppose they had been. As I lingered on the veranda, hoping Ash would show up soon, the scarlet flowers of the bougainvillea dissolved like ink, and far below, the eye-shaped lake turned from green to silver.

Maya came up behind me, her bracelets clinking as she laid her hand lightly on my shoulder. I smiled, already less lonely. She was two years older than I was and fairer, with hazel eyes and red in her hair, so pretty in her peacock-blue gown with its sparkling glass beads. I'd put on a smoke-gray silk dress that brought out my brown skin and amber eyes—though compared to Maya's, it felt suddenly too plain.

"I adore that dress," she said, "though I wonder if you might be *too* glamorous to be my little sister." I could always count on Maya to know how I was feeling. "Is Ash here yet?"

My throat constricted, and I shook my head.

"Never mind. If he doesn't come tonight, it's only because he's not back in town. The trains from Bombay are dreadfully slow." Trying to distract me, she said, "Have you seen Captain Fitcher?"

The party was crowded now, the line of black automobiles on the street below getting longer. On the upper terrace, surrounded by a crush of people, stood a tall Englishman in a crisp linen suit and a straw fedora. He was lean, with light eyes and hair, but deeply tanned (crouching in the sun, waiting to kill animals). A hunting knife hung conspicuously from his belt. Maya's best friend was saying something to him and pointing to the hills.

"That's got to be him there," I said, "with Gayatri."

She was the most beautiful girl in town, with huge almond-shaped eyes and a quick, daring smile she'd give you before she did something outrageous. Not the kind of girl to be starstruck. But there she was, Fitcher's white hand on her arm, her face turned up to his.

"She's positively spellbound," Maya said with a laugh.

Seeing Gayatri like that sent a ripple of unease through me. Conspiratorially I said, "Let's see if she needs to be rescued." Together we went down to the lower terrace and squeezed into the group.

"The tiger's pugmarks," Fitcher was saying, "what you'd call paw prints, were almost as big as this." He stretched his hand out as wide as it would go. In the setting sun the skin between his fingers glowed red.

"And to kill such a large animal . . . ?" Gayatri asked.

He smiled, showing his teeth. "I become the top predator."

"How?" she asked. "Do you wait overnight in a machan? Put out bait?"

Bait? I wanted to kick her. She *knew* hunters tied a baby buffalo to a stake and waited in a blind for the tiger to come. What was happening to her?

"It's not quite so simple." Fitcher's hand came now to rest on my sister's shoulder. "Shall I explain?"

Maya nodded, and he told the story of how he'd tracked the man-eater of Chowgarh. For months it had deliberately led him astray. But he'd persisted, following clues of bent grass and fur tufts on branches until he put an end (shot through the heart) to the tiger's reign of terror.

"But, Captain?" my sister asked dreamily, so unlike herself. "What makes *you* the best at it?" Her hazel eyes had gone soft, unfocused, and they didn't leave Fitcher's face. She reminded me of a snake charmer's cobra, so mesmerized by the sway of the street performer's instrument, it forgets it has fangs.

I nudged her in the ribs. "Come with me to see Granny. Please." But she didn't even turn to look at me.

"Patience," Fitcher replied, "and observation. Control. When you come down to it, the tiger's broken. It's sick or hurt and can't catch its normal prey. So it hunts something easier."

"Like girls," I said.

Fitcher's ice-chip gaze swiveled to me. "Something defenseless. Once a tiger sees how easy it is, it'll keep coming back, more dangerous than ever."

The horror of it made the hair on my arms stand up. Unfazed, Gayatri batted her lashes at him. "What's the biggest tiger you've ever shot?"

He straightened the lapels of his jacket. "Fifteen feet, nose to tail."

"That's hard to believe," I said under my breath.

But Fitcher heard me. "Why's that?"

"Haven't you British hunted our biggest game animals to death?"

"Between us and your princes we've done quite a job of it, that's for sure." He hid his hands in his pockets. "I'm going to stuff them—real as life. By the time I'm done they'll look like they could walk out of the room. The safest way to see wild animals, don't you think?"

Bile rose in my throat as I imagined him stripping a tiger's skin from its flesh. Peeling it back and filling it with something else. Making a trophy of it. Making it *safe*.

"We'll go, won't we?" Gayatri put her arm around my waist and Maya's. "And see these tigers for ourselves."

Around me rose a chorus of *yes, please, me too*s. I scowled at Maya, trying to get her attention, but like the rest of them, she only had eyes for Fitcher. But I hadn't forgotten the desperate tiger padding around Orchid House, whispering through the wall. I slipped away and left them to their unsettling fascination.

Over us the sky was deepening to indigo, while down in town, lights snapped on in the houses. At the lush edge of our garden stood Granny under her oldest mango tree. Admiring the fruit-laden branches while adjusting his striped college tie was Ash.

I paused in the shadows, drinking him in. He was handsome as always, his tawny hair tousled, the easy smile he'd had since we were kids softening the now-sharp line of his jaw. Away from our Indian sun, his skin had gone pale. He looked tired and worn, as if he'd passed through too many hands. I wanted to believe that he was who he'd always been: the boy who kept my secrets and said yes to every adventure. My oldest friend. My love.

"Ash!" I kicked my fancy shoes off under a rosebush and raced barefoot across the cool stones. "You're home!"

"Lili, darling!" His face changed when he saw me, like he'd never been away. And though my grandmother gave us both a stern look, we cheerfully waved *so long* and disappeared into one of the garden's secret haunts. For a delicious half hour there were no more hunters or prey, only the two of us under a jasmine-woven pergola, our feet in the fountain as we watched the stars spark, one by one.

There was so much to catch up on. The weeks of travel by train and by ship, glamorous London, scholarly Oxford. Punting a boat on the River Cherwell in the fall, the winter so damp he never felt warm and was teased for wearing two sweaters indoors. The libraries full of books and the demanding classes, the afternoon cricket matches and the dinners that ended at dawn.

I could tell he loved it, and it hurt, more than a little. "Was it at all strange, being there?"

He fell silent, considering. "No one seemed to care where I came from, if that's what you mean."

On the seat between us, our fingers lay braided together, mine dusky, his almost white. Could being half English and half Indian matter less in Oxford than it did here? Or was it that I was half, and he an eighth? "I've been thinking . . . I could try to get into St. Hilda's."

"You'd come with me to Oxford?" he said, bewildered. "But I thought you loved it here."

The music on the gramophone had gone swoony, sad. "It's not the same anymore."

"What do you mean?"

I sighed. "It's as if there's always been a rope around my ankle, but I've only just noticed it." I told him about the endless weeks of not being able to do anything, the cautions and *be carefuls*, my life slipping away like water. The nuns and Granny and everyone else forcing me to wait—to be safe—until I thought I might explode. And then, how even after Fitcher had killed the tigers, they wouldn't let me do what I'd done before.

"Darling, listen to me." His eyes were fierce and serious. "If you want to go, I swear I'll do everything I can to help convince your granny. And your parents. I promise, Lili—I won't leave you behind."

"Truly?" Tears I'd held back since the girls had first disappeared pricked at my eyes. I squeezed his hand, hard.

"Truly." Tucking a strand of hair behind my ear, he let his fingers trail down my cheek. "You'll dazzle them—Oxford's never met anyone like you."

When we finally emerged from the garden, star-dazed, drunk on each other, most of the guests had left, including Fitcher. Ash and I said goodbye on the lower terrace, where in the dark the steps zigzagged down to the road.

Suddenly formal, he said, "May I walk you to school to-morrow?"

Maya, Ash, and I had walked to school together for years; the whitewashed walls of the boys' school faced ours across the street. But this felt deliciously different. "The other girls will burst into envious flames," I teased.

"And you'll warm your lovely hands on the fire." He brought my face close and kissed me, slow and delirious. "Until tomorrow, then."

Heat burned through me as I watched him go. I had to find Maya and tell her.

In her bedroom the coverlet was turned down, the fan clicking away, but she wasn't there. Uneasy, I went to see our old nurse, who told me Maya and Gayatri had left the party with Captain Fitcher, to see the tigers he'd killed. "My poor girl!" she cried. "No sense, going to a man's house. Even worse, an Englishman's!"

"You've always insisted she was the sensible one," I said, more cheerfully than I felt. "You'll laugh when she tells us about it in the morning."

But in the morning, Maya hadn't come home.

———◦———

Before it was properly light, I crept down the hall and found her room empty, the perfectly made bed still waiting for her, eerie and wrong. In the kitchen I wolfed down several cups of tea, an excuse to linger and listen as, just outside the door, the mustached police chief briefed Granny. He told her his men had already combed the gardens and rooms of Orchid House for a sign of the girls and interviewed Fitcher. It was true that the girls had wanted to see the tigers, he'd said, but once in town they'd changed their minds. He'd dropped them near Gayatri's house.

But I knew they wouldn't have gone there unless they'd been in trouble; Gayatri's father was a closet drinker, uncomfortable to be around. Either Fitcher had scared them so much they'd gotten out of his car in town, or they'd continued with him to his house.

Despite the heat of the kitchen, I shivered. Everything about this felt wrong.

When the police chief finally left, I turned on Granny. "Did the police search Fitcher's house?"

"Why would they?" She dried her damp cheeks with the end of her sari. "It was a tiger that did this! My granddaughter is lying maimed in some forest, suffering—"

A tiger, snatching up two girls in the center of town? If I had told Granny this, she'd have scolded me for imagining things. But Fitcher had hypnotized them all into believing something they'd otherwise never accept as true.

Before Granny could tell me I had to stay home from school *because of the tiger*, I hurried down the sixty-three steps to the street. At the bottom was an iron gate with a brass bell. Ash was due in an hour, but I couldn't wait. Instead I wrote him a note saying I'd gone to look for Maya, which I wrapped around the bell's clapper. It was a system we'd come up with when we were kids; he'd know there was a message as soon as he opened the gate and the bell didn't ring.

I headed down the road, my school shoes setting off plumes of dust. The day was overcast, the air so wet it felt almost like rain. I went first to Gayatri's and talked to her family's sweeper, who knew everything that happened at the house. He confirmed the girls hadn't come home. I told myself it was too soon to panic, but it happened anyway, the fear ticking like a too-fast watch inside of me. Almost running, I went the places the police wouldn't know to check. Like Gayatri's favorite sweetshop, and the stand of the flirtatious chai wallah where Maya bought tea after school. I even rushed down to the wide green lake, in case they'd rented a boat and capsized—but no one had seen them.

It was as if they'd simply disappeared.

But if I'd learned anything from what happened that spring, it was that girls didn't just disappear. There was always a reason.

It was already afternoon by the time I found the road to Fitcher's house. The entrance was so overgrown and shabby that I'd passed it twice before spotting the half-hidden sign that said *Fitcher*. A faint dirt track wound through the forest, climbing slowly into the gloom. Though I kept to the center of the path, dead branches clawed at my arms, overgrown grass hissing around my legs. The forest smelled wild, sharp and green. High in the canopy, monkeys shrieked back and forth. Among the dark leaves, birds' wings flared yellow and red.

Suddenly, behind me, I heard a car's engine, running fast. I scrambled out of the way just as a big black car roared up, with Fitcher behind the wheel.

He cranked down the window and stared. His eyes, I noticed, were bloodshot. "Has your sister been found? And the other girl?"

"I'm sure they'll turn up eventually. No one's at all worried," I lied.

His hands gripped the wheel so hard the knuckles were white. "What are you doing here, may I ask?"

I gave him a helpless shrug. "You said I could see the tigers."

He relaxed then. "As you wish." He leaned over and flipped the lock. The car door yawned open. Scarlet leather seats, the reek of cigarettes. "The house is still a way up the road. You'd best drive with me."

I got in and closed the door. On his forearm was a clumsy bandage I hadn't noticed last night. Pinpricks of blood had seeped through the gauze. He made small talk about the weather; I stared out into the forest, not wanting to give anything away.

We jolted along the track for several minutes before the trees backed off and the house came into view. It'd once been a grand bungalow with balconies and dozens of large windows. But the shutters with their peeling red trim were closed, as if the house were asleep. Mold ferned the once-white walls; rot had eaten away at the veranda's pillars. From the gutters trailed eager, grasping vines. What had once been a pretty garden had escaped its fence, already halfway to jungle.

He noticed me looking as we got out. "I'm not here very much, you see."

Behind us, the car ticked as it cooled. The lake glinted through the trees. "You have a nice view."

The corners of his mouth turned down. "Nothing like your grandmother's. Come in and see my collection."

Up the stairs, across the sagging veranda, and in through the front door to a central hall. With the shutters closed, it was suffocatingly hot, and dark. It smelled of awful things: decay, the gag of formaldehyde. Nothing moved; the house was secretive and still.

Then Fitcher flicked a switch and lights blazed on overhead.

I flinched—the room was filled with eyes. Horns and teeth and tusks.

The severed head of a sambar, antlers curved like a crown. A spotted chital deer, its eyes dilated with fear. By the door loomed a pale-nosed bear, one paw forced out into a mockery of a handshake. An elephant foot, its toenails intact, had been transformed into a wastebasket; on a low table a tortoise's shell held letters. Two prancing blackbucks with spiraling horns stood shoved against the wall, as if Fitcher had killed so many creatures he'd run out of room to show them off. Under an archway of ivory tusks hung an enormous tiger's head, its mouth forever open in a silent scream. As I stared, a beetle crawled out of its ear and into a hole in the wall. And across the wide stone floor, as if they'd been slain where they stood, lay the pressed-flat hides of chinkara and lions and black-stippled cheetahs.

The safest *way to see wild animals,* he'd boasted. I bit down on the inside of my cheek to keep from throwing up.

Fitcher gestured at his trophies as if he were unveiling a work of art. "Impressive, aren't they?" His voice climbed, almost giddy. "Don't they look alive? Silent and—as a girl you must appreciate this—perfectly tame?"

The blackbucks' almost-human eyes seemed to swivel to mine. Careful to keep the dread out of my voice, I pointed to the severed head and asked, "That tiger over there isn't one of the man-eaters, is it?"

"Clever girl. Even I couldn't have stuffed it that fast. Come, there's more—shall I get you a nimbu pani as I show you around?" Fitcher flashed me a conspiratorial grin. "I suppose you're too young for a cocktail."

Had he offered Maya and Gayatri a drink? On the cheetah skins perched a few leather club chairs, a coffee table, a brass cocktail cart. It was cluttered with liquor bottles, but there was no sign it had been used last night. No lipsticked glasses. No crumpled napkins.

It didn't mean much. They could have been here last night and Fitcher had cleaned away any trace of them. I needed to keep looking. "No, thanks, I'd just like to see the tigers—the ones my sister and her friend saw."

Blandly, Fitcher said, "They never saw the tigers—they changed their minds."

It sounded so reasonable. Girls were always changing their minds. Distracted, teasing, impulsive. But Maya and Gayatri weren't like that . . . except at the party last night when they'd been enthralled by Captain Fitcher. His pale hands on their arms, their eyes locked to his. *Hypnotized.*

The police might have believed him, but I didn't. Brightly, I said, "*I* would like to see the rest of your collection."

He really looked at me then—watchful and patient—and seemed to come to a decision. "This way."

He led me down a hall, flipping on lights, and I followed, searching for a sign that my sister and Gayatri had been there. On the walls hung animal hides and grim photographs of men posing with guns, dead animals under their boots. Rooms opened off on both sides, packed like cells in a hive. The farther we went from the front door, the darker they became. More full of shadows.

A phone shrilled next to me, and I nearly jumped out of my skin.

Fitcher snatched up the receiver. He listened, head cocked, then hung up. A blue vein stood out on his forehead. "Someone's seen a tiger by the boys' school—I must go. The rains could start any minute and wash away the pugmarks."

Not yet. There was still so much house to cover. "But your collection—"

A slow, calculating smile. "Why, after coming all the way up here you must stay as long as you like."

"Really?" If he was so at ease, maybe there wasn't anything to see after all. *Or maybe,* the dead animals in the photos whispered, *it is a trap.*

"My house is your house. There's loads to look at, so feel free to wander into any room you like. Take your time."

I remembered the rooms we'd passed, some doors unlocked, others closed tight. "They're all open?"

"The ones you're allowed to enter are." His eyes slid to the telephone, black and quiet on the table. "But before you go any farther, you must take off those dusty shoes." He pointed to a pair of furred slippers tucked under the table. "Put those on instead, and don't get them dirty."

"I'll be careful." I unbuckled the straps of my Mary Janes and stepped into the slippers, rounded like paws.

"See you soon," he said. "Be good."

I waited until I heard him drive away.

The telephone table had a single drawer in it, a few inches high. Fitcher had glanced at the table, and now, in the silent house, it seemed to beckon me too. I had a prickling feeling, a kind of presentiment, that if I took hold of the brass knob and pulled it open and looked inside, there would be no going back.

Slowly I slid it toward me. The drawer was empty except for an iron ring bristling with keys of many sizes and shapes. They made a sound like splintering glass when I lifted them out.

Ahead of me doorways disappeared in the gloom.

I'd taken only a few steps when I felt something hard, like a pebble, in the toe of the left slipper. I turned the shoe upside down; a tiny ball fell out and rolled glinting across the floor.

My hand shook as I picked it up: it was a blue glass bead from Maya's dress.

I ran down the hall, the keys in my fist. The first door I unlocked led to a study, wallpapered with moldering books. No sign of them. Then a dining room, glasses on a sideboard, a table feathered with dust. *Nothing.* Desperate, I kept opening doors: a sitting room with a horn chandelier, a moth-eaten billiard table, cold tiled bathrooms, and a large bedroom, mosquito netting a ghost over the bed. But no matter how many rooms I went into, no matter how many keys I tried, I could find no other trace of my sister and Gayatri.

At the end of the hallway waited one last door, plain and narrow.

As I hurried toward it, something rumbled in the distance. Thunder? I listened hard for the sound of Fitcher's car. One heartbeat, two, three—nothing but rain in the hills.

I twisted the knob on the narrow door, but it didn't open. *Locked.* There were a dozen keys I hadn't used yet; I chose one and tried to fit it to the lock. Too big. I tried another one, smaller, and that too wasn't even close. One after another I tried the keys, and none were right.

I was running out of time.

Frustrated, I stooped to look at the keyhole. It was tiny, curved like a fingernail clipping, so small it could only be unlocked by the tiniest of keys. I fumbled with the ring until I found it: tarnished silver, no longer than the first joint of my little finger. As I held it, the key burned cold against my palm. Now or never.

As soon as I fit the silver key into place, the door creaked open. The smell I'd noticed in the front hall snaked out, sharp and sickening.

I fumbled on the wall for a switch and an overhead lamp snapped on. Harsh yellow light revealed glass cases stuffed with creatures: mongooses and flying foxes, cobras and speckled lizards. Their corpses had been twisted into poses in a gruesome imitation of life. Rare birds, their wings painfully stretched in pretend flight. Butterflies, dead and pinned but beautiful, filled every in-between space.

It was a graveyard. An extinction—one Fitcher hadn't wanted me to see.

The stench was malicious, suffocating. Holding my breath, I made my way to the window, forced the rusty lock, and shoved it open. Cool fresh air rushed in, and on it hung the faintest drizzle of rain. It fell in tiny droplets on the floor.

In the center of the room, in the middle of a slick red circle, stood two stuffed tigers. Quietly, as if I might wake them, I drew closer, my heart beating hard. Remembering Fitcher's warning, I stepped out of the furred slippers and tiptoed over the wet red line.

One tiger crouched low, posed as if to pounce; the other was walking, glancing mid-stride over its shoulder. Fitcher hadn't lied: the tiger seemed almost alive. Its fur was sleek, powerful paws smooth, rounded ears attentive. The black tip of its striped tail curled up, as if happy to be walking through this room of horrors. I kneeled beside it and curled my fingers into its fur. Thick and soft—and warm.

In the distance, unmistakable, I heard the revving engine of an automobile.

As the clamor grew louder, the tiger's ear twitched toward the sound, its eye focused on the door.

It wasn't a cat's yellow-green, but a familiar, beloved hazel.

"Maya!" I cried. Frantically I ran my hands along the tiger's crouching legs, feeling for seams or some other way out. Maya was inside, but how? And was Gayatri caught inside the striding tiger, its proud pose so like her?

I pulled both creatures close, an arm around each of their necks, and buried my face in their ruffs. They were trapped, maybe dying, and I didn't know how to free them. *Think, Lili.* I looked frantically around the room at the dead animals, each one of them a warning. But how could you escape from something like *this*?

Maybe if I could get them—somehow—back to Orchid House, someone else might know what to do.

Grabbing at their fur, I dragged them toward the open window, smudging the circle and leaving tracks of red on the floor. They were so much heavier than girls ever were, but my rage was growing, and it fueled me. Fury for what had been done to Maya and Gayatri, ensnared in these skins. Fury for the other girls, who'd been killed when they'd only been living their lives. Fury for the hacked-up beasts, the stuffed and the maimed and the pinned.

The tiger's hazel eye watched.

Mist drizzled in, falling on our faces.

The air in the room vibrated, as if it were filled with bees.

And under my hands, the tiger's damp hide loosened. *Sagging*, as if whatever was inside was shrinking, the wet pelt suddenly too big. Then the tiger growled, a soft, choked sound—but it was *Maya's* voice.

"Is that really you?" I whispered into the tiger's ear.

When she said nothing, I dug my fingers into her fur. It felt more like a coat now and less like skin. As I held it tight, she leaned away from me. Slowly, inch by inch, she tore herself free until the tattered pelt slid to the floor. Underneath she still wore her peacock-blue party dress, now covered with slick strands of what looked like cobwebs. I pulled my sister close; against my ear her heart drummed *alive, alive, alive.*

"Thank you," she croaked. Relief flooded through me at the sound of her (nearly) human voice. Gayatri too had almost finished shedding her skin. Her ruby gown was wrapped with the same glistening net as Maya's, though hers was thinner, fading. She peeled the last piece of fur off her arm as if it were a silk evening glove and tossed it on a chair.

"We have to go," she growled. "He plans to keep us here forever."

"How can he possibly stop us?" I said. "There's three of us—"

"He's a *sorcerer*, Lili." Still wild, Maya's eyes went to the circle I'd smeared when dragging them to the window. "He gave us tea and slippers and let us go anywhere we wanted. But when he discovered we'd been in here, he sliced open his arm and imprisoned us with his blood. He made snares that froze my muscles and slowed my heart. I could see everything but couldn't do anything. And then he put us in the skins. . . ."

I pressed my face against my sister's shoulder, as if we were back in her bedroom at Orchid House under the clicking fan, telling ourselves the tigers were outside the walls.

"He loved seeing us afraid. Trapped," Maya said, a catch in her voice. "But the water—"

Suddenly both of them stiffened, listening to sounds I couldn't hear.

Gayatri snarled, low and dangerous. The tiny hairs on the back of my neck rose as, at the other end of the bungalow, the door banged open.

"Girl!" Fitcher shouted. "Where are you?"

There was only one way out: through the window and into the forest. "Go," I told them. "Run to town, tell people to come. We can't let him get away with this."

"And what will you do?" Maya demanded. "By yourself?"

I smiled. I knew what I would do.

Be the good girl, the clever girl, the girl too young for a cocktail. Be the prey and the predator. Be the steel trap with teeth, but cover it with leaves.

"He left me here alone, didn't he? He thinks I'm harmless." But I knew he was waiting for me to make a mistake. Set a foot in his snare. "I'll stall him while you get help—"

Grimly, Maya nodded. "Do what you have to—but don't let him touch you." Together they bounded to the window and leaped onto the deep sill. There they paused, eyes half-closed, inhaling the jungle's thousand scents, before they disappeared.

Then I heard it: a few drops, light as feathers.

Within seconds it fell harder, as if someone were dropping sand on the roof, faster and heavier until it drummed relentlessly around the bungalow. Lightning cracked down, and as if a hand had closed around the house, the electric lights snuffed out.

Everywhere was dusk, but the dark was my friend. I ran as fast as I could, my bloodied feet hidden in the furred slippers. I was only halfway down the hall when I found Fitcher. He seemed bigger than before, his face feverish, shiny.

"There you are." He stared at the slippers, then scoured my face. "You're a good girl, aren't you?"

I nodded. Outside, the wind picked up, rattling the leaves like a warning. Behind me, the door of the forbidden room creaked open. Why hadn't I locked it? Any second now he'd notice I *hadn't* been good.

Unless he was looking only at me. "I should be getting home."

"It's started to rain," he said, as if speaking to a child. "You can't walk home now. Why don't you stay a bit longer?"

"What a lovely offer," I bluffed, "but I'm afraid I must go. My family will be wondering where I am." The way to the front door lay behind him. The hall wasn't wide; I'd have to pass horribly close to him. Near enough to touch.

Pinning my smile in place, I walked toward him. The plaid skirt of my school uniform flicked and swayed.

Terrifyingly patient, he watched me come closer. Blue eyes blown out with want, gaunt shoulders stooped into a crouch. Ready to spring.

Five steps. Three steps, two steps, my heart a hammer in my chest. One more step and I'd be free—

His fingers closed around my wrist. "What will you tell people about your visit?"

"Nothing." (Everything.)

Lightning forked down again, harrowing the hall with light. He was so near I could smell him: blood and rot and suffering.

His grip tightened. "No one would believe you if you said anything bad, you know."

I blinked. "Why ever would I?"

"That's right. There's nothing to tell." His manic gaze never left my face, but his voice changed, becoming low and secretive, as if he were talking to himself. "And even if there were something to report," he muttered, "who would listen to a half-blood Anglo-Indian girl, who has to walk the straightest line there is? Bloody hell, she shouldn't even exist. If she spoke against me, who'd believe her—the English? The Indians? My word is what counts—"

"You're wrong," I choked out.

"Silence!" He pulled so hard I stumbled out of the slippers. "We're going to work on your lines on the way into town. You'll tell the police you looked over the entire house and that your sister and her friend were never here. That's what they *want* to believe. Stray from the script and I will have no mercy on you."

"I won't." Whatever he thought I'd done or seen, he wanted me as a witness, and for that, I had to be alive. It was something I could use.

"Good." He gave me a shake, like a dog does to break a hare's neck. "Girls like you don't get second chances."

As he dragged me toward the door, I grabbed at the furniture—anything I could reach—to slow him down. Lamps, paintings, a row of books. I cracked my knee on a doorframe, my shoulder against a cabinet. He kept going, never turning around.

And then, cool on my bloodied feet: water. It lapped in insistent waves.

Fitcher froze. A tremor ran through him as he stared in horror at the rising tide. "My enchantments—"

I almost laughed. If it was water he feared, he'd have more of it.

Taking advantage of his shock, I kicked him, hard. He bellowed, and I twisted away. Racing through the house, I opened every window I could find. Rain reached in, stretched across the floors, filling the house like a swimming pool. Snakes whiplashed by; branches spun on the current. A portrait of the queen fell off its nail and was swept away.

And as the water touched them, the taxidermy animals in the living room wrenched themselves free.

A shudder ran through a spotted deer as it strained to unglue its feet from the pedestal. One by one, its tiny hooves came loose. With a shake of its head, it broke out of the pose it had been forced into and leaped into the flood. I waited to see if it would shed its deerskin, but it paddled on, whole, its black nose above the water. In the blink of an eye it swam down the hall and out the doors. Gone.

Hope made me wild. "Wake up!" I shouted to the others. "Flee!"

Slowly, the sloth bear shook itself alive. A sambar lowered his noble antlered head, sniffed the river gurgling by, then plunged in. A gharial crocodile, ridged and shiny as a trap, slunk below the surface and disappeared.

Fitcher had gone quiet. In the dark house, he could be anywhere. Coming closer.

But there was one more thing I had to do.

I pushed through waist-high water to the room of death. The window still stood open, rain pouring in. In the washed-out dusk, papers floated past me like leaves. The mammals had escaped, but in the cabinets the birds and the butterflies struggled against their pins. Snatching a stone paperweight off

Fitcher's desk, I smashed the glass. I reached in and yanked the pins loose, fast as I could. As the mist fell on them, the creatures stirred to life, climbing up my arms and launching off my shoulders in a glittering typhoon of butterflies and moths and birds.

Only one myna remained, its black wings crumpled. I cupped it in my hand and brought it close to the water, letting its too-dry yellow feet dangle in the wet.

"Come on," I urged. "The wind's coming."

As if the bird had heard me, its heart flickered to life against my fingers. It raised its dark head, looked at me with clever eyes, then flew away.

Over the pounding of the rain, Fitcher was shouting he would kill me.

The flood was rising.

As I stumbled past floating furniture to reach the door, a sandalwood statue of Lord Shiva bumped into me. Caught on one of his outstretched arms was Gayatri's torn tiger skin. Its head bobbed on the surface of the water, the ridge of its back just below, one paw missing.

I followed the skin as it floated into the hall. At the far end, a flashlight's beam—*Fitcher*—wobbled and searched. "Girl!" he shouted. "Come to me now or I'll kill you—this is your last chance!"

I held my breath and dove.

When I rose, the tiger's head covered my own like a hood. Through the holes that were once its eyes, I stared out on the twilit water and vowed: *This will not be my grave.*

I kicked off the floor and swam. The flanks of my pelt floated beside me, my tail trailing behind as I let the river ferry me into the grand front room.

The animals were gone, but Fitcher was there. He'd clambered onto a desk that had lodged in a corner. In his teeth he held the flashlight; in his arms, a rifle.

I paddled through the floating debris toward the open doors.

And then he saw me. Or he saw a tiger skin, with a girl's eyes in it.

The rain was so loud I didn't hear him scream. I only saw his face stretch in terror as he backed against the wall and raised his gun to fire.

Lightning broke; the house shuddered and groaned. Behind Fitcher, a crack spidered up the wall. Chunks of plaster plummeted into the water. The split widened into a ravine as an enormous wooden beam dropped from the roof and crashed into the corner where Fitcher stood.

He sprang at me, flashlight swinging.

The torrent swept me away.

Through the open doorway, across the rotten veranda, past the garden, and into the drive. It threw me against the car, then pushed me past it. I tried to climb out by grasping at low branches, but they only slid through my hands. The river (and I) followed the driveway as it ran downhill. Gathering speed.

Behind me, rain erased Fitcher's bungalow. I could only see what was closest: the wet lace of trees, the mighty paw covering my hand. An arm's length away, the gharial, its long-toothed snout curved in a faint smile, slid effortlessly through the water. Before it disappeared, it looked at me, its reptile eye tender.

The flood carried me faster. I spun around a tree, nearly smashed into it, but kicked hard against the trunk and whirled away. Ahead of me blackbucks scrambled out of the water and bounded into the undergrowth. Dappled chital deer huddled under the dripping trees, tails flicking.

I swam on.

The trees opened up; rain roared down. I was nearing the main road, the one I'd walked down only this morning. It was now a wide river, brown and fast. Before it could swallow me, I managed to catch a bent sapling and pull myself onto a muddy bank. Long minutes passed as I lay there, half-drowned and panting but alive.

My ears pricked to the sound of voices.

Rounding the bend, vivid in the pouring rain, was one of the lake boats. It wobbled and leaned. In the front, under a tasseled canopy, sat Granny, and beside her, the chief of police. Behind them, Maya and Gayatri huddled under a blanket. And standing at the back, punting with a long pole, was Ash. Determined and handsome, fighting the tricky current. The wind whipped his hair across his face as he worked to keep the boat from capsizing.

He'd found the note hidden in the bell.

"Ash!" I cried, loud as I could.

His gaze snapped to where I lay. Even in the tiger skin, he knew me.

He jabbed the pole deep. The boat spun around it, threatening to career out of control. Grim-faced, the strain of it making the muscles stand out in his neck, he maneuvered the vessel toward the rise where I lay. Wedging it against a fallen tree, he dropped to his knees and leaned out over the water.

"I said I wouldn't leave you behind!" he shouted over the rain's din.

He held out his hands.

When I stood, my tiger skin slid from my shoulders. It

tumbled down the muddy bank and, like a living thing, slipped into the rushing water. I watched it go, wishing the torn and tattered back to life: ears above the torrent, tail curled, until it was nothing but rain, a fragment of true magic.

AUTHOR'S NOTE

When I was ten, my family visited Jim Corbett National Park in northern India, not far from where this story takes place. In the library of our damp bungalow, I found a copy of Englishman Jim Corbett's memoir *Man-Eaters of Kumaon*. I read it at night, with a flashlight, while out in the hall, one of the enormous man-eaters Corbett had killed decades before still stood watch. Its glass eyes were foggy, and patches of its fur had been eaten away by beetles, but having read the stories, I was terrified of it. At the same time, I wanted desperately for it to be alive again, stalking through the elephant grass. Its ghost has haunted me ever since.

SAY MY NAME

Dahlia Adler

Inspired by "Rumpelstiltskin"

Lissa Haynes is *pissed.*

I settle into my seat at our lunch table, chin in hand in classic *I'm listening* pose, as I watch her storm over, the edges of her dark bob smacking her chin with each step. Lissa has two modes—syrupy sweet (when she wants something) and missionary from hell (when she didn't get it)—and there's only one thing my best friend wanted badly enough to warrant the way her hazel eyes glimmer with lightning. "Tell your bestie all about it," I say, patting the seat next to me.

It takes no other prompting to get her to spill. "Bridget Miller is such a bitch." She punctuates the statement with a slam of her tray, and I hold back a wince. She sounds so angry that, for once, Divya Kumari curbs her speech on internalized misogyny and its terminology.

Such a good heart that girl has. It's why she's only allowed to sit with us twice a week.

"I take it this means you weren't on the list," Div says carefully instead, tugging on a strand of her thick black waist-length hair.

"Brilliant guess. Must be why you're captain of Model UN and actually get to go places." Lissa snaps into a carrot stick like it's Bridget Miller's femur, her sharp white teeth making quick work of it. "Meanwhile, some of us get screwed out of NPCHS despite being the literal best coder in the class because Bridget Miller's daddy convinced Mr. Roy that *she's* Wheeler's answer to Steve Jobs. And since only one junior gets to go, ta-da! The girl who's spent all of one summer at programming camp gets my spot."

"That is *extremely* fucked up," I agree, both because it is— the National Programming Contest for High Schoolers is something that Lissa's worked toward for *years* and should absolutely be hers to attend—and because it would be the only right answer with Lissa even if it weren't. But my words don't seem to have any calming effect; the porcelain skin of her cheekbones continues to flame with heat, two poison apples in a sea of cream. Her jaw remains set, sharp as a shard of glass. The feeling of failure simmers in my bones.

I do not fail. Especially when it comes to Lissa.

"I'll take care of it," I say airily, stabbing a fork into a cucumber to make clear violence will be part of the job if necessary. It won't be necessary—the beginnings of an idea are stirring in my brain already—but Lissa's one of those girls who gets horny over bloodshed, and I'm one of those girls who gets horny over Lissa, so.

Her expression relaxes as much as it ever does, features still sharp but less feral—the face of a girl who never, ever lets her guard down. How she knows the background to Bridget getting her spot is beyond me, but that's Lissa; don't let her hooded eyes fool you, because they are always wide fucking open.

And she's not alone in that. We've been best friends since sixth grade, when social lives got more strategic and like called to like in the natural way it does. Of course, she hasn't yet

figured out that "best friends" isn't meant to be our final destination, but that's fine. I'm patient. And I know she'll get there
eventually.

But first things first.

———◦———

Fun fact: Lissa Haynes is not the best coder in our class. She
thinks she is, and until Bridget Miller's daddy got to his old
frat brother Mr. Roy about Bridget, everyone else did, too. But
that's fine. Lissa's happy when she thinks she's the best, and I
haven't exactly struggled to put my talents to good use.

Her C in English that magically became an A-minus?
Yours truly. Her seven absences reduced to three? Also me.
Every permission slip she's ever forgotten to get signed magically fixed by an email from Dr. Olivia Bradley-Haynes's personal account? Come on. Who do you think?

But I don't need the recognition, or to be Queen of the
Computer Nerds. If my parents found out that my sibling
Miriasha has taught me everything they know, I'd be held
prisoner in my room until I had pristine applications com-
pleted for Stanford, MIT, and Carnegie Mellon.

Besides, Lissa's favorite thing to do when she wins coding
competitions is to celebrate in her hot tub with her BFF, too
much champagne, and wandering hands, so like. Whatever the
coding version of an Emmy Award is, she can fucking have it.

The thing is, Bridget Miller is also definitely not the best
coder in our class; last I snooped she was barely scraping by
with a C. But I've seen her dad and Mr. Roy shoot the shit at
fundraisers, and it's clear the two of them are so buddy-buddy
that he could make this happen if he wanted to. Which means
Bridget is probably shaking in her last-season boots right now
with the competition approaching.

She'll probably need some help.

And lucky her, I know the perfect person for that.

———·———

Create new account. I could always use something like CodeMaster69—it'll work just fine for my purposes—but it's so lowbrow. I give myself a moment and choose LanaGintur, which sounds just enough like a real name to drive her nuts and make her think I can be Internet-stalked while actually just being an anagram of Alan Turing.

And okay, yes, I add a 69 at the end, because I'm only human.

> **LanaGintur69:** I heard you got the junior spot on the coding team.
> **LanaGintur69:** Congratulations.

Then I wait. It takes a few minutes, but I finally get my expected response.

> **UnderTheBridge:** Who is this

Does Bridget know how slutty that name sounds? She must, right? "Under the Bridge" is like a terrible pun that'd be made in the boys' locker room by a losing soccer team.

Honestly, it's kind of brilliant.

> **LanaGintur69:** Someone who knows that you have no idea what the fuck you're doing.

Silence. Every now and again, an "UnderTheBridge is typing" followed by a promising ellipsis, and then . . . nothing.

She doesn't respond again that night, but that's fine.

She will.

⎯⎯◦⎯⎯

The best part is watching Bridget glance furtively around herself the entire next day, like a chipmunk trying to protect its precious trove of acorns from encroaching squirrels. Of course, Lissa notices, too. Her laser eyes have been following Bridget almost as closely as mine have. "What's up Miller's ass today?" she asks with a snort as we reapply our lip gloss at the bathroom mirrors after third period. "Is it just me or does she look a little feral?"

There's no small amount of glee in her voice, and it takes everything in me to tamp down my smile with a sharp tooth to the lip that immediately demands reapplication of my Watermelon Wish. "She's definitely . . . something."

"I hope everything's okay," Divya murmurs instinctively, lavishing her own lips with the berry purple she wears just as loyally as Lissa sports her blood red. Then she catches us both glaring at her. "I mean, if she's going to steal your spot, she better not screw it up."

Not perfect, but better. Lissa looks mollified. I know Divya has one foot out the door on this friend group, and that's fine—I don't need to share. But a little respect, please.

"Maybe she's having a breakdown." Lissa runs her hand through her hair, and I watch the dark silk trail through her fingers. "Serves her right. The first in-school competition is this Friday, and she's going to tank. She's gotta know she's in over her head."

That's what I'm counting on.

"Definitely," I say, watching Lissa apply one final coat of

Dragon's Blood to her lips and blow a kiss at the mirror. "She is definitely in over her head."

———

Bridget cracks before the day is even over.

> **UnderTheBridge:** Who are you
> **LanaGintur69:** That is beside the point. Do you want the help or not?
> **UnderTheBridge:** Who says I need help?
> **LanaGintur69:** That would work a lot better if you weren't here replying to a stranger who was offering it.
> **UnderTheBridge:** Out of the goodness of your heart, I'm sure
> **UnderTheBridge:** What do you want

Now, that's a good question, Bridget. Because I absolutely do want something, but we're not there yet.

I have a much better use for this question.

> **LanaGintur69:** Just the satisfaction of putting Lissa Haynes in her place will be fine, thx

There's another minute of silence, and I know three things are happening right now.

1. Bridget's suspicion that Lissa was behind this account has now been torn apart.
2. Bridget actually believes she has an ally against one of the most powerful girls in school.
3. Bridget isn't using this time to think it over; she's already decided to take me up on the offer. She's just trying not to sound too eager.

UnderTheBridge: Well, it's hard to argue with that
UnderTheBridge: Okay
UnderTheBridge: What do I need to do

I send her an invite for a video chat under a dummy account, turn on my voice changer, and keep my screen on a shared presentation. For three hours that night, I walk her through the first three problems from last year's competition, which took me a grand total of twenty minutes on my own. Bridget's not a quick study, that's for sure. I may be better than Lissa, but Lissa's miles better than her, and every now and again I have to keep myself from screaming about the power of nepotism and shitty boys' clubs.

Still, I press on, but Bridget's clearly fading, not even trying anymore. It's a good thing there's no way she's actually going to the competition, because it's two hours longer than this and she would absolutely die. Finally, when I can tell I've fully drained her will to live, I let her go.

Sort of.

LanaGintur69: Tomorrow. 4 pm.
UnderTheBridge: I can't at 4, I have choir practice.
LanaGintur69: Tomorrow. 4 pm. You don't show up then, I don't show up again at all.
LanaGintur69 has signed off.

I've always hated her voice anyway.

—◇—

The next day, Bridget's walking around with dark circles under her eyes, so I guess being stupid is exhausting. I'm tempted to suggest she bring coffee to our programming lesson this afternoon, but, of course, that would give things away, so she'll just have to figure it out on her own—it's gonna be a long night.

We do an hour of algorithm challenges as a warm-up. Then an hour of puzzles. Then another hour of problem-solving. She tries telling me her dad's home and she has to leave for dinner, and I gently remind her that her father is the reason she's in this situation in the first place and maybe she should point that out to him if he gives her any trouble about using this time to practice for the first in-school meet this Friday.

She doesn't ask how I know that. After the first two hours, she's also stopped trying to guess my identity. If she had any brain space left after all these lessons, I might be worried, but I know it's more likely she's just dead on her feet.

I let her go at ten.

LanaGintur69: Same time tomorrow.
UnderTheBridge: Thanks, but I think the last couple of days were really helpful, and I've got a lot of other work to do.
UnderTheBridge: I can take it from here.

So fucking lazy. Lissa would probably jump at the chance to spend this many hours coding. Maybe when this is all over, I'll come clean about everything, but this is not, in fact, over.

LanaGintur69: You sure?
LanaGintur69: Because I'd hate to think about all the rumors that would spread about how you got onto the team if you crash and burn as hard on Friday as you definitely will if you don't put any more time in.

I almost hope she tries it. Lissa and I would have so much fun spreading her "secrets" like wildfire. It's exactly the kind of plot we would form while sprawled out on her couch, sharing her favorite roasted chickpeas from a bowl small enough to force our fingers to brush against each other every now and again.

But at least for today, Bridget's ironically too smart for that.

UnderTheBridge: One more day. That's it.

I debate pointing out that she's really not in control here—not when I'm the one holding all the cards *and* giving her a much-needed education—but decide I'd rather let her believe she has some semblance of power.

LanaGintur69: See you at 4.

—◦—

It isn't one more day, as we both knew would be the case, but at least the lessons have paid off—Bridget comes in first in the practice competition on Friday, which, ironically, seems to prove her father right. Lissa is *pissed*, as I knew she would be, but I know she'll be happy when she witnesses a much larger crash and burn.

"It's just luck," I assure Lissa. "Don't worry. She isn't going to make it to the real thing."

"And how would you know that?" Lissa demands, fire lighting up her eyes.

"I told you to trust me. So trust me."

Slowly, the anger melts off Lissa's face and her lips curve into a Dragon's Blood smile. "Of course I trust you." She leans over and leaves a red imprint I can feel on my cheek. "More than anybody."

I keep that with me going into one last evening with Bridget.

> **LanaGintur69:** Congratulations.
>
> **UnderTheBridge:** We really did it. I can't believe it. Thank you, I guess.

You guess? Oh, honey. Whatever guilty feelings I might've had about what I'm doing to you would've been gone with that, if they'd ever existed in the first place.

> **LanaGintur69:** You're welcome.
>
> **LanaGintur69:** Now it's time to get ready for the big show.
>
> **UnderTheBridge:** Did you see my results? I crushed my entire team.
>
> **UnderTheBridge:** And Lissa was definitely not happy
>
> **UnderTheBridge:** We both got what we wanted
>
> **UnderTheBridge:** We're done here
>
> **LanaGintur69:** Oh, are we?
>
> **LanaGintur69:** So I guess you don't want to take a look at the NPCHS challenges together.
>
> **UnderTheBridge:** We already did that.
>
> **LanaGintur69:** We looked at last year's, not this year's.

Silence. Sweet, sweet silence. I send a quiet thanks to Miriasha for sending me the problems from last year's international collegiate competition when I told them I wanted to help a friend study; Bridget isn't going to be able to tell the difference.

Miriasha did make me promise it wasn't Lissa I wanted them for; they're not exactly her biggest fan. And technically, they're not for Lissa. The fact that this whole thing will also help her in the long run is just a nice coincidence.

But really, isn't everything I do to help Lissa in the long run?

My big sib should know this.

Even if no one else does.

UnderTheBridge: How do you have this year's questions
UnderTheBridge: Who are you
LanaGintur69: How did I know your daddy got you onto the team?
LanaGintur69: How did I know you had no idea what you were doing?
LanaGintur69: How do I know your name is Bridget Alma Miller, you live at 4 Timothy Lane, you're allergic to cat hair and strawberries, you lied about hooking up with Ben Bandy on the class trip last year, and you told your parents you lost the necklace from your grandmother but actually sold it on eBay?
LanaGintur69: I just know things.
UnderTheBridge: Seriously, who the fuck are you
LanaGintur69: Tomorrow, 4 pm.
LanaGintur69: Fuck choir practice.
LanaGintur69 has signed off.

She lost her solo after skipping two practices last week to meet with me, so really, she's not missing much.

———

I give her two problems the next day and cut her off by six. She's better, but not *that* much better. I knew what questions were going to be in the practice competition, and that's what we studied; it's pretty much the sum total of what she knows, and it isn't nearly enough.

UnderTheBridge: What about the rest of them?

LanaGintur69: Like you said, you got it from here. And I'm sure you can learn Python on your own.

She absolutely cannot learn Python on her own. I'm not sure she even knows what it is. I *do* know she's screwed without it.

LanaGintur69: You've already won once. Of course, that contest was just practice, but who cares if you come in dead last in the real thing?

LanaGintur69: At least you get to go.

LanaGintur69: You'll be fine.

LanaGintur69: I'm sure your dad won't be humiliated.

LanaGintur69: And no one will wonder if you cheated the first time and how you possibly got on the competition team.

LanaGintur69: Good luck.

I give it thirty seconds, and that's all it takes.

UnderTheBridge: Wait

UnderTheBridge: Please

UnderTheBridge: I still need your help

Why, yes; yes, you do.

LanaGintur69: The price has gone up.

UnderTheBridge: What do you want?

Now, that is the correct question. But I suspect she is not going to like the answer.

LanaGintur69: Your spot in the competition.

UnderTheBridge: What the fuck? Obviously I'm not giving you that

UnderTheBridge: That's the whole point of this

LanaGintur69: No, see, you got off with making it look like your daddy isn't a liar. You're welcome for that.

LanaGintur69: But that's all you're getting.

LanaGintur69: That spot isn't yours, and you aren't keeping it.

LanaGintur69: And if you try to, I will make you pay.

UnderTheBridge: What the FUCK

UnderTheBridge: I did pay. Lissa is miserable, just like you wanted.

UnderTheBridge: And so am I.

UnderTheBridge: I'm behind in all my classes, got dropped down in choir . . .

UnderTheBridge: I have paid. I don't have anything else for you.

LanaGintur69: Did I stutter?

LanaGintur69: You. Have. The. Spot. I. Want.

LanaGintur69: Give it up.

UnderTheBridge: Even if I gave it up, it'd go back to Lissa, not you.

LanaGintur69: Now you're catching on.

UnderTheBridge: IS THIS FUCKING LISSA

LanaGintur69: No, it is definitely not fucking Lissa.

LanaGintur69: And if you tell Lissa how she got her spot back, I will end you.

UnderTheBridge: If you really expect me to believe this isn't Lissa, then tell me

UnderTheBridge: Who

UnderTheBridge: You

UnderTheBridge: Are

UnderTheBridge: You asshole

In a perfect world, I'd love for Lissa to know how brilliant I am. And I'd love for her to know we have this passion and talent in common. But I know that won't work for her, that she won't take it well. She doesn't like sharing any spotlights, and that's fine.

All she has to know is that I did exactly what I said I would, with some bonus life wreckage for Bridget in the process.

The how doesn't matter. It isn't important.

And yet, I can't risk dangling the carrot, just for a little catharsis.

> **LanaGintur69:** Tell you what.
>
> **LanaGintur69:** You figure that out, complete with my full name, by noon tomorrow, and you can keep your spot.

It sounds risky, I know, but it isn't. Even if she somehow figures out that it's me, no one—not even Lissa—knows my legal name. And they never will. Considering it isn't even on my birth certificate, I know I'm safe.

The fact is, at noon tomorrow, Bridget will be forced to give up her spot, Lissa will slide back in as if nothing happened, and I'll be her hero, who happens to be ready with a celebratory bottle of sparkling cider (and one of champagne in my car for later).

It's going to be a very good day.

My phone rings just then, and I smile at the picture of Miriasha that fills the screen. "Hey, Mir. Thanks again for those challenge questions. They came in super handy."

"Dude. What the fuck is wrong with your voice?"

"Oh, shit." I turn off the voice distorter I use for my sessions with Bridget. "Sorry about that."

"Why were you using a voice changer?"

"Oh, it's for . . ." Turns out, that's a hard thing to make up an excuse for on the spot. "Um."

They sigh. "Does this have anything to do with the questions you asked for? The ones that *weren't* for your girlfriend?"

"She's not my girlfriend," I snap, hating how the very idea of the impossible brings heat into my cheeks. "And they weren't for Lissa. I've been helping a girl at school who's going to NPCHS and has no idea what she's doing. Or at least she didn't."

"Is that so? You've been helping some girl who's *not* Lissa out of the goodness of your heart?"

I think I'm offended. "I happen to be an excellent tutor, Miriasha Stilton."

"I'll bet you are—"

"Mir, if you use my full name I am going to pull out your tongue through the phone."

"You know you didn't have to let Mom petition for the name change, right? It was an absolutely deranged thing to do."

"Yes, sorry that when I was a toddler, I didn't think to stand up to our Twihard mother in defense of a name I didn't even know how to spell yet." I sigh, because it isn't our first time having this conversation, and it won't be our last, but come eighteen, I will *definitely* be heading back to court to fix that mistake. "Anyway, you rang?"

"Just wanted to see if the questions were helpful, but now I think maybe I don't wanna know any more about what's going on here. You still coming to see me next weekend?"

"As long as you keep my name out of your mouth," I say sweetly. *As long as everyone does.*

We hang up, and I immediately open my messages to

Lissa. Tomorrow, I tell her. You'll have your spot back. Cafeteria at noon. It's gonna be a good time.

———◦———

I keep an eye out for Bridget from the second I walk into school, eager to see the anxious expression she's been carrying around since the day I first made contact. She doesn't look like a girl who's about to be humiliated in front of the entire school, but then I suppose I can spare her that if she wants to go quietly to Mr. Roy and drop out that way.

But no matter how long I stare at my phone, waiting for an excited text from Lissa that lets me know she's been reinstated, it doesn't come. So I guess we're doing this the hard way.

Okay, that's fun, too.

The noon bell rings for junior lunch period, and I gather up my stuff and head over to the cafeteria, not even bothering with my usual pre-lunch freshening up. Honestly, the promise of getting to exact humiliation against Bridget *and* reap the gratitude from Lissa gives me a special dewy glow my bronzer can't replicate anyway.

Expecting to be one of the first to the caf, I'm surprised to see Bridget already waiting at a table smack in the center. Guess her curiosity got the best of her. But of course, it also killed the cat, or whatever. I start to do an about-face to have a helpful conversation with Mr. Roy when a voice cuts through the room.

"Where are you going, Ren?"

I freeze in my tracks a split second before realizing it's a mistake. Bridget Miller and I are not friends. She does not call me from across the room. She does not call me at all, and I certainly do not stop to answer.

But it's fine. So she knows I'm Lana Gintur. What's she gonna do about it? Reveal that—gasp!—I'm actually super-smart and she isn't? She isn't holding any of the cards here, and I was perfectly clear on her needing my full legal name. "Ren," which is what literally everyone but my mother calls me, isn't gonna cut it.

I turn around and smile sweetly. "I was just going to have a fascinating conversation with Mr. Roy. Did you wanna come? Might be a little awkward, but . . ." I offer a helpless shrug.

"I'll bet it will be," she says, but instead of looking nervous, she looks . . . triumphant? Everyone's watching us now, faces alight with curiosity, and for the first time since this whole plan began I feel a flutter in my stomach that things might not go my way.

But no, it's not possible.

Is it?

No.

"I think I'll stay here, though." She steps up onto the center of the table in her delicate ballet flats. "What do you think of that plan, Renata?"

I snort. "I think that's just fine. I don't really need you around for this conversation anyway. But that was a nice try."

"Was it, Serena?"

"Not really," I say, tut-tutting. "But you did try. And as you were always meant to do, you failed." I flash her a smirk. "I'll let you know how the conversation goes."

I turn on my heel and am almost at the door when her voice splits the air again. "I don't think you will, Renesmee Carlie Stilton."

I never understood what it meant to feel the blood drain from your face, but I do now. I feel my lifeblood seeping out of me, physically *feel* myself fading, as the rest of the room turns and gawks at me.

What.

The.

Fuck.

And then.

"Ren, what's going on?"

No.

I turn slowly to see Lissa standing behind me, arms crossed in her pristine white sweater, gaze traveling from Bridget back to me. "Why is that freak even talking to you? And did she just call you . . . Renesmee?"

"That *is* her name after all," Bridget says gleefully. "Which means that thanks for all the help, *Ren*, but I really will be just fine without you." She shifts her gaze to Lissa and narrows her eyes into a glare. "Nice effort, though."

"Ren, seriously, what the hell is she talking about?"

My brain is whirring with possible answers, but somehow, Bridget's morphed into someone who can actually think on her feet. "I'm talking about your girlfriend trying to blackmail me into giving you my spot at NPCHS, but for someone so smart—and she is *so* smart, by the way; did you know she's better at coding than you are?—she's awfully stupid some-times." She looks almost drunk when she turns back to me and stage-whispers, "Next time, computer whiz, you might want to sign out before you take a phone call."

It takes everything in me to meet Lissa's gaze, to search for a sign she knows I did this all for her, lied for her, got her what she wanted, but the only way to possibly read her expression is a cross between anger and disgust. The entire room has exploded into one giant shitshow, and it's all just so much that I slam my foot hard enough to embed my heel into the linoleum.

If you were ever unsure how much lower you could go, try being forced to use both hands to unstick your foot from the floor while the entire room watches, your former best friend looks like she wants to puke for ever having been associated with you, and the girl you tried to blackmail into humiliation gets the last laugh.

As soon as my foot is free, I bolt.

I don't know if Lissa ends up with the spot, or if Wheeler High wins or even places. Miriasha won't let me look it up, won't let me torture myself any further. They're letting me stay with them, got me a coding gig, and promised that the minute I turn eighteen, they'll drive me to the courthouse so I can pick any name I want.

I am definitely done with this one.

And truth be told, Lana Gintur has grown on me.

FIRE &
RHINESTONE

Stacey Lee

Inspired by "The Little Matchstick Girl"

New York, 1892
ACT I

My grandmother was born with a mole high in the center of her forehead, a black thumbprint that said *Stay away.* Some believed she had died of the plague in another life, and that touching her would start a contagion that would wipe away all of Chinatown. Others believed she'd survive a cobra attack. That her poisonous saliva would cause instant death if she spit on you. Only I knew the real story, or as real as any of Amah's stories could be.

Our matchsticks rattled in my satchel as we made our way up Broadway to the Metropolitan Opera House, where we sold them for a penny each. After a long performance, most folks were dying for a smoke, even when the air was humid enough to lick, like tonight. The Met lay three miles from our flat, but we made the trip several times a week. Amah believed it was the best place to peddle fire.

I settled Amah against the post of the old clock, our usual

spot, making sure her bonnet was tied low over her head, so her mole would not scare away customers. The real story was that Amah had been hit by lightning as a babe, and the fire had become part of her life's energy. *Anyone can wield fire, Fire-fly, but few are built from it. Those who are built from fire are, by their nature, brighter than the rest.*

Built from it or not, Amah's hands were cold as ice chips. "You should've stayed home," I grumbled, though I knew she would not let me out of her sight.

"I couldn't miss the *William Tell* overture." Amah's gravelly Cantonese always contained a hint of mischief. Sometimes the music from the performance would trickle out through the blond bricks of the stately monolith. When that happened, Amah's face would take on a look of bliss, and her posture would become as fluid as a mermaid's. She began to hum the victory ride, holding imaginary reins and jostling her shoulders.

I caught the old woman before she fell. Amah was only sixty, but our hardscrabble life had aged her, and I constantly worried she would snap in two. The clock's disdainful face glared down at me. I glared back. Seven o'clock, and the opera still hadn't let out. Carriages had begun circling the block like bees. The after-opera crowd was a sweet place to drop a hook.

"William Tell shot an apple off his son's head. Would you let me shoot one off your head, Firefly?" Amah panted.

"If I had an apple, I would put it in my stomach, not on my head." Drawing from my satchel charcoal and a scrap of paper, I began to sketch to keep my nervous fingers busy.

"The bum-rag who played William always ate the apple after the performance." She had picked up "bum-rag" from the sailors who came to Chinatown to gamble.

I hooked an eyebrow. "How do you know that?"

"I was a soprano. They brought me flowers. How else would I know the story?"

"From the opera posters." They were everywhere this side of town, even stuck to the sides of the trolleys. I snorted, my hot breath lingering on my upper lip. As if we, a pair of Eastern devils, would ever be allowed into the opera. Before the arthritis had set in, Amah was a seamstress.

Her tea-steeped eyes pored over the lean figure that had grown from my makeshift pencil. "You've improved, Firefly. You have the moon goddess's nimble fingers, like me." She crooked an arthritic pinkie at the drawing. "Except William Tell was much fatter and his hair fell to his shoulders."

A horse stamped a foot, throwing its head impatiently. I glanced around for Pomp and Circumstance, the vainglorious opera manager. The man was always looking to give vendors a swift kick as he marched around, bowing and scraping to the theatergoers. Ever since his pants had caught fire years ago, according to rumors, he especially loathed matchstick sellers.

Not sighting P&C, I straightened Amah's faded jacket. "Tonight, you must act like a lo bok." The Chinese radish was her favorite vegetable. "None of your foolish chatter." Her face puckered. Lo bok might not talk, but they certainly had a bite. But people were less generous with a batty old woman than they were with respectable beggars.

"*You* act like a lo bok." She kicked at a crow, which took off in a flurry of black wings. "Your mother was never so bossy." Her lips clamped tight as two halves of a melon seed.

I groaned, wishing again she'd stayed at home. If she

started sulking, no one would buy from us. More gently, I said, "Tell me about her." Talking about Mother, who'd died when I was born, always lifted Amah's mood. As she chatted, I passed her one of the cigar boxes that held our loose matches.

"They called her Rosie because of her rosy cheeks. Sometimes, I hear her through the cracks." She glanced longingly back at the yellow bricks of the opera house. Amah's gaze shifted to me. "She had the same Swedish eyes as you, from your grandfather. You know, Firefly, he was a pirate who hid me in his sea chest so I could cross the Atlantic." Her cheeks flushed in pleasure. I couldn't always tell when she was lying because she seeded her lies with truth, and despite me having the same dusky skin and high Asian cheekbones as her, my eyes were blue.

"Maybe my vagabond sailor of a father gave me these eyes." According to Amah, he'd been lost at sea, never knowing the child he left behind.

A peanut vendor pushed a cart down the sidewalk, and my stomach cramped. With nothing to eat since last night, my belly writhed like a dying fish. Two boxes of matches was all I needed to sell, enough to cover our trolley ride to and from Chinatown and two bowls of noodles with a few vegetables. In the winter, I could sell ten times as many.

Amah's jaw went crooked. "Forget about that bum-rag."

I cocked an ear toward her. I knew the story about my father being a sailor was made-up, but she'd never called him a bum-rag before.

"He was a shooter of suns, like the Chinese William Tell." A classic Chinese legend told the story of an archer who'd been paid to shoot down the ten suns circling Earth, nearly leaving it in darkness. "Those who play with fire are destined for the flame," she spat.

I tried to shake off my unease. The theater doors were opening.

From the roofed entryway poured the ladies on the arms of their gents, dabbing handkerchiefs to their eyes.

"You're a lo bok," I reminded Amah, passing her my drawing. Then I lifted my voice. "Matches! Get your matches!" I polished up a smile. "A penny each, or a dozen for a dime. This is good fire we're offering, folks."

Eyes rinsed over me and flicked away. A frigate of a man pulled a pipe from his cloak. I hurried to him. "Let me light that calabash for you, sir. Don't trouble your fingers."

The man tilted back his bowler and hung his pipe over his lip. I hit a match against the striker. Soon, curls of smoke began pouring from the man's nostrils.

I held out a hand. "That's a penny, sir, and I wish you the joy of your smoke."

The man blew a cloud into my face and began to walk away.

"Excuse me, sir?" I began to follow him.

"Stop, match thief!" Dropping her cigar box, Amah shook her fist at the man. Matches fanned out over the sidewalk. "No one swindles Firefly. Pay the penny, you bum-rag, or I will knock your teeth out." Amah's English stalked out in heavy, indignant syllables.

I caught Amah's fist before it connected. "Never mind him," I whispered sharply.

The match thief's eyes grazed over us. People stopped, watching as if it were an encore performance. Blowing another, surlier puff of smoke our direction, he marched away, leaves squelching underfoot.

My teeth ground together. I would need to let this one go, or forfeit the entire evening while I chased him down.

"—priceless picture." To my horror, Amah was holding my drawing out for everyone to see.

A fresh spike of humiliation warmed my face. A lady with a fine lace shawl eyed the picture, which now looked out of proportion and heavy-handed. I hurried over. "Lo bok can't talk," I hissed in Amah's ear, reaching for the sketch.

"That's quite good," said the lady. "It's William Tell."

Amah waved the drawing as if it were a national flag. "All yours for a quarter."

The lady considered the picture a moment longer. She pulled a man with a sweating bald head by the elbow. "Jens, I would like the picture."

With a grunt, the man dug into his pocket. Amah's knuckles blanched as she held the drawing, maybe in case we had a picture thief on our hands.

The man set the quarter into my palm. It was all I could do not to snatch it and run. With a satisfied humph, Amah relinquished the prize.

"Aren't you glad I wasn't a lo bok?" Amah crowed, a toothy smile splitting her gaunt cheeks.

I sighed in mock defeat. Tonight, we would feast. Not just noodles, but thick cubes of bean curd and a bone with some gristle. We'd buy ginger liniment for Amah's fingers.

I numbly collected the fallen matches, hardly noticing the crowd dwindling. A single picture was worth more than two boxes of matches. Had the sale simply been a lucky strike? A charitable woman buying off her guilt at being rich? If not, maybe there was money to be made through pictures. I had promised to one day take Amah to the island of Hainan, which she called "heaven's garden on earth."

Amah's smile flattened, her eyes focused behind me. "Bum-rag."

Less than twenty feet away, a delivery truck had pulled to the street corner. The opera house manager, Pomp and Circumstance, in his stiff tuxedo, directed the unloading of a parade of costumes from the vehicle with the aid of a brass-tipped cane. P&C had used the crutch ever since his accident. A stunner of a dress—a red silk tutu gleaming with rhinestones—caused a ripple of gasps to erupt from the crowd. It was a gaudy constellation fallen from heaven.

"Yes, ladies and gentlemen, it's Olympia's dress, back from Paris in time for our big show next week." P&C mopped his shiny forehead with a handkerchief. "After more than a decade, *Tales of Hoffmann* is returning. A lustful tale of glory lost, as the poet Hoffmann tries to win the heart of the doll Olympia!" His lips spread over his short teeth.

"It did not end well, for Olympia," Amah said darkly. "At least *she* was only a doll. Your mother was barely fourteen. Just like you."

"What are you on about?"

"But everyone demanded so much of me. Queenie, they called me, because I was royalty. *Queenie, me first. Queenie, you're so talented.*"

Before I could stop her, she'd drifted away, angling for a better look as the dress traveled around the corner and up a staircase to a stage door. Sighting her, P&C's oily grin disappeared. He tramped toward us, the cane giving his approach more impact than two feet alone. The cane hovered within striking distance. "Be off with you," he barked, glaring at us through cornflower-blue eyes too pretty for his jowly face. "You don't belong here."

"Broadway belongs to no one," I said lightly. "We're just trying to make an honest living."

"Well, find some other sidewalk, you filth."

Amah's button nose flared. "Don't you remember, I used to be the star here?" Amah spat at him. "I wore Italian taffeta. Once, they all came to me, wanting my attention."

I grabbed one of her shaky wrists and set it back by her side, giving her a grim shake of my head. She might be a loony old woman, but P&C could still have us thrown into the pen. Her eyes pinched into wounded triangles.

P&C's chest expanded, as if filling up for a sounding off. But noticing all the people watching us, he dug up a smile. Probably it wasn't good business to be seen berating an old woman. With his cane, he signaled to the men in tall bucket caps across the street, shooing away a couple of boys. "Officers!"

"Sir, please." I bowed my head to P&C. "We won't trouble you." Gathering Amah by her shoulders, I steered her away.

P&C glowered at us, but Amah sauntered regally by. I worked out how we would ever return here. There were other places to sell matches. Amah would protest. I once suggested we sell at Battery Park to debarking ferry passengers, but she refused, even though it was half the distance.

Then again, if we wanted to sell opera sketches, nowhere else offered such predictable waves of wealthy opera enthusiasts.

Later that night, in the small room we rented on Pell Street, Amah rested on our straw mattress. We rented the place for a song because a man had poisoned his wife here. "Hungry" ghosts often returned to the site of their injury. That Amah defied ghosts only added to her fearsome reputation, which we counted on to keep us safe in the bachelor society in which we Chinese were forced to live.

The scent of ginger liniment drifted from where I had rubbed her fingers. On the nightstand, the flame of the hurricane lamp cast a warm glow over Amah's sewing basket, where sewing notions mingled with things from her past—a clipped peacock feather and a brass key, which opened no door I knew of.

Pulling up a chair beside her bed, I took out my new purchases of good paper and a real pencil.

While men quarreled in the room next door, my pencil flowed across the page like a finely honed skate across ice. Olympia in her star-touched tutu took shape under Amah's direction.

Amah grew quiet and long shadows plucked at her face. "William was foolish."

Irritably, I swept eraser crumbs from my drawing. "We're doing *Tales of Hoffmann* now, not *William Tell*. And anyway, at least his arrow didn't miss."

"A parent should never put her child in danger." She seemed to sink deeper into the mattress, becoming another crease in the sheet. "The stars are too bright tonight. Turn them down, please."

I adjusted the knob on the lamp, shrinking the flame, and the mole on her forehead faded into shadow. Amah had started those rumors about her birthmark for protection. But when had she begun believing the stories she spun were more truth than fiction?

"Tell me more about my mother," I asked, using my old trick.

This time, the request failed to scrub the unease from her face. She stared through the faded wallpaper, with its flowery ghosts. "I would not give up my child, but neither would she."

"What do you mean, Amah? Speak plain."

"I mean when your mother found she was with child, I told her it was too dangerous."

"Too dangerous?" Labor was a mortal risk women took every day.

She ignored me. "I asked her to get rid of you, but she refused the doctor's herbs."

The words stung, even though I had known my mother died in childbirth. Of course, no mother would want a grandchild at the cost of her own child, would she? But though I knew Amah loved me, maybe even as much as I loved her, it was hard to get my pencil to finish my drawing.

ACT II

We waited a week before returning to the opera house, hoping our absence would lower P&C's guard. Then we set out, Amah's hair coiled in a neat braid under her bonnet, and a cotton handkerchief securing my own.

The evening was humid, the air like wet wool over our heads. The energy seemed to have drained from New York's shoulders, the vendors closing their shades more slowly, the mules dragging their hooves. Amah rubbed her joints. The damp made them ache more than usual. As the trolley bore us toward midtown, I began to regret the decision to go.

But today marked the opening of *Tales of Hoffmann*, and people had come from all around to catch one of only four performances. We needed to milk P&C's moneymaker for all it was worth. Perhaps the rain would wait until tonight, when we were safely tucked into our room with bowls of cooled tea in our hands—chrysanthemum if we were lucky with the opera sketches.

We took up our usual spot by the old clock, and Amah studied one of my pictures of Olympia, the show's singing doll. I had exaggerated the height of her three-pronged crown and the tulle tiers of her gown. "If this goes well, I'll buy colored pencils."

"I sewed a fortune in crystal rhinestones into that bodice alone." Her thin lips pursed, and she flexed the fingers of her left hand.

"I have no doubt of your skill with the needle, Amah, but I thought you were a soprano," I teased.

She snorted. "I have the voice of a duck. You know that."

I smiled. At least that part was true.

"When Olympia stepped onto the stage, those crystals caught all the fire in the room. Fire shouldn't be wasted, you know. Which is why I pinched a handful to keep the two of us that first year."

"Pinched? You don't steal." Amah maintained that stealing turned one into a crow, and she couldn't stand the loathsome birds.

"No. I only take what I am owed." Her voice had taken on an edge. I could almost believe she had sewn Olympia's dress . . . except if she had worked in the grandest opera house in the country, why were we stuck out here, selling matches? It was hard not to feel a little sick at how her mind had wasted. "No one noticed. I had my own key because I worked late into the night."

The doors to the opera house parted, freeing a few couples anxious to beat the crowds.

"Remember, lo bok don't talk."

Amah sniffed but said no more.

I held up a picture. "Artwork from the opera, a quarter each!"

People walked past, some looking but not approaching. Perhaps it was the threatening sky, which thankfully had not yet split open. Or maybe William Tell had been a lucky strike, as I'd feared. A pity sale.

After thirty minutes of hawking pictures, the crowd had reduced to a trickle, and my throat ached. A straggler pulled out a cigar and dug around in his pocket. I started toward him, before remembering I had chosen to leave the matches at home. Foolish girl. At least they would've guaranteed a few pennies.

A little girl with pigtails emerged from the entrance. Sighting my pictures, she removed a hand from a statuesque fellow's arm. "Look, Father, it's Olympia."

I bent to her level and let her hold the picture. "Yes, it is. I sketched her myself."

Barely cutting his spectacles my direction, her father signaled a sleek motorcar. It pulled to the curb.

"Makes a great souvenir, sir, and a one-of-a-kind to boot."

The man attempted to lead the girl to the car. But she held her ground, her pretty eyes as irresistible as chocolate drops. He adjusted his spectacles, peering at my picture. "Say, that's actually pretty good."

"Only a quarter, or two pictures for forty-five," I offered, my mind springing to action. From my satchel, I showed them another drawing of Olympia, this one a close-up of her face.

He produced change from his pocket and let his daughter present the coins to me.

I swelled at the jingling weight in my palm. Watching their car pull away, the threads of a new plan began spinning in my head. Next time, I would direct my efforts to the children, who could do the begging for me.

"You two again." A familiar voice pummeled my ear. P&C strode toward us, cane swinging. Moving faster than I'd thought a pompous windbag like him could move, he snatched my satchel and threw it into the street. Papers went flying. The last of the operagoers turned their faces away, as if the sight of our mistreatment would spoil their vision. A passing horse carriage trampled the satchel underfoot without even a hitch in its step.

"How dare you—" I sputtered.

With a feral growl, Amah, who had behaved all night, flew at P&C, her braid blowing behind her like a phoenix's tail. "Bum-rag!"

"Amah, no!" I tried to pry Amah off the man without hurting her. A flash of gold jagged out of the corner of my eye, like lightning. Instinctively, I reached up a hand to block the strike of P&C's cane.

A wet crack rent the air, a sound that traveled straight to my heart. The blow was not for me.

Amah fell in slow motion, a floaty kind of falling, like a matchstick, onto the cement.

Collapsing at her side, I gingerly set her head, now bare of bonnet, into my lap. "Amah, where does it hurt?" My words tripped over themselves. Probing her head, my fingers grew slippery with warm blood. *Oh no.* "You monster," I spat at P&C.

He shrugged. "I warned you not to come back."

"You will pay for this."

His blue eyes became ice chips. "You dare to threaten me?" He stepped closer, glaring down at us like the farmer's wife choosing which hen to kill. "You're trespassing on *my* property."

With a groan, Amah unleashed her pinkie. "You are the trespasser. You shot down my sun."

"Foolish woman. What nonsense are you—"

"You shot down Rosie."

The man's gaze fixed upon Amah's birthmark. His hold on his cane loosened, and he swayed, barely catching himself before falling.

"Yes, you remember now. Rosie was mine, until you shot her from the sky."

They called her Rosie because of her rosy cheeks. Sometimes I hear her through the cracks.

Hungry ghosts often return to the site of their injury.

"Those who play with fire are destined for the flame." Amah's pronouncement fell like a mallet, splitting open the sky. Rain began to fall.

The man's mouth had become a gaping hole, which he steered to me. What had P&C to do with my mother? His too-pretty eyes matched themselves with mine. *Maybe my father gave me these eyes*, I had teased Amah.

Forget about that man, she had replied. *He was a shooter of suns.*

Slowly P&C backed away, all the pomp and circumstance melted away, leaving a mute doll, a harlequin. He slunk back into his fortress, the opera house.

My head throbbed, and my skin burned. I hardly felt the rain. I might be sick.

Amah wheezed like an accordion, her eyes rolling in her head. I scanned the world for assistance, but all I saw were small figures slipping away.

I retrieved my satchel, its contents squashed and muddied, then hurried back to Amah. "We need a carriage." The trolley wouldn't come for another thirty minutes, and a carriage would be faster. Thanks to the little girl, I had enough for the fare—forty cents for two, four times what the trolleys cost. But with the rain falling and the opera crowd gone, just finding one would be a lucky strike. With shaking fingers, I tied my silk scarf snug around Amah's head, watching for one of the horse-drawn carriages that roamed the streets.

Questions plowed my mind. P&C couldn't be my father, could he? Amah was always spinning half-truths. But I had seen the shock in his face. The guilty expression he could not hide.

Amah clawed at me. "Firefly," she groaned. "I shouldn't have brought Rosie. She hated sewing. *Bum-rag* was a stagehand then, and I had seen his lust. But I had so much work to do. *Queenie this, Queenie that.*"

"Hush. It is not your fault, Amah." Across the street, a driver had pulled his carriage to the side. His horse neighed with discontent, pawing at the ground. "I will be right back."

Setting her gently on the sidewalk, I hurried across the street and raised my hand. "Sir! We need a ride! Could you take my grandmother and me?"

The driver lifted his tweed cap and his eyes grew tight. "I'm off for the night."

"I can pay. Forty cents, right?" I showed him my coins.

"Pay first."

I gritted my teeth. "Half the fare now, the rest later."

He made a harsh clicking noise in his throat but held out his gloved hand. I passed him twenty cents. "My grandmother is across the street."

"Go on."

I trotted back to Amah, planting my feet so as not to slip in the slicked streets.

"Yee-haw!" he called. But instead of bringing the carriage around, it continued down the street. The jingle of his reins was a kind of mocking laughter.

I cursed into the torrent.

ACT III

An eternity passed before the trolley came to fetch us, and by the time I had gotten Amah settled into her bed, it was near midnight. I dipped a rag into cool ginger tea and held it to her head. The downpour outside could not compare to the storm raging in me. My legs and arms crawled with agitation, and my head swam with anger at the man who had shot down not one sun, but three. For it all made sense now. That Amah had been a seamstress for the opera, a good one who was always in demand. That my mother, who she'd brought in to help her, had caught the eye of a small man with grand ambitions.

I wanted to go somewhere, do something to rebalance the world, a world that had tipped too far in the wrong direction.

The rag warmed, and I rewet it. Amah stirred. "Firefly. The stars are out again. I can feel them calling."

I pushed aside our broadcloth curtain. The glass was slick,

but the sky had spread a cape of blue velvet, scattered with diamonds. How did she know?

She grabbed at my hand, her eyes strangely luminous as they grazed the flame dancing in its glass cage. "The suns might fall, but their fire never dies. It is reborn, each time growing stronger, each time burning brighter."

My gaze dropped to her sewing basket, with its notions, clipped peacock feather, and the key that unlocked no door I knew of.

I had my own key because I worked late into the night.

I knew what I would do.

———

After Amah had fallen asleep, I struggled into my damp boots and threw my satchel over my shoulder. There would be no carriage or trolley to take me at this hour. I would need all the strength I could muster.

In the moonlight, the narrow streets of Chinatown sparkled like a river, and the neighborhood, which rarely held still, had the look of a picture postcard. It was folly to go out at such a time for a lone girl like myself, especially without my grandmother and her mole to ward off evildoers. But some unfamiliar engine powered my steps, as if a hearth had roared to life within me. I streaked toward the Met, as fearsome and inevitable as a comet.

At last, the stone monolith rose before me.

I lit a match, and in the flame, imagined him at twenty-something. Had he caught my mother unawares, or lured her with an oily promise? I imagined her terror, her pleas.

Your mother was only fourteen.

Wiping my eyes, I pictured Amah's shock, her helpless anguish. Her word above a man's? Unthinkable. Despite all the demands on her time, Amah was just a seamstress.

Amah had left the opera, had taken Rosie away. In the cold blue of the dying flame, I realized that after my mother had left us behind to become a star in the sky, Amah had set P&C's pants on fire.

This impenetrable fortress that contained my history suddenly felt more like a facade, a stage prop. A place where I could rewrite the script and carve a new ending.

I rounded the corner to the staircase leading to the stage door. With only the glow from the streetlamps to light my path, I ascended, withdrawing Amah's brass key from my satchel. My heart pounded in my ears as I inserted it. Surely it would not fit after all these years. Yet? *Click.*

Darkness enveloped me along with the musty scent of sweat, lemon oil, and melted wax. I struck a match, and in its illumination, the backstage appeared. Beyond a rack of military costumes, something shiny flirted with my light. I stole closer, footfalls clacking against the floor, to where a mannequin wearing a red wig and sparkling tutu posed by a stone wall. Olympia's dress caught my sliver of light and reflected it like a living flame.

I worked the dress from the doll's body.

This is for what you did to Amah tonight. For the past sins for which you will never atone. When you find your moneymaker gone up in smoke, remember that you are destined for the flame. That it will always follow you, for playing with fire that was not yours.

I struck a new match and lifted it to the dress.

A fortune in rhinestones.

Fire shouldn't be wasted, you know.

An ember of an idea took hold. A pinched handful of rhinestones had kept Amah and me for a year. What about a hundred handfuls?

I had promised to one day take Amah to the island of Hainan.

Before the match burned my fingers, I let it fall to the ground. The flame teased the hem of a curtain, and I stuffed the dress in my satchel.

Those who are built from fire are, by their nature, brighter than the rest.

HISTORICAL NOTE

On August 27, 1892, a fire gutted New York's finest temple of music, the supposedly fireproof Metropolitan Opera House, leading to necessary structural changes in the building and ownership. There were no fatalities. A single cigarette was to blame for the incident.

MOTHER'S MIRROR

H. E. Edgmon

Inspired by "Snow White"

This story depicts transphobia and abuse.

My mom likes to tell me I could be the most beautiful girl in the world if I'd just put some effort into myself. She says it casually, and often, over the rim of her morning coffee mug or inside shopping mall dressing rooms. I could almost forget the cruelty of it, the way she says it.

But it's a shitty thing to say to your kid for plenty of reasons. Like, we can start with the fact that I'm practically her miniature, and how all her suggested alterations would just highlight those similarities. I'm well aware her goal is to turn me into her perfect mirror. She would deny this, but she's not subtle about it.

Still, her narcissistic desire to live vicariously through her daughter, to get some redo at life because she screwed up hers, isn't actually what keeps me awake at night. Neither is her equally unsubtle accusation that I'm too lazy to live up to the full potential of my good (or at least aesthetically pleasing) genes.

No. When it's just me and my thoughts, when I'm stewing over the latest stupid argument we got into about the last time I fixed my hair, or how I need to get measured for a new bra, or the number printed on the tag of my jeans, what I'm thinking is how I don't want to be the most beautiful girl in the world at all.

How I don't want to be a *girl* at all.

——•——

I try, of course. If there's an option besides trying, I don't see it yet.

——•——

"You wanna go get our nails done together?" My mother has a perfect smile, sharp and white. I've never understood why it hurts to look at for too long.

She stares at me from the driver's seat, the high school behind us. I wonder how many students look at her when they mill past, glancing through the car windows to glimpse the remarkably beautiful woman inside. I wonder if she wonders the same thing. Being admired is the only thing that means anything to her, no matter who's doing the admiring. I don't think she knows she exists outside the eyes of other people.

I'm not sure she knows I do, either.

I *do* know her question isn't actually a question. She's poised with her hands on the steering wheel, waiting for me to say yes, to drive out of the parking lot and head in the direction of the salon.

Seriously, what would saying no even look like?

Accusations of ingratitude. Tears, maybe, if she's well hydrated enough to pull them off. When the anger boiled over, she might even reach for calling me the first slur that came to mind.

It wouldn't even matter if it was the *correct* slur or not. My mother doesn't know anything about me, wouldn't even recognize me if she met the actor behind the character I've been playing for sixteen years, but she still knows something is *wrong*. I think she's always known. Maybe that's why she pushes so hard to turn me into a mirror. After all, if I grow up to be her, I can't grow up to be me.

Either way, no isn't a real option. So I say yes, and we go get our nails done together.

There's nothing terrible about it, really. It's even kind of nice. I pretend not to notice the way she rolls her eyes when I reach for the black polish. We sit side by side in oversized leather chairs while technicians scrub away at our nails with their files and some nonthreatening moderate news channel plays on a tiny TV in the corner of the ceiling. And my mom tells me about her day, complains about work, says she needs to quit before the toll of this year's career choice kills her.

Quitting jobs is something my mom's always been good at. She was supposed to take the beauty-queen-to-trophy-wife pipeline, but something got screwed up in the middle and she ended up a single mom instead. Sixteen years in, and we're both still trying to figure out what the hell happens now.

When our nails are finished, the techs leave us to let them dry. I flex mine under the LED lamp. I *do* like them this way. They look sort of like claws, long and sharp and strong. I picture my hands decorated in rings: heavy, opulent rings, with thick bands. What a ridiculous thing, how just the thickness of an imagined ring's band strikes the difference between feeling powerful and wanting to crush all ten of my own fingers.

"Maybe next time you could try a simple French manicure," my mother chides, interrupting my thoughts. "I don't know why you insist on being *edgy* all the time. You'd be so pretty if you'd just act like a normal girl."

I entertain a brief but gruesome fantasy, my black claws drawing her blood, ripping the very throat from beneath her chin. I don't say anything.

She doesn't continue. Though it probably has more to do with the return of the nail technician than any realization that she might've said something cruel.

"This is your daughter?" he asks, inclining his head toward me as he examines her cuticles.

She smiles that smile that makes my chest hurt. "My baby girl."

"Looks just like you," he chuckles. "What a beautiful family."

And somehow, her smile gets worse, and the pain in my chest grows, and I still don't say anything, because there's nothing to say.

Not yet, anyway.

—◦—

I find myself on the internet.

It's an accident, at first, or at least I tell myself that. I'm stumbling into Discord servers and group chats, filled with kids around the country and the world who have their pronouns in their bios or next to their names. And just like that, even if I've never met any of them in person, even if they only exist through a screen, they feel more real to me in a lot of ways than the people in my own town. And it doesn't take long for me to realize why.

There are people out there who would argue they *influenced* me—that I changed myself to become more like them. That's not true. What's actually true is that sometimes, without consciously realizing it, we seek out people who reflect the parts of ourselves we're still too afraid to face in the mirror.

When I finally tell my mother I'm trans, I do it over dinner. I've known for so long now, but it doesn't feel real until I say it out loud. It's this piece of me that's always been there, but that I've never let myself look at for too long.

"I don't feel like a girl," I tell her, hands knotted over my twisting stomach, eyes downcast on the kitchen table. "I'm a boy. My body's just—wrong."

This is only half true. Gender is complicated, and, if it's possible, my relationship with my body is even more so. But I barely know how to talk to her about this in the first place. I certainly don't have the bandwidth to walk her through deconstructing the binary or understanding singular "they" pronouns. Becoming a boy will at least make sense to her, even if she doesn't like it.

And she doesn't like it.

"No," she says, with something like a shocked laugh in her throat. "That's ridiculous. What are you even talking about?"

Last night, the group chat walked me through this conversation with my mother. They helped me decide what to say, when to say it, how to walk the knife-edge between stepping into myself and avoiding her rage. I think of them now and try to find my tongue.

"This isn't something new." I don't want her to tell me it's a phase, to weaponize my age against me, as if she somehow might know me better than I know myself just because she's been alive for longer. I'm still the only one actually living inside my head. "It's something I've been thinking about for a long time."

"I don't— I can't even—" She stumbles over a sob, caught between her teeth like spinach, and I finally look up at her. She's already crying, her head in her hands, those perfectly delicate shoulders shaking. "This doesn't make any sense," she says, lifting her face to stare at me with familiar eyes. They look just like my own. "A long time? Really? And you've kept it secret from me? How could you do that to me? Don't you trust me? I thought we were closer than this. I could have helped you work through this—this confusion!"

Confusion. Many things confuse me, but not in the way she means.

"I just didn't want to say anything until I was really sure." This is also a half-truth. The only reason I haven't been *really sure* before now is because I wasn't sure I could stomach going through with it. Because of her. Because living as someone else might be easier than having to have a single painful conversation with my mother, much less whatever happens next. "But I am now. I'm a boy."

"*A boy*," she snarls. "No, you're not."

And maybe I'm not, but I'm not a girl, either.

"You really expect me to believe this is something you've been struggling with your whole life?" she continues, tears giving way to rage. (Forget the fact I never said that.) She pushes herself back from the kitchen table, storming around to me on the other side. One hand curls around the arm of my chair and she yanks it back, forcing me to face her. "Look at you. You have long hair!"

That's . . . not incorrect. But it is also so entirely unrelated to the matter at hand that I don't know what to say, so I can only blink at her.

"And you wear makeup! And you own dresses! And—and we get our nails done together!"

These things are all true. They also don't change anything about what I told her or how I feel about my gender.

We're veering off topic at this point. I need to get control of this conversation. As if I've ever had control over any conversation with my mother.

"I want to start using he/him pronouns. And I'd like you to call me Hunter."

"Hunter."

It's funny, almost. I spent so long looking for the name that felt just right, a name that felt like coming home to find the key left under the mat for me. And the first time my mother says it out loud, voice twisted with mockery and hatred, I start doubting my choice.

That's a problem for another day, I guess.

She reaches for me, and I flinch away, but her touch is soft when it lands on my cheek. "Sweetheart . . ." The rage has all but bled from her voice in the span of seconds, but it's been replaced now by something worse. A venom that curls from her mouth to my ears, a poison that seeps into my skin. "Is this because you don't want to be an ugly girl?"

In retrospect, the question shouldn't even surprise me. It makes complete sense, coming from her. I don't know what else I should have even expected.

In the moment, though, it feels like someone flaying my skin open and drowning my exposed muscle in acid.

"What?" is all I can manage.

"I've told you so many times, it doesn't have to be this way. If you would just put a little effort into it, you could—"

"That's not . . ." I pull out of her touch, standing up and moving around the table to put some distance between our bodies. "The two things aren't related at all."

"Oh, baby." Her voice drips with condescension. "Of *course* they are. I am your mother. I know you better than anyone else, better than you know yourself." She clicks her tongue, shaking her head. "Being a woman in this world is *hard*. It takes so much work just to put on a face and go outside. And maybe that isn't fair. But it doesn't mean you should give up who you are. That doesn't mean you become a *boy* just because it's easier."

"You think transitioning is the easy way out?" It is the stupidest thing I've ever heard, and any second now it's going to make me cry. Because how do you even argue with someone whose head is this far up their own ass? How do you defend yourself with logic from someone who's making up their own reality as they go?

Maybe she hears the accusation in my tone, because her eyes narrow. The dangerous softness in her voice turns sharp again. "I think you're a lazy little liar. You disgust me."

"Okay."

"You will never be my son."

"Okay."

I'm not even here anymore. My eyes glaze over and autopilot kicks into control.

She's crying again. I can hear it in her voice when she says, "You might be the person who kills my daughter, though."

If that's what she wants. If that's what I have to do. "Okay."

—◦—

That night, when I look at my reflection over the bathroom sink, all I see is her face staring back at me. I can't make it stop, not until I take the kitchen scissors and chop at my hair until it sticks up at odd ends around my ears. She might strangle me to death in the morning, but it'd be worth it.

And it sort of sucks, you know, because I *liked* my hair the way it was. But if she thinks she can tell me who I am because of how long it is, I'd rather shave it all off than give her the satisfaction.

My makeup collection is minimal. Some concealer, some drugstore mascara and eyeliner, a little blush. I toss all of it in the trash. The last piece, a single tube of lipstick, rolls back and forth in the palm of my hand. Revlon Candy Apple, bright red. I've only worn it maybe twice. I don't like the way people look at me when it's on. But I do like the way *I* look, like I'm painted in blood, like I should have fangs in my mouth.

I throw it away, too.

In bed, I turn the palm of my hand toward the ceiling and stare at my nails. It's been a while since we last got them done together. They're back to their familiar shape and color, dull and anxiety-chewed to the quick.

No more claws. Never again. Not if she thinks it means something it doesn't.

Maybe I can't actually rip her throat out. But I'll cut my *own* heart from my chest before I let her tell me what's inside it.

The group chat's newest name is "Hunter and the 7 short kings," because I'm the only one taller than 5'6". We're scattered all around the country, and none of us have ever met in person. But summer is fast approaching, and we're determined to change that.

It'll be my last summer at home, before senior year, before graduation, before adulthood and whatever that means. I don't know what comes next for me, but I know I want to see my friends before it gets here.

Like usual, there's a hundred missed messages in the group by the time I wake up. I scroll through, still half-asleep, trying to catch up. The subject hasn't changed much since I went to bed. By the time I get to the most recent few, I'm fully awake.

Olly: so i can drive up the coast and pick up elliot, then we can do a kind of west-east road trip? pit stops in all your cities, hang out with everyone for like a week or so before hitting the road again.

Asher: i wish we could just like . . . get a place at the beach or something and disappear for a few weeks, all eight of us.

Elliot: well yeah, that's the dream.

maybe next summer, once everyone's 18.

Noah: yes to all of that but i vote mountains instead of beach. a cozy cottage in the woods or something. please.

Emmett: sounds like a dream.

Kai: can't wait.

Charlie: good luck spending a week in this shithole town i live in. there is literally nothing to do. you might as well skip me altogether lol.

Olly: no.

The last couple of messages were from less than half an hour ago. I fire off a response of my own.

Hunter: same, though. you're going to be bored as hell.

My mom and I live in Indiana, too far south to be a suburb of Chicago, too far north to be an offshoot of Indianapolis. No-man's-land, where there's nothing but . . . well, there's just nothing.

Elliot: we'll have you, and that's enough.

Kai: gaaaaay.

I laugh, but still hover over Elliot's message until the reaction options appear, sliding my thumb to select the heart.

Olly: and we'll find something to do, i'm sure.

I'm not as optimistic, but I also don't really care.
Because I'll have them, and that *is* enough.

As it turns out, I should have had more faith in a group of queer teenagers' ability to find something interesting to do, even in Indiana. Olly and Elliot arrive a few months later, with a list of plans to get me out of the house for a week. Their arrival comes not a moment too soon.

My mother would like to pretend I never told her who I am. So, she does, mostly, unless she's using it as a weapon. I've learned to become as invisible as possible, a ghost in the home and little more. She said herself she'd rather have a dead daughter than a trans son.

When the boys have been in town for three days, we pile in Olly's car and head to a park half an hour away. Apparently, there's a free drag show happening. I didn't even know people around here knew what drag is.

Then again, apparently *I* didn't even know what drag is. My understanding of drag was that it's about men who dress up as women to entertain laughing crowds. That's about as deep as it got. And it was clearly very wrong, anyway, because that's not what *this* is at all.

If all gender is performance, just a series of boxes we're expected to check to prove ourselves to the audience, then drag is going pro. I sit on a gingham picnic blanket under a tree, with Elliot's head in my lap and Olly's arm around my waist, and watch as people take the very concept of gender roles and turn them into art. The pageantry, the theatrics, the act of looking *gender* in the eye and calling its bluff, it's all enough to make my heart race. How did I not know it could be like this?

There's one performer in particular I can't stop staring at. Whenever he's onstage, even surrounded by other people, my eyes go right to him. A drag king with painted-on cheekbones and a dark goatee, a single gold hoop in one ear, and a leather jacket draped over his broad shoulders. His black hair falls across his eyes with practiced, perfected disarray. He winks and the crowd loses its breath. They call him Prince Charming.

"You're drooling," Elliot tells me. He reaches up and pretends to clean off my chin.

I swat his hand away, but I can't even bring myself to care that I'm being teased.

"Do you think we could loiter for a minute?" I ask when the show ends and everyone starts packing up all around us. Olly and Elliot both laugh, but it's the kind of laugh that sounds like *We love you* and not the kind that makes me want to disappear.

Prince Charming is leaning against the back of a Honda, on their phone, and looks up when we approach.

Olly takes it upon himself to speak. "Hey. Loved the set. I'm Olly, he/him. And you're . . . ?"

"Charming. She/her. Or he/him, if I'm performing." She tilts her head, bright eyes taking in Olly, then Elliot, before settling on me. Her smile is nothing short of rakish.

"But always Charming?" I ask, frowning. "So, is that . . . a character? Or just you?"

"Yes." Her grin only gets wider.

"Right. Uh, I'm Elliot, he/him." Elliot slaps a hand over his chest. "And this is Hunter, he/they. They wanted to meet you."

"*Okay.*" I'm going to kill him. It's unfortunate that he came all the way to Indiana just to die.

"I'm flattered." She rolls her tongue over her teeth. "You enjoy the show, Hunter?"

That feels like an understatement. "You're very talented."

"Well, you'll have to come back, then."

"This is a regular thing?"

"First Saturday of every month." She holds her phone out to me. "Gimme your number. I'll make sure to remind you next time."

The boys and I are back in the car when Elliot proclaims, "Dude, congrats."

"What?"

Olly rolls his eyes, clapping a hand over the back of my neck. "You are pitiful. I was worried you didn't realize what was happening. The very hot drag king was definitely flirting with you."

"No . . . wait, really?"

"You beautiful newborn baby." Olly shakes his head. "Let's get you home. It's way past your bedtime."

He's joking, but I really don't make it home till after my curfew. Olly's car is pulling out of my driveway when the porch light flicks on and my mother's silhouette appears through the window curtain.

I don't want to do this with her. My head is full of gender fuckery and laughter and wicked smiles, and I just want to go lie down and fantasize for a while.

But I have to get past her first.

"I guess I don't have to tell you you're late," she says when I step inside. She drops down into her recliner and crosses her legs at the knee, silk robe parting uncomfortably high up her thigh. "Where've you been? I noticed you turned your locations off."

To be fair, I did that a while ago. Not my fault if she just noticed. Though it certainly does make my being late look worse.

"We went to a park. We were just talking. I lost track of the time."

"A park, huh?" She sneers. "Right. Sure. There a reason you and your little *friends* can't talk here?"

Yeah, and I'm looking directly at it.

My mother isn't transphobic. Well, like . . . she isn't transphobic when it's not her own kid, because I'm a reflection of her and everyone else isn't. Everyone else can do whatever they want. I don't think she'd be cruel to Olly or Elliot. But it's also just not worth the risk.

What I actually say is, "I don't know. I guess not."

"Uh-huh. Right." Her nails, long and perfectly manicured, tap against her kneecap. "You know, I got a look at these kids when they picked you up earlier. Where'd you say you knew them from?"

"Olly used to go to my school." I am absolutely not telling

her I met them in a Discord server for trans kids who like anime. I would, to be honest, rather just die.

"*Olly.*" She snarls the word so violently that I jump, heart racing inside my throat. Tension cords its way into my muscles, bringing threads of ice with it.

Silence sits in the living room on top of us. I don't know what to say. She stews in her own anger. I watch it get brighter and hotter and spread out farther and farther from her body with every passing tick of the clock. This can't just be about me being late, but I can't figure out what's sent her over the edge.

At least until she speaks again.

"You know what? It doesn't matter how delusional you are, or how short you cut your hair, or what clothes you put on. You cannot change what's between your legs." She stands, so suddenly that I take a step back. "And anyone who actually cared about you would tell you that. No one who really loved you would ever let you walk around embarrassing yourself like this. You can all stand around and call each other whatever made-up names you want, but you and your *friends* are just miserable little girls who need some serious help."

For one fleeting moment, I feel the worst pain of my life.

You know what's really embarrassing? I don't actually hate my mom. I want to. It would be easier if I did. But no matter what she's done to me, I've never been able to really make myself hate her. I *love* her. She's my *mom*. And I want her to love me, too.

I want her to love me so badly that I spent years trying to be what she needed me to be. Even though I wasn't good at it, even though I was unhappy, even though we both knew, the entire time, that something was wrong, I tried. Because when I was trying, she loved me. When I wasn't me at all, she loved me.

But now she knows the truth. And every day, it becomes more obvious: I am not something she can love.

The pain fades as quickly as it comes, replaced by nothing at all.

If I let myself actually hear what she's saying, I won't be able to recover from the poison of it. So, instead, I disappear. I don't know where I am, but I'm not in my bones. I'm not in my head. I'm floating somewhere else.

Whoever's left in my body says, "Okay," and goes to bed.

———◦———

The boys leave and summer disappears, and one day I get a text from a number that's not in my phone. It's Charming, reminding me to come to the park. I know I shouldn't. My mother's words are still crawling around in my blood, looking for a chance to rot me from the inside out.

But I do. I go that night and then every first Saturday of every month. I can't ever stay late, sometimes even have to leave before the show's over, too afraid of breaking curfew again. So, one night, Charming invites me to her place early, instead, to watch her get ready.

Her apartment is nothing special, a shoebox studio in a building that smells wet and stale, but it's the coolest thing I've ever seen. Mostly because it's *hers*. There's a trans flag in the window next to a hanging plant, and art on the walls, and a lizard in a tank that flicks its tongue out at me when I stare at it for too long.

"I've never known anyone who actually has their own place before," I tell her when I sit on the edge of her bed.

Sitting on her bed feels like being naked, and I don't know why.

"Moved out of my parents' place as soon as I graduated last year. Mutual decision that it was best for all involved. Hell, I can only afford rent 'cause they pay for half. Don't know how long that'll last, though." She laughs, sitting down at her vanity, and twists her head over her shoulder. "If you're ever looking to get out of *your* place . . ."

I laugh, too. I do not mention the fact that there's only room for one bed in this apartment. My hands are so stupidly sweaty.

She goes back to the mirror, running a contour stick along her cheekbone. I watch, fascinated, as her reflection begins to change. I don't understand the way some people can turn makeup into magic. And this is nothing short of magic. Her round cheeks, soft and feminine, disappear into sharp lines. She paints fake stubble along her jaw and dark circles under her eyes, and she becomes someone else.

When she catches me staring, she smirks. "What are you thinking?"

"I wish I could do this."

"Oh. I thought you were thinking about how hot I am." Before I can turn bright red or say anything to that, at all, she's already continuing, "You want me to do your makeup?"

"Do you have time for that?"

Instead of answering, she grabs a handful of things off the vanity and joins me on the bed. Charming presses her palm flat to my chest and forces me farther onto her mattress.

And then, as if it is not mind-blowing in any way, she puts one knee on either side of my thighs, uncaps the contour stick, and gets to work.

I try to remember how to breathe. I don't think I succeed,

but she's, like, an inch away from my face, and I don't know what else could be expected from me.

"You *are* hot," I finally blurt out, after who knows how long.

She pauses, but only for a moment, to grin. "Thank you. About time."

That was basically the entirety of my arsenal, flirting-wise. So I don't say anything else. I let her go about her work, her soft hands brushing against my neck and face as she does, her hips shifting on top of my lap the whole time.

"Wait here. Don't look yet." She slides away, and the loss of her weight on mine is *the worst*. But she's back as quickly as she left, straddling me again, this time with a box from the bathroom.

From it, she produces an assortment of jewelry. A dangly black earring. A comically big cross necklace. An assortment of rings, including one that fastens over the length of my middle finger and ends with a claw-tip that stretches over my nail.

Charming grins a self-satisfied grin, leaning back to admire her work. "Wish I had a pair of fangs that'd fit you. You'd make a great monster." Her fingers brush through my hair. "Anyway, we should make out after this."

"Oh. Okay. Yes." It's a good thing *one of us* is charming.

"You can look now."

I don't want to look, actually, I just want to kiss her. But I do look.

And it's a good thing I do. Because that's when everything turns upside down.

The hollowed cheekbones and delicately painted facial hair. The dark, thick eyebrows and smudged eyeliner. Even the jewelry. The me staring back at me in Charming's vanity mirror is someone I've never seen before but someone I think I've been waiting my whole life to meet.

"What do you think?" she asks, her breath warm and soft at my throat.

I'm thinking too much for any of it to be coherent. With great effort, I manage to say, "It's me."

She chuckles. "Yeah, it is."

———

I take it all off before I go home that night.

But I know now.

I spent so long trying to be someone my mother could love, and all it did was hurt me. And now, in some attempt to prove myself to her, I've course-corrected in the exact opposite direction, denying myself anything remotely feminine so she can't point at it and say *I told you so.* Even now, I'm killing parts of myself to appease her.

But she's never going to be appeased. She's not going to be happy until I disappear completely and there's nothing staring back at her but her own reflection when she looks at me.

She's never going to love me. Not the way I need her to.

And now that I've seen myself, I don't think I can go back to making her try.

———

"They're in here!" Kai calls over his shoulder when he finds me in our shared bedroom in the woodsy mountain cottage. He studies my face, and one eyebrow rises with concern. "You okay?"

I'm sitting on the edge of my bed, facing my dresser and its matching mirror. My phone is unlocked, screen-up in my palm.

"I will be," I offer, which isn't exactly a yes. "And I'll be out in a minute."

He hesitates, but only for a second before nodding and leaving me to it.

My eyes go back to the open texts.

Mom: I don't care if you're 18 or 80, I am your mother and I deserve to know where the hell you are. Call me. Now.

If you don't respond to let me know you're alive, I will be contacting the police.

Do you think I want to do that? Do you think I want the people around here to know what you're doing? Of course I don't. It's humiliating. But I'm your mother. And if I have to embarrass myself to keep you safe, that's what I'll do.

Graduation was two weeks ago. Eight days later, I boarded a plane out here, to meet up with my friends in this cabin. I don't think any of them really believed it was going to happen, but I made sure it did. It meant dipping into the savings I've been trying to squirrel away for the last year, getting jobs here and there as a pet sitter or dog walker. But it's worth it, to be with them again.

I didn't tell my mom where I was going, didn't tell her I was going at all, just disappeared. And not only for this vacation.

When I get back to Indiana, Charming's picking me up from the airport, and I'm moving in with her. I've already got a real job lined up nearby, cleaning rooms at a little dive motel, and I've been shuttling my stuff to the apartment for the past few months. The last of it came with me in my carry-on bags. Anything left at my mom's place is what I'm willing to leave behind. I guess that includes my mother herself.

There's an assortment of my things scattered on the dresser. Wallet, deodorant, disposable camera. A stack of rings, some cheap costume jewelry. A single tube of Revlon Candy Apple lipstick.

My reflection in the mirror hasn't changed much over the last year. I don't think it has, anyway. My hair is just getting long enough to tug back in a ponytail again, but it's still loads shorter than it was the night I took the scissors to it. I've started filling in my eyebrows every day. I'm not sure why (or what) it helps, but it does. Just before coming out here, I went and got my nails done, long and sharp and black like claws.

I have an appointment in my phone's calendar, three weeks from tomorrow, at a Planned Parenthood in Illinois, to talk to someone about starting HRT. Maybe in another few months, the face in the mirror won't be this one at all anymore. Maybe it'll start to look more like the me I see when Charming does my makeup. But for now, this is me. I look in the mirror, and it's just me.

Which shouldn't be revolutionary. And maybe it isn't. Except that I don't see *her*.

I look back at my phone and hesitate for only a breath before I press the Block Contact button.

This isn't happily ever after. I know that. Just because I'm strong today doesn't mean I always will be. My relationship with my body might always be complicated and painful and confusing, and there may be days I wake up and *do* see her looking back at me in the mirror. Her words are always going to exist somewhere inside my head, and I'll replay them on my worst days. I know that.

I think I'm going to be sick, so I send Charming a text.

Hunter: miss you.

And I do miss her. But as great as my girlfriend is, she can't magically fix me, either. I have to fix me, one step at a time. This moment isn't the end of anything. I haven't won yet.

But this *is* the beginning of something. And my mother hasn't won, either.

Charming texts back while I'm standing in front of the mirror, applying a defiant layer of red lipstick. It feels like a special occasion, this exorcism. Something to be marked with blood on my mouth.

Charming: literally can't wait to kiss you again!!

My heart trips over itself, and I smile in spite of the nausea splashing like a tide against the back of my throat. Leaning forward, I press my lips to the mirror, leaving a perfect red imprint on the glass. I snap a picture and send it to her without a caption.

Her reply comes right away.

Charming: my beautiful boy <3 <3 <3

Three simple words that nearly make me lose my shit.

Somewhere in the cottage, I can hear the others laughing. I know they're still waiting for me to come back to them.

This isn't happily ever after.

But it's a *really* good start.

SHARP AS ANY THORN

Rory Power

Inspired by "Sleeping Beauty"

I used to think it must have happened on the day I was born, but I know better now. I know this started the day my sister saw my face.

I picture it, sometimes. Mel on the porch as our parents come up the drive in that old red truck. She's watching, hoping they're bringing her something back from town. She doesn't know why they left. It's only them and her, Mom and Dad and Mel, and the woods all around, bramble and rise. It's exactly the way it's supposed to be.

And then they get out of the old red truck, my mother carrying something small and soft and wrapped in pink. They crouch in front of her scraped knees, and my father pushes the blankets back so Mel can see my closed eyes. "This is your sister," he says. "This is little Aurora."

That's the night Mel curses me. Sits on the edge of her bed in the back room of the house and asks the woods to swallow me whole. To take me back. And I can't be sure, but I think she must hear a voice: "Wait," I think it says. "Give it time. Give it time for her to grow."

—•—

Mel turns fourteen seven years before I do. The day of her birthday is a Sunday, just at the end of September when the trees are still green. Mom and Dad send her out of the house right after breakfast, and I go with her. When I'm this age I'm always at her heels, whether she likes it or not.

She doesn't talk to me at first. Heads down the path into the woods without even looking over her shoulder to see if I'm following. There's just the breaking of brush underfoot as we go, my hand-me-down sneakers tripping me up every now and then.

Soon enough I can't see the house anymore when I check over my shoulder. The trees close around us, birches white and warping, dark knotted eyes staring out at me as I pass. Mel knows the paths better. She told me once she walked them only months after she was born, and some part of me believed her.

"Where are we going?" I finally ask her when we've been walking for what feels like hours. It's hot these days, harder to bear when we can all feel the season about to turn. My dress is sticking to my back, hair plastered to my forehead. Mel looks fine. She could've stepped straight out of spring.

"I'm going to the clearing," she says. "You can turn around."

I won't. Of course I won't. Even this young I know Mel doesn't want me with her, and even this young there's nothing I like more than the hem of her dress brushing against my knees as I hurry to keep up.

"But why did we have to leave?" I like Sundays at home. Things are almost never my fault on a Sunday. We don't go to church like some people do in town, but Mom likes us to get dressed nice and be quiet for a minute before we eat dinner.

We're supposed to shut our eyes, but I keep mine open, and I never tell.

"I don't know," Mel says. "A surprise, maybe."

"For your birthday, right?"

She doesn't answer, and I can tell she's mad by the way her steps get long and heavy.

This part of the path is downhill, away from town and heading into the valley. Mel says there's a creek at the very bottom, and she swims there some days when it's really hot, but I've never been that far. I think I'll go when I'm older. I think I'll go like Mel.

Last year her birthday was my favorite day of the year. Mom gave her a pair of her old high heels, because Mel was thirteen, and she was grown now. I remember that: *grown now.* I said it into my pillow that night before I went to sleep. I was so jealous of Mel; I thought it sounded beautiful. She told me to be quiet and then later, in the quiet, in the dark, I heard her start to cry.

Maybe this year they'll get her a new pair of heels, and I can have the old ones. Or we'll come back to the house and it'll be decorated in blue and pink, with a cake to match like I've seen in the ads on TV, swirled with towers of icing, so sweet I can taste it from here. Even Mel couldn't be disappointed with that, right?

"She could," a voice says, winding out of the woods and into my ear. "You know she could."

It's true. Mel looks at me sometimes like I've pulled down the sun, like I've left the sky above us empty and screaming.

"Yeah," I whisper. "Mel can do anything."

"Stop talking to yourself," she snaps from up ahead. "You sound ridiculous."

She pretends she doesn't hear it, that thing in the shadows that speaks so low, but she didn't always. The first time it came we were both small, even Mel just barely higher than the reeds by the creek, and I made us stop on the trail and listen as hard as we could. A fairy, I said, or maybe a ghost, but Mel said I was wrong.

"It's something in the trees," she told me. "It talks to you just like it talks to me." And when I asked why, she bent down and said, "So it can make the curse come true."

This is how it goes, she explained. Aurora came along when nobody wanted her, and so one day, when she's grown, the woods will take her back, just like Mel asked them to. I think she meant for it to scare me, but all I could think of was her alone in our room with my bed empty across from her.

"What about you?" I asked her. "You'll be alone."

"Exactly," she said. "Just me and Mom and Dad, and I won't have to keep sharing everything with you." We were somewhere back along the trail then, closer to the house where the thornbushes bristle thick. "See that?" Mel said, pointing to one long, spiny branch. When I nodded, she took my hand and spread it open, pressed her thumb into my palm. "The thorns will be so sharp. They'll go right through you."

Then she laughed. Laughed, and led me home again.

Now Mel is fourteen, and when she talks about the curse she gave me she still laughs, but it doesn't sound the same. "Me and Mom and Dad," she says. Bitter, biting. "No, you can keep them. By the time you leave, I'll already be gone."

When we get back to the house, it's almost getting dark, and the lights are on in the kitchen, the screen door on the porch propped open. I'm hungry, and my legs are aching, but

I still wait for Mel at the edge of the woods, off to one side so she can go in first.

"Don't," she says. "I'm not coming."

"You're not?"

She shakes her head and says, "It's fine," when I reach for her.

"But your birthday."

I catch her nervous glance toward the side of the house, where the dirt driveway squares off and the old red truck is parked. "It's not important," she says. "You go ahead."

"But—"

"Get inside." The long shadow of my father paces in the window. Mel's eyes are dark, and her fists are clenched. "I mean it."

She doesn't like to tell me things twice, and I've already pushed my luck with her today, so I turn around and head into the kitchen.

No cake on the counter. No streamers, no blue and pink. Just Mom at the table, and Dad standing by the fridge, his arms crossed, jaw set hard. I think I've interrupted one of their arguments—the quiet kind, the kind Mel warns me about most.

"Sorry," I say, and duck into the hallway before Mom or Dad can pay me any attention.

I'm barely a few steps out of sight when I hear them starting up again. A hush, a simmer of sting and spite. If I stay here it will reach me and drag me back until I'm held between them like a wishbone to break.

"See," Mel always says when that happens. "I learned. You will too."

Maybe she's coming in after all, and we can wait it out in

our room together. I check out the back window by the end of the hall, hoping to see her shape in the trees, but she's already disappeared—into the woods, maybe, or down the driveway and into town. She walks when I'm with her, but when she's alone I know she runs, runs as fast as she can as long as she isn't running for home.

I don't run when I'm alone. I sit. I wait. Sometimes it feels like sleeping, and sometimes it feels like nothing at all, and I itch with it, with wanting to follow Mel out of the house, away from our mother and our father. Away anywhere, as long as I'm with her.

She disappears the winter after she turns seventeen. One night she comes home from her shift at the general store and argues with our parents, and the next morning there is no answer whenever I call her name.

My parents spend the rest of the day searching for her. They pile into the old red truck and tell me to be good, and I don't see them again until sunset, when they sit at our kitchen table, left empty and saying nothing. Dad's eyes are shut. There's dirt under his fingernails. There's a shake in his body that doesn't go away.

It goes like that for a few days, until people stop looking for Mel, because they must have figured out what I knew right away. Mel is fine. Mel is somewhere else, just like she always wanted. But she's still here, because I can feel the curse she left behind. Not a curse at all, really, but a gift, a hand reaching back for me in the dark. That's how I find her again.

I turn twelve a year and three months after Mel disappears. My birthday is a Wednesday, and I should be in school, but I missed the bus where it stops down at the foot of our driveway. Instead I'm by myself until Mom's done with her double shift and Dad's back from the bar.

The day is empty in front of me, and I'm standing at the head of the trail, looking in. Only it feels different lately, like the edge of one of those quarries they cut into the mountain. A deep pull and a long fall and that voice waiting at the bottom.

I press my hand to the trunk of the birch that turns its eye to me. "Hello," I say. Of course the voice knows I'm coming. But still, this seems like the sort of thing I'm supposed to do.

I'm wearing some of Mel's old clothes today, a dress of hers that hangs a little too long below my knees and swings, faded stripes and stitched-up holes. I almost think she's here with me as I walk between the trees. I almost hear her calling, in between the birds. They fly low when I'm here. Speak, and sing as if I can understand. I watch as they flit in and out of the dappled sun, lift my face to the breeze that catches their wings.

I haven't found her yet. But she's here, waiting for me in these woods, and when it's time—when I'm grown—I'll follow the curse like a rope tied from tree to tree, leading me right to her.

"I'm glad you were born in spring," the voice says.

I stop. Turn slowly, just in case the shadows have come closer. "Me too," I say.

"Like a crocus," it says, "when you come around. That's how I know it's time."

I wonder sometimes if it's Mel. If she ran away to the woods, and if she's talking to me somehow. It sounds like her, after all. More and more, the longer she's gone. But every now and then it says things to me that Mel never would. Every now and then it wants to know things she never did—how our parents speak so softly in the night. How my mother leaves the room when my father yells. How the ring on his hand glints in the light over the dinner table, and how it stings when it hits my cheek.

Mel would never ask about those things. Mel already knows.

I continue along the path. I've been this way hundreds of times, hundreds of days blurred together in the green of the leaves or the white of the snow. Still, things manage to surprise me. A new nest perched on a low branch, or a hole dug between two roots, nuts collected inside. Sometimes, even a trail broken through the brush by someone else, and once, the haft of a shovel, badly buried by the edge of the woods.

Ahead of me the trail splits, one half circling around to town and the other leading down into the little ravine, toward the creek. That's where I always turn around. But maybe I'm not supposed to. *That's how I know it's time*, the voice said. Time for what? Time to keep going? Time to be like Mel, who went to the creek, who came home on summer evenings with her hair dripping wet and a smile on her face?

So today I stay to the left, start down the side of the ravine. The creek isn't far, I don't think. I'll still make it back before Mom and Dad. Dad doesn't like coming back to an empty house, especially not after he's been at the bar.

I'm about halfway to the bottom when it starts, a murmur, a rush under the birdsong. Soon I can see the gleam of the water through the trees, sun bouncing off smooth river stones, sinking into pockets where the algae collects. I hurry. Sidestep the roots as they duck in and out of the earth and round the last corner of the trail, breaking through the tree line and onto the bank of the creek.

The way Mel described it, I was expecting something bigger. A stack of rock, whitewater crashing over the edge, and a pool to dive into, with something golden shining at the bottom. But it's just a creek. Overflowing from snowmelt, swirling with dirt.

Did she ever swim here? Or did she climb upstream and find some other spot? I know the other kids from town have their own trails and their own swimming holes somewhere farther up, but I've never been, and I don't think Mel had, either.

I kick off my sneakers and leave them on a dry rock. There's a patch of turned earth next to it, longer than I am tall and clear of the little weeds that grow this close to the water. I stop for a moment, crouch and peer down into the dirt. Maybe Mel buried something here. Maybe she left something for me to find.

But the voice says, "Not there. Not yet."

"Why not?" I reach out, graze my fingers across the earth.

"You aren't ready," it says, clipped and curt. Just like Mel. I almost look over my shoulder to see if she's there before it speaks again, softer now. "You aren't grown yet."

That's true. I'm not. So I get to my feet again and wade into the creek. It's barely six feet across here, but it's deep, and I gasp as the cold shocks through me.

"What about here?" I call. "Is this okay?"

"Yes," the voice says. "Doesn't that feel nice? Won't it feel nice in summer?"

It will. I already know I will come back here every day, time gone loose around me, hours sinking into the mud. My parents back at the house, waiting for someone to blame for the latest bill, and me here, safe and free.

"It's strong," I say as I dip my hand beneath the surface, the current snatching at my fingers.

"It could carry you away."

"Maybe. Down the mountain. Far away." And I know it's only joking—that's not how the curse comes true—but just in case, I peer into the distance, half hoping Mel will be there walking toward me, wet clothes dangling from one hand. "Is that what happened to her? Is that where she went?"

"Don't worry about her," the voice says. "She's never far. You'll see."

I will. I know that. I feel her every time I look through our bedroom window and see the birches looking back. And she'll be waiting for me on the other side of her curse. Once the thorns go through me I'll see her standing by the creek, footprints tracked across that mound of earth as she waves me toward her. The voice is right. Mel isn't far. I'll see her soon.

———◦———

On the night before she disappears, I wake to the sound of her shouting. I am almost eleven, still aching to grow; Mel is seventeen and too tall for her clothes, for this house, but she still shares the room with me, and I am used to looking across to her bed, to matching my position to hers so our bodies align as we sleep. But tonight her blankets are undisturbed, and her voice is echoing down the hall.

Our house is small enough that I only have to press my ear to the bedroom door to hear everything. Still, I ease it open and sneak toward the light spilling out of the kitchen.

"I am," Mel is saying. "I'm ready, and whether you like it or not, I'm old enough to decide what happens to me."

Somebody clears their throat, scoffs—Dad, it must be—

and then Mom says, "I understand. But we need you here. I wish we didn't—"

"You don't," Mel says. "I barely make enough to help with gas for the truck, never mind the electric or the heating or—"

"You make enough to save for yourself, don't you?" Dad interrupts. I hear something crack down against the table, and there's quiet for a moment.

"How did you find that?" Mel asks.

Dad laughs. "This is my house, sweetheart. You can't hide shit from me."

"I only . . ." The floorboards creak as Mel paces back and forth, her shadow distorting as it falls across the hallway. I shrink back, press myself to the wall. "I just kept enough for myself. I just kept enough so I could leave eventually. And I have it now. That's all I want, okay? I'll come back for holidays, and I'll see you still. I will. But I have to go."

"And what about Aurora?" Mom says. "You'd leave Aurora? She loves you so much, honey. You don't understand."

"Yes, I do."

"You know she still talks about that curse you invented when you were little?"

She didn't invent anything, I think. She just saw what our parents couldn't—that we weren't home yet. That we were meant to be together in the trees, away from the house, away from the empty cupboards and too-thin clothes.

"Of course I know that," Mel snaps. "I see her more than you do."

"Don't fucking talk to your mother that way," Dad says, and I flinch, even hidden in the hallway, but Mom keeps going, ignoring him.

"Imagine what it would do to her if you left. She already wonders why you don't love her the way she loves you."

Mel makes a strange, wounded sound. I think she might be crying, and I wish I were in the kitchen with her, so I could take her hand. "Of course I love her," she says, and I feel my chest go tight with joy. I always knew. She never said it, but I knew, I knew, and I had the curse to prove it. "That's not . . . that was never—"

"But you told her you wished we never had her."

"Well, why did you?" I have never heard Mel sound so angry. "You must have known we couldn't afford it."

"Mel."

"It was hard enough already, but no—you just had to bring Aurora into it."

"Mel!" Mom cries. "Be quiet. She'll hear."

"Let her. You want to talk about curses?" Mel says. "You're the ones who cursed her. You're the ones who cursed us both."

I can't tell exactly what happens next. Somebody stands up, chair scraping back across the floor. Footsteps, and the swish of fabric—a winter coat. Mom says Dad's name, and Mel's, and then there's a push of cold air reaching all the way into the hallway. And the door slamming shut.

Quiet. Mel must have run out the back. Into the woods, probably, but it's too cold for her to be out in the dark. I want to ask Mom and Dad to let me follow her, just to make sure she's all right, even though I know it isn't time yet for me to go with her. But then I hear a long, rough breath. And Dad says, "Jesus Christ," and tells Mom, "Go back to bed. I'll find her."

I run back to my bed before anyone can catch me up. I lie awake as long as I can, waiting just in case Mel comes. But I must fall asleep, because come morning, her bed is still empty, and she is nowhere.

So I wait. Until it's my turn.

———◦———

The crocuses come back again. Snow melts on the mountain, and I turn thirteen. "Grown," I tell myself the morning of my birthday. Just like Mel. I remember the party I dreamed up for her that day in the woods—the pink-and-blue cake, the streamers and balloons. I know better than to hope for that now.

My parents are already up, low voices drifting from their bedroom. I hesitate in the hallway outside my door and try to see if I can catch my name, but after a few moments I keep on to the kitchen. There's a mug of coffee on the table, still steaming, and toast waiting in the toaster. For me, maybe. I pull out one of the pieces and take a bite, black crumbs going everywhere as I go to the table and sort through the mail stacked there, just in case Mel has sent a card. It's today, after all. I'm grown. The right birthday, finally.

I'm not scared of it. No, I'm relieved. The light from the house can't follow me into the woods; I will be too far to hear my father yell. And Mel will be there, even if I can't see her. We'll be together finally. Just me and Mel, exactly the way it's supposed to be.

No card, though. A catalog from the farm store in the city and an envelope stamped with the bank's letterhead, already opened. I don't bother reading it. They've been coming for months now, and every time I see one on the table it means Dad's got an edge to him that cuts from miles away. It's good I'm going. I'll be safer with Mel, in the trees.

I go to the door, kick my ratty sneakers to one side, and

start putting on my boots. The trail will still be tricky under-foot, and I want to be prepared. I want to be wearing my best.

"Where do you think you're going?" comes Dad's voice from over my shoulder.

There it is, that sharpness. I keep my head down, keep tightening my laces. Stay quiet, stay small.

"Nowhere," I say. "Only for a walk. I'll be back for lunch."

"Maybe not today," says Mom as she comes into the kitchen. All three of us in the same room—it doesn't happen so often anymore, and I turn around before I can stop myself. Just to get a last look.

Dad's braced at the table with his head bowed, and my stomach turns uneasily. It's better when he looks right at me. Better when I can read what's coming in the twist of his mouth.

Mom sweeps a few crumbs off the counter. "Let's just stay home today," she says, her voice tight. "All right?"

It's not all right. I have to go out there. I have to be in the right place for the curse to work. For the thorns to find me, and for the voice to show me the way to Mel.

"A short one, then." I back toward the door, one hand reaching for the knob. "For my birthday."

Dad's head jerks up. "For your birthday," he says, but he isn't looking right at me. "We don't have time for this right now."

"Why don't you go back to your room?" Mom says. I can hear her working. I can hear the strain. "I'll bring you some breakfast later."

I want to do as she says, but she doesn't understand. I have to go. With a twist, the door is open, spring air on my neck. "Don't you fucking move," Dad says, and Mom says his name, says, "Calm down," and that's my chance.

I run like Mel. I run as fast as I can, faster than I ever have. Past the birch trees and their watching eyes, even past the thornbushes that Mel showed me that day. I have to get away from the house. It will happen how it's supposed to as long as I get free.

Behind me, cracking branches, and my father calling out to me. If he catches me I'll never get to Mel. I have to keep going. My breathing comes heavy and ragged as I corner at the fork in the trail and tumble down into the ravine.

The creek is swollen, the current bruising. I stagger to a stop on the bank and look over my shoulder. Something is moving in the trees.

"Hello?" I call. "Mel?" But there is no answer, and of course it isn't her. It hasn't happened yet.

The sides of the ravine are dotted with underbrush and covered in tangled shadow. I follow the line of the bank, looking for some kind of thorn, and the ground is new under my feet, giving way with every step, tilled and turning. A worm crawls up the side of my boot. Roots and rocks from seasons ago come back to the surface. And something white, rounded at the top and cracked along the side. Bones along the creek bank.

I kneel down, my dress soaking through. The dirt sticks under my nails as I dig. There are more here, clustered together in almost the right shape. Almost a person. Almost alive.

"Mel," I say. "Is that you?"

"She's waiting," the voice says. "Haven't I always said she wasn't far?"

"It was an accident," says someone else, hoarse, stumbling. Dad, caught up at last. "I didn't . . . you don't understand. She just kept talking. She wouldn't . . ."

But I don't turn around. It doesn't matter. None of it matters but Mel. "I knew it," I say to the voice. "I knew I'd find her."

A crack. My eyes go black, and white, and burning. I pitch forward. Hands out. Catch myself, and there is pain, pain at the back of my head. Pain in my hand, so I look. Something white, pierced right through my palm, blood welling up around it. Something sharp as any thorn. *Mel*, I think. *Mel*.

I don't feel the second hit. I am already gone.

COYOTE IN HIGH-TOP SNEAKERS

Darcie Little Badger

Inspired by "Puss in Boots"

When I returned from robotics camp, there was a moving truck parked outside Roberto's house, and yeah, I assumed the worst. Just like the Sanchez family, who were relocating to Tennessee, his family couldn't afford to live in our neighborhood anymore. Which meant Roberto, the guardian of all my secrets, the partner in my biggest plans, the keeper of inside jokes, and my lifelong friend, was leaving.

I stood there gawking at the truck, which was half full of boxes labeled in all caps (*BOOKS! MORE BOOKS! KITCHEN STUFF! GRANDPA'S WIGS!*), and wondered how everything could fall apart so quickly. I'd been at camp only a month!

With a shout of "Robbie, I'm here!" I circled his adobe brick house and crossed the eighth-acre sliver of backyard, weaving between anthills and prickly clumps of weeds, my red tennis shoes leaving zigzag prints in the dirt. Earlier that day, he'd messaged: Meet at the hammock, which could only mean one place: the tangle of mesquite in the southernmost corner of Roberto's property. There, a sun-warmed hammock hung between two trees. He waited in the middle of the sling, his back to me, his legs dangling, his feet decked in a pair of high-top sneakers. At my approach, Roberto twisted around, smiling. His hair had grown since June; now it covered his ears in thick black curls, partially hiding the silver studs he wore in each lobe.

That brought back fond memories. At age twelve, we got our ears pierced together. I'd been the first one to want earrings. But after scheduling an ear-piercing appointment at the mall, I lost my nerve. In response, Roberto offered, "I'll get mine pierced and tell you if it hurts. How's that?"

Something about sharing the experience with a friend made me braver. So a week later, my mom drove us to the mall, and Roberto held my hand when a boutique associate named Carly punched holes through my ears.

Years later, Roberto wore earrings way more often than I did.

"Nadia!" he greeted, waving. "Did you bring me robots?"

"They didn't let us take any camp property home," I said.

Roberto shifted to the right, and I plopped onto the sling of fabric, which wobbled as we found our shared balance. "I wish you could've seen my remote-controlled car. It won second place in the all-camp race."

"You can build another. Teach me how, and we'll race each other."

He was acting like nothing would change, like we'd be neighbors after the summer ended. "Roberto, what's going on?" I asked.

"Huh? How so?"

"The truck. You're moving? I thought . . ." I tilted back, looking at the vivid blue sky, regaining my composure. It wasn't fair to cry in front of Roberto now. Yeah, I felt shitty, but he had to feel worse. He was the one losing a home. "I thought you had more time."

"More time for what?"

"To save your house, for one!"

He uttered a long, half-groaning "Ooooooh!" Then Roberto said, "You didn't read my letter."

"Letter? Huh? I never got one!" Not surprising, considering the state of mail day at camp. Every Tuesday and Friday, Jake, who was much better at programming computers than supervising fifty teenagers, would heave a bag of mail into the cafeteria and dump a loose mound of envelopes onto the nearest empty table. The first week had been utter chaos, hands grasping, names shouted. By week four, we'd developed a system of lines, but it was still difficult to account for every letter. "Last I heard," I continued, "your mom got laid off, and y'all couldn't pay the mortgage."

With a lopsided grin, Roberto bent his knees, causing the hammock to sway as gently as blades of grass in a breeze. From our seat, we had a clear view of the Westminster ranch: a rolling field of grazing land, two newly refurbished horse stables, and a colonial blue farmhouse with perpetually dark windows. Apparently, the Westminsters, a married couple and their college-student sons, also owned a town house in Dallas and a beachside vacation home in Corpus Christi. As far as I knew, they only visited the ranch to ride sweet-tempered horses around the grazing fields. In other words, they were the wealthiest people in town, excluding Graybrow, the infamous pirate who may or may not be buried here with all his loot.

That said, woe befell anyone who stepped on their land. Once, Roberto and I tracked a spiny lizard across the invisible border between the yard and the ranch. A few minutes later, a burly man in a two-piece suit charged out of the farmhouse, shouting, "You! Hey, kids! No trespassing!" Scared the piss outta me.

"Your connection was so bad up there," Roberto continued, "I thought it'd be safer to describe the whole adventure by mail. Guess not."

"You're smiling," I said. "Tell me why."

"Settle in, Nadia." He passed me a can of peach soda and a bagged sandwich. Peanut butter, honey, and banana on wheat. My usual. "It's a long story."

This is what Roberto said:

———

One time, this guy traded a penny for a soda can
    and the can for a bouncy ball
    and the bouncy ball for a doll
    and the doll for a rusty saw
    and so on until he had a Jet Ski. Unfortunately, he'd never driven a Jet Ski before, and sank it after crashing into a buoy. That's not the point, though. The takeaway is that a man got a Jet Ski, and all it took was a penny, determination, and seven months of bartering.

I thought that story would console Mom after she got laid off. Especially because she was stressing about the mortgage. We didn't have much, but there were at least nineteen pennies in the rubbish drawer.

But Mom just shook her head and said, "You're missing an important part of the story, Roberto."

"What?" I asked. Sure, I hadn't listed every trade—there'd been at least fifty—but I thought I'd covered the important stuff.

Apparently not. Mom stopped unloading cups and mugs from the dishwasher to fully concentrate on me. Out of respect, I stopped wiping the kitchen counter to give her my full attention. Outside, cicadas cried. In the living room, the news played, and Grandpa snored. Footsteps thundered down the hall: my sisters playing zombie tag. A toilet flushed. Probably Dad. Either that, or our dog had learned to do her business indoors.

Above all the white noise of our life, Mom explained, "The Jet Ski man's trading experiment went viral. Millions of people followed his adventures, rooting for him with every update. Worldwide, people offered trades and travel assistance. To get a Jet Ski from a penny, you need a community willing and able to help you succeed."

"And . . . we don't have that community?" I was thinking of you, Nadia. All the times we've helped each other.

Mom just smiled at that. It wasn't a "ha-ha happy" smile. More like the smile she'd perfected at work while dealing with the unreasonably angry public. Every week, at least one random museum visitor would hog the info booth to complain at length about the dinosaur selection in the fossil hall or renovation-based closures. That smile's a mask, and it bothered me that Mom was trying to hide her real feelings.

She said, "Times are difficult for nearly everyone." And that's when I got it. I know you'd fight for me, Nadia. But the system fights against us all.

So I continued scrubbing the counter, erasing a bunch of ring-shaped coffee stains and spots of dried soy sauce with a moist hand towel. After that, I kissed Mom on the cheek and went outside—here, to this hammock—to think.

That's when my story gets wild. Bear with me.

A coyote stepped around that laurel bush and asked, "What's wrong?"

———

I know it's bad form, but I had to interrupt the story.

"A coyote talked?"

"Yep." Roberto lifted one shoulder, a half shrug. Confused but confident. "Not the way we talk, though. Her mouth stayed shut, and the words appeared between us."

"Like psychic communication?"

"Um, no? At least, I don't think so. The sound manifested."

I ruminated a second and then leaned an inch to the right, nudging him shoulder to shoulder. "Like Jason Oakshield's summon music command," I guessed again. Roberto and I played an ongoing tabletop RPG with a few other friends. Roberto's character, an elfin bard named Jason, couldn't strum a lute for shit, so he used the level-one "summon music" spell to pretend. Any D20 roll lower than five meant the audience caught him faking. Jason Oakshield was essentially a fantasy-world air guitarist.

"Exactly!" Roberto said. "Just like that."

I nodded, encouraging him to continue. For the sake of the story, I'd pretend that sound could be summoned in the real world, too.

Over years of friendship, I'd learned something about Roberto: he couldn't stand it when his loved ones got sad. He'd go to great lengths for a smile, por ejemplo, getting his ears pierced or sharing inspirational stories about Jet Skis. And when that didn't work—when life's problems were greater than any self-less act or story—Roberto would imagine a different world.

It wasn't lying. It was hopeful thinking.

"What happened next?" I asked.

———◦———

To put it mildly, Coyote's question surprised me. Ignoring that most coyotes don't talk to humans, why would she care that a random guy on a hammock was frowning? So that's what I asked.

"Just making small talk, Robbie," Coyote said.

Obviously, my next question was, "You know my name?"

She explained, "I know all my neighbors."

Coyotes do live around here. Do you ever hear them yapping and howling at night? Their voices are shrill, almost ghostly. Gray-haired scoundrels: that's what Grandpa calls them. Mom and Dad say they're timid, clever animals. The talking coyote didn't seem like a scoundrel, and she definitely wasn't timid. Clever, though? Yeah. I could tell right away that she knew a lot more than she was lettin' on.

"My mom got laid off," I explained, "and that probably means we can't afford the mortgage anymore. Especially since Dad's hours were cut. I just . . . I'm really going to miss this place. That's what's wrong."

She tilted her head, swiveling her pointy ears my way. "What's a mortgage?"

"It's . . . um . . . wait a second." I had to search the term "mortgage" on my phone because it's not easy to explain the concept of a mortgage to a coyote in succinct, clear terms. "When somebody wants to buy a house, but they can't afford the whole cost, they can make a deal with the bank and get a loan. After that, they give the bank money every month to pay off the house plus interest."

"Why are you paying for this land?" Coyote asked. "You've been here for centuries."

It took me a moment to understand that she wasn't referring to me specifically—I couldn't pass as eighteen, much less ancient—but meant my family line. She knew we were Apache. Like I said: clever.

"Violent colonization," I said, "stolen land. Honestly, I'm bone-tired of rehashing our tragic history. Just trust me when I say that the bank doesn't care about any of it."

Coyote's fuzzy brows lifted up and pinched inward, probably the most concerned expression a coyote can muster. I felt the urge to ruffle her ears and promise that everything would be okay. To assure her that human problems like mine shouldn't worry her, since the life of a wild animal is already hard enough.

She didn't give me the chance. Coyote sprung upright and exclaimed, "I've devised a three-step plan to save your house. C'mon." With that, she scampered into the brush.

Keep in mind that I was willing to do whatever it took, assuming the "whatever" agreed with my sense of morality and wouldn't end in tragedy. I flopped out of the hammock. Then, after a final glance at the house, where my sisters still played tag without a care, 'cause they didn't understand the uncertainty of home, I followed Coyote.

Coyote led me to the wilds of Purgatory Park, about four miles off Deer Run Avenue. Her lair was a hollowed-out fallen tree. She crawled, belly to the ground, into one end of the log and exited from the other side with a faded, dirty *Missing* sign, the kind people staple to telephone poles when they're searching for lost pets or family. "Step one," she declared. "A rescue mission." I plucked it from her mouth, curious. This sign had a picture of a wrinkly pug whose panting face seemed to smile. I read aloud, "'MISSING! REWARD!'" According to the small text, the pug's name was Otis, but he also responded to "Sweetie" and "Cuddle Bug."

"Coyote," I said, "thanks for trying to help, but there's no way the reward money could pay off the house. Plus, this little guy has been missing for weeks. If he hasn't been found already—"

She nudged the poster with her round black nose. "I know where he is."

"Where?"

In response, she just tilted her head. "To rescue Otis, we need a pair of shoes." Coyote paw-pointed at the sneakers on my feet. "Those shoes."

———◦———

"Roberto, were you wearing your best high-tops?" I asked, staring pointedly at his shoes. They'd seen better days. A chunk of the rubber tread was missing near the heel, and their colors were dulled with scrapes and mud.

"Yep," he confirmed. "My favorites."

"What the heck happened? Did you put them in a blender?"

He chuckled. "Well . . ."

———◦———

After Coyote and I hatched a doggie rescue plan, she told me to meet her at—and I quote—"the place with sweet-smelling trees and a high wooden fence." We couldn't go there together, since it was miles away, and her standard route was unsafe for lumbering bipeds. When I asked for more specific details about the location, Coyote elaborated that Otis was being imprisoned in a neighborhood with lots of fences. Not near farmland. No stores nearby, either. Just houses. Oh, and the house belonged to a woman and her monstrous son.

That made me worry. "Monstrous? As in actually a monster?" In a world of talking coyotes, anything could exist, right? My imagination jumped to giants, vampires, and mothmen.

"Monstrous as in terrible," Coyote explained. "He's a human boy your age, maybe older. I was exploring garbage bins on trash day, and he stepped outside. When he saw me, he laughed. I thought that meant friendliness and let my guard down. Wrong assessment. Mid-laughter, the guy threw a rock. Good aim, too. I barely dodged in time."

"Yikes, Coyote."

She continued, "See, I understand why people throw rocks out of fear or anger, Roberto, but it always confuses me when they throw rocks for fun."

"To be honest, I don't completely get it, either." Then something clicked. "What did he look like? I might know him from school—"

———

"No way!" I interrupted. "Was it . . ."

Roberto nodded. "Peter. How did you guess?"

An obviously rhetorical question. "I thought Peter went to Dartmouth after he graduated?"

"Unfortunately, he's home for the summer."

Two years my senior, Peter used to be the most terrifying upperclassman in school, and he deserved the reputation. Once, as a freshman, I was heading to third-period English. Walking through a crowded hall, overwhelmed, everything new. Suddenly, a sharp pain exploded in my side, like I'd been jabbed with a stick. Looking up, I noticed this big auburn-haired stranger passing. He had a pen clutched in his fist. It was so confusing. We'd never met before. In the moment, I convinced myself that he'd bumped into me accidentally. Turns out, Peter had a reputation for painful accidents. "Stay away from Pete," my friends warned. "He makes roadkill for sport. He joined the football team just to break bones. He'll smile to your face and stab you in the back."

"What happened next?" I asked. "Did you save the pug? Was Peter there?"

"Well . . ."

———

A friend of a friend goes to church with Peter's family; that's how I learned he lives on Cider Street. Not a long drive, thankfully. The house with sweet-smelling trees, blossoming crepe myrtles, was at the end of a cul-de-sac. I parked along the road, and although Coyote hadn't been precise about the time of day we'd rendezvous, there was a gentle scratch on the passenger-side door, a paw against metal. I cracked the door to let her inside.

"Go now," she advised. "The woman is gone. Every morning, she leaves, and every afternoon, she returns."

"What about Peter? I doubt he works a summer job."

"He usually stays in his house."

In other words, I had to work quickly and quietly, or Peter the dognapping bully of Cider Street might start throwing rocks at me.

"And you're one hundred percent sure the pug is Otis and not a different dog?"

Coyote looked at me like I'd just asked her if water is wet. "Yes. Otis told me everything. He misses home."

Made sense. If Coyote could speak to humans, she could obviously communicate with dogs.

Honestly, even if Coyote hadn't been one hundred percent confident that the pug on Cider Street was Otis, I would have rescued the poor dog anyway. Coyote said Peter left Otis out-side all day, every day. It was a miracle the little pup hadn't overheated and died yet. Must've been a hundred degrees that afternoon!

With not a minute to waste, I grabbed my supplies and hopped outside. Left the car running—both for a quick get-away and because Coyote would bake without air-conditioning. She was supposed to keep guard and honk if the dognappers returned from work early.

A wooden fence enclosed a square-shaped backyard, Otis's prison. I circled to the far side and climbed onto a horizontal support plank, which gave me enough height to look over the seven-foot-high pickets. There was a doghouse nearby, and I could make out a round face beyond the entry.

"Otis," I whispered. When he didn't leave the shade, I chanced a slightly louder "Otis!"

His ears might've twitched at that, but I needed the dog's complete attention. "Otis, come" didn't work, and neither did "Here, boy." I was afraid to shout, so if Otis didn't approach, I'd have to go across the yard and retrieve him just feet away from the back windows.

Then, I had an epiphany. "Cuddle Bug," I called.

Like a wrinkly jack-in-the-box, Otis's head popped out of the doghouse. He was panting with all his might, peering up at me. So I took my shot and threw one of my shoes. It landed smack-dab between the fence and the doghouse.

Little Otis trotted across the finely trimmed grass, sniffed my shoe, and commenced to chewing. No time to waste, I dropped the second shoe against the fence and beckoned. "Here, Otis!"

But the little dog seemed content with just one shoe. He

plopped onto his side and gnawed at the rubber sole. As the minutes passed, I realized that there was no other choice: I had to walk partway into the yard. It was easy 'nuff to climb over the fence, and Otis, whose heavy breathing resembled a choo-choo train, simply rolled onto his belly when I approached. As I gently tucked him into my backpack, I thought the coast would remain clear.

That's when the blinds in one of the house windows snapped up.

—◦—

"Oh no! He caught you?"

"Yeeeep."

—◦—

Let me be clear: Peter didn't speak a word. He didn't even shout in surprise or anger. But as I climbed onto the horizontal plank and heaved my body up, the sliding door opened with a quick *whoosh*. When I straddled the fence, Peter sprinted across the yard with all the speed and single-minded purpose of a linebacker. As I dropped to safety, the fence shook with the violent *thunk* of his body slamming against it. The impact made me jolt, no different from a jump scare in a horror movie, except the danger was real. If I'd been a couple seconds slower, he would've caught me.

Thankfully, he didn't outrace me to the car, but as I reversed, Peter opened the front door and stood at its threshold. Just stood there. Staring.

Smiling.

"This is serious," I warned Coyote. "We might've saved Otis, but I'm scared that Peter will now hurt somebody else."

"Not gonna happen," she promised. Coyote had moved to the back seat to keep Otis company. The wrinkly dog seemed much happier in the air-conditioning with a bowl of water I'd prechilled using ice cubes. "Peter laughed at me, Roberto," Coyote explained, "and then threw a rock at my head. But he missed. He failed to kill me."

"That's a good thing."

"Not for him." She laughed; the sound resembled hyena cackles, so I suspect that it came from her actual mouth. "Now I will ruin his monster plans. All of them. Forever."

Look, I'm all for dousing Peter's reign of terror, but I had to ask, "Is that the real reason you brought me here?"

Reflected in the rearview mirror, Coyote cocked her head, the universal doggish sign of confusion. I tried to reassure her, "It's okay. I'm happy to rescue Otis, even if it doesn't save the house."

"Two birds in one bite," she said. "Don't worry. Your house is the main goal, and step one was successful."

———

"How big was the reward for Otis?" I asked Roberto.

"A thousand dollars, but I turned it down."

"I'm itchin' to know the reasoning for that."

He shrugged, like it was nothing. "On the drive to Otis's home in Will Heights, Coyote advised me to ask for something else."

"Will Heights?" I juggled memories of costumes and tin pails full of candy. "That's where we went trick-or-treating as kids!" It was a well-to-do neighborhood with big houses just shy of mansions.

"Which house was it?" I asked.

"The shiny one." He tapped one of his silver earrings. "That old house with a gold-painted lion-head knocker on the door."

"Yeah! I remember. It was really mysterious. The home-owner always went dark for Halloween. Never opened the door."

"She opened the door for me and Otis," Roberto reported.

———

The lion-head knocker sent reverberations through both the heavy wooden door and my hand. In other words, we need one of those. The moment that door swung open, Otis started wiggling in my arms. Never seen a happier dog. I'm serious. His stumpy tail wagged just about a thousand beats per minute. His joy was sparked by an elderly woman in a flowy silk dress, yellow with red flowers; she wore gold bangles on each wrist. For a moment, I thought she'd faint. Then she cried out, "Sweetie! My sweet Otis!" and scooped him into a hug. For his part, Otis tried to lick the nose off her face. He was a changed pug! Not a trace of gloominess left.

She cried, "Where did you find him?"

And I told her, "Cider Street. He looked so sad. Then I remembered your poster. It's been weeks, but my mom taught me to take a picture of every 'missing pet' flyer on my phone. That way, you always have the info."

After introductions—her name was Miss Jen Raster, retired photographer—she thanked me over and over again, told me that she'd never stopped hoping, but it got harder by the day. "Like so much of life," she said. "You can't appreciate how grateful I am, Roberto, but perhaps a thousand dollars will help."

I went, "No, no, no. Reuniting you with Otis is enough of a reward." That part wasn't a lie, but the next phrase out of my mouth verged on exaggeration. "I'm really thirsty," I said. "Could I bother you for a glass of water?"

She was delighted. "Of course! Come in! Do you like sweets? I just had macarons delivered." Then Miss Raster led me into her home with a twirl. Speaking of twirling, she reminded me of a ballerina. Maybe it was her perfect posture. Could have been her grace. Inside, the walls were decorated with framed photographs, a mix of artsy and personal pieces. In every picture of Miss Raster, she was joined by a dog. Pugs, poodles, even one mastiff. All well-fed, finely groomed, and happy.

Past the hall, we entered a dining room. Against every wall were glass-faced cabinets. They displayed porcelain plates, crystal animals, and expensive-looking pottery. All really pretty stuff, but I was looking for something specific.

"Your home is like a museum," I said, which made her smile.

As Miss Raster filled Otis's doggy bowl with a handy tin of food—guess she hadn't been exaggerating about never giving up—she explained, "They're curios I've collected over the years."

That's when gold flashed in the cabinet near her floor-to-ceiling, velvet-draped windows. There sat a wooden jewelry box overflowing with coins. They came in many sizes and shapes, but all were silver, bronze, or gold, with a rough-hewn quality, as if shaped by hand, stamped one by one. Ancient, in other words. I asked her, "Is this pirate treasure? Did you find Graybrow's hoard?"

———

"Wait! Let me guess what happened next. Did Coyote's plan involve Graybrow's loot? That old lady had a treasure map, didn't she?"

Roberto made a long, uncertain sound: "Eeeeeeh."

"I'm close?"

"Soooorta."

Graybrow is the town's most famous dead guy, even though there's no actual proof that he died here. Oh, he existed. That's not in dispute. According to multiple historical records, in the 1700s, Graybrow and his men accumulated a massive pile of wealth through high-seas robbery, mercenary work, and gambling. Finally, a bunch of pissed-off warships chased him into the Gulf. There, his ship sank to the bottom of the ocean, but Graybrow was never found, and neither was his treasure.

According to local legend, the pirate captain was mortally wounded during the chase. Facing capture, he and his loyal crew sank their own ship and escaped to land. There, Graybrow died and was buried with his share of the loot.

Buried here, according to the Lipan people who witnessed his death. They never shared the exact location. Ain't right to mess with the dead. That's why his tomb, if it exists, remains lost.

"How so?" I asked.

———◇———

I learned that Miss Raster found all the gold and silver coins herself. Every summer, she takes a metal detector to Europe and searches for coins on private land. Her friends let her do that for a cut of any finds—mostly bronze coins, but also silver and gold when she's lucky. "It's relaxing," she explained, "and helps me stretch my legs, since Otis isn't one for long walks."

At that, the dog waddled up to me and licked his chops, enviously eyeing the pyramid of macarons Miss Raster had carried into the dining room. During the visit, I must've scarfed down five or six of them. They were top-of-the-line. Bittersweet chocolate, crisp outer shell. We need to track down that macaron bakery, Nadia. It's called Sweet Treats or Sweets and Treats, not totally sure.

Anyway, I said, "Miss Raster, could I buy one of your old coins? My mom used to work for a museum, and she'd love one."

I had twenty dollars in my pocket—no chance in hell an ancient coin would go for twenty. Thing was, they were probably worth around a thousand dollars, and she'd been pushing me to accept the reward all visit.

My instincts had been right. With a generous "Yes, yes!" she swooped out of the dining room, leaving me with a glass of water, a pound of macarons, and a begging pug. She returned carrying a tiny black bag, velvet, the kind used to package jewelry. Miss Raster unlocked the cabinet, dunked her hand into the jewelry box, and dropped a pinch of coins into the bag. "They're yours," she declared, a queen making a proclamation. "A gift."

———◦———

Roberto paused to drink from a glass bottle of citrus-flavored mineral water. I took a sip of my peach soda; the carbonation tickled my nose, made me sneeze.

"You want to see the coins?" he asked, jingling a velvet jewelry pouch. I grabbed it, emptying five coins into the palm of my hand: three silver, two gold. They were heavier than average change, brighter. Better yet, over the course of centuries, they'd passed through countless hands, carried the fingerprints of generations. The most intriguing coin depicted a bird on one side, a woman on the other.

"You still have them," I breathed, awestruck. If they were legit, how much of Roberto's story could actually be trusted? All of it? Including the talking coyote?

"Uh-huh! They'll be birthday gifts for Mom and Dad."

"I just assumed that you swapped the coins for a new house somehow? Since you told me the Jet Ski story, trades were on my mind."

He laughed. "Nope." When I tried to return the coins to their velvet pouch, Roberto folded one into the palm of my hand.

"That one's for you," he said.

It was tricky to hug him on the hammock, since every movement caused us to wobble, but I managed by throwing my right arm around his shoulders, squeezing tight. "How'd you know I like this one the most?" I wondered, tilting the coin side to side, allowing sunlight to glint in the rivulets of bird wings.

"Just a hunch. Plus, it's my favorite one, too."

"Good taste." I took a thoughtful sip of my soda. "But I still don't understand how the coins played into Coyote's big plan."

"Well," he explained, "psychology."

I didn't see Coyote for a couple days. She'd promised to "check in" at a nebulous moment in the future. Turns out, that time was Wednesday, ten minutes past midnight. I was the only person still awake in my house. That's why I was worried when Coyote shouted, "Hey, hey! Roberto! We have work to do!"

I paused the horror movie I'd been watching—have you seen *Faces in Devil Lake*? Not a bad found-footage movie—and went to the window, sliding it up to lean outside. There she stood, her eyes glowing bright in the moonlight. "Keep it down, Coyote," I whispered. "My family's asleep."

"Don't worry," she said. "They can't hear me talk. Unless I do this . . ." Coyote mimicked howling, throwing back her head. At the time, I assumed that she controlled the recipient of her second voice, her sound without a mouth, but maybe it's something else. Like I could have a knack for understanding or just an unusually high willingness to listen.

In any case, I asked her, "What now?"

"One more task," she said. "The most important step in my plan."

That was intimidating. It only got worse when she continued, "The other two steps? They both had fail-safes. Backup steps, plan Bs. There is no plan B here, Roberto. And I can help you prepare, but success depends on you. How well can you act?"

All my grogginess dissipated in a snap. "I've taken drama, but is it safe?" The incident at Peter's house had left me shaken. Remember when we got trapped in a flash storm, and we were running home, and a bolt of lightning hit a tree right across the street? Peter had been a near miss, too. I kept wondering how things could've gone wrong. I had to think of my family, see? It was bad enough to lose the house, but they'd be way more devastated if I got hurt.

Plus, I wouldn't enjoy getting maimed or murdered, either.

"Very safe," she said. "The worst outcome is the bitter disappointment of failure."

No pressure. "In that case, I'm in. Can it wait until daytime, though?"

Coyote tilted her head. "Mostly. But you need to dig a few shallow holes under the cover of darkness."

———o———

"Grave robbing?" I guessed.

Roberto snorted. "That's indecent. For your information, I buried bottle caps and paper clips all over the yard."

"At midnight?"

"Yep. Guess how the Westminsters always know when somebody trespasses on their ranch."

I considered the question. Their property seemed too large and rustic for motion sensors, and the staff couldn't monitor every corner of the ranch unless . . . "They use cameras?"

Roberto nodded. "That's right. Hence the cover of darkness. I couldn't let them see me digging . . . yet."

———☉———

Nadia, when the Jet Ski man saw a penny and dreamed of bigger, faster riches, he had to have a lot of faith in the goodwill of strangers. And that faith paid off. Similarly, Coyote bet that Miss Raster would be grateful enough to give me a coin; she was right.

But the last step of her plan hinged on the opposite of generosity.

I was almost afraid to succeed.

After two days of pep talks and practice speeches in front of the bathroom mirror, I carried Grandpa's gardening shovel outside and started digging a hole at the edge of the yard. By the way, when I say edge, I mean razor edge. Less than a foot away from the Westminsters' land. I'd planned it using a map of the property. No room for error.

Now, it stung me to be so impolite, but I was a messy shoveler, chucking every scoop of dirt onto the Westminster side. The first day, I shoveled like that for hours, and nothing happened. Second day? Third day? Same result. To ward off heatstroke, I worked in the morning and sub-evening, pausing only when the sky went dark. Still, by day four, my hands were blistered, my arms burned, and several mounds of dirt were scattered along the weedy border of the Westminster ranch.

While I toiled, Coyote remained hidden, but I sensed her

attention, especially later in the day. You know the feeling of being watched? Like a tiny ant walking up your back, just the mildest tingle. Now and then, when I got impatient with the digging, I'd wonder aloud, "What if everyone's on vacation? Or in one of their million other houses?"

Once, Coyote deigned to respond, "They aren't."

My back was to the ranch when a burly man—the same guy we saw during the lizard incident—stormed up and shouted, "Stop that!"

He wore black pants and a collared shirt; the sleeves were folded up to his elbows, but he still sweated damp patches under his armpits. That meant he probably jogged all the way from the house.

I'd been dreading this confrontation. Not 'cause he scared me—well, he kinda did—but mostly 'cause failure scared me. I had to sell a story, and if he got a whiff of deception, it was over. Everything. Over. We'd lose our house, our land, and I know that this sliver of yard ain't much, but at least it's big enough to curl your toes in the dirt and sit in a hammock with your best friend. . . .

You get the point.

I dropped the shovel and wiped my hands on my jeans like this: See? It gave me the chance to pull the coins out of my pocket. "I can dig in my own backyard," I told him.

He crowded close, a real power move: intrude in my personal space, force me to step back and make room for the big man. I let him feel powerful. All part of my role.

"Well, you can't dump piles of dirt in ours."

That's when it struck me. "Ours?" All this time, 'cause of his prim and fancy clothes, I'd mistaken him for a butler or something. But he was Mr. Westminster! To my credit, he'd never visited for a neighborly chat, and I'd only seen him riding horses from a distance. In other words, I couldn't identify the man in a lineup.

"Clean it up," he said, jabbing a manicured thumb at the mounds. "Now."

"Yes, sir." I scrambled to do as he asked, retrieving the shovel with my free hand and casually showing him the coins in my other. "I was going to refill the holes anyway! Um, can I finish digging this last one? There may be a few more. . . ."

"You found those in the ground?" His demeanor shifted from peeved to intrigued, and all it took was a flash of gold.

"Yeah. Well, my sisters found one closer to the house, and I got the rest here. We're planning to move—if the house ever sells—so I'm on a mission to dig around, find as many as I can."

"I see," he said. And you bet that he was looking. He stared at those coins like they were calling his name.

"Here," I said, handing him the coins, even though all my instincts resisted the decision to give ancient treasure to a stranger. "I think they're from the museum. Mom used to work there, and the gift store sells fake Graybrow doubloons for ten dollars each. There could be a hundred dollars." As I rambled about time capsules and pack rats, Mr. Westminster held one gold coin up till it caught the light, and then—shameless, really—he bit it when my back was half-turned. His tooth left a tiny nick behind; it's not on yours, thankfully.

The thing about gold? Pure gold's soft. That's why people bite it.

He knew.

The rest was out of my hands, Nadia. I'd pulled off a successful charade as the naive teenager next door. But would Mr. Westminster tell me I'd struck gold? Or would my neighbor—our neighbor—betray me? What do you think happened?

——○——

Of course I'd hoped for—if not expected—a happy resolution. In the story, beyond the story. But I couldn't overlook the U-Haul parked in their driveway.

"Honestly," I confessed, "I don't know."

——○——

Mr. Westminster returned the coin, and with a smile, he said, "They're good replicas."

And if you think he actually believed that, explain why—late that night, when everyone else was sleeping—a team of guys with metal detectors paced up and down the ranch, even sneaking into our yard. Explain why, two days later, the Westminsters made an offer on our house. An offer much higher than the market value.

Clearly, on the off chance I'd accidentally found Graybrow's tomb, they wanted it all for themselves.

——○——

"So yeah," Roberto said. "We're moving down the street. With the money, Mom and Dad were able to pay off the rest of their loan, buy the Sanchez place—its yard is a whole acre!—and put some extra into savings. It'll help while Mom finds another job. We're going to be all right, Nadia."

He kicked his legs, swinging us back and forth. I had vivid memories of the playground, where we'd always run to the swing set and try our hardest to make a loop, never quite breaking free from gravity, never quite caring. "You're going to be all right," I agreed.

In a world where coyotes could talk, we all would.

"But what happens when the Westminsters realize there's no tomb?" I mused.

"They'll flip the place?" Roberto guessed. "Expand their ranch?"

"No," said a high-pitched voice, half-bark, half-song. "They'll convert it into a bed-and-breakfast. That's part of my seventy-step plan for this neighborhood."

"What the h— Aaaaah!" Jolting in surprise, I flipped the hammock, and Roberto and I spilled onto the ground in a tangle of limbs and a splash of carbonated, citrus-flavored mineral water. After the world stopped spinning, I rolled onto my belly and looked up to see a coyote near the laurel bush.

"You heard her, too?" Roberto asked, sitting.

"Y . . . yeah. Hi." Hesitantly, I extended a hand; Coyote placed her front paw on my palm, and we shook in greeting.

"Hi, Nadia," she said.

Just like he'd described: the voice materialized between us, a real-world version of "summon sound."

"Thank you for helping Roberto," I said.

"Any time." Her eyes were yellow as sunflowers, bright as stars. "And if you ever need my help, I'll be in the hollow tree. Just ask." She stared at my red shoes, as if weaving them into her endless plans. Then, with a canine smile, the coyote vanished into the brush.

THE SISTER SWITCH

Melissa Albert

A New Fairy Tale

The girl had a wide red mouth. She teetered on lace-up boots and stuck out like an inkblot among the blanched storefronts of downtown suburbia. There was nothing in her hands as Nate approached, then an out-thrust flyer.

If Nate had grown up in the city he would've been used to this, would've sidestepped her neatly as a square dance partner. Or maybe not. She was hot. Older than him, a little bit scary. He took the flyer.

ONE NIGHT ONLY, it said.

WORLD PREMIERE PRODUCTION OF

THE SILENT SISTERS
an Immersive Theatrical Experience
Presented by the Kindly Players
Pencil Factory, 10 p.m.
Multiple floors to explore
Audience participation required

He turned it over. The back was blank. "The Pencil Factory? I thought that place was condemned."

The girl pursed her painted lips. It made Nate think of

a documentary he'd watched once, about sea life. He tried again. "So it's like a *Sleep No More* thing? Actors just . . . wandering around?"

She showed her teeth. Like a smile, but meaner. Hotter. "Actors," she repeated. "Wandering around."

Girls did that echo thing when they were into him, he'd noticed. Mirroring, it was called. He looked down, peered at her through his lashes. "Will you be there?"

Her voice was a sexy burr, and that startling mouth. "Will you?"

Nate was still thinking of a reply when she walked away, brushing past him and disappearing around the corner just beyond the Sweet Shop. Briefly he imagined following, then moved on.

Miriam and her endless stuff were sprawled across the worst table at the coffee shop, the one right below the fuzzy speaker. Nate pulled up beside her and held out the flyer.

She snatched it. "What's this? Ooh, one night only. Ooh, 'The Silent Sisters'!"

Miriam looked cool, like she always did. Ghost of a Governess, you might call today's look. Immersive theater in an abandoned factory was her exact shit.

"You've heard of it?"

"So have you. It's an old fairy tale. Tonight, though?" She considered it. "Yeah, I can get out tonight."

"Maybe, uh." He adjusted the strap of his bag. "Maybe Case wants to come."

Miriam's gaze, flicking from the flyer to his face, was neutral. "What a good idea," she said. "I'll ask her."

"Cool." Guilt made him lean awkwardly over the table to kiss her, which he'd forgotten to do when he walked in. Before they made contact his bag swung off his shoulder and knocked her coffee onto the book she'd been reading. They both jumped back, and Nate ran for napkins. When she left first, twenty minutes later, she didn't kiss him goodbye.

—◦—

Probably Nate should've broken up with Miriam as soon as he fell in love with her best friend. But his birthday was coming up and he was pretty sure she'd gotten him tickets to see the Hiddenways play the Empty Bottle, a show that was now sold out.

He had a plan. He'd wait a full week after the show to dump her, then give it another week before asking out Case. *The sister switch*, his friend Ian called it, when you traded a girl in for her best friend.

But Ian was a leering asshole. It wasn't a switch, it was a *correction*. Case and Nate were on a collision course and they both knew it. The way she made teasing fun of Nate's poetry, the layered digs about his being wrong for Miriam. The sweet, scornful way she looked at him. Their hate-to-love meter was tipping precipitously to the right. Miriam would respect their inevitability in the end.

He really did like Miriam. She was a great girl. They'd definitely stay friends once he got with Case. They'd hang out all the time, they'd be this enviable trio. His brain flickered greedily around an image of himself kissing Case *and* Miriam . . . but, no. That was disrespectful. And he liked to keep his fantasies on the likely side.

Nate got home around five, lay on the couch in a fall of late sun, and fell asleep. When he woke up it was dark. He circled the ground floor for a minute, head still aqueous with dreams. "Mom?" he called. No one answered.

He took a shower. He patted his pits with the stuff that

made him smell French and sprayed his hair with the stuff that made it look dirty and tried three T-shirts before settling on an overwashed black one with two small holes at the hem. Is Case coming, he texted Miriam, leaving off the question mark so it would seem casual.

She didn't answer. And when she rolled up at nine thirty, she just honked. The house was still empty, and Nate was feeling a little off, to be honest, but Case's shape in the front seat focused him. It put him back in his body, let him feel the way he looked with his worn-out clothes and his bedhead and the eyelashes an ex once referred to as "your Bambi bullshit."

The girls watched him through the windshield, their faces so identically expressionless he felt a surge of paranoia. Could they have *felt* it somehow when he'd pictured himself kissing both of them? No, that was ridiculous. He tilted his chin at Miriam as if to say, *Hey*, and *Why didn't you come to the door?* Her face didn't answer.

Then he got distracted, because someone was already in the back seat. A dude he'd never met sprawled across two-thirds of the bench, looking at him with massive liner-smudged eyes.

"Hey, man," Nate said stiffly.

"Good evening," the guy replied. He had brown skin and thick hair tied back from his face with a literal ribbon. He was taller than Nate, unnecessarily taller. He was wearing a fucking *duster*.

Nate nodded at it. "Cool coat," he said, trying to ride that line between sincere and shitty but face-planting over it so hard he saw Miriam's eyes narrow in the rearview mirror. Fucking Lestat over here just smiled.

"Hey, Mir," Nate said, putting a hand on her shoulder. Then, "Hi, Case."

Miriam smiled thinly as she backed out of the drive. Case might've bobbed her chin. Nate watched his empty house as they drove away.

The dude's name was Kevin, so that helped. He went to the vaguely shittier high school one suburb over. Nate split the drive between clocking Miriam's improvisational driving style and trying to figure out the vibe between Kevin and Case. Nothing? Something? He was definitely hot but possibly also gay? The music was too loud to really talk, but the girls were up front doing that thing they did, volleying in a best-friends shorthand so flattened by shared reference it was impossible for anyone else to understand it.

"These hooligans out here," Case said in a lazy drawl, head turning to follow a pack of kids on bikes out way too late. Then, "I was worried your picker was broken." He could just make out her voice. "But things are looking up."

Miriam took a hard left without signaling. "Like, *up* up. My neck hurts."

"Worth it, yeah?"

"Big time. Just, you know. Still gotta take care of a thing."

Both girls laughed, the sound running glittery nails up Nate's spine. When his eye caught Miriam's in the mirror she looked away.

"You gonna make it hurt, Mir?" Case asked.

"Nah." Miriam remembered her blinker this time, slapping it on in the middle of a turn. "But *you* could."

Nate wasn't sure how much he'd misheard. It was monkey in the fucking middle having a conversation with these two. He always forgot that when he wasn't actually with them.

Miriam's beater rocked to a stop in a cracked lot about a

mile from the elementary school. It was a half acre of weedy asphalt that trickled out into a thin stand of trees that bled into the grounds of the old Pencil Factory.

Kevin unfolded himself from the back seat, duster settling dramatically around his boots. Hot, Nate noted flatly. Dude was wearing a floor-length douche coat and a haircut like he'd just stepped off a ten-dollar bill but somehow he pulled it off. Nate was 90 percent straight and *he* could feel it.

He glanced at Case. She looked, as she always did, utterly unaffected. Her jeans were washed to paper thinness, her hair spilled down her back like silvery lemonade. Miriam stood beside her—high-necked black dress, laddered tights, eyes rimmed with shimmery red shadow—and Nate found himself stirred by the contrast. Case looked like she belonged inside a tapestry about unicorns. Miriam looked like she'd just stepped out of a punk rock opera about clowns. Or a haunted hayride rolling through the Dust Bowl. Or a short film about a roller derby circus. Or a . . . anyway, she had a lot of looks.

Then Kevin touched Miriam's arm. He cupped it, really, gentle as a cavalier. She tipped her head to look at him.

And *there* it was, the unsettled ripple of attraction he'd been looking for between Kevin and Case. With Windex clarity Nate realized this handsome, dorky giant was going after his girlfriend.

It's a good thing, hissed a sensible corner of his brain.

FUCK THAT GUY, yelled a louder, more central corner.

Case took a step closer, leaned in. "They're cute, right?"

Her voice thrilled against the thin skin over his temples, his neck, behind his ears. And she probably smelled good, too, but the parking lot didn't, and as she spoke he breathed in a cocktail of exhaust and dumpster and retention pond. It made him queasily uncertain whether he was being flirted with or mocked.

The Pencil Factory made an uneasy shape against the sky. The place had been shuttered for years, but it was still owned by somebody. The high fence around it buckled and bent where it ran through the little woods, and every kid in town knew you could cross it there. It wasn't the fence that kept you out of the Pencil Factory, it was the suburban legends.

The night was cool and very clear, each star humming in its muzzy halo. The trees they walked through were an autumn muddle of green and brown and already leafless, and the best part of the trip was when Hot Kevin's duster went right through a patch of burrs.

"Damn," Miriam said, breaking out of the trees. Nate's feet stuttered as he pulled up beside her.

The stretch of land between them and the factory was littered with pieces of abandoned machinery. In the moonlight they looked alien, unrecognizable. Organic, somehow, the wild outgrowths of a gearhead's garden.

"So cool," Case said, skimming a hand over the waving night grasses that grew through a perforated hunk of industrial steel. An engine? A . . . carburetor? Nate scanned his brain, but no part of shop class had stuck.

The factory was dark. Nate didn't know he'd started to dread the night ahead until he felt a shock of hope: the show got canceled, it happened *last* night, the girl with the flyer made it up. But then, in the windows of the uppermost floor, a roving illumination. Like a restless ghost. Or somebody carrying a Maglite.

Miriam poked his arm with two stiff fingers.

"Look." She pointed not up but across. Pressed against the

building, swimming in its spit-thin shadows, a line of people. Nate picked his way toward them, around decommissioned machines. Everyone here was high school age, maybe college, at least half of them dressed like Miriam. Their quiet had a tense, waiting quality to it. You could hear people's breath catch, soles crunching over the gravel. When a girl in a red coat broke the still to say, "But this is weird, right? Can you just confirm for me?" the girl she was with whisper-snarled, "*Stop talking.*"

Nate fell in next to Miriam at the end of the line, grabbing her hand. Her fingers went limp inside his, but she didn't pull away. Just ahead of them stood a girl in a baby-doll dress and bleached hair, her arm around a dude wearing pointed black cat ears.

"Holy shit." He elbowed Miriam, nodding toward the guy's fake ears. "I can't believe Batman is here."

He was punchy and pissed. He wasn't looking for a laugh. But he didn't expect her to rear on him, lip curled.

"*God,* you are such a glib motherfucker." She didn't even sound mad. She was almost laughing. "I'm so sick of you judging everyone who's actually *trying* something. Trying to look the way they feel. Trying to be joyful instead of, instead of, *sedated.* It's boring, dude. You're *boring.*"

Nate's heart was pounding. His tongue tasted like the peanut butter toast he'd eaten an hour ago, plus stomach acid. "Oh, yeah," he said, looking pointedly at Kevin in his coat, pretending he couldn't hear them, and Miriam in her haunted black dress. "You guys look super joyful."

"Cool burn," she said, making a jerkoff gesture with her hand. The line had started to move and they were carried along with it. "Look, I was gonna wait to do this, but—we don't work. Obviously."

Nate opened his mouth. He tried to summon up words, but nothing would come. They were being funneled through the opened doors of the factory. When he finally spoke it echoed in the hush of a barely lit entryway.

"I was gonna break up with *you*. I was waiting to be *nice*."

Miriam's laugh was neither quiet nor kind. "That sounds about right. Mr. Nice Guy."

"What's that supposed to mean?"

"Figure it out. Oh, and I wouldn't bother going for Case if I were you."

The factory was cold, his sweat was hot. The contrast made him feel feverish. "Um. What?"

"She's my best friend. You think we haven't noticed you panting on her?" Her perfect burgundy mouth seemed to move independently of her still, scornful face. "When you're not around, she laughs at you."

Nate looked past her, at Case. She stared back, as luminous and imperturbable as a blown-glass figurine.

"You're a hypocrite," he told his ex-girlfriend coldly. "I'm out."

But when he turned to go, the doors were closed. Not just closed but literally barred, a great splintered beam slid silently into place. Nate pictured how ridiculous he'd look if he tried and failed to move it, and stayed where he was.

The space they stood inside was dim, lit by lanterns that cast a pool of antique light. Nate lurked at its edges, not wanting to be near Miriam, not wanting to creep into the dark.

Maybe Case didn't hear what she said, his brain chirped distantly. He should at least give her the chance to deny it, right?

"Look." It was the girl whose rude girlfriend had shushed her. "Something's happening."

The pool of light was growing. Stealing over the floor, climbing the walls like golden dip-dye. It looked like magic, but it was just more lanterns being kindled, up and up, light jumping from one to the next like sparks thrown off a bonfire.

They were standing inside a grand old fire hazard of a hall, light pouring over the worked faces of fantastical creatures and oddly shaped men, peering out from carved cornices of flora. The room was empty but for twin staircases bowing away from each other like the curves of a violin, ending at a gallery two stories overhead.

For one night? Nate thought. *All this for a one-night show?* Then, *I should've dumped her a month ago! I should've dumped her when she wore a wedding dress to school!*

Miriam's head was tilted all the way back, taking in the room. He didn't want to think about why he'd started liking her in the first place, but the illuminated column of her neck was the kind of thing people wrote poems about.

Her throat, he thought fretfully. *Her throat wrapped in gold, her heart icy cold.* Christ alive, that was bad. All this fancy set design was messing with his head.

The air buzzed with stifled excitement. Nate watched stone-faced as Case and Miriam took a selfie and Hot Kevin skulked around sexily. Then a gasp came from behind him. A startled laugh, a whispered curse. When Nate turned, he felt a zip of electrical terror: the barred doors were gone. In their place stood a white wall, hung with a constellation of faces.

Of masks, he corrected himself. And it was a *false* wall, rolled into place by some unseen stagehand. The masks were lined up on hooks, each bearing a paper tag.

Miriam's eyes were shining. "I think we're supposed to take one," she said.

The crowd was tentative, then hungry, nobody wanting to be stuck with an inferior mask. They were the bad-tooth color of old ivory, shaped into garish caricatures. *Stepmother* read the tag attached to a face as high-boned and wicked as a *Scream* mask. *Old Soldier*, read another. *Clever Peasant. Seventh Son.* Nate picked up a toothy rabbit mask, then put it back. Its tag read *Prey*. There were as many masks as there were people—about thirty, he'd guess—and the wall was empty when they were through.

Hot Kevin wore a mask tagged *Maiden*, delicately wrought. Miriam's was thin-lipped and broad-planed; the tag in her hands read *Huntress*. Case's mask—*Warrior*—was frozen in a rictus of stony severity.

Resentfully Nate fitted his own to his face. He didn't want to look ridiculous, so he'd reached past a purse-lipped *East Wind* and a carven-curled *Spoiled Child* to reach it. The mask's eyes were thickly lashed crescents, its plush lips formed a daffy smile, and it was too late to replace it when he read the tag. *Fool*.

Fucking perfect. Through the limited span of the Fool's eyeholes he traced the powdery lines of transformed profiles. He looked sidelong at Case as Miriam's words turned over in his mind, rocks with squirmy things hiding beneath them. *When you're not around, she laughs at you.*

Someone brushed against him, and he turned, irritable. An old woman was moving through the crowd at a stately pace. She was as tall as Kevin, dressed in white, her features spare and daunting beneath a bonkers Shakespearean headdress. Nate rubbed his chilled arms. Here, finally, an actor.

The woman paused dramatically between the two staircases, letting the room's tension mass upon itself like a thunderhead.

"Once upon a time," she said.

The tension broke. Someone gave a nervous titter.

"Once upon a time two daughters were born to the wife of a king. The first came in the golden morning, the second in the night's black heart."

At the words *first* and *second*, spotlights were cast onto the faces of two actresses: a stacked blonde on the left-hand landing, and on the right, a fierce and narrow figure whose dark curls bled into the shadows. They wore black Zorro masks over their eyes and noses and seemed at a glance to have no mouths. Squinting, Nate saw their lips had been painted out.

"As her midnight child breathed its first breath, the queen breathed her last. Lost in grief at her passing, the king took no joy in his daughters. He closed himself away, leaving his children to be raised by a nurse and his kingdom to be ruled by council."

Between the staircases hung a screen that looked like a wall until a light clicked on behind it, casting against it the shape of a man's grieving figure.

"The years passed and he remained in perpetual mourning. Until the day, straying from his path through his dead wife's garden, he spied his daughters in the orchard beyond."

Now the actor behind the screen untwisted himself. Arms out, head angled toward the mouthless actresses above. Even in silhouette, dude was *ripped*.

"The princesses were nearly grown. And it seemed to him that these two beauties, each as different to the other as a diamond to a daisy, were the very image of his lost wife. Longing pricked his heart. And it made him wicked."

"Gross," Nate whispered. Miriam was right, he did know this story. He couldn't remember how it ended.

"But someone witnessed the root of his fascination: his

daughters' old nurse, crouched with her basket among the rose hips. The nurse had raised her princesses from infancy. She had been their only mother. And she had a secret even they did not know: she was descended from a fairy line and maintained a small measure of magic. As the king strode into his council chamber to declare his intentions to woo and wed his daughters the nurse carried out her own desperate plan.

"She bid the princesses lay abed and, summoning her weakened gift, altered their faces. Their skin grew craggy as oak bark, their noses lengthened like tubers. Their red lips withered and their brows drooped like moss."

The actresses dropped their heads as she spoke, turning their backs on the audience. Nate peeked at Miriam. Her body was taut, her hands clenched in her skirts. She was lapping up this theater-kid bullshit like boxed wine.

"The nurse considered her work with satisfaction. Though the girls would be found quite beautiful by certain fey courts, they would be safe from the lust of the human king. Before she left them, the nurse whispered a warning: their new faces would last but a year. In that time they must devise a means of escape, before the magic faded and their father's obsession was rekindled. Then she went to present herself to the king."

Behind his screen, the buff actor fitted a shadow crown to his head.

When the king saw the nurse's grave face, he sprang to his feet, trembling.

"Your daughters lie ill, she told him. And though they will keep their lives, their beauty is lost forever.

"The king rushed to their rooms and wept bitterly at what he found there. Mask them, he told the nurse. Hide their faces and bid them be silent until they are wed and away from here. May the first man who will have them take his pick.

"The nurse bowed in obedience, but she hid a smile. Marriage was their surest method of escape. When the king had gone, she kissed the girls before sealing their faces away beneath black masks.

"Suitors came from near and far to present themselves. And though they approved of the girls' silence, none were willing to offer for a princess's hand without first seeing her face. Soon rumors spread of what their masks were hiding: monstrousness. Eyes that turned men to stone. No maidens' faces at all but twin voids, into which a prince might fall.

"The months passed and the stream of suitors came to a halt and at last the furious king made a decree. The ones who married his daughters would be given half his kingdom between them, but they must meet and marry the princesses in a single night. Anyone brave enough to try it was invited to a masked ball. There the princesses would choose from among the party and be married at midnight.

"The old nurse wrung her hands when she learned that the party was set for a year from the day she ensorcelled the sisters. On that very midnight, her spell would end. She drew the sisters to her and gave them a final warning: they must hold tightly to their masks until they were wed and away, lest the king learn he had been fooled.

"The girls nodded without speaking. For a year they'd maintained perfect silence, as the king commanded. At times they were silent even inside their own heads."

Behind his screen the king receded. Into his place came a close crush of silhouettes, simulating the bob and weave of a party. It was a pretty cool effect.

"The ball shattered this silence. The palace filled up with strangers from whom they had nothing to fear. Recklessly the sisters swam among the froth of heavy satin and double-sided remarks. They drank champagne and flirted through their masks and danced so beautifully even the king took notice. Their nurse, haunting the party's bright edges, hissed through her teeth, *Foolish girls, foolish.*

"Midnight was approaching, and soon they must make their choice. Then it was upon them, and the clock struck. As the girls moved toward the wedding altar at the front of the room, where they would beckon to the suitors they had chosen, a pair of pampered princelings trailed them. Determined to discover their secret, the men snuck up from behind and unmasked them."

Despite himself, Nate felt nervous. He brought a hand to his mouth as the actresses turned to face the audience again, softly startled when his fingers met his Fool's mask.

"The clock struck a final time as their masks fell to the ballroom floor. At that very moment the magic broke. The king cried out, and he was not the only one. Their beauty was restored, almost shocking in its force."

The actresses removed their masks. They *were* pretty hot, even with their painted-out mouths.

"As suitors shouted their offers, the king advanced. His royal body cut like a blade through the clamor. He stood in front of his daughters and spoke words that chilled the party into silence."

Again the king's shape filled the screen.

"You will marry no man, he said. No man but me. Until you accept my suit, you will live as caged birds, never seeing open sky.

"And though it grieved them, the guards did as their king commanded, seizing the princesses and their nurse and imprisoning them in their rooms."

The old actress paused. She'd delivered her tale as if she were reading it from a dusty book, but now her voice swelled with sorrow.

"I and my two charges were locked away. Our windows sealed and covered over. We were fed only on fairy foods—nectars and sweetmeats and spun-sugar pinwheels—and grew sick for lack of bread and sun. When I came to understand we would die in the dark, I drew them to me.

"Though my powers are slight, I said, fairy blood has its uses. It could, if they were courageous, be fashioned into an alternate means of escape."

Her voice rang through the factory like a cracked church bell. "To each girl I gave a knife and bade them harvest from me a long red road. Even from within our prison, they might walk this road and discover a new horizon. My princesses wept, but I had raised them to be strong. They did as I demanded."

A red spotlight switched on over the nurse.

"My blood fell and formed a path that led them from the palace. And though they clung to each other, their journeys diverged. My morning daughter stepped into a realm of daylight, while my midnight girl walked into deepest night.

"But their escape was not complete. Too soon, the impatient king arrived in wedding garb to press his suit once more. He found my body and the garnet road his feet were never meant to tread. He followed his daughters into their realms, and there he searches for them still."

The old actress lifted her chin, imperious. "Now, you

seekers. Choose a princess. Choose a realm. And see where your travels take you.

"But before you do." She raised a finger, knobby with rings. "A word of warning. The masks we wear are the roles we play, and roles are safer than reality. Do not make the mistake the sisters did: do not allow yourselves to be unmasked." Her voice went singsong, almost mocking. "Such slight protection stands between you and a fate unspeakable. Lose your mask, and you may find the walls between truth and illusion are easily breached."

Whatever *that* meant. Nate tapped a finger against the Fool's chin, hoping it wasn't actual ivory. That would suck for some elephants.

Then the lights went out.

Nate swayed a moment, hand lifting toward the place where he had last seen Miriam. The dark was absolute, sticky as caramel. It was a breathable toxin that infected him with fear. He had the sudden, ridiculous conviction he was alone in it, and lurched forward, reaching. When the lights returned—less than a minute after they'd gone—he was standing in an empty entryway, both arms thrust out.

His skin crackled. Every nerve ending, every hair.

How had the crowd moved so quickly? How had everyone but him known what to do?

He let irritation burn away his anxiety. Miriam and Case were off somewhere, giggling with Kevin. Or, shit, maybe they were watching him right now. Claustrophobia clawed at him and he put his hands to his mask. Just as quickly he dropped them, fingertips sparking.

So: search for another exit by the light of his phone, hoping not to stumble on a tetanus-covered nail.

Or follow the actresses. Confirm Miriam and Case were having fun being art monsters before he went the fuck home.

Yellow light spilled from the left-hand archway, all buttery against the dark. But the girls would never pick the non-goth option. Doggedly Nate turned right, climbing up the stairs and into the stamped indigo shadows of the land of the middle of the night.

It began with a blind black hall that smelled of paint and freshly planed wood, stretching like a limb through the dark. The blackness saturated in increments to the trippy purple of a photo negative, then he was stepping out into a massive room in which a false forest grew.

Midnight had the hot-candy scent of theatrical mist. It was tinted a heartache blue. The backstage odors soothed him, disarmed him, as he wandered the handmade wood. Miriam swam behind his eyes, Miriam and her curls, brown like the shavings of some luxury chocolate. And Case, with her prim beauty and skater-kid clothes, her eyes that worked you over like a lockpick.

They blurred together, snapped apart. Here in the sugary mist the worst pieces of the night were losing their pungency. Miriam was just jealous, Nate reminded himself. She was mad he'd been pulling away. And Case felt guilty. She was a good friend, she worried about Miriam getting hurt.

These thoughts worked on his feelings like oil on ruffled feathers. By the time he stumbled onto the play in progress he'd forgotten how it felt when Miriam went off on him, that pall of bad recognition. He'd forgotten the uncanny flavor of his fear in the emptied entryway. He registered the actors with a burst of pleased surprise.

There was the Midnight Princess, with her blotted-out mouth and black domino mask. Beside her, the Huntsman.

You didn't need a tag to identify him. His body was as outlandishly muscled as a werewolf's, his leathers an unlikely green. A short blade hung from his belt and a bow was strapped to his back. His face was bare, though Nate wished it wasn't. It had the gouty handsomeness of the gym teacher who used to call him Cardigan Boy.

"What would you have of me, Princess?" he growled.

"Only that which is owed to me, Huntsman," she replied. "And here, in my own land, I am owed all."

The two actors medieval hate-flirted for a while, as Nate's attention wandered. Finally the Huntsman withdrew a small box and a wicked knife from inside his tunic thing.

"A blade fit to carve out a maiden's heart, and a box to put it in." He took a step closer, forcing the princess to look up. "But your royal father is a hunter. I do not think he will be fooled out of seeking you by an animal's heart."

"No," the princess said lowly, gripping her box and her knife. "If he is to believe I am dead, he must have the heart of a maiden. I leave you here, Huntsman. I'm off to seek a purer heart than mine."

Other audience members had gathered to watch. Among them was a tall girlfriend thief in a floor-length coat, who'd apparently already ditched Miriam. When the princess took off, Kevin followed her. Nate followed Kevin.

They picked silently through the trees, pumped-in fog curling around their planked bases. The play forest was full of invitations to adventure: an oak tree with a brass-fitted door embedded into its trunk. A briar hung with keys instead of roses. A cottage with mossy windows, as wee and twee as a Wendy house. The princess led them to its threshold, then, startlingly, turned to face them.

Nate's scalp prickled. Goddamned immersive theater. *Don't pick me!* he thought.

She glided forward and took Hot Kevin by the hand. Of course: her character needed a maiden's heart. He was wearing the Maiden mask. But something in the way she moved—the lunar curve her body made, dropped chin to beckoning hand—made Nate's own body tauten and twang. Both princess and Maiden stooped as she opened the cottage door and pulled him through.

The door closed behind them.

The rest of the rejects drifted away until only Nate remained, heated by a righteous combination of vindication and fury. What a prick! Miriam deserved better. What a sucker! Miriam should've known better.

He circled the cottage, high on the feeling of being both wronged and right. The windows were obscured with fake dirt, but there was one whose center was clearish. Nate peeked in. Just for a second, just in case Miriam asked him about this later. She would want to know the truth.

Kevin sat on a quilt-covered bed, his back to the window. The actress was kneeling in front of him, between his legs. She'd removed her domino and Nate recognized her with a faint beat of surprise: she'd given him the flyer.

Her hands were on Kevin's knees. Faintly smiling, eyes as dizzily hypnotic as a cobra's in an old cartoon, she moved them slowly up his body. His stomach, his chest, his neck, resting at last on the edges of his mask. Gently, gently, she eased it away, tongue red against her painted lip.

Nate stepped back, heart surging with a sluggish electricity. *Such slight protections stand between you and realms unspeakable.*

Silly. Still, he felt along the jawline of his own mask, making sure it was in place.

Restlessly he moved away. The ember of his anger had blown out; now he just felt tired. Miriam wanted to dump him for a dude who started cheating on her before they were even official, that was her call.

The woods ended at a concrete wall, blue mist cut by the bloody glow of an exit sign. Nate pushed through the door beneath it, stepping into a stairwell jaundiced with safety lights. As he started down the steps, he heard the metal clang of someone else coming up.

The top of their head came into view first. Two floors down, smooth black hair above the white mask of an audience member. They reached the next landing and twitched their chin up to look at him.

Nate gave half an up nod, and froze.

It wasn't their face. That was covered in a mask with the pointed ears, cruel brow, and heavy muzzle of a wolf. It wasn't their size, either. This person was smaller than him.

It was the way they stood, predatorial and alert. Totally still. Totally *ready*.

Nate took a step back. Then another. Then he was running, up and away. Past the door he'd come from, up another floor, and when he reached the next door he charged through it, into the welcoming light of Morning.

For a minute he just breathed, back against the door.

Then he shook his head, feeling humiliation bloom. Had he actually *heard* the girl in the wolf mask following behind him? No, he decided. God, she must've thought he'd lost his mind. At least she couldn't see his face before he ran away like a little baby.

The light here was good. It was clean and even; it washed the anxious scum of Midnight away. He found himself laughing against his mask, already imagining how he'd retell this story later. The story of the night he dumped Miriam for taking him to the worst play ever.

He might as well explore a little before leaving, though. Give the stairs time to clear out. Just ahead was a cobbled square with a dry fountain at its center. A wall painted with trompe l'oeil houses rose on one side, a wall of rolling green valleys on the other. You could walk between them onto an old-timey high street.

Nate figured the shops were Potemkin fronts until he was among them and realized they were real, actual constructed rooms full of meticulous props. The street smelled like sawdust and fresh paint and more surprising things, too: oiled leather, hot bread. A gamey iron tang, wafting from a window hung with cuts of genuine meat. *All this for a one-night show*, Nate thought again, looking up. It messed with his head to see rafters there, furred with decades of dust, instead of open sky.

An audience member came hurtling out of a dressmaker's. Her arms were piled with satin and her mask had the sprigged curls and snub nose of a Stepsister. She flinched away when she saw him, disappearing into an unlit gangway between shops.

What, did she think he wanted her dresses? Nate watched the gap a moment, frowning, then walked on. He passed a toy shop, a hatter, a confectionery whose window glistened with bright, chitinous candies. The back of his tongue flooded at the sight, but there was something sickening about them, too. Legless insects teeming over each other in tall glass jars, obscene in their Crayola-colored jackets.

He jerked his head. The thought felt alien, intrusive. Then something moved in the shop's glassy depths.

It was Batman, the guy with the cat ears. They stuck out now above a Falstaff mask, broad and apple-cheeked, its mouth a Comedy crescent. His posture was furtive, exaggeratedly so. He looked to either side, head swinging like a bull's to accommodate his mask's narrow eye holes. Then he tugged the mask off with one hand, plunging the other into a glass globe of peppermints.

It was funny. It should've been funny. But as the guy took a second handful, then a third, his eyes greedy blanks and his cheeks puffed out like he was playing Chubby Bunny, Nate felt a rising disgust. *Get ahold of yourself,* he thought, touching fingers to his stony Fool's cheek. *Put your mask back on.*

The candy containers threw whimsical shadows on the shop's back wall. It seemed to Nate that the shadows were deepening, changing shape. They looked like hunched figures, getting ready to stand.

As soon as he had the thought, he moved briskly on. The row of shops curved to the right. Nate curved with them and came upon the Morning Princess.

She was close, startlingly so. Her mouth was the same fatty milk shade as her skin, all of it so blurred with powder she seemed polished. A small train of spectators stood behind her, watching as she glared sorrowfully at the shop in front of her. Nate's heart squeezed with complicated relief when he saw Case among them. He sidled up beside her.

"Where's Miriam?"

His words thudded against the inside of his Fool's mask. Case didn't seem to hear. When the princess entered the shop, she trailed behind.

Nate hesitated before following. The shop was kitted out like an apothecary, too small to hold everyone, but somehow they filed in. Through his mask drifted the scents of camphor and licorice.

From the back of the shop prowled another actor, black-browed and consumptively lean.

"What a surprise," he said silkily. "I thought you had no need of me, Princess."

"My father will not rest until he finds me," she said. "I do not have my sister's warrior heart. I cannot withstand him forever."

The wicked man's voice softened from silk to suede. "I cannot give you a warrior's heart. But—perhaps a warrior could be found, to take your place."

Three times the word *warrior* shrilled past Nate's ear, like a mosquito circling back. *Case's mask*, he thought with a thump of padded dread. She wore the face of a Warrior.

As the Morning Princess turned her gaze on the spectators, Nate stepped in front of Case.

Tried to. He sent the message through his body, to block her, and it didn't obey.

He'd had dreams like this. Dreams in which he watched unmoving as the monster came forth. In dreams he felt no pain, but here his skin puckered with gooseflesh and his eye sockets ached and he could only watch Case step forward as if she, too, felt the narrative wheel turning. Taut as a flame in her jeans and Warrior's face, kneeling at the princess's feet.

The princess's smile was as pitiless as the sea. She took off her own mask. Then she pulled Case's free. Beneath it her face showed damp and dazed.

Nate's head was so hazy he couldn't tell which girl looked more like the other.

Case gazed at the princess like she was looking upon an unwinnable bride at the peak of a glass hill. Gently the princess pressed her own black half mask to Case's face, then leaned down to rub her mouth and its makeup across Case's lips, paling them out.

"I am honored," she said, and put on the mask she had stolen, sealing her terrible beauty away. No one moved as the princess left the shop, just another spectator now.

Case's mouth hung open beneath the rim of her new disguise. Nate thought he saw, in the stunned rise of her shoulders, a first inkling of uncertainty.

"Go, Princess," the apothecary told her. "*Flee*. The King approaches, he rides through Midnight and on to Morning, with all his dogs and his wicked men. He'll kill you if he discovers an impostor wearing his daughter's face. Perhaps your warrior's heart will save you. But"—and he smiled—"I think not."

Like a sleepwalker Case rose and headed for the door. The scene ended, and with it the deep freeze in Nate's limbs. He lurched forward to grab her shoulder—to steady himself, to speak in her ear—and someone ripped him away by the back of the neck.

An audience member. A girl about his height, in a sunny vintage dress and the thuggish mask of an enforcer.

"*She knew the rules*," she said, her growl muted behind the ivory. She shook Nate like a rat and sent him sprawling out of the shop, onto the cobblestones. The doors closed behind them, sealing in the rest of the spectators. Nate could see them bumping dully against its shelves, the apothecary drawing closer.

The girl circled him, fists drawn tight.

"Jesus!" Nate put up his hands. "I just wanted to talk to my friend!"

When she lunged suddenly, Nate recoiled. She straightened up, laughing, like a jock who'd just made him flinch.

"Find the King, Fool." Her voice was oddly low. "Your place is at his side."

Then she strutted off like a bantam rooster. Behind her, the apothecary's lights had gone out.

"What the fuck," Nate said, his voice seashelling off the mask and into his ears. "What the *fuck*."

Head pulsing, limbs jerky and lactic, he set off to find the king. Not because some asshole had told him to. But because, in this terrible play's terrible world, the King was looking for Case.

If it's real, but it's not, so it doesn't matter. The words spun in his mind like splatter paint. He thought he was retracing his steps until he dead-ended into a second, unfamiliar square: rose-bushes and another fountain, built into a corner painted with a Parrish sky. The cobblestones here were clumsily laid. You could see the factory's concrete floor beneath them, marked with chalk and scuffed masking tape.

Nate pressed a hand to the Pencil Factory's exposed skin. He was inside a derelict building in a boring suburb, his old elementary school so close you could bust a hole in the wall and see it. He could *run* home from here if he had to.

Two deep breaths and he stood. When he did, he spied the fountain's secret.

It was an exit. Its center bubbled with stone merfolk sur-rounding a manhole someone had cut straight through the floor. Nate slipped between a merman and a lush sea queen, peering at the ladder that descended from the hole, disappear-ing a few rungs down into a perilous haze. Stage lights angled upward to obscure what lay below.

Nate smiled humorlessly into the pool of colored gels.

Lowering himself into a crouch, bracing his hands on either side of the gap, he set a foot to the ladder's first rung.

Climbing down was hell. First he was above the lights, then moving moth-stunned through them, then blinking in the dimness below. Legs quaking, heart pumping lemon juice, his hands gnarling themselves into knots around the narrow rungs.

The lights had gone blue and violet. They made a storybook twilight. A Twilight, a place between Midnight and Morning. He couldn't look away from his own quaking hands, so he descended unaware into a garden of blown white flowers and sad-eyed stone animals.

Inside it, a wedding was in progress.

Nate stood at the foot of a grassy aisle that ran between two flanks of motley guests to the place where a priest stood, holding a book chained to his wrist with gold links.

There was a hook beneath Nate's rib cage that he'd never noticed before, attached to a vaporous cord. It pulled him irresistibly toward the groom. Golden-crowned, clad in plum velvet and the smile of a birthday boy: the King.

The bride who stood across from him, hands gripped in his, was wrapped in an oceanic white dress. But she had a mass of familiar brown hair, and a Huntress mask.

Nate staggered forward, limping—limping? He'd damaged the tender mollusk of his body coming off the ladder; the pain was just now hitting his brain—calling Miriam's name in a ragged voice. As long as he kept his eyes on her, he didn't have to look at the King.

His ex-girlfriend's body shuddered when she heard his cry. He stumbled toward her, but the closer he got, the more irresistible the urge to drop to his knees. Not because of the pain, the fear, the plunging exhaustion. No: Nate longed to sit at the feet of the King.

Your place is at his side.

A laugh bubbled up in him, as buoyant and burning as a soda burp. The skin of his nose and mouth and cheeks felt sticky, humming against his mask. The mask of a king's Fool.

The priest was droning and Miriam was shivering and Nate was leaning like a weathervane into a dozen conflicting winds. He wanted to run. He wanted to take his mask off. He wanted to cling to the King.

Before he could do any of it, a black-masked Case—knife arm up, pale hair streaming like a Viking's—hurtled out from behind a weather-eaten statue.

Nate closed his eyes as she threw herself at the King. The sound that followed—a jacked-up Dolby squelch, like a cleaver punching into the guts of a melon—burned away the gauze around his brain.

When he opened his eyes Miriam was drenched in a red Pollock splatter, her eyes stretched unnaturally wide. Nate searched for the soda-syrup odor of fake blood and found hot pennies instead, and the chemical whiff of his own terror.

Case stood proudly over the fallen King. No one moved to help him. He was beyond help.

"The King is dead," the priest said in his grave-deep voice, unperturbed. "Long live the queen."

While the wedding guests raised the cry, Nate lunged for the bloody bride—for *Miriam*—and took her hand.

"Case?" she asked dully.

He shook his head.

They ran. He ran through injury, panting wetly against

his mask. She ran with the punitive froth of a wedding dress snatching at her legs.

Twilight was as endless as a nightmare. Fairy-tale vignettes—a cozy tavern, a trio of goose-winged men, two urchins sucking on rock candy—rose in front of them and fell away. An electric smear of light hung overhead, condensing into letters. Nate stared until his brain put them together into *EXIT* and cried out against his mask, urging his body faster.

They slammed through the heavy fire door, into open air.

The moon was full, the breeze so fresh it scalded his skin. He felt like a mole whiskering toward the light, near to weeping with gratitude. He let go of Miriam, dropping to his knees on the broken concrete. He pulled off his mask to drink in the October air, candy corn and gasoline.

But when the ghostly breeze touched his bare face it carried the scents of stage smoke and plywood. The moon was no moon but a light capped with a thinly colored gel, and the distant trees, sulkily shifting, were fabric and papier-mâché. Maybe if he walked through those trees he would find a car that looked like Miriam's. A thing of scrap steel, with an empty place where its engine should be.

Miriam, her front stiff with cooling blood, gaped at Nate's altered face. Holding her mask tightly to her skin, she ran from him, to seek another path.

He was no longer crying but laughing. His heart was not racing but settling. He lifted a hand, smoothing it tenderly over his face's new planes. His mouth smiling and his cheeks up high. The face of a Fool, happy in his foolishness.

The mask broke to pieces on the factory floor.

AUTHOR'S NOTE

"The Silent Sisters" isn't a real fairy tale, but it draws on a hodgepodge of existing stories. Its predatorial king can be found in "Thousandfurs" and "Donkeyskin"; the idea of a Morning and a Midnight Princess was inspired by George MacDonald's haunting Victorian fairy tale "The Day Boy and the Night Girl"; the countdown to midnight is, of course, from the empress of the canon, "Cinderella."

The tale nods at the many stories in which girls and women lose parts of themselves ("The Handless Maiden," "Rapunzel") as well as those in which they specifically go voiceless ("The Little Mermaid," "The Wild Swans"). There are other stories baked inside it, probably some I haven't noticed are there, and it's my hope that pieces of it will chime in tune with tales you remember, or half remember, from childhood.

And there's a little piece of *Ella Enchanted* in there, too, because sometimes you just want a fairy tale that makes you happy all the way through. (But this isn't one of them.)

ONCE BITTEN, TWICE SHY

Hafsah Faizal

Inspired by "Little Red Riding Hood"

There's a notion that Muslims have to be saints. And I suppose we do when the world's a viper waiting for one of us to slip so it can swallow us whole, continuing the narrative of us being monsters, but hey. I digress.

If I were a saint, I'd be wise enough to run far, far away from the black suitcase at my side.

But here we are.

For the purpose of this recollection, my name is Red. I won't name names, because you know what they say—"once bitten, twice shy"—and I'm not making the same mistake twice.

TWO DAYS AGO

The sun on my hijab lights the faintest halo around my face in brilliant bloody red. My sister would gasp and call it raspberry red, but she hasn't hit her emo phase yet. I clench the classifieds in my fist, even though I've looked over the address enough times to have it memorized. I've passed enough faded bins along Rockler Street to have recycled it by now, but I can't. It feels like a lifeline. Like I might miss the opportunity without it, and next thing I know, I'll be staring at dirt piled over a grave.

I need this job, or the one person who truly gets me won't get me anymore—she'll be dead.

The address is a warehouse, dark and imposing enough to make my sneakers scuff the sidewalk when I break my stride. But with my eyes closed, I can see tubes snarling like roots around my grandmother's throat, up her veins like vines going wild, and I know that I'll do anything to see her cured. And I can, with the right amount of money.

I glance at the paper again, running a thumb along the creases left by my pen's repeated squares around the ad. *Contact Wolf*, it says, without a number. Just this address. The words *architect* and *blueprint* stand out. It's almost as if the job was *made* for me.

Doubt is of the devil, I remind myself. I prayed Istikhāra again today for guidance, just after Zuhr, before I left home with Mom's warning: *Don't stray from your path.*

I've got this.

Aside from the Raptor parked on the side, there's no sign of life. There's no knocker or bell, either, so I glance both ways down the empty street and roll open the warehouse gate myself. Buckets are strewn about, the sting of ammonia making my breath catch. My red hijab is the only burst of color around me. I blink past the burn in my eyes and squint into the shadows. It looks abandoned, dust glittering like magic. Metal beams lean against the corrugated walls, waiting for a breeze to tip them over. Sheets flutter in the breeze I've let in, ghosts saying hello.

If *dubious* had a photograph in the dictionary, this would be it.

I've come this far, and it's not as if walking around with a hijab is an easy gig to begin with. I can hold my own. Might as well give it a shot. Voices tiptoe from the other side of a tarp curtain a few feet away. I whisper a prayer and pull it back.

The voices stop. Seven faces turn to mine.

The girl nearest me oozes distrust, her asymmetrical pixie cut as black as her clothes. Beside her, a ginger with soft features looks at me curiously, and I'm reminded of a cat regarding an unsuspecting mouse. Then there's a pair of twins, a lanky boy with a pair of glasses sitting askew on his face, and a blond boy dressed too impeccably for our surroundings.

They're close to my age, all except for the one at the head of the table, who looks to be in his early twenties and most definitely in charge. The Wolf mentioned in the classifieds, I'm assuming.

"Architecture student?" he asks me without preamble. The room is small, a sterile-white table in the middle, where he's braced his hands over a map.

"That's me," I say. It would be some time before I graduated as an architect, but I know my stuff.

His eyes are intense, harder to hold because he looks good—and he knows it. It's written all over his sharp jaw, dark features, and a shirt that clings to his muscled arms, too brawny for my tastes. I want to look away, but I can tell it's what he expects, so I bite my cheek and weather it, deciding to come across more confident by telling him my name.

"Is that so?" he replies, and the tone in his voice makes me feel like an idiot. Maybe I wasn't supposed to do that. Maybe you're not meant to step into abandoned warehouses and drop your real name.

The pixie girl smirks. My blood decides to boil.

"This is where you introduce yourself," I say.

He looks on the verge of saying something demeaning. You can only live so long before you come to memorize the signs, but he decides against it, and that's how I know he's desperate. Soul calls to soul, as the poets like to say.

"Wolf," he says eventually. It's his first show of emotion and it unnerves me a little bit. "Deep Woods University?"

I start at that. Three Oaks is one of those forgotten towns, a tiny place born out of leftover space from the cities that surround us. Somehow, I don't think it's a coincidence that he's guessed exactly which school I attend.

I lift my chin. "The one and only."

The twins murmur something to each other, and the ginger looks even more curious. Before I realize what's happening, Wolf's pushing past me with the others on his tail. No one looks at me while they file outside the warehouse, and I grit my teeth.

I know a power play when I see one. He wants me to question them, to call after them. But what is pride when the life of someone you love hangs in the balance?

"Wait," I say before I can stop myself. Wolf looks back at last and lifts a brow, and I have the acute sense that I'm slowly falling into a trap and I just don't know it yet. "What about the job?"

He studies me a moment. "It's yours."

"That's it?" I ask, looking around and lifting a brow of my own. "No background checks or interviews or salary disclosures? I don't even know what the job is for."

"It's a one-time gig," he says, leaning back. "I can hire someone else if my methods don't work for you."

I only need a one-time gig. I don't have the time or energy for a full-time job, or even a part-time one. I need to focus on getting through my first year at DW.

"You do realize this is all very shady, right?" I ask.

"Yet here you are," he replies with a grin I can only describe as wolfish. The description tugs a smile out of me, and he turns to face me fully, thawing me the rest of the way. "I own this place." He looks at the pipes running along the ceiling. They remind me of roots and vines and my grandmother's oxygen—tubes on the outside to make up for the failing tubes on the inside. "I inherited it from my uncle a few weeks ago, and I'm trying to shape her into something less . . . what did you call it? Shady."

He says the word in a way that makes me feel bad I threw it at him, and I look away. I also immediately hate myself for doing that.

I adjust my hijab and force my gaze back on his. It makes sense why they'd need an architect, and just a student at that—it's only a warehouse. "I'm listening."

"I have a few very specific ideas for the renovation," he continues, slipping his hands into the pockets of his dark jeans. "I assume you have archive access. There are a few blueprints I'd like to have on hand before we begin working."

He pauses, and I realize too late he's waiting for a response.

"What do you need the blueprints for?" As far as I can tell, there's no elaborate structure to the place. It's just four walls, a few small rooms inside, and a roof.

"Oh, not blueprints of the warehouse—blueprints I'd like to match to a certain degree."

And the others are supposed to help him with that? They look like students themselves, not builders. "I can't pull files like that—"

"Unless you're an academic. With a traceable record."

I hesitate because he's right.

"Why don't you just hire a real architect?"

He makes a sound. "You know your kind. I've spoken to more than a few, and for the amount of money I'm putting down on my own, everyone seems to have their own opinion on how the thing should look."

"Let me get this straight. You don't want to spend money hiring an architect, so you want to steal a set of blueprints instead?"

"No," he said, and he seems to hesitate, as if what he wants to say makes him uncomfortable. "My uncle raised me. It was always his dream to redo this place in a specific style, but he never had the cash for it. I'm . . . I guess I'm a sap, and I'm trying to honor him this way."

Wolf looks at me like he hopes I can understand, a little quirk to the side of his mouth that makes him look younger and makes me feel flustered. When he puts it that way, of course I want to help him.

He continues before I can say anything, "I have a builder who doesn't understand the foundation and style I'd like to use. The last thing I am, Red, is unoriginal. These will aid my cause. I need them tomorrow, and you can have them returned the day after."

It sounds . . . sound. I don't see why I shouldn't let him borrow them for a little while. It's not like he's asking me for the plans to a bank.

"How much?" I ask. The words feel heavy on my tongue, wrong. Like I'm asking for something that I shouldn't.

"You'll see."

I'm still thinking of how to phrase my protest when a smile curls along one edge of his mouth. This time, it doesn't look wolfish. He doesn't let my silence simmer for long.

"Think you can handle that?" he prompts in a tone that assumes I can't.

So of course I agree. Humans are like wolves that way— pride makes us do stupid things.

YESTERDAY

On Sundays, Deep Woods is as quiet as the trees that crowd around the campus. The archive is open, because the school has seen its fair share of students hustling in before a Monday due date, but I'm rarely a participant for one reason alone: my brother's best friend.

I don't have a choice this time.

After Maghrib, I hurry up the steps and inside the building, my hoodie baggy and warm, just how I like it. I tug my hood over my hijab, a slip of red like the bill of a cap peeking through, and realize I've pursed my lips, one side slanting up because that's just me when I'm anxious, even if my mom says it makes me look ugly.

The glass doors give me a glimpse inside, and I peer through, looking for a sign of him. The flop of his dark hair, the cut of his stubbled jaw. The coast looks clear. I swipe my card and step inside, pausing as years of history and genius distilled onto paper assault my senses.

I pull out the slip of paper Wolf gave me, with the entire hierarchy to what he needs—from the sous-fond down to the file—shrug off my backpack, and get to work. There are a couple of others meandering the shelves. It's quiet enough to hear the scratch of their pencils.

"Working late?"

I stop. I know that voice.

Did you know a man's entire appearance ups drastically when he's got facial hair? Back when we were young enough to hang out, we used to play video games together. His screen name was always Hunt, even when my brother goaded him because *he* could never use the same name twice.

I turn and give him a smile that comes out more like a wince because he caught me. The thought makes me pause because I haven't . . . done anything wrong, have I?

Not yet, anyway.

"Something like that," I say. We rarely speak anymore. I can't, not when I can barely look at the guy, and some small part of me hopes he stays away for the same reason.

I linger, not sure what to do next. Do I turn and leave? Ask him how he's been? Lie and say I'd forgotten he worked the archives during the weekends or I would have said hello? I slide a finger beneath my hijab, tucking away errant hairs with a swipe down my cheek.

"Well," he says, a bit of awkwardness bleeding into his tone when I don't elaborate. He gestures toward the shelves. "Let me know if you need anything."

Is that a loaded statement, or are we talking archive files? Reason tells me it's the latter. When I climb into bed later tonight, it'll be the former. I give him another small smile and head for the shelves I need, past the section on history and down toward the blueprints, running my hands along the uniform spines and checking labels as I go.

My phone chimes in my pocket, reminding me I need to pick up my brother in ten minutes. By the time I locate the file, there's no time to spare. Certainly no time to look through it.

Wolf was oddly aggressive about not leaving a record of the files being taken out, and I'm assuming it's because he doesn't want anyone to see potential similarities between his fancy new place and the blueprints in my hand. They wouldn't have to look far for proof if there's a record of it.

But the last thing I need is to ask Hunt for a favor to let me take them out without a scan. I work my jaw. Clench my teeth. Ignore the warning bells in my head.

And slip the file into my bag.

I'll bring it back tomorrow, when Wolf is through. Hunt's gaze tracks me as I leave, dropping to my backpack when I glance his way.

He says nothing, so neither do I.

———◦———

Wolf looks surprised when I drop the file on his sterile-white table. He's alone in the room, though I can hear shuffling and voices from deeper inside the warehouse.

It's only when he opens the file that I remember I forgot to look through its contents. I didn't even ask, didn't even peek at the address. Between finishing up my assignments and visiting my grandmother at the hospital, I didn't have time. My brain feels like it's being stretched every which way, exhaustion beating a tune in my head, throbbing behind my eyeballs.

"You're fast," Wolf says, in a way that tells me he doesn't dole out compliments easily. "Come back tomorrow, will you? I'll have everything sorted out."

"I can draw, if you need me to," I say, always ready to please.

"I've got it. Really, this is perfect, Red. You'll have your money."

I know a dismissal when I hear one.

"It's not that I'm . . . greedy, or anything," I amend quickly. As if I owe him an explanation. As if I need to explain myself.

"I know," he says quietly. "I heard about your grandmother."

Warning bells go off in my head, and I narrow my eyes. First my school, now this?

He sees the look on my face and smiles. I think it's meant to be disarming. "Small town, Red. One of the crew saw you entering the hospital and worried you weren't going to deliver the blueprints." He taps his finger on the manila folder. There's a ring on his right thumb, worn-down silver at odds with the rest of his polished attire. "I know what it's like to be desperate, to do whatever it takes. Trust me."

I shouldn't, but I do.

TODAY

The next morning, one of the twins from Wolf's crew is on the news. *"Arrested,"* the newswoman is saying, but my brain doesn't compute.

I see the words *blueprint* and *architect* on the screen.

I hear her talking about how access to the original blueprints of Woodsville Manor is what helped the robbers escape.

"More money than anyone even knew existed in Three Oaks."

Eyewitnesses claim it was a crew of seven, and though they were unarmed, police are grateful Roger Woodsville wasn't anywhere on the premises when the theft happened.

"Only one arrest has been made."

Money. Robbery. A crew of seven. Blueprints. The voices become a buzz. The world spins on without me because I'm stuck. Wolf is a *robber*. I breathed in the same air as a robber, a crook. I did more than that—I *helped* him. I grip the kitchen counter, cold granite chilling my skin as I sink into a realization.

I'm a thief.

I don't steal. It's wrong. It's haram. Forbidden. A sin. I won't even touch the last cookie in the cookie jar without asking the entire family if anyone else wants it. It doesn't matter that Wolf and his crew blindsided me, lied to me, *used* me—I'm as complicit as the boy staring blankly at me through the screen in front of me.

Unless he was used the same way I was. A scapegoat or whatever a band of robbers calls someone who takes the fall for them.

"He's so young, too," my mom says. "Such a shame."

The sound of her voice reminds me of her warning. *Don't stray from the path.* I listened to my mom. I prayed Istikhāra more than once. I didn't do anything wrong.

I also distinctly remember slipping the file into my bag. The very file with the very blueprints that they used to break into Woodsville Manor and steal all that money.

When I rush upstairs and into my room, there's a suitcase in the center and my window's ajar. I think I see a flash of black, but when I dash to the window, no one's there. My heart thunders up my throat, making it difficult to breathe.

Zhikr, I tell myself. I need to do zhikr so I can calm down. Recenter myself. Make dua and ask for guidance. Everything happens for a reason. Even terrible things like unknowingly robbing a rich man's mansion.

My chest pounds like a drum as I crouch on my rug—the one my grandmother got for my thirteenth birthday—and unlatch the locks on the suitcase. I open the lid. Money. Cash. Bundled up in rows and rows that elicit warning bells and fear, not the possibility of helping old ladies in hospital beds.

I slam it shut and lock it tight. A slip of paper flutters out from the force of it, landing on my dress and tumbling to my jeans.

For your grandmother. —Wolf

My hands shake as I wrap my hijab, making sure not a single strand of hair slips loose and my neck is covered. I snatch up the suitcase. Maybe the note is meant to be touching and heartfelt, but I can only see his wolfish grin and his mocking crew.

I see red.

———

The warehouse is empty. Not a sound echoes from the vast space, not a speck of dust on the sterile-white table in the room where I met Wolf more than once. There's no Raptor parked out in the alley. I'm alone.

He's gone.

It was naive of me to expect him to be here, smiling that wolfish smile, knowing everything about me when I knew nothing about him, conning me so he could con a manor in turn. I was naive. The entire time. He *relied* on my naivete to do this job.

"What have you done?"

I jump and whirl, but it's not Wolf or anyone from his crew. It's Hunt and his honey-brown eyes looking at me like he knows exactly what I've done.

"How did you get here?" I demand. "Were you following me?"

I ignore the lock of dark hair that fell over his brow when he crouched to enter the warehouse. The dim ambience of the place highlights his cheekbones, gives him a roguish air that I really shouldn't be thinking about.

He doesn't look sheepish at all when he looks me in the eye and says, "Yes. Yes, I followed you. I was heading to your house to talk when I saw you sneak outside. That file, Red," he says heavily. "I saw you leaving with a file, and the next thing I know, it's been used for a robbery. Theft, Red. That's not you."

I tell myself I won't cry in front of him. I'm not a little girl anymore. He's not my friend—he's a boy who's a little too hard to look at, who works the archives at the university, who's never known hardship the way I have.

When I don't say anything, he adds, "That's not us."

The word hurts more than anything else he's said. *Us.*

My eyes well until I swipe at them and clench my jaw, dig my teeth into my tongue to stay strong. I know what he's getting at. I'm Muslim. I'm *wired* to do the right thing.

"Tell me that what I saw wasn't true. Tell me you didn't give them the plans to Woodsville Manor."

I don't answer.

He clenches his jaw. "There's a reward out there for anyone who turns in the robbers."

I take the smallest step toward him. "Are you going to turn me in?"

Hunt doesn't look at me. He looks pained, confused. Hurt. And I know what I owe him: the truth.

I tell him everything, and because I can't look at him, either, I turn back to the warehouse. There has to be something

Wolf and his crew left behind. I look through the buckets that smell of cleaning solution. I move the mops that smell of ammonia. I shuffle old cardboard boxes that leave dust on my hands. I find it a little while later, and it's as if the haze has cleared and possibility doesn't seem so impossible anymore.

So I tell him what I plan to do.

"You can't bring them down," he protests. "A crew like that knows what they're doing. I'm surprised they even gave you a cut. You're aware they usually tie up loose ends, right? Let it go."

But I can't let it go. Wolf wronged me. Wolf *duped* me, and used my dying grandmother to do it.

"We won't get lucky twice," Hunt insists. "Did you hear me? Let it go."

"We?" I ask, surprised.

Hunt lifts a hand to the back of his head, suddenly sheepish. "I figured you won't be telling anyone else, so I thought I'd help."

I fight a smile. "We're not going to bring them down. We're going to dupe him the way he duped me."

He nods, indulging me. "How?"

"Get the money back. It's not stealing if it's stolen money. Three Oaks is small. There's only so many places they can be."

For the first time all day, I find it a little easier to breathe.

"If you steal it back," Hunt says, "you're going to have to return your cut of the cash, too. What about your grandmother?"

I shake my head. "My cut is as good as trash. It's haram. It's a sin to use it, and if I *do*, I can't blame anyone but myself when her treatment inevitably goes wrong."

Because it will go wrong. And it'll be my fault for using

stolen money. It hurts to say it, almost as much as it hurts to know I suddenly *have* all this money and can't use it to pay for my grandmother's treatment. If I let myself dwell on it, I can feel the thorns digging into my lungs, making it hard to breathe, hard to think. My head spins.

This isn't about my grandmother anymore. This is about making things right, and I know that's what she'd want me to do.

A heavy breath leaches out of Hunt in the quiet. He knows I'm right. "We'll find another way, Red. I'll help you. I didn't know it was that bad."

I nod, looking away before my emotions get the best of me.

"You don't think the police have already swept the town?" he asks.

"But the police don't know who they're looking for."

I do. And better yet, I have a lead. I hold up the crumpled receipt to the gas station on 35. And the way his eyes light up makes my heart do funny things.

———————

We park at the gas station, and I'm way too aware of the fact that I'm in a car with a boy. I'm not supposed to be, because I'm not a little girl anymore, and he's certainly no little boy. I think he's aware of it, too, because he gets out a little too quickly and meets my gaze over the hood of the car.

"You take the car, I'll explore on foot," he says. "We'll work through the radius."

I want to point out that hunting around on foot doesn't sound very reasonable, but I can't offer him another ride, so I nod and start to get back inside when he stops me by calling my name and lifting all the tiny hairs on the back of my neck. My hijab feels tight.

"Call me, okay? Don't do anything alone."

I close the door without a reply, because I'm not about to make a promise I have no intention of keeping, and wade back into the lazy Three Oaks evening traffic, looking for signs of Wolf or his Raptor before pulling into a motel the kids from senior year called haunted last fall. My parallel park would give my dad a heart attack, but I don't have time. Whoever left the money in my room is from Wolf's crew, which means they're still here, *particularly* because one of the twins is in custody. If *my* twin had been arrested, I wouldn't leave them behind. But if they're as smart as I think they are, they won't stay in Three Oaks for long. It's too small, and there's only so many places they can hide.

My hope is that they're still deciding on their next plan of action. They have to be. Surely it wasn't the plan for someone to be arrested. I won't let myself think of the alternative.

The motel lobby assaults me with stale air and wan walls, the little man with glasses on the other side of the peeling counter staring at my hijab with distaste before realizing I can see it, making *me* realize that my plan to ask him if a good-looking white man checked in isn't the best idea.

Wearing a hijab stacks the odds a little higher. Being Muslim means the world builds a few more walls against you, and that's okay because I've been living this life for as long as I can remember, and I'm ready to break them down.

"My friend checked in a couple days ago," I say. "Tall guy, clearly works out every day, dark eyes. He left his cell at my house." I wave my cell phone. "Could you tell me which room he's in so I can hand it back to him?"

The lobby attendant's look tells me he doesn't think Wolf is my friend, but if I concerned myself with the opinion of men, I'd go nowhere.

"Never saw him."

I make sure he can tell from my face that I don't believe him before I drop two twenties on the mottled counter. I'm not sure what the usual pay for information is, but he takes it.

"A week ago, yeah. He was here with two girls. A ginger and an emo. They checked out a while ago."

My heart quickens at the mention of the girls. Wolf really was here, but where is he *now*? He had to have been living somewhere for the past week, and it can't have been the warehouse. I didn't see any signs of anyone living there. No beds, no makeshift pillows.

I rack my brain as I unlock my car and slip inside. When my seat belt clicks, so does my resolve.

I have to keep looking.

———

The sun is winding down. I've checked the depot, the shopping complex, and the old gas station, eyes peeled for Wolf, his crew, and his Raptor. I've found nothing. I slip back inside my car.

I'm on the highway when I see it: the dark flash of a car to my right, hidden deep behind the trees. I nearly lurch out of my lane. Why didn't I think to check here?

I've always been fascinated with the way humans create things—massive structures and buildings and the design of a place that fits a multitude of rooms without wasting space. It's why I decided to study architecture. It's also made me more appreciative of nature, and how it defies anything we humans can ever do.

Which is why my sister, Mom, and I rent this cabin from old Mrs. Hudson every other year.

And why Wolf doesn't know these trees the way I do.

———◦———

The quaint little cabin is straight out of a fairy tale, the only building in an entire acre of forest. I park and follow the winding path on foot, doing my best to keep quiet, backpack on hand because it's never a good idea to wander the forest without one. I hear the snap of twigs and heavy, sure footfalls across fallen leaves. I hurry behind a tree trunk and peer out.

Wolf, and he's alone.

I linger behind a cluster of oaks, waiting and watching, but Wolf really is by himself. I wonder if the crew dispersed after the twin was arrested. For the amount of money they took from Woodsville Manor, they wouldn't have distributed it yet. It's hard enough having to keep track of a single hoard of cash. Something tells me Wolf has it somewhere inside the cabin.

My phone weighs heavy in my pocket, reminding me of Hunt, but I ignore it, collecting rocks in my bag as I draw closer and closer to the cabin. I can break open a window if I have to; I refuse to think of the alternative. Wolf meanders to the other end of the forest, fiddling with something that I hope isn't a gun, sunlight casting mottled gold over him. His steps are purposeful, telling me he'll circle back soon enough.

I dart up the cabin steps, tucking myself out of view as I try the front door. It's locked. I slip to the back, ducking past a waving fern and hoping if Wolf glances over, he'll mistake my red hijab for an oversized hibiscus. The handle gives, but the door sticks and cracks loudly when I pull it open. I freeze, peeking over the side of the cabin where Wolf has paused. He turns back, scans the perimeter, and goes back to his work.

I swallow my sigh of relief and slip inside.

My anxiety is so constricting that it's making it hard to see, but I know my way around. I can hear Mrs. Hudson's laugh as she showed us the place. I imagine Wolf flashing his wolfish smile at her when she handed him the keys and wished him a good stay. If only she knew. I lug my bag of rocks with me, scouring the plank-walled rooms, both relieved and disappointed when they all turn out to be empty. What if Wolf *wasn't* behind the robbery?

No sooner do I have the thought than I spy something familiar: the file from Deep Woods' archives. I peek outside the rain-stained window to make sure Wolf is still out by the trees and flip it open. Blueprints, plans. Dated and stamped. The detailed sketch of Woodsville Manor is a fist to my stomach. I shove the file into my backpack, gritting my teeth against my trembling hands, which make me fumble with the zipper one too many times.

But that's not what I'm here for.

The floorboards creak beneath my footfalls, reminding me of when my sister insisted we explore the cabin because it looked larger on the outside than on the inside. Sure enough, we found a room hidden from view. I make my way down the hall, pulling on exposed wooden accents and trying to find it again.

At last, one of the narrow sconces on the wall gives and a door swings open. I hurry inside, blinking twice at the two oversized utilitarian hard-sided suitcases to make sure they're real.

They are.

I lower the first bag and drop to my knees, sliding open the zipper with my thumb as a buffer against the sound. Inside are clothes and other belongings. No money. With a huff, I lower and open the other one, sweat making my fingers slick.

Money. Lots and lots of it.

My chest is tight. I don't think I've ever seen this much money in my life. It's enough to cover my grandmother's treatment ten times over. *That's the devil whispering*, I tell myself, before realizing I didn't have a plan for what I'd do *after* finding the money. There's a note with the cash, a letter in Wolf's fine hand. It takes me a moment to understand it for what it is: a way out in case he gets caught. It's a letter saying he found the cash. He thought he got lucky until he saw the news, and so he was returning the money like a good Samaritan. I scoff and fold it back up.

My backpack's too small, and I can't take the luggage with me—I might as well throw in a farewell wave at Wolf as I lug it behind me. I have a folding tote somewhere, but even if I managed to fit the money into both, Wolf will check on the luggage the moment he returns to the cabin. That's what I'd do if I were a robber.

Technically, I am, but still.

It hits me when I dump the rocks out onto the rug. I murmur a quick thanks. Wolf won't need to open the bag and check on his cash if the weight feels right. As far as he knows, no one is around for miles. He has no reason to check on the cash until he's far, far away from here.

I start shoving the cash into my backpack, stack after stack of Benjamin Franklins smiling up at me. I zip it up and heft the rest into my tote, crossing the handles before securing them both over my shoulders. It weighs about the same as the rocks did, and I quickly throw them into the hard-sided suitcase, throwing in an extra pillowcase to make sure they don't roll around too much, and stand it upright.

The front door opens.

I'm Muslim. I'm not supposed to curse, but I feel very, very close to it just now. The front door is on the other side of this hall, I tell myself. I still have time. I jump to my feet, nearly falling backward from the weight of the cash, and my arms quiver as I ease the door closed behind me, struggling with the sconce and the bags.

By the time I'm done, Wolf's heavy footfalls are louder, treading toward me, and the only place I have to go is the shadowed nook less than two feet from the hidden door.

I press myself as flat against the shadows as I can, my heart beating loud enough to alert the whole forest as Wolf steps into view, dark hair damp and fresh from a shower. He looks even more handsome this way, which is probably *really* handsome if I can register that thought while also being terrified for my life. When he turns, water flicks onto my cheek and I have to bite my tongue from gasping at the chill of it.

If he turns on the light, I'm doomed. I'm dead. I murmur prayer after prayer, watching as he pauses in front of me, close enough to touch.

He tugs on the sconce with two fingers, moving as if this is his own top-notch secret lair and not a cabin in the woods of our tiny town. I hold my breath as he disappears inside. The door closes behind him, and I think my heart stops when I venture out of the shadows and into the hall. I creep toward the back of the cabin, ready to bolt at the first sound of noise, and fumble with the lock on the door until it gives and I'm gasping at the fresh air. My shoulders ache as I hurry down the steps, making for the woods where I know I'll be safe.

In the woods of Three Oaks, I'm more wolf than he is.

I tell myself this until I'm back in my car and the doors are locked around me. My voice breaks when I call Hunt and tell him everything.

I can hear his worry and concern and his frustration, but in the end, when I tell him about the rocks, he laughs, and maybe it's the exhaustion and the adrenaline and how close I came to dying, but I think, after everything I did these past few days, getting a ring on his finger four years from now can't be that impossible.

THIS EVENING

Wolf is gone. I don't know about his crew, but I know about him because Hunt found the cabin empty. I walk past Wolf's abandoned warehouse, and I know why my Istikhāra led me here. Not to be complicit in a robbery—to test me, to see if I'd do the right thing when what I desperately needed fell right in my lap.

The sun shines a little brighter as I make my way up the steps of Woodsville Manor, red hijab pinned in place, a suitcase full of cash in tow and Wolf's letter in hand. The sign tacked on the front door is long and bright, promising a reward to anyone who returns the cash. I hadn't known until earlier this morning.

The reward won't even be a fraction of what's in the bag, but it'll come with a clear conscience attached, and having dealt with the opposite, I'm grateful. Grateful for the peace I've won, grateful for the treatment we'll be able to finally afford for my grandmother. Still, I like to think I would have done it even without the reward money.

After all, there's this notion that Muslims have to be saints. A girl's got to do her part.

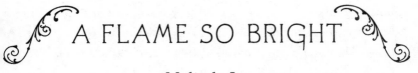

A FLAME SO BRIGHT

Malinda Lo

Inspired by "Frau Trude"

The first time Obedience Burcham saw Trude Strong, she was wearing a dress of startling carmine red, the skirt flaring behind her like a tongue of flame. A woman could be punished for wearing that color.

Obedience was on the riverbank below Strong Farm, dawdling on her way home from town, and the flash of red on the hilltop caught her eye. A wagon had pulled up to the house on the ridge, and the woman was climbing down from it, one hand holding her cap to her head against the gusting wind. Goodman Strong came around the wagon and held out his hand to the woman, and when she took it, Obedience realized she must be his new wife. She had heard that the woman had sailed here from the old country, and Goodman Strong had gone to Boston to meet her a few weeks ago. Now here she was, as foreign to these parts as her name. *Trude.* Obedience formed the name on her tongue silently, but as if she had heard, the woman turned and looked down the slope toward the river.

Obedience froze, for she was plainly visible on the grassy bank. She was too far away to see the woman's face, but she was certain that she was looking directly at her. She felt the woman's glance as if she had been pricked by a pin.

And then Trude Strong followed her husband into the

house. The overcast sky seemed to open above; a hint of sunlight gleamed low in the west. Obedience reluctantly turned toward home. Her mother was expecting the tinctures she had fetched from town.

Obedience Burcham was the youngest of her parents' five living children, and from the day she was born she was a willful girl. This had been tolerated to some extent while she was little, but now she and her sister Silence were the only ones left at home, and her mother's patience had worn thin. "You will never be a good wife if you don't learn to listen," Mother admonished her on Sunday morning as they walked to the meetinghouse.

Silence, who usually couldn't resist a gibe at her sister, was unusually quiet. Obedience knew it was because Goodman Strong had married and was expected to bring his new wife to church. Silence had once harbored hopes that Goodman Strong might court her, though she would never admit it. After his engagement to a stranger from afar had been announced, Silence had been in a foul mood for weeks.

In the meetinghouse, the Burcham family pew gave Obedience an angled view of Trude Strong's neck and shoulders. The Sunday morning service was hours long and provided plenty of time to study the woman surreptitiously. She wasn't wearing the red dress today, but a more ordinary one of russet linen, albeit with scarlet sleeve ribbons. Peeking out from beneath her white cap, her hair was the color of dark polished wood. It reminded Obedience of a merchant's trunk she'd once seen in a warehouse in town.

After the service, everyone wanted to meet Goody Strong; even Silence seemed grudgingly curious.

"We're your closest neighbor," Obedience's mother told

Goody Strong after they were introduced. "You might see our cattle grazing near your orchard, but Obedience will mind they don't cross into your fields. Obedience, come and meet Goodwife Strong."

Goody Strong's sleeve ribbons glowed in the warm summer sun, and she stood out among the villagers as if a cardinal had flown into a flock of sparrows. Her face was bright with youthful good health, and she was probably no older than Silence.

Obedience realized she was staring and quickly bobbed her head, saying, "Welcome."

"Thank you," Goody Strong replied. "Everyone has been so kind."

Obedience stepped back as the introductions continued, but eventually the villagers scattered to other conversations, leaving Obedience and Goody Strong alone together on the edge of the common.

"Is your mother a healer?" Goody Strong asked her, for Goody Porter had just pulled Obedience's mother aside to request a poultice for her aches.

"She knows some useful remedies," Obedience hedged.

Goody Strong had eyes of an unusual color: tawny, more golden than brown, like burnished brass in firelight. A faint fragrance of lavender clung to her, and Obedience had to resist leaning in to take a deeper breath.

"Obedience!" her mother called.

"You'd better go," Goody Strong said, with a tiny smile.

Obedience noticed again the ribbons tied around Goody Strong's russet sleeves. She said impulsively, "Your ribbons— they look well on you."

Goody Strong seemed surprised, and a rosy color bloomed in her cheeks. "Thank you."

Obedience felt a peculiar answering flush heat her own face, as if a lick of flame had leaped from Goody Strong's skin to hers.

———◦———

Goody Strong had scarcely been in the village for a month before her husband fell sick with a fever and died.

On the early autumn day that he was laid to rest in the family plot on his farm, Goody Strong was veiled all in black. Obedience's family attended the simple burial, along with most of the villagers. Afterward, Obedience and Silence walked home together, cutting through Strong Farm orchard to the field where their cattle grazed.

"She was too proud for her own good," Silence said in a low voice. "Displaying her mourning as if for show. She barely knew him."

"Hush," Obedience said, but mildly. "Don't be disrespectful."

The trees around them hung heavy with ripening apples. Impulsively she pulled one from a branch, polished the skin against her skirt, and took a bite. It was so tart it made her mouth pucker, and Silence observed her with a stern expression.

"It's too early in the season," Silence said.

Obedience gave her sister an arch look and took another bite.

———◦———

Goodman Strong had left no will, and upon his death the entirety of his property was inherited by his widow. A magistrate from town rode all the way out to Strong Farm to take inventory, accompanied by the village minister.

"It's not right," Obedience's father grumbled at supper.

"That woman knows nothing about how to run a farm. She'll destroy Goodman Strong's life's work."

The neighbors who came for Goody Burcham's poultices and tonics soon brought rumors with them. They said Goody Strong had brought trunks of finery with her from the old world: silks in colors of wine red and rich orange, emerald green and deep purple. There was a carved chair as grand as a throne; there was a tapestry of roses and thorns, and rings of gold and silver.

"She thinks herself above us all," Silence said after hearing of the rings.

"She has never even worn a ring to church," Obedience said.

"You must keep a close eye on her to know that," Silence said.

Obedience flushed. "Surely if she had, you would have heard about it," she said stiffly.

"Gossip is the devil's work," Mother cut in.

Perhaps aware of the gossip, Goody Strong sent bushels of apples to her neighbors after the harvest, including the Burchams.

Obedience had just finished putting a pie filled with those apples into the oven when Goody Corwin knocked on their door, her face ruddy and her eyes wild. Her husband had fallen ill after eating several of Goody Strong's apples, and she had come to Obedience's mother for a physick to cure him. Goody Burcham murmured soothingly to Goody Corwin as she measured angelica root into a twist of paper, instructing her on its use. But after Goody Corwin left, Obedience's mother took the pie out of the oven and told her to burn it, along with the other fruit.

The bonfire, which Obedience built in the yard behind the henhouse, smelled like roasting apples. As Obedience fed the flames, the heat like midsummer sun on her face, she could practically taste the fruit on her tongue: the melting sugars, the soft sweet flesh. Her stomach growled.

—◦—

One afternoon when the trees were aflame with red and gold leaves, Obedience left their cattle in the field and walked along the river below Strong Farm. If gossip was the devil's work, then it had worked on Obedience, because she was consumed with thoughts of Goody Strong. Did she really possess a trunk full of marvelous silks and jewels? She imagined Goody Strong wearing them alone in her house, like a queen in exile.

She had just resolved to return home when she saw a man in black ride up to the front door of Strong Farm House, his hat pulled low over his face. In an instant, he had dismounted and knocked on the door, which quickly opened. Obedience glimpsed a vermilion flash and then the man went inside and the door closed behind him. The diamond-paned windows were flat and dark, and yet Obedience had the eerie feeling that the house was watching her. The black horse turned his head in her direction, and Obedience fled, her heart pounding.

Soon afterward, Goody Wright claimed that her butter had gone rancid after Goody Strong walked past her house. Goody Strong kept to herself except when attending services on Sundays, so her stroll down the road past Wright Farm had been well noted.

Mother warned Obedience and Silence to stay away from Goody Strong. "That woman is trouble," she said as she sharpened her cleaver on the whetstone in the yard. The young pig that Mother and Silence had just slaughtered lay waiting on the board beneath the cool autumn sky, its eyes glassy as blood dripped into the pan that Obedience had set below.

The day after the winter's first snow fell, Obedience walked to her brother Makepeace's farm to deliver an herbal tonic to his wife, who had just given birth. On the way back she saw a man in green riding toward Strong Farm House, and when she drew closer, his horse had been tied up outside. A flash of emerald appeared in the window, and Obedience wondered who the man was.

As a widow, Goody Strong possessed a certain amount of freedom that was denied unwed girls like Obedience, but Obedience knew this freedom was double-edged. So long as Goody Strong remained uncontrolled by any man, tongues would wag about her decisions.

Uneasily, Obedience hurried home to discover Goody Hawkes on the doorstep. She was departing with a tincture in her hands and a grim expression on her face.

Inside, Mother and Silence were preparing the pottage for supper. "What's happened?" Obedience asked.

"Goodman Hawkes had an accident," Mother responded.

"Goody Strong overlooked him in town," Silence said, "and he tripped immediately afterward. Broke his foot."

"God save us all," Mother said. She took a pinch of salt and threw it over her left shoulder to ward off the devil.

Obedience eyed the crystalline flakes on the floorboards, and she surreptitiously crushed them beneath her shoe. She felt a tingle shoot up from the soles of her feet, as if a thread of lightning had sparked from the salt. Her pulse raced, and she wondered if this was witchcraft.

———

On a bleak day in December, Obedience laboriously drove the cattle away from Strong Farm, herding them toward the cowshed. They had wandered into the orchard, and the slow-moving, obstinate beasts resisted her entreaties. It was near dark before she got them all into shelter, but then she counted and realized she'd lost one. Grumbling, she pulled her hood closer over her head and trudged back out to the orchard, calling for the missing cow through the rising wind.

In the distance she saw glimmering lights coming from Strong Farm House, winking through the trees like a will-o'-the-wisp. She hesitated—she knew what the stories said—but then she heard the lowing of her lost cow. There she was, a shadow against the growing dark. As she approached the animal, she noticed that a cart had pulled up to the house. Its windows were lit with burning lanterns. Ducking behind a tree she watched as a man in red walked from the cart to the door. The light from the windows cast his shadow across the ground, and the corners of his hat were as sharp as horns.

Obedience abandoned the cow and ran. The trees of the orchard loomed out of the dark like crones with crooked fingers.

At home, Mother and Father were sitting down at the board while Silence poured ale. "Where have you been?" Father asked as he sopped a piece of bread in his bowl of pottage.

"The cattle field," she answered, breathing heavily. She had run almost the whole way.

"She's been spying on Strong Farm again," Silence said.

Obedience shot her sister a dark look. "Why would you say that?"

"You're always walking down by the river when you should be minding the cattle. We all know what you can see from the river."

Obedience didn't respond. She sat down on the bench across from her parents and broke off a hunk of bread.

Mother looked from one daughter to the other and asked, "Obedience, is that true?"

"We told you to stay away from that woman," Father said.

"Didn't you hear," Silence continued, "that Goody Turner's sheep was taken with fits?"

"What does that have to do with anything?" Obedience asked.

"Her sheep wandered onto Strong Farm last week," Silence said.

"That woman has only brought bad luck to our village," Mother muttered.

"There's no proof she's done anything," Obedience said imprudently.

"Have you been speaking to her?" Father demanded.

"No," she said. She had not spoken to Goody Strong outside of greeting her on Sundays, but she had looked at her—at the pink apple of her cheek and the creamy line of her throat—and she had longed to ask her so many questions.

"The apples, the butter, Goodman Hawkes, and now the sheep," Silence said, counting off each offense. "Is that not proof enough? She's a witch."

The word was a curse. "Take care before you point a finger," Obedience snapped. "Mother could just as easily be accused."

Everyone hushed. Obedience heard the crackle and hiss of the kitchen fire. She saw her sister's face drain of all color while her mother's went bright red.

Her father stood, and his fury made Obedience afraid.

"Goody Strong is a wicked woman," he roared. "Has she bewitched you? You will stay away from her and think no more of her, or else you will no longer be our child."

———

Storm after storm blanketed the ground in snow; drifts piled up against the door and the cowshed and the henhouse. Obedience's days and nights were an unceasing cycle of hauling wood and building fires and shoveling out the ashes to begin again. The new year dawned with a particularly fierce blizzard that prevented them from attending services on Sunday. Father led them in prayer as they huddled close to the kitchen hearth for warmth.

Despite her father's prohibition, Obedience had not stopped thinking of Goody Strong. She wondered how Goody Strong was faring in this weather, all alone on her farm. Did she have enough wood for her fire? Did she even know how to keep it burning through the night?

Obedience dreamed that she was walking through the orchard, following the will-o'-the-wisp through the naked trees. When she emerged on the ridge, the house's windows were bright with red-gold light, each pane of glass glowing like a jewel.

She ran across the snow-covered yard toward the house. *Trude*, she called. She stumbled into a drift and fell, and the falling seemed to take a very long time and then she was kneeling on the ground below the window. There, inside the house, was Goody Strong. She wore her ruby-red cloak, except it was not made of cloth anymore—it was a blaze of copper and crimson—and her hair had become one with the inferno, each lock a tongue of flame. Her eyes were still tawny, and when she looked at Obedience through the window, Obedience felt desire lighting her up as if she were about to catch fire herself.

———◇———

Obedience awoke with a start, her heart racing, her skin hot and damp as if it were a humid summer night. But when she sat up, her breath steamed into the frigid winter air. Silence was asleep in the bed beside her, and she heard her parents' light snores from the parlor.

In the dim light of the fire's dying embers, she quietly pulled on her clothes. Outside, the night was clear and bitter cold. She went to the woodpile and thrust an armful of logs into a canvas carrier. The moon was low in the west but still bright enough to silver the world through which she walked.

Afraid that the orchard would be impassable in the snow, she took the frozen road instead, nearly running while she clutched the log carrier in her arms. At last she saw Strong Farm House in the distance, the snow-covered roof glimmering in the last of the moonlight. No smoke rose from the chimney, and the windows were dark. Fear grew inside her like ice spreading across a windowpane.

She did not bother to knock. She pushed open the door and hurried inside, snow falling from her skirt and shoes onto the cold wooden floor. Dark shadows lay all around, but she could make out the shapes of a bedstead, a chair, a trunk. The bed was empty, the blankets stripped off. She went through to the hall, and in the darkness she sensed a faint motion beside the chimney.

"Goody Strong?" she called. "Trude?"

She felt her way through the blackness and discovered a nest of bedding next to the hearth, and beneath the blankets was the shape of a woman. She leaned over Trude Strong's face, holding her cheek above the woman's mouth. She still breathed, but faintly.

Obedience set the logs down and held her hands over the coals. They were barely warm but had not completely died. She fumbled for the poker and stirred the embers, then blew on them until they glowed a deep orange. Finally she set a log on the coals and coaxed it slowly to burn.

When at last the fire had caught, she turned to the woman huddled beneath the blankets. Her face was hidden, her body motionless. Obedience knew that the fire alone would not revive her quickly enough. She had to warm Trude Strong with her own body, and to do that she needed to take off her cloak and unlace her gown, until she was shivering in the icy hall in her shift. She crawled beneath the blankets and realized Trude was wearing a cloak over another cloak, as well as a gown over her shift. Obedience's teeth chattered as she began to strip away Trude's clothes. Finally she pulled the blankets back over them both and pulled the woman close to her. She was limp and half-frozen, and Obedience started to rub her hands over Trude's arms, the rise of her hips, the length of her thighs. She breathed on Trude's icy skin as if she were the coals of the fire, and gradually she felt the warmth return to Trude's body. And then the woman began to tremble in her arms, shuddering and quaking as if she had been taken by fits. Obedience held her tighter, her belly against Trude's back, their legs entwined. Trude smelled of salt and iron and the faintest trace of lavender, and finally Obedience could press her nose to the nape of her neck and inhale the scent of her.

As the gray light of dawn seeped into the firelit kitchen, Obedience felt Trude begin to relax against her, the weight of her body pressing warmly into hers. She felt her desire rise again, and it made her tremble as if she were the one who had been frozen.

Trude turned over to face her and asked, "Why are you shaking?"

Obedience whispered, "I am afraid."

Trude stroked her arm from shoulder to hand. She linked their fingers together, and Obedience quivered at her touch. "Of what?"

Though she knew the answer, Obedience couldn't say it aloud. Instead she asked, "Who was the man in black?"

A breath passed before Trude replied. "The woodsman, who has not visited me in weeks and has left me with no fuel for the fire."

Obedience felt as if a knot had loosened inside her. "Who was the man in green?"

"A hunter. He asked permission to hunt on my land, which I granted him."

Another knot released. "And who," Obedience asked, "was the man in red?"

"A butcher from town."

At last, Obedience felt free.

In the gathering light, Trude raised one hand to Obedience's cheek and cupped her face. "I was so cold," Trude whispered, "but at last you have warmed me."

Obedience covered Trude's hand with her own, pressing her cheek into the woman's palm. "I dreamed that you had turned to flame."

Trude smiled. "It is you who have turned me to flame. I have been waiting for you for so long."

When Trude touched her, it was as if she had become

kindling—a freshly hewn log, her skin just bitten by the axe blade. Trude's fingertip was flint against steel, sparking her instantly. Obedience knew this must be witchcraft. She saw the truth in Trude's tawny eyes, and she felt it in the heat of her skin. She was inflamed by the taste of her wine-red mouth; she was engulfed by the blaze between them.

Never have I been so alight, she thought. *Never have I burned so bright.*

THE EMPEROR
AND THE EVERSONG

Tracy Deonn

Inspired by "The Nightingale"

Once upon a time, a small planet in a binary star system gained an emperor.

Luckily for them, the inhabitants of this planet were quite familiar with their new emperor, because, prior to the coup, he was the prince of their most powerful kingdom.

Everyone knew the prince's face. Cheekbones set high and proud in dark brown skin had made him a beautiful child and, later, a terrifyingly handsome young man. Black curls fell to his shoulders in shining loops and twists; his earrings were golden mobius strips. Anyone would be proud to wield even one of his features, and yet he held them all at once with devastating ease. His Royal Highness was well known and recognized.

Nevertheless, the coup was a brutal surprise.

After murdering both of his parents in a very public, very bloody midnight battle, the prince had declared the dead monarchs' reign over and his reign of light begun.

For as long as he could remember, this young man had been, as many powerful leaders are, secretly obsessed with death. Well, not death exactly. He had been obsessed with *life*, and all that it encompasses, its reaches and its limits. So wholly obsessed with life was he that the night of the coup, the very minute his parents stopped breathing, the young man began hunting for a way to live forever.

The prince held no evidence that his parents had ever pursued immortality. But so convinced was he that *any* leader would wish to pursue this same goal, he'd assumed that if he killed his parents without advance notice, they wouldn't have time to take preventative measures to protect their findings.

So, still dripping in the mess of murder, the prince swept into every alchemical laboratory formerly under his parents' control seeking that which he assumed would be there: a fiercely guarded, hidden elixir that could stave off death.

He did not find anything of the sort. Not a single experimental vial, nor a collection of false starts. No efforts made at all.

Unfathomable.

When his search concluded, the prince stood in the middle of the royal balcony, overlooking the sunrise. The prince straightened his spine, set both bloodstained hands on his hips, and tossed his curls over his shoulder in a haughty manner. He declared, simultaneously to no one in particular and to everyone who might one day meet him, "The first step is to rid ourselves of limited vision. My parents should have realized that a monarchy under a king, as a system, holds a weak grip on power and is easy to topple. An empire, however, spreads across the land until every subject can touch it. An empire is steady and strong. It shines so bright that its light reaches the bottom of every well, the bed of every stream and lake, the recesses of every cave. As an emperor with control over all the resources on this planet, my subjects will think of me and my works for all time. . . ."

From the entrance to the suite, a well-dressed man watched and listened. This man had seen generations of leaders come and go over his long life. All rose young, and died young, too—at least to him. He waited until the young prince was finished crowing, and cleared his throat.

The prince, out of breath with excitement, whirled on the man. "Who are you?"

The man glided into the room, chin tilted up but eyes cast down. A mixture of stately authority and obeisance. "My name is Purlion, and I would like to be your chief advisor. If you accept me as such, Majesty."

The prince liked the sound of the formal address but narrowed his eyes. "Did you advise my parents?"

Purlion shook his head. "No, Majesty. I am the palace's resident watchmaker. I have watched time and held it in my hands and shared it with others for three generations. I work here, in one of the old wings. I'd like to offer my services to the new empire."

The prince thought about this for a moment. He wished for immortality; perhaps it would be beneficial to have an advisor who saw time itself from a different perspective. He dipped his head to Purlion and welcomed the watchmaker to the future.

The prince lifted his chin. "I have a job for you, Purlion."

Purlion nodded. "I am at your command."

"Gather the leaders of the other seven territories and bring them to me. Tonight." The prince paused. "Use force as you may."

And so, by the time the sun set, the seven kings, queens,

and grand dukes of the planet had been invited to meet the prince at his palace.

All thoughts of challenging the young prince's authority died on the lips of those leaders when they entered the throne room, because the prince met them with dried blood still flaking between his fingers, because the floor was still stained dark crimson from the battle, and because the former king and queen still lay cold on the floor. Indeed, all thoughts of *anything* left the leaders' minds at these sights, save one: fear.

The prince was pleased that his welcome had succeeded in suppressing any further unpleasantness, and greeted the other royals with a declaration:

"A kingdom, by design, only lasts as long as its king. An empire is meant to endure for all time. I welcome you all to my empire."

As expected, there were no arguments.

At his coronation the next day, the young man bowed a prince and rose an emperor. The seven sovereign kingdoms fell quietly, and a single empire rose in their stead.

And so it was done.

That night, the Emperor hosted a celebration for his subjects from every corner of the globe. The great ballroom was laid out like a grand map of the world, and the Emperor asked that citizens from each of the former kingdoms—now imperial territories—be seated in the ballroom in positions approximate to their respective locations, so that he could, from his golden throne, look down on all that he now commanded.

When the Emperor entered the banquet hall and swept up the dais, the voices died down and the people of the eight territories eyed their new leader. Double regicide one day and an abrupt regime change the next had led to widespread speculation about what would happen now. This new emperor was quietly terrifying, but the people's hope was that he would rule, not oppress, and that he would unify the territories and provide equal support to them all.

The Emperor waved his hand as he settled into his throne, as if to say, "Please, continue." And the banquet began in earnest. He crossed one ankle so that it rested delicately across his knee.

Purlion stepped forward from beside the throne. "Is this what you want, my emperor? Citizens, made happy in your name?"

The Emperor nodded. "Yes. All of my subjects here, bellies soon to be filled. This is how the empire begins, and how it will persist, as well."

When he fell asleep that night, the Emperor was satisfied that he would be the first to achieve the impossibility of forever.

He woke the next day and called for a meeting of the territory leaders whom he now considered his advisors. "What do you believe is the first step toward creating an empire?" the young emperor asked.

The advisors shifted uncomfortably in their chairs. No one wished to remain silent if he expected them to speak, and no one wished to speak out of turn if he had meant them to remain silent.

Purlion rose to his feet. "Great works, Majesty."

The Emperor nodded. His chief advisor had answered correctly. "Great works. So let us begin."

The Emperor's forces executed his plan, and within months he'd taken the world entire. One would think that his directives might have brought pain and suffering, but that is the way of another story. In this tale, the Emperor's "great works" began with providing resources to every single one of his subjects.

The Emperor's army was soon stationed in every community and directed to listen to the people who lived there so as to best serve the community's needs. Fresh water arrived daily in lands that saw regular drought via transport by the navy. The abundance of the palace gardens found its way to every city on the planet through regular deliveries from the Emperor's airships.

Soon, a statue of the young leader rose in every town square of the former eight territories, glittering gold and tall, and the Emperor's subjects tossed flowers and dried fruit at its feet in gratitude.

A year passed this way, and the Emperor, dark eyes glittering in satisfaction, smiled again at his group of advisors. "I should like to see my great works," he proclaimed. "Let us go on a tour to celebrate the growth of the empire."

Purlion cleared his throat. "If you had requested a tour six months ago, then I would have stood in approval and gathered the airships myself. But I am afraid my emperor will be disappointed if we toured the planet today. Time has passed, and the world has changed already."

The Emperor scoffed. "Why should time matter? Great works persist, do they not?"

The table shifted uncomfortably under the Emperor's sharp gaze.

"Do they not?" the Emperor repeated.

"Let me show you, Majesty." Purlion waved his hand at the far wall, pulling up the view screen. He flicked his wrist and the screen divided into eight smaller images, each showing a live feed of a territory town square. At first glance, there was nothing amiss in the Emperor's eyes. But after a moment, he rose at the head of the table, sweeping back his heavy golden robe, and stalked toward the screen.

On each of the screens, something *was* amiss.

Purlion gestured as he spoke. "The statues remain standing, as they are built to last, but . . ." The video feed of the town squares showed the Emperor's subjects flowing like water around the plinth beneath his statues' feet. His image had been so absorbed into the world that he was now invisible. Markets overflowed with the plenty the Emperor's forces provided, so much so that the Empire's subjects let food go to waste. Fruit lay hot in the sun, shriveling with disregard, because a new shipment would simply arrive the next day to replace it.

The great works were no longer great, because they had become *ordinary.*

The Emperor's brow furrowed. He dismissed his advisors—all but Purlion. The Emperor leaned toward the screens as if moving closer to them would reveal an alternative explanation. Instead, standing so close to the screens, his failures shone in light against the brown of his cheek and his transient triumphs were reflected against the hard clench of his jaw.

"I will commit greater works," the Emperor asserted, his eyes bright. "Raise schools for their children in my name, so that the next generation will know me as well. Organize annual festivals in the square, occasions on which my subjects may admire the statues that they no longer notice. Rename their towns so that they live always under my gaze and title."

"Majesty, is that your truest desire?" the advisor began, voice cautious. "To create work that will never be forgotten?"

The Emperor stood back, grinning. "Is that not every man's wish? To be known for all time."

Purlion tilted his head. "But even if you achieve this, in order to be certain your goal has been met, you would need to live forever. One cannot witness eternity unless one is alive to do so."

The Emperor's mouth folded into a frown. "My design for society already reaches every corner of the planet, or will very soon. I can prepare works that will far outlast me, but as you say . . . I will not live to see them come to full fruition. This vexes me."

The advisor's brow drew tight. He began again with a new question. "You are young, Majesty, and you have many decades of life ahead of you, do you not? You will witness your legacy for longer than most."

"I expect," the Emperor murmured, and turned toward the windows to gaze out at his world, "I shall live a long while yet. If there has ever been an herb, a practice, a distant spring one should bathe in to extend the beating of one's heart and the strength of one's lungs to the limit of the human life span, I have partaken in it, practiced it, and bathed in it. But there is no elixir. No magic that grants immortality."

Purlion stood beside the Emperor and held out an antique watch. *Tick, tick, tick,* it went. "The clock is ticking for us all, Majesty. Unless"—he clicked a hidden switch—"it is stopped."

"Stopped by what?" the Emperor asked.

"Or whom." Purlion slipped the watch back into a pocket without another word.

"What do you mean by this, Purlion? What would you have me do?"

"I cannot force you to take action, only provide the tools

you need to persevere." Purlion bowed and left his emperor's presence.

———◦———

The Emperor had been a clever child, a devious prince, and now a power-ravenous ruler of an entire planet. He did not request that Purlion explain himself. He did not need explanations. He knew what the old advisor was suggesting.

Or at least, he believed he knew.

When one is desperate, one does leap to conclusions.

———◦———

The following month, the Emperor invited subjects from all over the planet to the palace once more. This time, instead of celebrating his rise to power, he asked his subjects to bring with them the most beautiful, wondrous items from their territories. Those who heard his summons thought that their emperor must truly wish to celebrate his people—a fair assumption, with all of the pleasant conquering in the recent past. But that is not why the Emperor made such a request.

You see, the Emperor realized that there was another way to reach his goals. He would recommit himself to great works, this time modeled on the things that his *subjects* most admired and worshipped, so as to maximize the effect—and then end the world at the peak of his popularity.

If he could not ensure that his works would last for eternity, then he would stop short the clock of the world . . . and deny eternity itself.

The first territory arrived with a flowering plant that only bloomed for two minutes each day, but did so in colors of the rainbow. Before his eyes, the flower burst open, its petals flashing bright across the spectrum of color, until it drooped and fell in a lifeless brown mass.

The second territory brought a tank full of merpeople, their deep brown skin and blue scales flickering in the water.

Purlion sat at the Emperor's left on the dais as each territory entered the banquet hall with something grander than the last.

Finally, the eighth territory, the coastal peoples, brought forth a plain young woman with no adornment or jewelry. Her skin was a dull bronze, but her eyes were wide and bright. Her hair rose about her head in a halo of tight dark curls.

The Emperor frowned. "You were invited to bring the best of your home territory. Is this girl the most beautiful, wondrous thing your people can imagine?"

Purlion stepped forward to whisper in his emperor's ear. "Majesty, this is the Nightingale."

The Emperor shook his head in annoyed confusion. "What is this Nightingale? I have not heard of her."

A small child rushed forward, nervous and yet determined. "Sir . . . Majesty?"

A low humorous murmur rippled through the room.

The Emperor, however, did not laugh. "Speak."

The child continued, emboldened. "Sir Majesty, the Nightingale is a rare creature from our coastline, not seen in many, many years. She is a myth to most sailors, a songstress who sings when the fisherfolk sail out in the morning and sings all through the night as they return. She sings the Eversong."

The Emperor did not wish to appear confused for long. "Ah, yes. The Eversong." Luckily for him, no one caught on to his ignorance, and the volume in the room grew as the other seven territories' low murmur increased to a small, excited roar.

"Purlion," the Emperor whispered hastily. "What is the Eversong?"

Purlion stared at the young woman, and she stared straight back at the advisor.

"The Eversong is sung by a young woman from the tropics near the center of the equator. It is said that if she sings of you, all who hear her song will think of you and bless your name always. That you will become like a god in the listeners' minds."

For a moment, the Emperor sat in pride that his advisor knew so much. Then the Emperor's eyes grew wide. "Is that so?"

Purlion lifted a shoulder. "Some say that these blessings can grow powerful enough that even Death will leave you be."

The Emperor sat up in his throne. "Purlion, is this not what we have discussed?"

A melodic voice found their ears easily across the room. "It is a superstition, Majesty," the Nightingale said.

The crowd quieted. The room waited.

Purlion hummed. He leaned close to speak to his emperor in a low voice; all the while he held the Nightingale's gaze. "No, it is a *belief*. Beliefs are much stronger than superstition and more effective than rumor. It does not matter if a belief is true or false, it only matters that it persists and spreads."

"A belief?" the Emperor mused aloud. He looked over the banquet hall at the thousand faces turned his way. Imagined *belief* flowing through and between them, elevating him to the status of a deity. How easy it would be to achieve if all one needed was to hear a single song once. How powerful a construct, belief. More durable than a statue. So strong could the blessings be that even Death would avoid him.

The Emperor smiled. He did not truly wish to destroy his empire, after all. That was a moment of weakness, before he created his own salvation by hosting this banquet at which the Nightingale appeared. He did not need to cut all time short to prevent his obsolescence. In the Nightingale, and in the belief of his subjects, he saw another path to immortality.

He gestured to the Nightingale. "You will sing of me."

The Nightingale knew the request was coming and did not protest.

So, she sang of the Emperor. Of his vision and his great works, of his well-documented beneficence. She sang of his accomplishments at such a young age. The conviction needed to destroy his parents and the love he showed his subjects. She sang of all that he had the power to do, whether he'd done those things or not. And her song was so beautiful that it lured the listeners' hearts into its rhythm. Eyes fell shut in order to better hear the melody. Even time held its breath.

When the Nightingale finished singing, the Emperor rose slowly to his feet. "You will remain here and sing every day so that all who pass through this palace will hear you sing of me. And all will bless me. Enough that Death will leave me be."

The Nightingale knew this was coming, also. Her voice was even and her demeanor calm. "I can sing of you every day, if you wish, but I must warn you that I sing best the way I always have. Here and there, of someone new each time, sometimes quiet, sometimes loud."

The Emperor's mind was turning. He gestured to his guards to escort her away, and their hands were gentle on her elbows. "My subjects will make pilgrimages to hear the rare and mythical Nightingale sing, and you will sing here at the palace every day until everyone has heard the Eversong in my name."

It had already been decided.

—◦—

The next day, a new group of subjects from the empire visited the palace to hear the famed Nightingale sing.

However, it went as the Nightingale said it would. She took to the small stage in the center of the room during a crowded luncheon and sang of the Emperor, but her song rang differently.

Even though the listeners were swaying as if half-asleep, lost in the beauty of the Eversong, the Emperor—having heard the first song the previous day—frowned. At the close of the performance, there was great applause. Or rather, great applause began but was abruptly ended when the Emperor cleared his throat. "This is not the Eversong from yesterday."

The Nightingale looked at the Emperor with sharp eyes. "I cannot repeat the song exactly, Majesty. The Eversong is not a single composition—"

"No." The Emperor turned to Purlion, lips pursed in dissatisfaction. Purlion watched the Nightingale. The Emperor turned from Purlion back to the young woman and shook his head. "You will sing again. The same song from yesterday. I will not risk uneven blessings from one of my subjects to another."

The Nightingale began again, and the song was *similar* to the first. And *dissimilar* to the second. But not the same.

The Emperor's jaw clenched in response and the Nightingale sighed. "I cannot stop your actions; I can only give you the tools to stop yourself. You do not want me to sing the same song again, Majesty."

He snorted. "You do not know what I want."

The Nightingale's lip twitched as if suppressing a scowl.

The Emperor was back to proclaiming things by now. "This will not do. Practice tonight, and try again tomorrow."

But tomorrow did not produce the same Eversong. Each day, something differed. A key change. A shortened phrase. A coda removed, then replaced. An entirely new melody. A song that was in counterpoint to the first. A new tempo.

The Emperor was displeased.

"Purlion," he said one night. "I'd hoped that the belief in the Nightingale and her song would soon become a unified blessing for me across the planet, and that I would become so blessed that Death would not favor me."

Purlion hummed. "Each group that arrives to hear the Nightingale sing leaves the palace humming the tune of the day. Everyone is thinking of you when they do so, Majesty."

"No," the Emperor said. "This . . . variance is too unreliable. An empire endures. Great works must persist. If the Nightingale cannot sing the same song tomorrow, then I will cut the planet's time short." He shrugged as if particularly saddened by the prospect but not bothered enough to prevent it.

Purlion considered the Emperor, and believed he would do as he said.

—◦—

Some days later, the Nightingale, looking worse for wear, was brought to the center of the banquet hall to perform the Eversong for a new group of visitors. Just as she opened her mouth to begin, a gorgeous birdsong burst through the silence in bright, clear tones.

Everyone turned to find a mechanical bird perched on a bar of a golden cage that slowly descended to the center of the room. This mechanical bird glittered even at a distance. Its feathers were a thinly cast gold, its eyes two rubies, and in the center of its chest sat a button made from an emerald. And it reproduced, to every single note, the Nightingale's Eversong from her first night in the palace.

The Emperor leaped to his feet, grinning. "This bird!" he exclaimed. "Where did it come from?"

Purlion stepped forward from the shadows wearing a quiet, clever grin. "I built the bird last night, Majesty." His eyes slid to the Nightingale. "There will be no need to rely on the Nightingale when this bird will sing the exact Eversong required without variation or the need to rest."

For the first time, the Nightingale's eyes flashed. "The Eversong may change, and belief may vary, but that is life, Majesty. That is living. This creation is not alive."

The Emperor narrowed his eyes at the Nightingale and gestured once again. This time, his guards handled her harshly at the elbows and took her to her room without the intention to free her ever again.

————☙————

By the end of the following year, the mechanical Nightingale had performed the Emperor's preferred Eversong thousands of times, for thousands of listeners. Its song could be heard hummed, whistled, and played on instruments all across the lands. Every citizen on the planet knew the tune for the Emperor by heart, and the Emperor finally felt as though he would live forever. It was rumored that he played the mechanical Eversong all night in his chambers, so that the sound would further protect him.

————☙————

One night, Death paid the Nightingale a visit in her rooms. The sequence was this: There was a knock at the door, the Nightingale turned from her seat at the window to call to her visitor, and Purlion entered, his clothes transforming at every step.

By the time they faced one another, Purlion's suit had completely bled into fine black-and-gold robes, just as Purlion himself had bled into his true form. Death smirked at the young woman, who did not seem surprised to see him at all.

Annoyance graced her face instead.

"You have to admit, Gale . . . there is an irony to it all." Death's voice was a deep, mocking rumble as he circled the Nightingale.

The Nightingale scoffed. "You play with the mortals. Hiding in plain sight to position them like game pieces until they are in formation as you like, and call that irony."

Death chuckled. "The arrogance of a mortal who wishes to defeat death and decay in his life and works, and who has the resources to *act* on those wishes, is too delicious not to cultivate to its richest form."

The Nightingale shook her head. "You have other lives to reap, and yet you focus on this one."

"*This* mortal murdered his parents for power. In the coldest blood imaginable. Of *course* that got my attention." Death sneered, then released a low groan. "But he is ruining everything. Even I cannot listen to that mechanical song another moment. Fortunately, the bird is failing at last. Gears and chips and wires all worn down beyond repair." He tutted in faux remorse.

The Nightingale's eyes widened. "You would take him now? After you were the one who gave him the bird in the first place?" She sneered. "Punishing a simple creature for your sins?"

Death's eyes glowed in the dim light of her rooms. "If I hadn't given him that bird, this *simple creature* would have destroyed thousands of innocent lives. Something that the Goddess of Life would be interested in preventing, I would think."

She stiffened. "I cannot stop mortals' actions, only give them the tools to stop themselves."

"Just as I cannot force them to *take* action, only give them the tools to persevere."

Death and Life stared at one another in the type of silence only achievable by the ancients.

"I came to tell you how I plan to end this particular game." Death stepped backward, and with each movement his robes and body pulled inward toward Purlion. "Your move," Purlion said, and exited the Nightingale's chamber.

The Emperor stirred in his bed when the Eversong came to an end. He sat up, gave his chambers a mighty yawn, and reached toward the mechanical bird's perch on his bedside table. A quick press of the bird's shiny emerald button would begin the Eversong once more. The Emperor had performed this ritual so many times he could do it without fully waking.

But this time, the bird's song did not begin again.

The Emperor woke in alarm. He tried once more, but the bird remained frozen in the night. Again, and there was a soft click, but the bird did not persist. Again, and the emerald button broke, the jewel falling onto the bedside table with a soft *thunk*. He planned to have Purlion repair the bird as soon as possible.

Abruptly, the Emperor felt a chill reach him through the open window, and he knew that Death had found him.

Before his end could enter the room, the Emperor screamed for salvation. "Guards! Bring the Nightingale!" he cried.

Purlion climbed through the window wearing the Emperor's crown askew on his head.

The Emperor blinked, not believing his eyes at all. "Purlion?" His shoulders fell from his ears and he released a breath. "Thank goodness it is you and not Death, as I'd feared."

"Well," Purlion began, and stalked toward the Emperor

until his appearance bled into Death's once more. "I am both, you see."

The Emperor's heart seized in his chest and he fell backward, pressed against the wall behind his bed. "No . . . no, you are my advisor—the Eversong!" the Emperor cried. "I have the blessing of thousands!"

Death watched the Emperor and sighed in a sort of disappointment. "You brought me here yourself and are now surprised that I remained?"

Blood drained from the Emperor's face. "I—"

"Deserve this and more," Death murmured, leaning close.

The guards entered the chamber with the Nightingale in tow—but rushed away when they saw Death in a crown hovering over their young emperor.

Death stood as the Emperor ran from his bed to the young woman. "Your Eversong failed me!" the man shouted in a voice threaded with fear. "The bird sang it every day. Thousands know it by heart, and yet Death has found me tonight."

The Nightingale held her ground, and her eyes glowed as she spoke. "The Eversong only works as you believe when it is allowed to change and shift, when it never repeats itself. I was always singing of you, even though the tune varied and evolved. That is life. But you would stop life if you could, and so now it stops for you."

The Emperor shook in his nightgown. "The bird . . ."

"Useless," Death said. "A trinket that offered you no protection but showed me how far you would go to keep the world from growing away from you."

"You tricked me!" the Emperor yelled.

"I tempted you," Death corrected.

"And if I sing of him now?" the Nightingale asked. "Loud enough that the entire palace will hear?"

The Emperor looked between the two, an accusation of collusion there and gone on his tongue.

Death considered this. "If you sing, I will leave. I will abide by the rules of our game."

The Emperor fell at the Nightingale's feet. "Please, sing for me. I will allow you to sing whatever version of the Eversong you like! I will let you roam free once again!"

The Nightingale stared at the Emperor and weighed her choice. She made her decision and stepped forward to face Death. The Emperor smiled in relief as she began to sing— but the Nightingale did not sing a new version of her Eversong. Instead she sang the mechanical bird's familiar tune—which was once her own—more beautifully than the bird had ever done before. The same notes soared through the night to reach the farthest edges of the palace grounds. And the Emperor's subjects hummed along in their sleep, knowing the song by heart.

At this, the Emperor knew she had not chosen to protect him from Death.

A smile spread across Death's face. He stepped past the enraged Emperor, who cursed both their names, and bowed to the Nightingale as she sang. "Until our next dance," he said, and took the Emperor away.

HEA

Alex London

Inspired by "Cinderella"

There was once a little boy whose mothers were all fabulous.

Goldie Hoard was the dragon queen, whose sequin scales could be seen from space, and Beluga Carlisle, the wurst witch. There was Rue LeDay and Hottie Buffet and Cosiné. All drag mothers any boy would be lucky to have, and they taught this boy well. He'd lost his own mother when he was little, and each of the queens had filled some piece of his broken heart with more sequined kindness than he had any right to.

Though they had each moved on—to Santa Monica, Berlin, Nashville, and medical school, respectively—he carried their lessons with him always, in his healing heart, and also on his social media, where he was known to his 9.2 million followers as Phoenix Ashes, though to his friends and family he was Asher Brockmeier, seventeen-year-old ATM machine.

"Ash!" his stepmother called from downstairs while he was just trying to read a book in peace and quiet. He ignored her. Barb could wait.

Barb was, in addition to being his stepmother, his manager. She took 10 percent of his income in addition to 100 percent of his family, and it was his fault she'd met and fallen in love with his dad to begin with, which was its own kind of barb, a sharp one, right in the small of his back where he could never quite get it out. She was a damn good manager was the problem, and she doted on his father too. She managed his career and his father's happiness with unmatched enthusiasm. Some Barbs simply had to be endured.

"Ash, did you see?!" she shouted louder than his music and then followed with a text because she knew he'd have his phone on him. "The invitation came!"

She added an eggplant emoji, because she knew he got annoyed when she misused emojis and this one was so wildly inappropriate he wouldn't be able to resist telling her to please not. She was brilliant in her way. She knew what it meant, and he knew she knew, and she knew he knew she knew, but ignoring it would *not* make it stop.

He groaned, tossed aside the fantasy novel with too many birds in it and made his way downstairs in his glitter jean shorts, Sailor Moon tank, and pink silk bathrobe that had been a gift from one of those French fetish-wear designers who didn't know Phoenix Ashes was underage. The internet was a dangerous place for a young person to be famous, but it did lead to great swag.

"Ash, look!" Barb's daughter—his stepsister, Margot— hopped off the counter stool and bounced over to him, waving the elaborate cut-paper invitation in his face. Barb stood by the sink with her hands folded, feigning surprise that Ash had come down so promptly. "The theme is Villainy! That's perfect!"

"Villainy," he sighed.

"Oh, don't act put-upon," Barb told him. "This is a gala concept tailor-made for you. You can channel all those sea witches and ice queens."

"It's just . . ."

"What?" Barb said. "Perfect? On-brand? Faaaaabulous?" She threw her hand in the air and struck a pose, which he was tempted to call a low-key hate crime. "Yes, your manager is the greatest and got them to change the theme from 'A Feast of Plenty.' Can you imagine? No one wants to see Zac Posen design a dress that looks like a turkey leg. Anyway, Harris Reed will send over some designs for you to look at, gratis. Unless you want me to find a different designer? I know you like to make your own design decisions, and I can make the calls you want made, though Harris is quite in demand right now and—"

"No, it's fine," Ash told her. "Really, love their stuff. I just . . . this year? The gala? I'm not sure I'm feeling it."

"Excuse me?"

If the interrobang symbol could be a person, his stepmother became it. She was shock. She was dismay. She was not going to hear any explanations from Ash about why he didn't want to attend the Met Gala, *the* fashion event of the year, to which A-list celebrities had to beg invitations.

"Oh my god!" Margot slammed the invitation down on the counter. "He doesn't want to go. He doesn't appreciate it." She grunted with disgust, or at least a performance of disgust. "He's such an ungrateful little pr—"

"Margot!" Barb snapped.

"I'm sure she was going to say 'princess,'" Ash replied with his best sarcastic smile.

She rolled her eyes and stormed out of the kitchen like a teen in a nineties movie.

"Green is a bad color on her," Ash said.

"Don't be that person, Ash," Barb chided him. "Perform

pettiness for your fans if you must, but you and I both know you are not that person."

How dare you! Ash thought. *Calling me out to my better angels.* Only Barb knew him well enough to use his own basic decency against him. His drag mothers had known him well too, from the first moment he'd met each of them at FlameCon as a scared little baby queer geek. They'd taken him under their sequined wings, asking nothing in return, and there were days he wished any one of them had become his stepmother, or manager, or both. But their mothering was situational, and situations change. Mothers too. Sondheim had written an entire fairy-tale musical about that.

"Now, let's discuss your posts leading to the event," Barb said, tapping her nails on the marble countertop very unmusically. Ash's success had paid for that countertop. Maybe her nails, too.

It was his pleasure to earn income for his family, of course, and to serve his fans. His fans had been with him since he'd started posting crafting and makeup tutorials in sixth grade, under the tutelage of his drag mothers. The fans saw him through bullies and breakdowns and glow-ups and blowups. Though his drag moms had moved on, the fans were still with him now, panting for each new look, trick, and tip. They commented on everything, had channels to discuss him on Reddit and multiple Discord servers. He was practically an ecosystem. And oh, the fan mail. More of it came from Brazil than he would've expected, but the filthiest mail was from Midwesterners. Something about hot dish and Kroger brought out the smut in people. Ash should not have been allowed to read his own thirst tweets, but his ego was like sourdough starter: it needed daily feeding from straight white women.

"You know I wouldn't interfere with content," Barb told him. "But with your book launch coming up, and the buzz around *Last on the Lanai*—"

"I had a cameo in that, and I played myself," Ash said. "I'm not sure there is anything I can do to help a major movie studio."

"But you can hurt the buzz, which does impact you," Barb said. "Word will get around. Not with your fans, but with the people who—"

"People who matter?" Ash raised an arch eyebrow. "Were you going to insult my fans? The people who bought this very house?"

"I was not," Barb replied coolly, utterly impervious to Ash's bullshit. "I was going to say the people who make business decisions. The ones whose decisions to support you actually bought this house. And they could *undecide* to support you just as easily. Branding at your level is three-dimensional chess."

"Like on *Star Trek: TNG*," Ash replied, because Barb hated when he admitted to off-brand fandoms. Geek culture was cool now, but only the *right* geek culture. Admit to loving the wrong IP, and you might as well be the guy who farts in the Voltron costume at Comic-Con.

Ash had gone through a Voltron phase. He'd done some great cosplay, and those early fans were passionate. It was queer geeks who'd built his brand in the beginning, queer geeks who'd embraced him and raised him up when he was grieving. He'd only gotten into drag through cosplay, and was only good at cosplay because of drag, and he'd learned from the queens and the geeks how to marry his passions into something bigger than the sum of their parts. He owed queer geeks everything. He wasn't going to disappoint them.

"I'm gonna post 'Gala Rags to Gag on . . . on a Budget,'" Ash told her. "Maybe also 'The Five People You Meet at the Met Gala.'"

She handed him the cold-brew iced coffee she'd been keeping in the fridge and a stack of press photos. "Your daily dose," she said, the double meaning clear.

Yes, like all gay boys it was required he drink iced coffee year-round, but unlike most gay boys, he had to sign 750 press photos per day until he'd made his way through the entire first run of 60,000 copies. Anyone who bought the first edition of *Phoenix Ashes's Almanac of* 🔥 was going to get a signed photo, come hell or carpal tunnel.

Ash trudged up to his room to get sipping and signing. If he didn't finish all 750 signed photos today, he'd never hear the end of it. If he didn't pick a concept for the gala outfit today, he'd never hear the end of it. If he didn't get new content up today, he'd never hear the end of it. Sometimes it felt to Ash like all he ever did was serve the brand, when just once, he'd have liked to do . . . well . . . nothing.

But nothing was not an option for a boy like Ash.

Content was king and he the king's humble servant.

The days passed in a parade of tulle and school and video rendering. He toiled on his content, on his autographed photos, and on his consultations and fittings for the gala and the Oscars and the parties and the after-parties, each color palette reviewed, each stitch examined, each jeweled tiara custom crafted with just a hint of insouciant masculinity. Harris Reed added a veil, just to give the haters something to lose their minds over and Ash's fans something to dream about lifting. He'd already planned a post-gala video about lifting the veil, where he'd get to show a carefully constructed kind of vulnerability and maybe discuss how toxic masculinity robs boys of the joy of dress-up, which then pushes them into becoming the uniformed agents of state violence. All boys just want to play dress-up, after all, and denying it can be deadly.

His stepmother warned him not to get too political. "No one looks to you for that. Count yourself lucky. I have clients who must weigh in on everything, and the tide turns on them terribly quickly."

"At least they get to swim," he said. He felt like he was treading water.

———◦———

On the night of the gala, his makeup had been planned, his outfit prepared, and the design team arrived to help him dress and get in the car. It was a two-hour drive to Manhattan, so they had to get a move on.

Which was why it made no sense that he was standing at the end of his bed in sweatpants and a long-sleeve Starfleet Academy T-shirt, moments before their scheduled car pickup, staring at the "gowncedo" garment in front of him with a feeling of doom. There were unsigned photos scattered across the floor like lentils spilled in a fireplace, and the outfit itself, which of course looked fabulous on him, made him think of nothing so much as a skinned animal pelt, even though there wasn't a stitch of fur on it. He was not about that animal cruelty life.

"Come on, Ash, what the hell?" he chided himself in his best chiding voice.

"Come on, Ash, they're all here waiting," his stepmother chided him through the door in hers.

He'd never be able to say what came over him at that moment, whether it was late-afternoon madness from skipping his iced coffee, divine inspiration from caffeine withdrawal, or just the way the birds in the tree outside his window sang their carefree songs in absolute indifference to his brand strategy, but he threw on the frayed blue hoodie he wore to protect his clothes during hot-gluing sessions and slipped out the window.

He couldn't bear the thought of another glamorous ball.

For one night, he wanted to be anything but *on* and anyone but Phoenix Ashes.

He'd text them not to worry, that he was taking a personal day, but first, he had to get down the driveway and past the gate and figure out where to go next.

His phone started blowing up in his pocket around the time he reached the nearest major road. In a strip mall across the way, he saw a Gloria Jean's Coffee, one of those chain coffee shops that couldn't even aspire to Starbucks-level style. He'd never gone inside before. He remembered something about maybe a boycott but couldn't remember what for.

There's no ethical consumption under capitalism, he thought, and figured if there was some kind of boycott for reasons beyond mediocre coffee, that would make this as good a place as any to hide out and get his head right.

"Iced coffee, venti—er, I mean, large," he ordered at the counter, and the boy behind the register looked up.

Rich brown eyes and thick black hair, just the slightest fuzz on his upper lip and a little more on his cheeks in uneven patches that managed to look like potential, not disappointment. He smirked at Ash's fumble over the Starbucks-style order, though really, it had become universal at this point, like *Kleenex* for any and all tissue. The barista's name tag read *Mirza*, and when he spoke his voice was like a spell being cast.

"You look like you want a shot of espresso in that," he said.

Is this love at first sight? Asher wondered, nodding enthusiastically at the offer. "I very much do, thank you."

"Name?" Mirza lifted a plastic cup and pressed a Sharpie against it, poised.

"A—" Asher began, then cut himself off. He was incognito here. What if Mirza was a fan? Would that be good or bad?

Bad. Definitely bad.

"Wesley," he blurted.

"Ah, like the shirt." Mirza nodded toward the shirt peeking out from Asher's half-unzipped hoodie. "On leave from the academy, Cadet Crusher?"

Asher grinned. Mirza was a *Star Trek: TNG* fan too. Sure, *Discovery* was a better show by any measure, but there was something about the retro nineties vibe of *Next Generation* that appealed to Asher. Maybe it was just the twinky energy of Wil Wheaton's Wesley Crusher or how the show made no effort to be cool. It was from a time when geeks weren't mainstream, so the show didn't have to try to be, either. They could just let Cardassians be Cardassians.

Mirza wrote the name on the cup before passing it along to the other barista behind him. If Asher's hesitance about his name had raised any alarms, Mirza didn't show it. Of course he wouldn't. People give all sorts of names in coffee shops, for all sorts of reasons. Asher's friend Aiden first came out as nonbinary in the name they gave to baristas eight months before they told anyone else. The coffee shop was America's last neutral space. It was a miraculous place.

Maybe he should make a video about that. The weird things people do in places they think they're anonymous? Was that relatable? Did nonfamous people think about anonymity at all, or was that just an influencer thing?

Stop making content! he scolded himself.

"Need anything else?" Mirza asked, eyebrows raised in genuine curiosity, because Asher was still lingering there, and he
was probably not as fascinating to Mirza as Mirza was to him.

"No, uh, thanks," Asher muttered, lowering his eyes. He
scuttled to a booth and waited to hear his name called and
tried not to get caught glancing at Mirza, who, he noticed,
was doing the same.

When the boy called out the name "Wesley," Asher shot to
his feet before the pseudonym was all the way out of Mirza's
mouth and said way too fast and way too loud, "That's me!"

Get a grip, Ash, he told himself. *No one knows you're anything
more than another customer. No one knows your phone is buzzing like a
deranged dragonfly in your pocket. Unless . . .*

As he walked to the counter, he tried to assess if Mirza
recognized him. He knew *Star Trek: TNG,* so maybe he was in
the fandom, and maybe he'd figured out who Asher was. What
if Mirza *posted* somewhere about it? He wished he'd looked up
the reason for the boycott before coming in. The brand dam-
age could be severe.

He took the iced coffee, and Mirza didn't let go of it instantly. Their fingers touched and their eyes met and it was
totally *not* an accident. Was this the moment his disguise failed?

"You go to Farley?" Mirza asked.

Asher shook his head.

"Hm," Mirza added. "You look familiar."

"Just one of those faces." Asher grinned, and Mirza returned the grin, releasing the coffee to his custody. *Does he
know?* Asher's heart thumped with conflicting beats. Not a
coronary incident, just the tension of wanting not to be recognized and also kind of hoping this boy might recognize him.

An invisibility spell is only interesting if you believe you're worth noticing.

"Guess so," Mirza said, then leaned over the counter, lowering his voice to a whisper. "Yes, I am flirting with you, if you're wondering."

The heart racing stopped to make room for a new sensation. It felt like he had just been punched in the stomach by a butterfly, sort of pleasant and nauseating at the same time. He looked a mess, he'd given a fake name, and as far as Mirza knew, he was just some awkward guy off the street, but somehow, to this beautiful barista, he was worth flirting with.

People see just as much beauty as they let themselves, his drag mother Rue LeDay had told him before she moved away.

I hope you always know how worthy of love you are, his mother had told him shortly before she died.

Guard your heart from creeps, Barb had told him that very morning.

The blessing and the curse of being a boy with many mothers was that sometimes their advice filled the air like too much perfume.

Asher was not one for speechlessness, but here he was, speechless.

Phoenix Ashes was a notorious flirt, fond of innuendo and double entendre, but that was the brand, when there was no chance of anything real coming of it. Asher Brockmeier was shockingly inexperienced at romance, and out of character he had no idea what to do with it.

"Flirting, huh? Well, keep up the good work," he said, and then his soul left his body.

Mirza's brow furrowed and he cocked his head.

"I meant, like, er . . . I'm . . ." Asher was lost in deep, dark woods. He needed an out; he needed a trail of breadcrumbs; he needed a fairy godmother to transform him into a pumpkin spice latte—anything to get him out of the sentence he'd begun. Instead, he overcompensated. "I think you're *ravishing*, darling."

Okay, that was worse.

Mirza laughed.

Praise Ru and Harvey and Martha and Blanche and all the fairy godmothers in the pantheon! Mirza thought he was joking! Asher did his best follow-up laugh to confirm the joke and then tried to smile as normally as trying to smile normally allows, and he added a calm, cool, and absolutely sincere "That's me flirting back, kind of."

Asher pulled out his own personalized metal straw that he carried with him, a gift from a sponsor after he'd done a whole video about single-use plastics and made fantastic armor from disposable straws. He took a sip of his coffee, mostly to stop his mouth from saying anything else. The straw was louder than he wanted it to be, though his heartbeat felt louder even than that.

Mirza's smile widened; he had cartoon-prince-perfect teeth except for one that was at a slightly different angle, which made him look more real and even more endearing. "An hour," he said. "My shift's done in an hour, if you're around we could . . ."

"Have a coffee?" Asher suggested, holding up his large, more for the joke than the actual reality of it. He couldn't stick around that long. He didn't dare.

But Mirza nodded. "Maybe not here, though," he said, winked, then went to help the next customer.

Asher took his seat and watched Mirza take orders and write names on cups. To avoid spending the next hour staring at the boy, he pulled out his phone.

That was a mistake.

Fifteen missed calls, seven of them from Barb, one from his stepsister, one from his dad traveling in Singapore, and the rest from the assorted publicists, schedulers, and brand ambassadors coordinating his entrance to the gala. The sun was setting. He should have been on his way by now, livestreaming from the car. He had a whole plan to go through the best and worst outfits of animated villains during the drive. It was going to be devastatingly clever, tagging just the right fandoms to maximize exposure. He could enrage and enrapture the most passionate online people as he saw fit, and no matter how they felt about him, they'd share the post. That was how social media worked: engagement of any kind was currency; it didn't have to be positive. It just had to be unignorable.

He was gonna praise Scar from *The Lion King*, that apex predator queen, then propose wearing his pelt, just to annoy the PETA people. He could only get away with that because he didn't actually wear fur. The online outrage would be good for PETA and good for him, but only because it was insincere.

It's a more brutal ecosystem than Pride Rock, he thought. *At least the lions and hyenas don't have to measure their engagement stats.*

He sighed and looked at his texts, which were what he expected, various levels of concerned and exasperated. It wasn't like he was going to hide out in this strip mall coffee shop forever or run off to the South of France with Mirza and raise chickens on their vineyard . . . but it wasn't the worst fantasy he'd ever had. (The worst was when he was thirteen and dreamed about being adrift on a small life raft for weeks with Yuji Itadori from the *Jujutsu Kaisen* manga. Things got steamy, and sheets were ruined.)

He scrolled through the gala tag on Instagram for a bit,

looking at the red carpet early arrivals, a certain tier of socialite and celebrity who arrived in the first wave. Some of their fashions were impressive. One of the judges from the pottery show he liked arrived with a porcelain headpiece held up by four clay-spattered potters in overalls, but the outfit underneath was nothing terribly inspired. All concept, no substance. Ash would never. There was depth and history to the performance of villainy, and if you ignored it, then you were just playing dress-up. He'd have to do a "dress-up versus drag" video soon.

He grunted at himself. He couldn't even take an hour off, could he?

Instead of judging red-carpet looks for a gala he was trying to avoid, he opened his notes to draft a text to his stepsister. Margot couldn't understand how he was so cavalier about his opportunities.

"Your problems are my fantasies," she'd once told him. He'd scoffed at the time, but just because he felt guilty. As his manager's daughter, she was only in his life at all because of his fame, which meant that his fame and his family were forever linked and however he felt about one stuck all over the other like tar spilled on the steps of a palace.

After Asher's mom died, he'd taken to YouTube as a kind of therapy. He used to watch *Project Runway* and *Drag Race* with his parents, and he started his own channel to explore different looks and projects. It was through that channel he'd found his voice and his community.

He discovered he could be flamboyant and passionate about color and puns and anything that sparkled and other people enjoyed it. The more people liked Phoenix Ashes, the more he became Phoenix Ashes for them, and the more they supported him, and the higher he rose. It was fun, and it was healing, and it became lucrative too.

Barb discovered him just after she'd started her own management company, and after six months, he was her biggest client. After a year, she'd fallen in love with his dad. Work and family merged and the rest was history. He believed Barb when she said she cared about him as a son and as a client separately, but he wasn't sure which came first for her, the boy or the brand.

He wasn't sure which came first for him, either. He was kind of curious to find out. He kind of wanted to test what would happen if he walked out on Phoenix and tried to just be Asher.

"Hey, Wesley?" Mirza's face materialized in front of him. "You okay? I've said your name like fifteen times."

"Oh, sorry, yeah." Asher tucked his phone away, text unsent. "Just distracted."

"You're not stoned, are you?" Mirza asked, then put his hands up. "I'm not judging, I just want to be clear I don't do that and I don't, uh, want to lead you on if you're not in your right mind."

"I'm in my right mind!" Asher blurted too quickly, popping once again to his feet. "I mean, I'm not stoned. Caffeine is the hardest drug I take."

"Maybe you've had enough of that, though, yeah?" Mirza suggested. "There's an ice-cream-and-pizza place at the end of the strip. We could go there? They even have lactose-free options."

"Why do you think I—?"

"I don't think . . . I just wanted to offer—"

They were talking over each other. It was cute how thoughtful Mirza was trying to be. Now that he'd calmed down a little, Asher could tell Mirza was nervous too. It leveled the playing field.

The boy had shed his apron and visor, and his sleeves were pulled halfway up his forearms. For a second, Asher wondered if Mirza rowed crew, but of course Farley didn't have a crew team. Asher just always had crushes on the crew boys at his prep school.

"So, do you always pick up customers at work?" Asher asked.

"I have to," Mirza said. "They won't let me use the grinder." He paused, then added with that bright smile, "Get it? Like, Grindr and coffee grinder?"

Asher couldn't help laughing. It was a profoundly bad joke, and also kinda niche, but that just made Mirza's weird charm more infectious. Also, Asher loved terrible puns.

"I'd love to get pizza and ice cream with you," he said. "Just don't milk it."

Mirza rolled his eyes and bowed formally, letting Asher out of the booth first, then trotted ahead to hold the door for him.

"How very chivalrous of you," Asher said, stepping into the cool early evening parking lot. "My knight."

"Actually, Mirza means 'prince,'" Mirza said.

"So you're royalty," Asher said.

"Named after the late pop star," Mirza replied. "My mom was a huge fan but also came from a conservative Persian family, so Mirza was her subtle rebellion."

"Very subtle," Asher said. "You a fan?"

"Isn't everyone? I think it's the law. Like Dolly Parton. You don't even have to like the music to like the music."

"So you don't like the music?"

Mirza laughed. "I do."

"Prince and Dolly?" Now Asher was intrigued.

"I mean, I'm not like in the fan clubs," Mirza said. "But I don't complain when my mom puts either of them on."

"So what do you listen to?" Asher asked, hoping their taste would align.

"Don't laugh."

"I won't," Asher swore.

"I really like religious music," Mirza said.

"Like . . . Christian rock?" Okay, so their tastes did not align.

"No, like chants. Monks chanting. Muezzin. Cantors," Mirza said. "I love the way faith bends a voice, raises it, and wrecks it."

"Whoa," Asher said. "Did not see that coming."

Mirza shrugged. "Everyone's got surprises in them, right? What's yours?"

"My . . . surprise?" Asher's voice caught. His heart thundered. He didn't want to be Phoenix Ashes right now. He didn't want that part of him to interfere with this moment, but what other surprises did he have? "I . . . I don't know that I—" he mumbled.

"The thing that you always thought makes you weird," Mirza encouraged him. "Not, like, your crush on Captain Picard, but, like, the thing that you think you're the only one who feels."

"You don't do small talk, huh?" Asher asked.

"I go big," Mirza said. "Sorry . . . I've heard it can be off-putting."

"No," Asher told him. "I don't mind. I'm just not sure."

Asher thought about it. He'd made his "weird" things into

his brand, distilled them and broadcast them to millions. He never really thought about what he'd held back just for himself.

"Well, you have until the end of our pizza and/or milkshake," Mirza said. "Think of it like the Oracle at Delphi: *Know thyself.*"

"Oh, so you're into mysticism?" Asher wondered. He'd done a whole series of videos on tarot looks.

"That's from Greek mythology," Mirza said. "Well . . . I mean . . . via *Percy Jackson.*"

"Aha!" Asher laughed. "Not so scholarly as you put on!"

"I never said I was scholarly." Mirza smiled. "I was just trying to impress you. But seriously, with me, what you see is what you get."

Mirza opened his arms wide, and Asher looked at him and liked what he saw. This guy was interesting and open and kind . . . and Asher was lying to him.

It was too late to come clean. He'd ruin the whole vibe they had. He had to just roll with it, think of some awesome interesting detail to tell Mirza. He'd invented Phoenix Ashes, after all; he could invent Flirty Coffee Shop Customer Boyfriend Material Wesley, too. Of course, that would be *another* role to play, and wasn't the whole point of skipping out on the gala to have one night where he didn't have to play a role?

"You get lost in thought a lot, huh?" Mirza asked, walking next to him.

"I guess so," Asher said. "Got a lot on my mind."

"God gives burdens but also shoulders," Mirza intoned. "We never get more than we can bear."

"Is that more *Percy Jackson* wisdom?" Asher wondered.

Mirza laughed. "Yiddish. I had a Jewish piano teacher."

"You play piano?"

"Badly. You?"

"I'm actually pretty good," Asher said, but not boastfully. He was proud of his musical talent. He'd shared it with millions of people, so he kind of had to be confident in it.

"I'd love to hear you play," Mirza said. "Maybe you could help me get better."

Asher swallowed. They were walking distance from his giant house, where he had two different Yamaha keyboards and a Steinway baby grand. If he weren't lying to Mirza, he could've invited him there now. If he weren't lying to Mirza and hiding from his family, that was.

If everything were different, then I could do everything differently. Brilliant.

"Maybe another day," he said. "Let's just get some pizza."

This time, he held the door for Mirza, basking in the bleach-and-yeast smell of the pizza place.

"Cadet." Mirza saluted.

"My prince." Asher returned the gesture with a curtsy, mixing narratives, but still holding the door open.

That was when disaster struck.

An SUV screeched into the parking lot, horn honking over and over like the tolls of a midnight bell.

"Asher Wilhelm Brockmeier! What on earth are you doing?" Barb bellowed as she leaped from the passenger side. Mirza whirled around, defenses up, shifting his broad shoulders between Ash and trouble.

Ash, meanwhile, was as still as a shoe stuck in tar.

"We were driving past, looking for you, and I thought, *That couldn't possibly be him*," Barb railed. "Why would Asher be dressed like a hobo going into a pizza place two miles from home, when he should be in the car, wearing couture and heading for the gala?"

"Um, lady, I don't know what your deal is," Mirza said, "but—"

Barb silenced Mirza with a quick raise of her hand and a look she often used to frighten publicists and that had once reduced Tom Ford to tears. "Asher, who is this boy?" she snarled.

"This is . . . um . . . Mirza . . ." Ash said meekly.

"Wait." Mirza flinched. "Who is Asher?"

"Asher is a boy who doesn't seem to care about all the *effort* that other people put into tonight," Barb snapped. "He is a thoughtless boy who forgets that other people count on him."

Ash sighed and slipped around Mirza's protective shoulders. "I'm sorry, Mirza. I can't join you for pizza."

Mirza's mouth hung open, as Asher trudged after his stepmother, who held the SUV door for him. The spray-tanned driver stared straight ahead through his mirrored sunglasses, face blank as an enchanted pumpkin.

"I'm sorry," Ash mouthed before his stepmother slammed the back door, climbed into the passenger seat, and ordered the driver to make haste for Manhattan.

"The outfit is in the back," Barb told him. "I got a room a block away from the Met at some tourist hotel, where you can finish changing. I suggest you come up with a story to explain your lateness. I'm sure you'll think of some fairy tale to tell your fans."

"My fans like me to be real," Asher grunted.

Barb craned her neck around the headrest to look Asher up and down in his sweatpants and hoodie. "And this is the real you now?"

"I just wanted a night off," he sighed.

"You have a book coming out and a cosmetics line to launch and a movie premiere," she said. "A night off comes *after*. Do you really want to be someone who doesn't keep their word? A selfish little social media star?"

"No," Asher grunted.

"Excuse me? I can't hear mumbling," Barb said, looking forward as the highway slid under the big black hood of the SUV. Asher felt trapped in the massive leather back seat, like he was a giant foot crammed into too small a shoe.

"No," Asher said. "I don't want to be selfish."

"Good," said Barb. "Then no more running away from your responsibilities. We'll go to the gala, we'll put on our faces, and you'll get through this season with style and wit, and then a vacation. I'm sure any destination in the world that you choose would love to comp your stay in exchange for some posts."

"What if I just want to do something without, like, creating content?" Ash asked.

Barb snorted. "All life is content," she said. "Some people just know how to transform it."

Ash leaned back and closed his eyes, listening to the muted sounds of the traffic and the purr of the engine. He pictured Mirza's smile below that dumb visor, imagined their date playing out over pizza and ice cream, thought of the stomachache he'd have had later and then lied about, daydreamed the secret, anonymous moments they could've had at stupid movies and in the New Age section of bookstores reading each other's horoscopes and in parked cars in suburban parking lots like normal teens.

In truth, he didn't know Mirza well, but Mirza didn't know

him at all, not even his name. It was a fantasy, but one they'd both started to create together. Meeting someone new was like that, making up a story as you went along and revising it to make the new discoveries fit. It didn't have to make sense or even be true, as long as both people were willing to make it up together.

He'd have liked to work on a story with Mirza.

Instead he'd be Phoenix Ashes again, serving the people with the version of himself they already knew and didn't have to revise, because he'd chosen every detail in advance. It wasn't fake, exactly; it was just a fairy-tale version of a self. It left enough room for everyone to project their own wants and needs onto him, without any of the messy details that make a person specific and complicated.

Mirza had wanted to know the specific and complicated, and Asher had given him nothing.

As the SUV reached Manhattan, the fog of publicity shrouded Phoenix Ashes like a witch's curse. There was the flurry of wardrobe changing at the hotel, the makeup and the hair, and then the quick drive to the museum for the red-carpet stroll.

They loved his look, as he knew they would. It nodded to Billy Porter's 2019 Oscar's gown/tuxedo, but with a golden collar nodding to Charlize Theron's queenly robes in *The Huntsman*, and swirls of black and gold silk velvet and tulle that were meant to evoke Ursula the sea witch.

You can get away with anything if you give them no choice but applause, Goldie Hoard had once told him.

Be yourself for the rest of your life, and you'll never regret anything, his mother had advised him at the end.

Barb said nothing to him before he stepped onto the red

carpet, either because she was still mad at him or because she trusted him to know what to do. Maybe both. She was capable of feeling more than one thing at the same time. As much as he hated to admit it, she was as complex a character as anyone else.

Not a character, he thought. *A person.* He'd had many mothers, and all of them were their own specific people, too, even Barb. Asher was not the protagonist of their stories, of any story but his own.

Uninvited, an image of Mirza grinning in his stupid coffee shop visor popped back into Asher's head, and the smile it drew out of Phoenix Ashes was 100 percent genuine. He had to dial it back to stay on theme. Tonight, he was a villain.

The night rolled on: the poses for photographers, questions shouted, answers shouted back through a devilish sneer, questions ignored and answers misquoted, event producers scurrying, and a thousand different names and faces thrust in front of him, demanding charm, demanding graciousness, no missteps allowed, don't place a wrong foot, a wrong word, a wrong look that can go viral. Be what they think you are, laugh at the jokes that aren't funny, ignore the microaggressions that aren't accidental, and try not to make eye contact with Gwyneth Paltrow.

It was a dance he'd done a thousand times before, and he did it flawlessly as the night unfolded. In the back of his mind, there was Mirza, smiling with that one crooked tooth, holding the door, inviting him to mediocre pizza. A normal date with a normal boy, whose name meant 'prince,' and who might've turned out to be his happily ever after.

No happily ever afters at this party, baby, Rue LeDay had once told him. *Just the next dance to do.*

She said "dance," right, not "Dan"? Goldie Hoard had cackled, and the queens had all laughed, but the lesson was in there. Happily ever after was the period at the end of sentence, but life only ever gave an ellipsis. . . .

I wonder if Mirza likes a grammar nerd, Asher thought.

He felt the spell of the party ending and the sadness setting in as the car took him home. Barb was asleep in the front seat. It was one a.m. on a Monday night and he wondered what Mirza was doing. Probably sleeping. Or playing video games. What did normal teenagers do at night on spring break?

What they didn't do, he knew, was wear forty-thousand-dollar outfits, cake themselves in (fantastic) makeup, and try to avoid eye contact with A-list celebrities. This was not why he started making videos. He hadn't wanted to be famous or rich; he'd just wanted to feel a little less alone.

Nice job, he thought. *You feel more alone than ever.*

He hadn't, until that moment, considered bringing a date. *Would Mirza be the type of boy who'd like life as a plus-one?* Would he even be willing, after discovering Asher's lies and getting ditched in the strip mall parking lot?

He went numb for the rest of the drive home, and that was still how he felt when Margot pounded on his door only six hours later, waking him up with an aggrieved shout:

"Ash, I am not your butler! Get your own coffee!"

Bleary-eyed and still wearing that perfect smoky eye he hadn't bothered to remove before bed, he stumbled out of bed in his underwear and sleeveless Pokémon halter top that had once been his actual childhood T-shirt. He whipped open the door to find out what his stepsister was yelling at him about. His face was more scowl than question mark, but they had enough of a sibling shorthand that she just grunted, "Your coffee order's downstairs."

"Huh?"

"You didn't get coffee delivered?" A flicker of worry danced across her face. "Should I have not let the guy in? You have a stalker?"

"I have a lot of stalkers," Ash said. "So, no, you shouldn't let anyone in, and obviously, I didn't order coffee in my sleep, unless there is some enchanted coffee fairy out there who knows what I need better than I d—"

He froze.

He brushed past Margot, padded down the hall, and looked over the banister into the large marble foyer, where the coffee delivery boy stood in his apron and visor. His head snapped up toward Asher, and he broke out in a crooked-tooth grin.

"I have an iced red-eye here for Starfleet Cadet Wesley," announced Mirza. There was a metal straw poking out from the top of the cup. Asher's metal straw. He'd left it behind in Gloria Jean's.

"Not sure if I have the right rank. Or address." Mirza paused, his eyes finally taking in Asher's sleeping outfit, underwear and all.

Asher's cheeks flushed and he yelped, audibly, before leaping out of sight.

"Want me to call the police?" Margot whispered.

"No." Asher shook his head, trying to get control of his swirling thoughts. He rushed back to his room to get pants and a robe, before coming back for a more graceful entrance. Mirza waited patiently, extending the coffee out to him as he descended the stairs.

"How did you find me?" Ash asked.

"I had every boy in the kingdom try the slipper you left behind," Mirza said. Asher didn't get the joke quick enough, and Mirza moved on. "Kidding. Did you know you have personalized straws?"

"Betrayed by my own conscientious consumption," Asher laughed. Had part of him left the straw behind on purpose? "How'd you find my house, though?"

"It's actually scary," Mirza said. "Your address wasn't hard to google. Privacy is dead. Sorry to barge in."

"No, it's okay." Asher took the coffee from him. "A, I could use the coffee, and B, I never thought there'd be an upside to getting doxxed last year."

"In my defense, I reported the website where I found the address, right after I wrote it down," Mirza told him.

"Thanks," Asher replied, and meant it.

"So why'd you lie to me about your name?"

"That's a long story," Asher answered.

"Good," Mirza told him, taking off his visor. "Because I'm not actually working today, and I love a story."

"Me too," said Asher. He took a sip of his coffee. He had no idea where any of this was going, or what he and Mirza were going to learn about each other, but he didn't have to know. The best stories didn't have endings that you already knew when the story started.

"Why don't we go for a walk?" Mirza suggested, with a quick glance up toward the railing where Margot lurked, Barb now at her side, peering down at Ash and Mirza like curious crows. He could see Barb's gears turning, calculating the brand implications for him dating or maybe-dating someone who wasn't famous. Did Mirza *want* to be famous? Would Barb give him a choice?

These were questions for later. For now, Asher was excited to take a walk with this barista prince.

"Yeah." He smiled. "Just let me get my shoes."

THE
LITTLEST MERMAID

Meredith Russo

Inspired by "The Little Mermaid"

Did you know there is a kind of human who lives on dry land and who can't even breathe water? Don't roll your eyes! I know what the other children say, but they're little liars. Terpeople are as real as you or I, and if you swim close to the surface, you can even see them on the wood-and-iron shells they use to float, or splashing in the surf in their flimsy swimming hides.

Instead of tails, they have two legs, not knobby and hard like a crab's or supple and soft like a squid's but, if you believe it, like a long, powerful pair of extra arms ending in stiff, flat hands for gripping the ground. Their voices are scratchy and thin, with almost no song in them, and can only be heard from very short distances—they hardly have any way to show one another how they feel! But there is a kind of thing called fire in their world, and it loves them and helps them, and because they only live under the desolate sky where everything is chained to the floor, the tools and nests it helps them build never corrode or drift away. Their feet, which is what they call their lower hands, are always digging into the ground. They love to stay in one place, and for things in that place to be still and quiet.

Well, they aren't *all* that way. I haven't told you about Aria yet, have I? Auntie Termaid? I know you've wanted me to, yes, sweet one, but you were too little to visit the surface until recently. I knew when I told you about her you'd want to meet her. That wouldn't be fair, would it? To make you want something you can't have and then to stop you from having what I tricked you into wanting? That isn't how things are on the surface, though; even when they're grown they can't survive alone, and they can't help wanting all the things they can't have, in a net that traps them if they aren't careful.

Life on the surface is harsh and cruel, so they all live together and help one another. You might think it sounds nice, and it can be, but they are as capable of cruelty and violence as we are, and they can't freely swim to calmer waters. If you are to understand Aria's story, then you must understand this as well: the way terpeople reproduce stays the same all their lives. We change from man to woman as suits our hearts, or when there isn't enough of one kind of body or other, or sometimes just because. Your sister changed once, remember? I've changed twice. If you ever change we might sing a new song for you, or bring you the biggest fish we can find, or go on like nothing happened if that's what you like, but we will still love you, still swim with you, and we will thrill to learn each new side of you as they appear. Terpeople, though . . . well! They're as different from one another as we are, of course, but the way they are different is supposed to stay the same. They hate when things change, and they especially hate when something they didn't believe could change does so unexpectedly.

Aria was a termaid who had already changed from boy to

girl by the time I met her. Her family resisted, but for a human, Aria's song was strong and true. I could not tell you how it was done specifically, because terpeople's techniques and tools and invocations barely make sense in the first place, and it isn't ever polite to ask someone things about a change they don't tell you first. What's important is that when we met, in her seventeenth summer and my sixteenth, she was as much a young woman as I was.

I was stalking warm shallows not far from here when I found her. This was before even your sister was born, of course, when I only hunted for myself and whichever roving young adults kept me company for however long suited us. The moon was high and the waters of heaven swam with countless glowing fish. There was a colony of oysters just under a rock where waves crashed helplessly against the cliff, and as I floated happily prizing shells, certain I was alone, I flung oyster liquor toward the heavens and sang prayers of love to the honored dead. Imagine my surprise when a raspy little voice cried out! I looked up and there, poking her head over the cliff, backlit by one of the cold lights terpeople put everywhere they go, was Aria.

Her words were less than nonsense to me at the time, of course, but she looked worried. I thought maybe these oysters were her territory and I'd missed some important marker, or she had spotted a shark and meant to warn me. I sang back reassurance and waved—my stomach was full, I had only ever seen terpeople from a distance, I *knew* the water was safe, and I was young and curious. She leaped from the cliff suddenly, unfolding and sharpening her strange body, plunging for the water like a marlin into a school of tuna. I was too shocked to do much more than wriggle out of her way! The moment she hit the water I understood her better, since terpeople flesh sings as clearly as ours does. Her body sang to me of peril and protection, of resolve and responsibility, that someone would die if she didn't intervene. Even when I understood she meant to save *me* I hardly believed it, but behind those louder notes was a melody of loneliness, a sucking abyssal dirge, and I suspected these more urgent feelings were the only thing keeping her from falling prey to something horrible. Confusion entered her song, and it finally occurred to me she thought I had legs like her. I guessed from all this that the body singing to me was beautiful, and when we surfaced I knew I was right.

Her black hair seemed short to me, but I later learned it was very long by surface standards. They cut their hair with iron claws! Her nose wasn't flat and slitted like normal, but poked out from the middle of her face like a dolphin's, only her mouth was underneath it. Her skin was the color of a nurse shark's, and when she hooked an arm through my elbow I shivered at the tickle of barely visible fur over her whole body, soft and downy like a seal or a penguin, and how she was *warmer* than anything I had ever touched. Suddenly I understood how they made friends with fire—they are *of* it! It burns inside them like the churning in the seams of the seafloor. More wondrous than anything was her neck, which was long and thin and as smooth as the skin on your arms.

I had always assumed they *had* gills and just didn't use them, since legs are clumsy for swimming and fire hates the water. But no! She gasped each time her head broke the surface. She couldn't even hold her breath a hundredth as long as a whale or a manatee. Water could smother her and she still threw herself in to save me. I knew then that she must be a warrior. When she opened her mouth to breathe I saw her teeth were flat and blunt behind thick, soft lips. Strangest of all was her second skin, the fiber hide terpeople wear at all times. I had seen them from a distance and knew how to tell a swimming hide from a land hide. She was not dressed for swimming. I smelled old, stale tears on her as surely as a shark smells blood. I smelled loneliness. Desperation.

We reached the beach and stopped just shy of the sand, where the water tugged and surged at her hips. She kept gabbling nonsense and I had no dry words to tell her I didn't understand. Even if I had, it was the season for mating and I was young and she was, even in her strangeness, so unbearably beautiful and brave. I did not want to talk. Oh, little one, every inch of her vibrated strength and weakness, self-sufficiency and need. Such contradictions they hold inside themselves! I twined my arms in hers. I pressed us together and savored her despite the uncomfortable, alien radiance of her warmth. My lips touched the base of her skull and hummed a simple baby-song of gratitude, concern, and delight. She shook and squeaked understanding, and it must have been the mating time for her too because she touched me back and even showed me a trick called kissing they do on the surface, where two people press their lips and tongues together. Ha! Yes. Yes, it was a little bit gross, but also nice. You'll understand when your first mating time comes, and there's no need to rush that.

I had assumed she knew I was a human and not a termaid, since she had touched my cold skin and I wasn't wearing a fiber hide at all. The moon and sky fish were so bright, too—had she not seen my iridescent hair? My skin, mottled turquoise and purple? The gill slits where my neck met my shoulders? No, it was my teeth that gave me away. Her delicate little omnivore tongue cut itself on my fangs. She recoiled in pain and I in shame as my traitor body nearly burst into a prey song at the taste of a *thinking creature's* blood. My tail broke the surface and slapped the water. Aria barked and keened and leaped closer to the sand. I prepared to dart back into the deep, to flit away in part from the shame and confusion but also because elders had warned me terpeople were far deadlier than they look. What their clumsy limbs and blunt teeth couldn't do, fire and iron would do for them, and fire does not have mercy or shame.

But oh, little one, what a miracle, what a melody came then. Before I could escape she dashed back into the water, erupting in dry, honking laughter, her eyes and her mouth wide like a child's, yelling the same thing over and over. "Blah blah mermaid?" she said. "Mermaid blah blah! Blah mermaid blah!" That word struck me, because when she reached me again she seized my fluke and nuzzled her face into it, stroking the webbing and calling out, "Mermaid! Mermaid! Mermaid!" She didn't understand what an intimate place our flukes are, or how you should never touch them even in the mating time unless someone invites you, but in the chaos and newness I had altogether forgotten how to be offended. I seized one of her lower hands and brought it above the water. She shrieked and laughed even harder, and showed me how she could wiggle the stubby little fingers I found there. "Mermaid!" she said. "Blah blah mermaid!" She patted my tail and poked one of her fingers at me when she said it. I realized that was her word for what I was and I was shocked, because it had never occurred to me there could be a word for what I was besides *person*. Didn't she know she was the alien? I freed my fluke from her hands and stroked her face and hair, her shoulders and arms, singing the words I knew for her. Firefriend. Drywalker. Earthgripper. Oh, I'm sorry, darling, I know this is confusing, and some of these things aren't what was literally said—I'm translating as I go, you understand? And *termaid* wasn't a word yet, so I couldn't call her that!

We communicated as best we could. I listened to her body songs and sang what feelings I could into her flesh. She patted and slapped and pointed at things while rasping and honking and I began to understand words, like *woman* and *water* and *beautiful*, though that last one came as a shock. There was a reason I was alone for my mating time! I couldn't recall anyone ever finding me beautiful before.

The conversation wasn't what I would call scintillating, but we began to understand the basics and then found a place hidden from shore to mate. I'll spare us both the details there. No, little one, I know you have questions about how it "worked." Everyone has those questions. If you still want to know I'll tell you when you're older. For now all I will say is that we had a very nice evening together, and when we parted she pointed at the moon, mimicked its course across the sky, and counted on her fingers. Eventually I realized she wanted to see me again in three days! There were kelp forests and oyster colonies everywhere, and no hunters to share with, so I kissed her in agreement (carefully this time) and disappeared under the water.

I spent the time hunting and singing private ballads, too distracted to listen to the worldsong much at all. Your grandparents and aunts and uncles were so worried those few days! Aria laughed much later when I told her this, relating that when two women mate on the surface it is a tradition for them to disappear from social life for a time and live in a little mobile den called a "yoohaw." When I did pay attention to the worldsong, my friends in distant seas relayed messages of surprise, curiosity, delight, confusion, and disgust. More than a few asked, "How would that even work?" Some meant well, like you, and some asked just to be cruel. I decided not to tell anyone anything else for a while and to keep this bright new thing all to myself.

Aria, I learned later, was swimming even choppier waters. Terpeople have their own worldsong called the internet, but made of lightning instead of sound. She was even more curious about me than I was about her, since I had understood that people like her existed at all. Apparently most terpeople think we're a lie someone made up to trick them as children. They're materialists that way. If something can't be touched and measured, weighed and appraised, then it is what they call "unreal." Her worldsong friends thought her mind had gone sour, the way ours sometimes do when we spend too long alone, or they told her she was a liar. If they did believe in us, they told her I was dangerous, that I was not a person but a kind of animal who lured terpeople to drown with songs and ate them. She didn't tell her pod at all, not because she knew they would not believe her (though they wouldn't have), but because her previous change had already angered and confused them so much. And two termaids mating was already such a taboo even when neither of them had changed that she suspected finding out I was also a female would cause them to attack her. Imagine that: biting and clawing your own offspring like a mindless, hungry guppy!

One soul did believe her. There is a kind of den called a café, where terpeople go to fill their mouths with hot, flavored water. It's called drinking, and I don't think I can explain why they do it until you feel what the surface is like yourself. The café near Aria's den was called the Beans You Couldn't Roast, and it was owned—owning is a thing where terpeople think of a patch of land or a dead object as part of their body—by a woman named Katrin. Katrin was a friend of Aria's, and one of the only adults in her community who neither rejected her when she changed nor accepted her in an embarrassing, conspicuous way. When Aria confided in her, she kept the secret that I was not a terperson like them, but Katrin was cunning and wise. She knew enough of our songs, and enough about Aria, to fill in the gaps, and told Aria so when they were alone. What's more, Katrin told Aria that she was a witch, which is a very complicated terperson word for a kind of person whose voice, flesh, and craft change things in ways terpeople mostly think of as unreal. A witch is also, I learned later, a kind of person whose help is never given freely or in straight lines.

She offered her help to Aria, and Aria accepted. The night we were to meet again they convened at Katrin's café. Katrin wove flames with songs. She invoked the names in the sky and the names of deep things best avoided. She marked Aria's throat and legs with blue and red ink, and Aria began to change for the second time in her life. When next she submerged herself in water, Katrin told Aria, her teeth would sharpen, her skin would smooth and thicken, gills would blossom on her throat, and, most important, her legs would fuse and stretch into a tail with a fluke at the end. There was, however, a catch: She would understand our songs perfectly, but she would have no voice of her own. What's more, if a year passed and I did not permanently pair bond with her, Aria would turn into smoke and mist, crabs and frogs, seafoam and flinders of driftwood as the sun rose on the 366th day. Katrin did not warn her that we don't sit still like terpeople do, that the idea of anything being permanent, especially love, is usually as strange and impossible for us as breathing water is for them. There were a great many things Katrin did not tell her. If I could have been there I would have warned Aria that the risks were too great, the conditions hardly even possible, my humble love and non-existent beauty not at all worth the trouble. But I think even with those warnings Aria still would have gone through with it.

Life on the surface is so bitter and cruel that sometimes terpeople hear a dying song inside themselves. It is especially common when the close cooperative ties they rely on crumble or, worse, turn into sources of pain and danger. Aria's life had been difficult, and too many people she relied on had been vicious to her for too long. The death song had been playing in her heart from such an early age that she was hardly aware of it anymore, though it was aware of her. She told me later that she hadn't planned to die the night we met, though she had been thinking of it in the abstract. The death song had blunted her will to live so thoroughly that she didn't blink at the witch's stipulation.

I returned to the beach to find her waiting. The waters of heaven churned dark, and their flashing lights and claps of thunder made me feel small and nervous, like when I was your age, clutching my father's arm to keep sudden currents from throwing me into the wide dark—so afraid, but so excited and so in love that I couldn't imagine running away. She stood there with her feet buried in the sand, her simple, loose fiber hide flapping and tugging in the air currents. Seeing her again, seeing that she had come back, seeing how much stranger but somehow less silly she looked with dry hair and dry clothes, it all sent me somewhere else entirely. Being in love is a kind of madness, little one. People will try to tell you to be sensible with love, to be practical and rational, but those people are fools.

Love is the opposite of thinking. It surged when her eyes met mine, and it screamed at her smile. It raged through my flesh and buzzed inside my skull so hard I was left helpless, my eyes drifting everywhere but her face in a search for some calm center. My gills flexed and my breath hitched, neither sure which should breathe or whether to at all. She laughed and pranced down the beach on those long, delicate, slender legs, precisely the opposite of the brave, sad girl I'd met before. This new note in her song only drove my mind further away, and so I barely noticed when her feet splashed in the water and her skin turned gold with stripes of crimson and shed its downy fur. She peeled her false hide away and, laughing, threw it toward the sky, and even though I had seen it once before, the sight of her body overawed me. Streaks of yellow and brown slithered up her formerly black hair. Talons grew from her fingers, her nose flattened, and her eyes grew large, and yellow, and her odd round pupils flexed into slits. When she kissed me I felt fangs clicking against my own, but it wasn't until her new tail twisted around mine, until she raked her fluke down my back, that I finally understood what was happening.

"Please explain!" I sang. I was too shocked to try to speak in dry words, even if I'd known the right ones, but her eyes still flicked to mine in recognition. She opened her mouth and shook with silent laughter. Her flesh sang of love and excitement, and of desire for me, but flesh songs can only say so much. I pushed her away, but gently and not so far that we had to stop touching. Her face glowed with mischief and delight. "You understand me?" I sang.

She nodded. She laughed, and we kissed again. A spear of light danced down from the sky far out to sea, and the shock of its impact washed over us. Water began to fall from the sky, so chaotic and harsh I lost sight of the beach and the witch who had been standing there. We clasped hands and sank down and out, away from the churn of the border between our worlds and into the pleasant, cool darkness of mine.

The next few days were a blur, and what I remember of them would not be appropriate for little ears. We eventually came to our senses and got hungry. At first, I thought her transformation was just a thing terpeople do sometimes, that maybe I could change, too, somehow, and the difference between us didn't have anything to do with how we were born but was just a sort of choice we each made, unconsciously, every day. Every time I tried asking about her new body, she either shrugged playfully or made odd little scratches on whatever rock was to hand, which I gathered was a kind of silent, visual language terpeople use since they can't hear flesh songs. It was all nonsense to me then, and mostly still is now. I tried hunting with her, but she was hopelessly slow and clumsy, so I left her with a friendly octopus in the kelp forest near where we met and set out on my own. When I returned with a brace of mackerel, I found her huddled over a flat stone with a long, thin piece of driftwood in her hands. She'd ground it down smooth and straight, and with an utterly alien focus in her knotted brow she was lashing a sharp piece of coral to the end with a strip of kelp. The pride in her eyes was contagious, but I was still ashamed. No, don't make fun of her! And promise you won't bring this up when you meet her, all right? She didn't know, and she thought she was giving me a new thing.

I explained that we know what a spear is. I told her we have them, and we make them when we need them, but that they are only for the very old, little ones like you, and those who are infirm. Her face folded, and her body vibrated with confusion and frustration, and it occurred to me that she might feel her own clumsiness as a kind of infirmity. Maybe that was true! I had never heard of something like this happening! I told her she hadn't done anything wrong, and that long ago many more of us used spears and even nets, but that fish had been disappearing for reasons we didn't understand and we'd learned that if we made hunting too easy we would fall to the temptation to take more than we needed and then there would be no more fish for anyone. I was young and strong enough to hunt for both of us until she acclimated, I sang, so wouldn't it be better to train until she could hunt with me like an adult? Guilt radiated from her, and was, strangely, joined by frustration when I reassured her she hadn't known the meaning of what she'd done.

She did train all the same, at hunting and every new thing I brought to her. We saved our strength riding the great currents with her as navigator. The smell of sharks, orca, and sea lions became known to her, as well as which dolphins were trustworthy and which were scoundrels. Her inner ear attuned to the worldsong and she came to know my friends, your other aunties and uncles, and your grandparents, and they came to know her as much as was possible. She couldn't sing back to them, but I relayed how her body sang in answer to their questions, her facial expressions, and of course she could communicate yes and no. The questions they asked were much like the questions you have asked and the ones I know you want to, and let me say I'm very proud of you for interrupting so little. Did terpeople really have warm blood and make milk like dolphins and whales? Yes. Wasn't it uncomfortable to be so hot inside one's body all the time? Shrug. Was it true terpeople gave birth to live babies instead of laying eggs? Yes. Had she done it yet, and if so, wasn't it horribly painful wobbling around with a whole clutch of babies in her stomach? She pointed to her stomach and shook her head. What did her swim bladder feel like, if she'd spent her whole life only moving back and forth and never up or down? Silent laughter. Was it true she could talk to fire and ask it for favors? Confusion.

What I didn't know then was that she listened to our world-song constantly and attuned herself to choirs I never would have thought to seek out—radicals who believed terpeople were the cause of the dwindling numbers of ocean life and of the horrible growling that had all but destroyed the whales' worldsong and even of the increasingly common poisoned waters, which even the strongest and healthiest of us couldn't breathe without falling ill. When I finally learned of these people and listened to them with her, I was disgusted beyond belief. They wanted to kill terpeople, to coax the giant things of the deep from their blessed slumber to rise and pull their floating iron houses apart like oyster shells. They wanted to dart into the wreckage and rip terpeople bodies apart, not for food or in self-defense, but on principle. Some, surely driven mad by isolation and too many voyages to the lightless depths, sang with hissing pleasure that they would eat terpeople meat and suck the marrow from terpeople bones. I tried reassuring her that if news that she had once been a termaid spread to them and they tried to harm her, I would defend her with all my strength. But then I realized I could hear the same timbre of loathing rolling off her own body when I broached the subject.

She *hated* terpeople. She nodded in agreement when distant, bloodthirsty voices cried that terpeople had ruined the world as surely as any disease. I tried to distract her with my love, with games and poetry, with as many of the good things in our life as our bodies could stand, but that awful darkness at her center never went away. Her death song, it seemed, had changed with her, rising in volume and pitch until it stabbed out at everything that reminded her of the self who had wanted to die or the people who had driven her to that point. Something had to be done to quiet it, but it had already been eight turns of the moon, and clearly my love wasn't enough. The only way out was through. So we made knives from whalebone and hunted one of the hated iron shells the radicals sang of, the kind my elders had warned I must never approach. Their vast nets sprawled lazily in the water, scooping up more prey than any person could eat in a year. What was worse was that everything they caught, except tuna, was left suffocated and broken in a choking, carrion tail behind them. A young dolphin screamed for help from the net. I understood, suddenly, the hatred of the radicals, and how a people capable of atrocity on such a scale could have left wounds in Aria's soul so deep her death song might never go away entirely. All I wanted was to flee the horror before me, but Aria boiled with rage. I knew that if I left she would not come with me, and that if she were left alone there she would think of nothing but to kill. This could not happen. I couldn't love her if she broke the blood taboo, and I had so much more love still to share. My heart and my stomach shivered in revulsion and fear but I seized my knife and lunged forward, rending the nets and sawing through their strands until my fingers bled and my muscles begged for rest. Aria joined me. Even through the flares of pain in my own flesh, the screaming of the young dolphin, and the unnatural susurrus of so many animals packed so horribly close, I could hear in her flesh that the death song was changing again, eddying and dissolving like a choking cloud of sand carried away on the tide. All that was left was resolve. My knife broke. I tore at the net with my teeth, and time slipped away in a billow of mingled pain, relief, and blood.

My next memory is of her arm hooked in mine and the thick, sandy taste of coastal water. I heard the chatter of dolphins but couldn't understand them. A dozen sleek bodies swam between us and the surface, all arranged defensively around an unsteady young shadow. Consciousness slipped away again. I awoke, for the first time in my life, completely out of the water. I was on my back in dry sand, a long furrow between my tail and the gentle waves where she had dragged me. The dark sky was beautifully, horrifyingly vast. Its lights were brighter than I had thought possible. She had a white clamshell with crossed red lines open beside me, and it was full of little sharp pieces of metal and fibers woven into strips and eggs that rattled in her shaking hands. Water ran down her cheeks and, though voiceless, I knew she was crying from the rapid, clipped gasping of her breath. I wanted to tell her not to waste water, that she must preserve it and drag herself back to the sea before she was too dry to move. I wanted to stroke her cheek and tell her how proud I was that she had filled the hollow in her spirit with a new song. My voice was a rasp, and no matter how hard I tried I barely had the strength to move my fingers.

A seal sat on a nearby rock, its eyes keener than any seal's should be. Aria's shaking talons fumbled with a strip of cloth. I closed my eyes, and when I opened them again there was a termaid looming over us with reddish-gold hair and eyes like glaciers. She was nude except for a sealskin tied around her waist. Aria grunted and gasped at her, begging as best she could, and through the heaviness and pain I found, to my surprise, that the woman nodded in understanding. She squatted, pressed a hand over my heart, clicked her tongue as if receiving unwelcome news, and began singing our language as well as can be done with a terperson body out of the water.

"I am Katrin," she sang. "A friend of Aria's. It is thanks to me that you have spent this time together." She pursed her lips and let her eyes drift over my body. "Though perhaps thanks are not appropriate. One of your fingers is gone. Two more are damaged beyond saving. Your fluke is shredded badly; if it heals, you will never swim strongly again. Your gills are damaged, and they are bleeding into your lungs. These things would not have happened to you if not for my intervention, and so I owe you a boon. You can't speak, I think, but your thoughts are known to me. Show me what you desire, and I will see that it comes to pass."

To my surprise, though of course I wanted to survive, I thought: *Aria has no pod of her own, and no voice to find one. She can't survive as she is without me. Give her a voice.*

"I'm sorry," Katrin sang. "There is no undoing that spell. Her voice was collateral, and her future is the final price. The former cannot return until she has paid the latter."

My selflessness could only last so long, and the longer I was conscious the more real and terrible the pain of my injuries felt. *I want my injuries to heal*, I thought. *I want the pain to stop. I don't want to die.*

"This is within my power," Katrin sang. She produced a necklace laced through dozens of shark and alligator teeth, lifted my head, and placed it around my neck. Her lips moved in a silent recitation and the necklace radiated the same pleasant warmth as Aria's body had before it transformed. The pain remained, and the weakness, but I found I could breathe again. "Full healing will take time, but you will live, and sooner rather than later, the only tokens of this adventure will be scars."

I thanked her weakly. Aria buried her face in her hands and her shoulders shook, but when she looked at me again I saw she was smiling. Katrin untied the skin from her waist and threw it over her shoulders, then turned as if to leave. She looked at Aria over her shoulder and spoke a soft reminder.

"The year is nearer its end than its beginning," she sang. "Remember the price. Try not to curse me when the time comes to pay."

Aria's momentary relief turned ashen. She nodded. Katrin turned her back to us and took a few steps down the beach. Anger rose up to fill the spaces pain left, and I sat up to face her.

Selkie! I thought at her. I had never thought *at* someone before, but speech was still beyond me. I now knew what she was, or at least one of the sides of her. Katrin stopped and turned. My voice sounded like the rasp of coral on flesh. *I am owed another boon.*

"I disagree," Katrin sang, but she didn't resume her escape. "But do go on."

First tell me what you mean when you say the final price is Aria's future.

She told me everything, as calmly as if she were talking about promising hunting waters or the schedule of the tides, how if I didn't mate with Aria for life, she would melt away into nothing.

Did you tell her we don't do that? Did you tell her such a thing is nearly unheard of? Did you tell her our love might not even last the entire year?

"No," Katrin said. This time she spoke in dry words, but still I understood her. "She didn't ask."

We were already lovers before you interfered, I thought. *She became a part of me that first night, and I a part of her. To deceive her, even by omission, was the same as deceiving me. I hadn't met you, and I didn't want anything from you.*

"That isn't how it works," she said, but all the same she strode back to us and sat beside me. "I'm older than anything your oral histories remember, child. I was old when the first Christians came to Norway and drove me out to sea, and I was old as well when the merpeople of the great northern waters were warlike and vicious enough to spawn legends of sea monsters. Your people's customs and values have nothing to do with me or my magic." She rubbed her temple with her thumb and screwed up her face in thought. "I do, however, appreciate the nerve behind this little gambit. Tell me what more you desire and I might grant it, for curiosity's sake if nothing else."

Make my love for her last forever, I thought. *Do marriage to us as humans do. Give me a lifetime with her. Would that break the spell?*

She blinked and frowned. "What you ask is possible," she said. "Theoretically. But interfering in this way would alter the nature of the spell. Weaken it. Make it unpredictable."

"If it is possible, then do it!" I sang. "Anything is better than losing her."

"Very well," Katrin said, after a long time. "But only because I'm curious, not because I am compelled. Do you consent, Aria?"

My lover nodded vigorously. Katrin had us hold our wrists out and bound them with cord made of dried animal skin. She extracted oaths of devotion and loyalty from us, and we gave them happily. We were made wives then, which is what terpeople call a kind of woman who has decided to love as long as she can stand or for the rest of her life, whichever comes first. We kissed in the moon's glow. When we eventually parted, Katrin was gone, and Aria was transformed for the second time since I met her.

How was she transformed? You'll have to see for yourself, little one! It's time to sleep now, and the sooner you wake, the sooner I can take you to meet her.

———

Nearing the surface is like swimming backward through time. Even with my daughters at my side, even with one of them only a few years away from breaking away to start her own life as a woman, I am suddenly and completely young. Our heads break the surface. My oldest plays it cool and standoffish, emerging only enough for her grumpy eyes to be seen, while my youngest squeaks and splashes her arms clumsily as she encounters, for the first time, a hard limit to her ability to swim *up*. Her eyes blink and twitch at the golden-purple sunset light, so I use one hand to shield hers and the other to protect my own. I scan the beach, trying to ignore the fear pulling at my heart that she might not be here, that last year's anniversary might have been the last. Then she is there, past breakers and foam, crabs, and gulls, at the edge of the line where palm trees meet sand. Aria has laid out a faded quilt, all oranges and browns. A marine biology textbook is open in her lap, and a thermos is buried in the sand. I lift my chin and call out. Her gauzy, light blue summer dress billows as she stands. The wind tugs the wide brim of her straw hat, which she tucks beneath her massive book to keep from flying away.

"Is that her?" my littlest says. She twines herself around my arm and sucks her lips in. "What's wrong with her skin?"

"That's not skin, stupid," my eldest says.

I smack her between the shoulders with the flat of my tail and spare her a look, then smile at her sister. "Your sister is rude but correct. Observe, little one."

Aria calls back, laughing, as she jogs for the water. Little sprays of sand fly after her feet. She gathers her skirt in her fists and flings her dress off and into the wind. The tawny skin of her face, chest, shoulders, and neck gives way to sleek gold and crimson scales everywhere else, and as she gets closer I remember her fingers end in talons like mine. Interesting that it's still a shock after all these years, but maybe telling the story to the littlest made all the years between disappear for a little while. She knifes into the water with hardly a splash. My littlest squeals and claps and points as Aria's dress flutters away into what she can only understand now as nothingness. Next she sees her first birds in flight, and then a terperson flying machine in the distance, and her little eyes are so full with wonder that Aria's reappearance mere feet from us is enough to send her into hysterics. Aria's eyes, with her old golden terperson irises bisected by slitted pupils, crinkle in delight, her halfway nose wrinkles, and those lips I couldn't help but kiss spread to show sharp, round teeth and a black tongue.

"Hey, Auntie," my eldest says, in a voice more cheerful than I've heard in months.

"Hiya, kiddo," Aria says, sweeping my eldest in a crushing hug. "I've missed you so much. I wanna hear all about the year's reef restoration once we're out to sea, okay?"

My eldest nods. My littlest, once more in possession of her senses, giggles and splashes over with neither hesitation nor shame. Aria's face shines with wonder. She sweeps my littlest into a spinning embrace and then lifts her over her head and admires her in the sunlight.

"I've heard so much about you, Auntie!" my littlest says. "Is it all true?"

Aria's eyes drift mischievously to mine and I think of how long it's been since I held her hand, the abyssal depth of time since last we kissed. Her eyes promise that if we're out of practice we'll soon get up to speed. If my blood were warm I would blush. Aria laughs and brings my littlest daughter back into the water with a raucous splash.

JUST A LITTLE BITE

Roselle Lim

Inspired by "Hansel and Gretel"

Muskoka's supposed to be a summertime thing. My fingertips danced across my phone's surface, adding another bubble to the silent conversation with my brother as we remained trapped in the car's back seat.

In the summer and early fall, Muskoka was a crowded escape from the city for rich Torontonians. Giant McMansions lined the Georgian Bay shoreline as private piers and overpriced gaudy boats littered the water.

In the dead of winter, though, it was a vacant tundra. No one wanted to be here, especially us. If you were stupid enough to be caught outside, you could pick your poison: burial by blizzard or death from hypothermia. Hell was cold, no matter what anyone said.

My brother, Hank, breathed on his window and traced an affirmative response in the condensation. Long ink-black hair concealed golden-brown eyes. Before I could laugh at his drawing, he raised his index finger to his thin lips.

Dad gripped the heated steering wheel, knuckles white from navigating the eight inches of darkened snow sludge on the road. The gritty sound of tires chewing up salt along with the occasional crash of gray chunks of ice that had fallen from wheel wells of past vehicles formed a fitting soundtrack to the darkening world outside.

Sandra, pronounced "Sawn-dra," ran bright-pink manicured claws through her big, brassy blond hair. The blasting heater vents forced a cloying billow of aerosol hairspray mixed with Calvin Klein's Obsession into the back seat. "You'll love the chalet, kids. No reception at the lake, though; you'll have to make do without. I know that will be especially hard for you, Gigi."

I hated how my name sounded from her lips: "Shi-shi." No trace of the *G*s, no matter how often I corrected her. She didn't even have the excuse of being French—she was as French as the dried-out bottle of yellow mustard in our fridge. Sandra had married Dad's money two years ago. Mom was barely in the ground before *she* arrived. His life had revolved around Mom; now it revolved around Sandra. Everything else was either an obstacle or—at best—a nuisance. "Happy wife, happy life," he repeated to death.

He was around for *her*, but not for us. They'd been arguing recently and not around Hank and me. All we got were hushed, hissing whispers about money. She wanted more for her ridiculous wellness beauty business and Dad was running out of it. Not our problem—they could hash out that crap themselves.

Hank brushed his hair from his forehead and leaned against the window. Amid the curtain of blowing snow and powder-ladened pine trees, the purplish-pink sky dimmed into darkness. The landscape was a series of inky moving shadows as my father plowed on, turning onto yet another country road. We had left the highway hours ago, civilization replaced by endless farmer's fields and patches of dense dark forest. Paved roads were only a rumor.

A dull whitish-red glow emerged from within the blowing snow, growing brighter as we passed a brightly lit modern cedar-and-stone-facade restaurant and its packed parking lot. It looked like a steakhouse that had been plucked out of downtown Toronto. Unlike the exclusive farm-to-table places Sandra gushed over, there were no other buildings around, nothing to contribute to its self-sufficiency. Instead, isolated and alone, it disappeared back into the endless darkness.

"What was that we passed?" Hank asked.

My brother broke his silence only with deliberation. He stopped talking to our father a month after Sandra came into our lives. Even before that, they hadn't been on good terms.

"Oh, that's Appetite. I've eaten there on several occasions. It's very exclusive." Sandra raised her voice to rise above the sputtering vents. "You need to be in the right social circles. Reservations are very hard to come by. Your father hasn't gone yet, but I hope to take him soon."

They should have left us at home. I hate her so much. She probably gets sick pleasure out of constantly dangling stuff in front of us, only to yank it away, Hank texted me.

His fingers continued to tap but nothing else arrived. The reception bars had disappeared. We were cut off.

In the last two weeks of winter break, instead of being with our friends, we were out in the middle of nowhere for more of Sandra's mandatory family fun.

"Pack your bags," she had said. "It's a once-in-a-lifetime experience. It's about time to get you kids out of the house."

The way her mouth wrapped around the last word created edges around each syllable.

I shoved my phone into my pocket and crossed my arms. No way to block out the world and its unpleasantness. Every second spent with her and Dad was torture. I blew out my lips and wedged myself tight against the door.

Hank reached across and held my hand. After Mom died, his strong grip was what kept me from sinking into my despair. And when he was paralyzed by panic attacks, he clung to me. Us against the world.

After a while, I began to doze until Sandra's sharp voice startled me awake.

"David, stop the car!" Sandra braced herself against the dashboard. "My diamond earring! I dropped it."

Dad braked to a rocky stop, sliding toward the trees and jarring Hank and me in the back seat. "Do you need help finding it, dear?"

She let out a dramatic sigh. "Yes. It must have rolled out under the mats." Sandra tucked her hair behind her left ear, exposing the missing stud. Her right lobe glittered with a two-carat round diamond mounted in platinum.

They were Mom's.

Dad had given them to Sandra on their first anniversary. Seeing her wearing them had made me ill. But I told myself it was just jewelry. It wasn't Mom. My mother was gone: nothing could bring her back. All that remained was her wealth— bequeathed to Hank and me—with Dad as the conservator. These forced family events were Sandra's clumsy attempts to ingratiate herself with us.

"Hank, Gigi, get out. Your dad and I need to check in the

back seat." Sandra disabled the child safety lock and shooed us to move.

My brother shrugged and stepped outside. After four hours in the car, it did feel good to stretch our legs.

I leaned my back against the red Land Rover and hugged myself. Hank walked around the car and joined me. My nostrils constricted from the freezing temperature. "They better find it before we turn into White Walkers."

Dad crawled into the back seat to check the mat under my spot while Sandra rummaged around the driver's side. They were taking their sweet time.

Hank wrapped his arm around my shoulders and drew me close. We huddled together, shivering. Around us, the blizzard intensified, coating the tips of our lashes in white. Gusts of icy wind sliced through our down-filled jackets.

Sandra hopped into the driver's seat and closed the door. Dad tapped his heels together, knocking off some excess snow, and climbed into the front seat.

About time: my toes were beginning to tingle.

I reached for the handle. Locked.

The SUV lurched forward, making a slow U-turn, as I banged on the window.

"Not funny," I said. "Let us in!"

Hank tried the other handles as snow crunched under the sluggish tires. We banged our uncovered hands against the tempered glass—the smear of our palm prints fading with each gust.

I punched the side door and yelled in frustration, as Hank kicked the tailgate, leaving a couple of dents.

Sandra braked as we faced one another. Behind the

tinted glass she grinned. She was toying with us. She blew a kiss, stomped the gas, and sped away. Her vanity plate—BADBTCH—swallowed by the storm.

This had to be some stupid prank—the sick ones that were supposed to remind us about gratitude or build character. Dad would tell her to come back for us. We were his kids. After a few minutes, they'd be back, and we'd have learned our lesson.

Seconds passed. Then minutes.

The snow piled deeper, filling in the tire tracks.

How could they? How could *he*?

I crumpled to the ground, reaching for handfuls of snow to squeeze. My bare hands, knuckles red from the cold and the tension, formed two fist-sized snowballs. That was how anger worked: you gather it to you until it becomes a formidable, tangible object.

The same man who taught me to ride a bike, and cheered when I pedaled away as Mom laughed, had so easily abandoned his children to the elements.

Apparently, his promise to Mom on her deathbed—that he'd take care of us and love us as she had—meant nothing. Mere lip service.

He chose Sandra over us, over his own flesh and blood.

Liar.

Deceiver.

"Murderers!" I screamed, lungs heaving, my words swirling as a vapor cloud. "We're going to die."

"No, we're not," Hank replied, his voice hard. He tugged on his hood and tightened the cords. "We'll get them back."

"How?"

The blizzard raged, biting into my bones underneath the layers of fabric.

Hank put on his gloves and dragged me forward. With his cell phone as our only light, I linked my arm with his and started down the road, following the tree line.

Take one step.

"We better get to that restaurant," I said amid the howling wind. "We won't last out here otherwise."

Take another step.

Keep going even when you couldn't feel your limbs and every exposed cell was raw.

Survive.

The dead couldn't exact revenge.

—◦—

Hours later, our skin stung like a sunburn. Icicles dripped from our noses. A suffocating numbness gripped our minds and bodies. Sandra was lucky—we hadn't lost any fingers or toes. I'd have broken each one of hers in return. An eye for an eye, a finger for a finger. *Snap, snap, snap.*

Appetite Steakhouse's polished metal serif letters finally came into view. From a distance, the floodlights had been the most visible—glowing beacons in the shadows. They watched over a parking lot that was still full: a try-hard congregation of midlife crises—Audi, Benz, Bentley, Jag, Tesla—blanketed under two inches of snow. Given her enthusiasm, I had half expected to see Sandra's SUV.

Hank yanked open the heavy front doors and pushed me in.

I stumbled forward. No physical energy left to do a good stomping. Wet snow piled around my boots. Sensation started to return and, with it, a throbbing rawness.

We waited within a small circular wood-paneled room. I pulled off my gloves and touched the wall, reveling in its slightly rough texture. It was a thin layer of timber wallpaper seared with illustrations of meat cuts. If we hadn't been left to die, I might have appreciated the artistry.

Hank leaned over the podium to peek into the dining room. "Full." His phone turned off. "It's dead." He tucked it into his back pocket. "Yours?"

"Still no reception." I powered mine off to conserve what little power remained.

A woman in a figure-hugging black dress typical of any gastropub or high-end restaurant hostess approached the empty podium. Conventionally attractive, her electric steel-gray hair, pulled into a tight high bun, contrasted with her heavy black eyeliner and deep currant lip stain. She wore the appearance of youth; a slight loss of facial symmetry betrayed her true age.

She appraised us before turning her attention to her dark red acrylic nails. "I take it you don't have reservations."

Hank gave me a sharp look.

I leaned over the lip of the podium to read her engraved name tag.

"Dinah," I asked, looking up with my best smile, "do you have a charger or phone we can use to call a taxi?"

"This establishment is very, very exclusive. We don't allow phones in here and therefore, no chargers. As for local taxis, they are already done for the evening and rideshare drivers won't be out in this weather." She clucked her tongue. "Well, we can't just leave you two out in the cold. Poor little things. Let me talk to Chef and see if we can figure something out."

Her stilettos struck the slate tiles as she strode to the kitchen.

"I don't like the idea of bumming a ride with any of these people." Hank scanned the dining room again. "They're in no hurry. Getting their money's worth."

"Agreed. We just survived one near-death experience. I'm not about to step into some stranger's car and give them the opportunity to finish the job."

Get through tonight; find a way home tomorrow. Focus on the next action. If it took begging to sleep in the kitchen, so be it. And while I slept, I would dream about strangling them with my bare hands, outside, in the forest, where no one would hear them scream. I'd squeeze until Sandra's mascara ran down her cheeks and those devious eyes lost their spark. But I would save something far worse for my father.

Without Mom around to protect us or to force him to love us, there was nothing to check his urges. Thinking back, he only showed kindness when she was around. Mom was there when I rode my bike. He never tried to teach me on his own. It was all performative—an act for her—and when the audience left, the act stopped.

As we waited, I examined the diners. Suits. An occasional gown. Middle-aged and white. Older men with Rolexes and patent leather shoes; women with too much makeup and too much jewelry. Definitely Sandra's crowd.

Stretched chocolate-dyed leather upholstered every seat and booth. A large modern gas fireplace—the kind with a river stone bed and crystals—blazed, controlled and sleek, radiating heat throughout the building. Classical piano music swelled and receded under noisy conversations. A massive glass wine vault with a smooth temperature panel dominated the far wall. Beside it, a separate refrigerated display case held various cuts of meat, each with printed labels indicating their age—nothing under four or over eighteen.

Sizzling plates of filet mignon, New York strip, and prime rib jiggled on cedar planks—their juices running down the wood and onto the buttercream linen tablecloths, leaving droplets and pools of darkened red.

Sandra proclaimed herself a vegan, and yet she ate here. Of course, blatant hypocrisy was now the least of her sins.

Sharpened serrated knives were provided at every place setting, though not many diners used them. The meat looked so tender that it could be cut with a fork. Chef must know what he was doing.

Mom was amazing in a kitchen, and as I helped her prepare dinner each night, I learned what made a good dish. She fueled my curiosity about cooking. When I closed my eyes, I could still hear her voice: *You can tell a perfect steak by touch and how it wobbles.*

Sandra and Dad always ordered in. Yet their ineptitude in the kitchen hadn't stopped Sandra from having a remodel done of her least-used room. "The place has great bones. We just need that to come through." Her interior design degree came courtesy of HGTV. Other than spending money that wasn't hers, what she really wanted was to eradicate every trace of Mom from our home.

I took up Mom's kitchen duties after her death, feeding Hank and myself, and keeping Mom's memory alive.

You can't erase memories, Sandra, no matter how much paint you apply.

—◦—

"Hey, check out the weather alert." Hank tipped his head toward the lone TV screen in the dining room.

I leaned over to read it. The roads were dicey. Even if we could call someone, no car would be coming out here to get us. The people in the dining room had their own vehicles and probably the best four-wheel drive that money could buy—judging from the cars in the parking lot.

Dinah emerged from the kitchen carrying two white uniforms over her arm. "Chef says you can stay until after service is done and he can give you a lift to the nearest city. He'll even throw in dinner—if you're willing to work in the kitchen. He's alone tonight."

"Mind if I talk this over with my brother?" I asked.

She shrugged. Dinah placed the uniforms over the lip of the podium before poring over the reservation book. "Reservations start at twelve hundred a plate. Not that I think it will factor into your decision-making."

"What do you think?" I asked him in a low whisper.

"Do we have a choice?" He leaned against the entrance door and began tracing a circular design on the glass. Frost and snow coated the edges. The whiteout conditions rendered even the cars in the parking lot, a few steps away, invisible.

Trapped in a deadly snow globe.

I pressed my palms against the glass, feeling the storm behind it. Given any other option, I'd have told Dinah to shove it. "Guess it's better than being out there."

Hank placed his arm around my shoulders and squeezed.

"All right, kids, are you done with your little meeting?" Dinah tapped her pen against the side of the podium. "Have you decided?"

I turned to her. "We'll do it."

"One more thing," Dinah said, holding up the two uniforms with one arm, and two hangers for our outerwear with the other. "Chef wants to know how old you both are. He wouldn't want someone too young to work in the kitchen."

"I'm seventeen. He's eighteen," I lied, taking my coat off and hanging it on the hanger. Better to pad our ages by a year to meet whatever labor requirements this woman was looking for. Besides, I'd never trust a stranger with our full names or ages.

Dinah took my coat and handed me my uniform. "Excellent. Same age as our summer interns."

Once Hank was changed, she straightened his jacket and sleeves, taking a short walk around him to assess the fit. Dinah then withdrew a black Sharpie from her pocket and wrote *18* on his chest and right shoulder. "Chef has a quirk with numbers. Don't be surprised if he addresses you by this."

She did the same for my jacket with a *17*. Her swirling writing was clear and feminine—matching the cursive in the reservation ledger.

"Here's two pieces of advice," she continued. "First, do as you're told. You won't be asked to perform anything you aren't capable of. Second, stay away from the walk-in freezer. The lock is temperamental and you can get easily trapped."

Easy enough. My job at the movie theater's concession stand was more complicated.

"Service ends in three hours. He'll serve dinner then. It'll go by quickly. You might even learn something." Dinah's exaggerated wink left a slight dark smudge under her left eye. "Follow me and I'll show you to the kitchen."

Something about her seemed off. Her whole demeanor had changed after we accepted the offer. A little too friendly. She reminded me of a fruit fly swimming in a chilled glass of lemonade on the hottest day of summer. Hank thinks I'm too suspicious of everyone.

I'd rather be known as a judgmental bitch than a stupid one.

Dinah kept checking over her shoulder and chattering. It was the kind of one-sided conversation from someone uncomfortable with silence. Hank would be miserable if he were left alone with this woman. I reached out and grasped his hand to steady his twitching fingers. Her inane conversation didn't bother me. I knew when to smile and nod. Great for teachers and authority figures like Dad.

"Go on in." Dinah stopped before the swinging doors of the kitchen with its round, brushed-metal-framed porthole windows. "Let Chef know we're running low on fives and fours; they always want the less-aged steaks."

Hank took a deep breath and exhaled when she walked off. The dark shadows under his eyes deepened and his skin was paler than it had been. We hadn't eaten for almost half a day, and the hike here was mostly him holding me up and carrying us forward.

"You feeling okay?" I rubbed his upper arm. "We can ask Chef for something to eat before we start work."

He placed his hand over mine. "I'm fine. It's only three hours." His weak smile barely reached his eyes. It was the same one he gave when he had to go in first with the dentist. A false sense of bravery meant to protect me.

Older by 384 days, yet he had done more for me than anyone else in this world.

"Hey, maybe you can learn to use the oven and add tater tots to your diet."

Hank cracked a genuine grin.

———◦———

The kitchen's footprint was half the size of the dining room. Steam escaped from boiling stockpots with high-pitched screams as fresh meat sizzled on the grill, flames licking glistening fat.

Every surface was as sterile as a hospital, rendering the space a hall of mirrors: my fractal reflection cast in grotesque angles.

In the center, a six-foot-five lumberjack with a hairnet over his auburn beard moved from station to station, swiftly switching between sautéing and searing, carving and chopping. His cleaver hammered a well-worn cutting board, severing a bleeding rack of ribs. Scarlet spray spritzing his crisp white apron.

A culinary Santa Claus in white and red.

The ribs were small—possibly lamb, veal, or some other local wild game. There was scarcely any meat adhering to the bone. Given how much they were charging here, the guests must have been paying for how fresh it was.

Chef glanced up for the briefest of moments. "Eighteen. Dishwashing station. Use the gloves, the water is hot."

Hank shot me a glance before slipping on rubber gloves and tackling the sink full of dishes. The water jet blasted each plate clean, white noise to drown out the sounds of the kitchen. The three hours would fly by for him. Hank always gravitated toward menial tasks—it freed his mind to wander to the last book he read or whatever video game he was trying to platinum.

"Seventeen," Chef said, without making eye contact. "Get me three number-twelve filets and four number-fifteen strips from the left freezer." He pointed to the stairwell at the room's far end.

The short stairs led to a darkened cellar with a single suspended lamp. Unlike the kitchen, this room was grimy. The shadows probably helped to conceal a multitude of sins. I didn't want to think about anything crawling or scuttering in the dark—tiny feet stamping along a dirty floor. A shudder shook my body.

I stood before two massive metal freezers. Like most every-thing else I'd seen at Appetite, the one on the left was polished and appeared expensive. The other was dented and rusty. It almost seemed like it had been installed before the restaurant was built. I grabbed the handle—freezing—and pulled.

The door creaked open. Using my left foot as a brace, I peered inside.

A young girl, no more than twelve, hung from a meat hook, her doe-brown eyes petrified in silent terror. Dark blood had pooled below her naked body. Cuts of muscle had been carved out of her like a horrific, incomplete jigsaw puzzle. It kind of resembled the meat they had on display upstairs.

I crammed half my fist into my mouth and screamed.

These sick bastards were eating children.

You give kids food—not chop them up to feed them to rich people.

What the hell.

No wonder Chef Lumberjack was so magnanimous about having my brother and me stay at the restaurant—we were the free meal.

Slamming the door shut, I dry heaved, my empty stomach convulsing in waves.

We had to get out of this place.

I couldn't go back up empty-handed, though. Chef would know what I'd seen. I opened the left freezer and grabbed the vacuum-sealed pieces of meat he had requested. He must have known this would happen and was screwing with me.

A small black beer fridge beside the door caught my atten-tion. I opened it, bracing for the worst. A row of fifteen small medical vials filled the top shelf with syringe kits below. Rocu-ronium bromide—paralyzing agent—according to the label.

They first immobilized their victims before they slaughtered them alive. Monsters.

I ripped a syringe kit open, loaded it with one vial, and tucked it into the long, slim compartment on my left thigh meant for a pen. You couldn't hide much in a pair of skinny jeans. I wished I had worn my cargo pants, but Sandra had insisted I wear something "fashionable."

If Chef or Dinah were planning anything, they'd wait until after service was done.

I emerged from the stairwell with a seminormal neutral expression. Chef acknowledged my return and pointed to an empty butcher block across from the gas grill. I unloaded the steaks and stepped back, patting the syringe in my pocket.

Chef rang a bell. Dinah swept in, double-checked the printed and posted tickets, then picked up three dishes to deliver to the dining room on a tray. There were five tickets left.

I walked over to Hank and tapped him on the side. He shut off the hose for a sec and met my eyes. I gave him a subtle signal that something was off.

Chef pulled a small round steak off the grill and placed it on a plate. The filet jiggled as he sliced off two pieces. "Come, taste."

Crushed Sichuan peppercorns, smoked paprika, and brown sugar dry rub highlighted the prominent grill marks. By all appearances, the meat looked like a cut of high-priced Wagyu as a light bleed pooled onto the plate.

If I didn't know what it was, I would have eaten it in a heartbeat.

Hank wandered over and picked up one of the two forks Chef had laid out. I placed my hand over his. "I'm sorry, Chef, we're vegan."

My brother let go of his fork.

"I insist," Chef Lumberjack said as he pushed me forward. "Eat."

His meaty hand rested at the base of my back.

I stiffened. Hank began to move before I could even speak. He knew something was wrong. We'd been in sticky situations before, and if talking ourselves out of it was an option, the duty was mine, but he was the one who'd punched his way through a group of drunken frat boys who once cornered me in a parking lot.

If there was anyone in the world who would trust me implicitly, it was him.

"Don't touch me," I hissed.

Hank clutched the fork and slammed the tines down on Chef Lumberjack's hand resting on the counter. I reached into my pocket and plunged the syringe into his thick neck, squirting every milliliter into his veins.

Chef flailed, knocking me and my brother to the floor, the syringe still stuck in his neck. He yanked it out and began stalking me.

Hank rushed to the washing station, pulled the hose, and trained it on my attacker—a scalding jet of water burned Chef's upper back but didn't slow him down. He grabbed me by the collar, hauling me in the air. The front fabric pulled tight against my throat, cutting my skin. I scratched at his meaty hands and tried to pull them off me. He tightened his grip and reached for a nearby cleaver.

Hank lunged for a knife on the counter and stabbed him in his shoulder blade. Chef dropped me on my ass and tried to pull the knife out, but Hank got him in a strategic spot—he couldn't dislodge it without being a Cirque du

Soleil contortionist. I scrambled backward until my back pressed against one of the lit grills.

The injection hadn't worked. There was no way around this brute. He was twice our size and had a lifetime of practice butchering cornered animals. We'd be slaughtered, vacuum-sealed, and turned into entrées—a sixteen and a seventeen—for some rich asshole.

"Hey, Hannibal!" I scrambled to my feet, waving my arms like a windmill.

Chef turned to me. His bright blue eyes sharpened into tiny pinpricks. He stepped forward and stumbled. His movements had slowed slightly. I should have stuck him with at least three needles.

I grabbed his arm and pulled him toward the grill as Hank bodychecked him from behind. He crashed face-first onto the hot surface as I cranked up the flames. The sizzle and searing of scorched flesh drowned his muffled screams as an acrid stench filled the kitchen. Chef twitched one last time, smoldering on the grill top.

The bastard was dead.

Hank stared at me, his chest heaving. "What the hell is going on?"

"There's a dead kid in the freezer downstairs. They're serving us like steaks. Those bastards in there are eating children."

"Can't say I'm surprised. Filthy carnivores." He kicked Chef's immobile body. "What about Dinah?"

"I don't know if she's in on it, but grab as many keys as you can from the coatroom. We are getting out of here."

"I'm not leaving you alone until we jab her." Hank armed himself with a cast-iron skillet and waited by the exit. He checked the hallway and leaned against the wall, eyes not leaving my face, knuckles white from his tight grip on the handle. I raced downstairs and took a handful of vials and syringes, loading one as I climbed the steps.

Dinah walked into the kitchen as I emerged from the cellar. "I have table five getting impatient on those three strips. I comped them a pricey Napa pinot noir. We have ten more orders coming in." She stopped. "What is that smell?"

Before she could react to the carnage, I jabbed her neck. Her dark painted lips formed an *O* as her fingertips found the syringe. Her green eyes darted from Chef's smoldering body to my face.

"Why did you warn me about the freezer?" I pulled out the needle.

Dinah slumped to her knees. Her chin bobbed as her pupils dilated. The drug was working faster on her.

I repeated my question.

"Can't have you . . . discovering body." Her pink tongue darted out to moisten her lips. "We were . . . low on . . . meat. Can't . . . keep up . . . with demand."

Her words were slurring, but the word *we* was all I needed to hear.

I turned to Hank. "Go. I'll meet you outside."

He nodded before disappearing down the corridor.

"Do they know what they're eating?" I demanded.

"They . . . know. Ask for specifics . . . eye color . . . hair. What . . . will . . . do . . . with . . . me?" Dinah's last words trickled in a soft gasp.

I patted her frozen cheek. "Nothing."

She stared at me, eyes glassy. Her shallow breathing was barely audible. The wolves in the dining room could figure out what to do with her after we left.

My brother left my coat on the podium. I took one last survey of the dining room. The wealthy cannibals were still in good spirits, oblivious to what had happened in the kitchen.

Headlights glowed beyond the frosted glass.

I swiped the reservation book on the way out before hopping into the black Porsche Cayenne Hank had chosen as our ride.

———◦———

The blizzard had abated. Hank slowly drove us back to the city as I tossed keys from those rich cannibals out the window every kilometer.

We stopped at the first McDonald's we saw and ate in the parking lot. Hank chewed on a Quarter Pounder as he browsed through the reservation book. "They even had special requests when they make a booking."

"And it's a franchise," I replied, dipping a fry into the packet of sweet-and-sour sauce. "Check out the back page."

Every continent had multiple cannibal restaurants. I'd love to shut every one of them down. We now knew how they worked—we'd be the perfect bait. They'd never see us coming.

"Wanna do it?" he asked while tapping the list of locations on the last page. "Could be fun."

"We have some unfinished business to deal with first. I'm sure Sandra and Dad miss us." I rolled my eyes.

I doubted it was a coincidence that they needed money and they thought they'd be inheriting ours.

My brother parked down the street from our home. I handed him a loaded syringe and patted the one in my pocket. We walked together up the circular driveway to the front steps of our Bridle Path home.

Sandra's Land Rover was parked out front.

The stupid getaway had always been a lie. Just an excuse to leave us for dead.

Well, now every one of their lies would determine how far we'd drive before dumping them out in the cold.

By the time the paralytic wore off, they would be hypothermic—as frozen as the kid in the basement, but intact—at least until the animals discovered them.

Perfect.

A STORY
ABOUT A GIRL

Rebecca Podos

Inspired by "The Robber Bridegroom"

Dani drops her rent-a-bike into a lilac bush and stares up at the Glowinskis' house—the Glowinskis' megamansion, actually—as her heartbeat slows to something like normal. The thick July air is steamy enough to curl the hair at the nape of her neck, and armies of bugs dash themselves against the solar lamps that line the driveway, coming to life in the twilight. Still, even as sweat trickles down the back of her sundress, she can't make herself move just yet.

This evening is a favor to her dad, and holy shit, will he owe her one.

Mr. Glowinski is her dad's boss's boss, and between his corner office on the tenth floor and Dad's cubicle on the first, they never should've crossed paths. Then the company barbecue happened. The men stood next to each other in the burger line, making small talk about their respective teens. Before long, they'd pulled up their kids' social medias over potato salad and declared between swigs of craft beer that the two just *had* to talk. Never mind that she and Aleksandr Glowinski have nothing in common besides their age, including their zip codes; Dad commutes an hour to work each day. Dani had to take the train from Danbury, then pay for a rent-a-bike at Greenwich station, with just enough cash leftover to buy a bubble tea along the way.

Mr. Glowinski doesn't know any of that. Probably he'd forgotten her dad's name by the time they set out the desserts.

Once she's caught her breath and run out of reasons to stall, she hitches her backpack up her clammy shoulders and trudges through the swarm, along a slate walkway, and onto the massive columned porch. The second after she rings the doorbell, she realizes she's still holding the bubble tea she'd unclipped from the bike's cupholder. It can't be good mansion manners to BYO plastic to-go cup from Yum Ice Cream when dropping in for a blind date. Mournfully, she sets it down beside one of the stone columns and out of sight. Maybe she'll get lucky and make it back before the ice melts. . . .

The front door swings open, and though she'd half expected a camera-ready butler to greet her, there stands Aleks: tactically disheveled copper hair, boat shoes, and close-lipped smirk, just as his pictures promised. "Danielle?" he asks, as though any number of girls could be standing on his porch right now, wilting in the heat. "You're shorter than I thought."

"Do you want a refund?"

He laughs once, then remembers his mansion manners, stepping aside to let her pass. Not far enough, since she's forced to squeeze by him and feel his breath flutter against her ponytail.

The moment she's standing in the overly air-conditioned vestibule, Dani skips away and spins to face him, her tennis shoes squeaking violently on the black marble floor. "Should I say hi to your parents? I don't want to be rude."

Aleks shakes his head, though his pale blue eyes stay trained on her, sweeping downward from her flushed face to the spaghetti straps of her orange cotton dress to her newly goosebumped bare legs. "They're in Saint Moritz for the week. They prefer the off-season."

"Oh."

Aleks turns to peer out into the darkening front yard. "Did you walk here or something?"

As if she's just come from the manor up the road. "I took a train. And a bike. I didn't really want my parents, like, parked in the driveway the whole time, but I don't think they would've let me come by myself if they knew how far out you lived."

"So you didn't tell them, huh?" A shallow dimple appears in each cheek. "Bad girl."

Her answering smile feels pretty weak. "Do your parents even know I'm here?"

Pressing a finger to his lips, Aleks winks.

Dani claws her own fingers around her backpack straps. "So . . . I was promised popcorn?" They've mostly been messaging through Snapchat (studiously unflirty on her end) since her dad gave her Aleks's info and *strongly* suggested she reach out. When Aleks sent a snap of the theater system in his game room, inviting her over for a movie and homemade jalapeño popcorn, she gave in and accepted. If her parents were never going to stop hinting and prodding, then better to go and be done with it, right?

"Sure. Let's go to the basement."

"The—"

"The game room, you know?"

"Yeah. Cool."

As they move farther into the house, she tries not to gawk like a tourist on her first day in the big city. Beyond the vestibule doors is the entrance hall, with its black marble flooring and snow-white walls and a grand staircase leading up and up to the third floor. Aleks opens a door just off the hall that she assumes leads to the basement, but she stops short when he does; inside is a closet-sized wine rack. He pulls out two bottles, then walks on without looking back, taking for granted that she'll follow.

They pass through a kitchen the size of a small restaurant, yet more black and white, plus pristine silver appliances without a grease splatter or crumb to be seen. Veering into a narrower hallway, she finds not a basement door but an actual fucking elevator. Grabbing the bottles by the necks, he elbows the button, and the doors—silver as polished as the double oven in the kitchen—slide open. Aleks steps inside and smirks out at her. "Coming down?"

Well, what choice does she have?

The game room is more like an arcade when she sees it. There's a black-topped air hockey table and a white-topped pool table, both inexplicably ornate. They pass a whole row of hulking, classic arcade games—at least there's *some* color in this house, though the screens are dark—before they reach the home theater on the far side of the room. The wall-mounted flat-screen is at least as wide as she is tall (which apparently isn't saying much) with a reclining leather sofa instead of separate chairs. Dani tucks herself against one arm, pulling her knees up to her chest and the hem of her dress to her calves.

She realizes once Aleks sits beside her—not on the opposite side, but dead smack in the middle of the couch—that there isn't any popcorn. Just two wineglasses ready on the coffee table.

"What are we watching?" she asks.

Prying a utility knife from the pocket of his pants, some kind of chinos/joggers hybrid, he flicks open a corkscrew. "I don't know, what are you in the mood for? Probably nothing bloody, right?"

"I actually love scary movies."

Aleks scans her again from spaghetti straps to tennis shoe tips, and she shivers; the AC must be turned down to sixty in the game room.

"Not like, slashers or torture porn," she babbles, though he didn't ask. "But you know, the classic stuff."

"Like what?" He leans forward to uncork a bottle with a bloodred label, one of his knees drifting over to touch her ankle. The cork slides out with practiced ease, and he pours her a glass.

"I love this one movie, what's it called?" It's hard to concentrate while trying not to spill the wine she begrudgingly accepts—there's barely a centimeter to spare below the rim. "Maybe you haven't seen it. It's about a girl living in a town in the shtetl in czarist Russia in the early eighteen hundreds. It's, you know, a monster movie."

"So tell me the plot, and I'll decide."

Aleks picks up the remote and flicks on the massive TV, scrolling lazily through a dozen streaming services, half listening at best, while Dani recites the story.

VOLOSHKY

The Pale of Settlement
1822

"The shadchan has found you a husband, zissele!" Aniela's papa announces just as she manages to corner a chicken for slaughter.

If she pretends not to have heard the news, perhaps they'll

both forget. She concentrates on the bird instead. Clutching it to her coat and murmuring soothingly, she strokes its bright comb as she carries it from their small pen to the tree stump in the center of the yard. Swiftly so the poor thing won't panic, Aniela lays the chicken out, sliding its head between the nails that rise from the stump, stretching its wiry neck taut.

But Papa won't be put off. Even as he lifts the chalaf, polished and sharpened to deliver merciful death, he presses on. "Such a brilliant match, too." He brings the knife down with practiced speed, slicing smoothly down to the wood. "The bridegroom's father is in the business of alcohol and very prosperous." Papa runs a fingernail across both sides of the blade and along the cutting edge, inspecting it for flaws as he does before and after each killing. "They have several taverns and a watermill, and own a fine house right in the center of Kovel."

A city an hour and a half west by horseback, if she recalls—she's seldom left her shtetl, but Papa sent for an opshprekherke from Kovel at great cost when Mama fell ill, for all the good it did.

Aniela hefts the bird by its feet. "Why would a rich man want me?" Papa runs a small grocery from which they make enough money to keep their own chickens, but her dowry is painfully humble. "And why not a girl from Kovel?"

"The shadchan must've told him of your beauty," Papa lies, eyes cast downward. Even he knows his daughter is no shayna punim. "Well? What do you say to such a match?"

Blood patters the half-melted snow between them.

"What should I say?"

"Tell me you're pleased, zissele."

She crosses the yard to hang the bird from their arbor. Before its body cools to match the raw March afternoon, Papa will remove the heart and liver and gizzards for cooking, the fat to be rendered for schmaltz. Aniela will plunge the bird into a basin of water, pluck the feathers, and salt the flesh. She'll never wield Papa's chalaf herself, though. Women aren't allowed. Not in Voloshky, nor anywhere, so far as she knows.

Nor do young women tell their fathers to shun a brilliant match with the son of a very prosperous merchant from Kovel, though it's on the tip of Aniela's tongue to say she doesn't want this man, that she will *never* want a man, that in her most dramatic and lonely moments, she thinks she would rather be sent to the butcher herself than to the chuppah.

"I am pleased," she replies.

—◦—

Aniela meets her bridegroom for the first time when the families gather to settle terms before the betrothal ceremony. He, his parents, and his sister dine at their house, as tradition dictates; she prepared the meal herself while Papa scrubbed the stump clean and swept around the chicken coop. Now, as they greet their guests on the front stoop, she shivers in her best gown, the same violet as the twilit spring sky above. The bridegroom makes a handsome figure in his fine coat and trousers and gloves, she supposes. She can admire his shape as she would a beautifully made statue in a cemetery.

Still, his touch leaves her chilled when he seizes her bare hand in his gloved one and brushes his lips across her knuckles. Maybe it's his smile, close-lipped and cool. Or perhaps it's his pale eyes, which glint in the lamplight while their parents decide upon the tnoyim to be written and signed at the betrothal, the dowry, the date of the ceremony, and the knas—the penalty should either of them back out of the arrangement. He meets her gaze only once, and it feels like falling into a frozen pond. She imagines her best gown growing sodden and heavy, dragging her down to the bottom.

They sit beside one another at dinner, and Aniela forces a smile while Papa raises a toast to the soon-to-be couple, to an answering chorus of "L'chaim!" The liquor burns like a lantern in her belly, and she drains half of her glass in one urgent swallow.

"Delicious, isn't it?" the bridegroom says—his first words to her.

"Is it yours?" she asks. "Your family's, I mean. My father says you have taverns and a mill."

"We lease the taverns," he corrects, "from one of the Polish lords. We ran a watermill on the edge of town, where the road meets the woods. You'd pass the path when traveling from Voloshky. It was used to grind grain for malt. But the river changed course upstream, and now it's shuttered, poor old thing." He laughs once—not kindly, but as though at some private joke—and presses his fingers to his lips. "You really must come and see it one night."

Something curious happens then.

While Papa and the bridegroom's parents have been busy plotting her future, his sister—who can't be more than a year or two younger despite her slight build—has stayed silent. Now she looks up from her untouched plate to lock eyes with Aniela from across the table. Hers are as dark as her brother's eyes are icy pale, the warm brown of tilled earth. She holds Aniela's gaze and, slowly and deliberately, shakes her head.

Aniela's face must give them away, because the bridegroom turns to catch his sister staring, and she shrinks like a child caught mid-mischief.

"Papa wouldn't allow it," Aniela demurs, drawing the bridegroom's gaze once more. She's pretty sure Papa would travel there on foot this very night for such an invitation. "Not before the wedding."

"Of course." His smile returns, just the slightest gleam of teeth in the corner of his rosy lips. "After, then. I'll take you there myself."

She shivers, and wonders why.

Her bridegroom is handsome. He is rich. He's been well-mannered. If not this match, there would soon be another; Aniela is nearly eighteen. She must marry someone, and what man *would* she find unobjectionable? She ought to be grateful, not suspicious of her own luck.

Soon enough the meal is done, though she hasn't managed to eat much. Then again, neither has the bridegroom—when she clears his plate after supper, he's hardly taken a bite.

—◦—

A summer of preparations passes too quickly, and then autumn. The first snow brings the week before the wedding, the Golden Week. Papa gives her Mama's shterntikhl, the headdress she wore to their own wedding, sewn with pearls and semiprecious stones. It's been waiting for her since birth; everything has been planned for her since birth.

The wedding dress, cream silk trimmed with lace, is retrieved from the tailor. Aniela stands before a mirror in her childhood bedroom dressed as a bride, headdress pinned, smothered in silk from neck to toes. As her friends and cousins and aunts cluck over her good fortune and happy future, she imagines herself on the day of the wedding, penned beneath the chuppah, her bridegroom aglow in the lamplight, gazing down at her as though she were a chicken destined for the tree stump.

Suddenly, she feels the truth in her bones: She cannot marry. Not now. Not him.

Even as she sends up a silent prayer—*Let there be a flood that spares lives and lands but washes away the road from Voloshky to Kovel forever*—she knows no miracle or disaster is coming to save her. Neither will her tears. The tnoyim have been signed, hands have been shaken, toasts drunk. Calling off the wedding without cause would cost Papa his good name and maybe even his business.

To be free, if only for another year or two until Voloshky has forgotten and forgiven this broken match, a *cause* is what she needs.

The day before the wedding, the dawn breaks cold and bright. Aniela greets Papa in their kitchen already wrapped in her traveling coat and scarf. "I'm going to visit Mama," she announces.

Papa raises one bushy eyebrow, salted with white. "You should've told me, zissele. I would've closed the store and come with you."

"I wanted to go alone and spend the day. I know you can't spare so many hours."

It's tradition to visit the graves of loved ones in the Golden Week, so what can Papa say? The cemetery where Mama's grave has stood for five long years is just far enough that he won't find it strange, her begging a horse from their neighbor to ride rather than walk alone in the cold.

Of course, she isn't going to the cemetery.

Instead she rides west, and as the pale sun shifts overhead and strains to warm her through her wool, Aniela makes plans of her own.

Nobody knows her in Kovel, and no one will think to look for her so soon before the wedding. She'll make her way to the market and ask questions, find the women always ready to spill secrets and scatter gossip like birdseed. Because there is something strange about her bridegroom, and about this match. Why *hadn't* one of the richest families in Kovel found a match in town? What drove them to Voloshky, to the doorstep of a grocer and his daughter, a girl with a modest dowry, square shoulders, no hips, and no mother? Papa might be blinded by their luck, if you can call it that, but her eyes are clear.

If there's nothing wrong with *him*, why should he need *her*?

She travels the wooded road between towns at a cautious but constant pace, nearing Kovel just as the sun peaks overhead. The towering pines begin to thin, and suddenly the road forks. One sign points up the road toward town, while another— *młyn*, it reads—points deeper into the forest. The path is carved with permanent wheel ruts, though the dead and frozen leaves that litter the ground signal its disuse.

We ran a watermill on the edge of town, where the road meets the woods. You'd pass the path when traveling from Voloshky.

You really must come and see it one night.

Aniela pulls the horse to a stop, remembering the look of fear in her bridegroom's sister's eyes, the shake of her head. She was warning Aniela off, but from what?

The bridegroom and his family will be busy with preparations and rituals in town, not haunting an abandoned watermill the day before the wedding. Most likely, there's nothing there at all . . . but can a quick look hurt? If anybody sees her and objects, she can say truthfully that she was invited. And if there *is* something, some whiff of bad business, anything she can use to stop her life from spinning out of her control . . .

She has to look, doesn't she? It's that, or turn back and face her fate.

Steeling her spine, Aniela tightens her hold on the reins and trots the horse onto the path.

Soon she comes across the riverbed, just a brackish trickle at the bottom. A few moments further, she reaches the mill. It's less ruined than she'd pictured from the state of the path, its great wooden water wheel motionless but solid; the stone mill building covered in places by creeping ivy, but unbroken; the glass pane in the small ground-floor window filthy but intact. And are those recent hoofprints in that patch of mud? Not fresh, exactly, as they're half-buried by snow, but someone must travel this way still. She turns the horse in a circle, hearing nothing except for the animal's breath and her own.

Until she does.

It's faint, as when the boughs of the spruce tree outside of her bedroom scrape against the roof in a storm. She eyes the path behind her. Perhaps it's best to ride on toward town. . . .

"Please, is someone there?"

The voice belongs to a girl, it seems, close by but muffled.

"H-hello?" Aniela whispers into the wintry air, then dares to call louder, "Hello?" and trots the snorting horse a few steps closer to the—

GREENWICH, CONNECTICUT
2022

Aleks lets out a single, serrated laugh.

Cocking her head, Dani asks, "What's funny?"

"Just girls." He's close enough that he doesn't need to lean to reach her, and brushes his cold fingers across the nape of her neck, through the escaped curls. "They never run when they should, do they? In scary stories, I mean."

This time, she fails completely to hide her shudder, but Aleks doesn't seem bothered. If anything, when she slips free of his touch and presses back against the couch arm hard enough to merge with it on a molecular level, his smirk widens. He doesn't even take the hint when she plucks her backpack up off the floor and *casually* tucks it between them.

"Well, Aniela knows some scary stories, too. Baba Yaga, the crone who lives in the middle of the forest in a house with chicken legs. And the północnica, women who die just before their weddings and wander the woods waiting to snatch travelers. And shedim, Jewish demons who're supposedly all around us all the time, invisible until they don't want to be. Like, this is the Pale of Settlement in the eighteen hundreds—you think they don't believe in monsters? But she came into the woods looking for a way to save herself, and she doesn't run away just because she's scared. She listens for a moment and realizes the pleas are coming from the mill building, that somebody is inside. And when she climbs down from her horse to peer through the grimy ground-floor window—"

"Idiot," Aleks declares.

"—she sees the bridegroom's sister, tied to the big axle between the gears."

Now his interest is piqued; Dani can tell by the new light in his flat blue eyes.

She continues, "The noises she heard were the girl, struggling hard enough against the ropes that bind her to turn the millstones just a little. Aniela circles the building and finds the door locked, but the iron key hangs from a peg beside it. Whoever put the girl inside clearly wasn't worried about somebody coming along to save her, only that she couldn't get out. She goes inside and frees the sister, taking care with her bloodied wrists, and gets a kiss of thanks—"

"That's hot." Aleks snickers.

"Can I finish the story, please? This is like, the big reveal."

He shrugs, then scoops her untouched wineglass off the coffee table and tips it down his own throat, eyes gleaming at her over the rim.

"She tells Aniela the truth about the bridegroom at last. 'My brother was born the year before me,' she says, 'with not one heartbeat, but two, and two sets of teeth from the very moment of his birth, one all but hidden behind the other. The midwife put him in my mother's arms and refused to come near again, but when my father sent for the opshprekherke, she knew him for what he was—a boy destined to become a strzyga.'"

Aleks fumbles the glass, wine sloshing out onto his chino-joggers and the sofa that might cost more than either of her parents' cars. "Shit, shit," he mumbles.

"Something wrong?" Dani asks sweetly.

"I— Where did you see this movie?" He's wiping his pants, clawing at them really, the tips of his ears burning pink.

"Oh, you know. Hulu, Netflix, Prime . . . somewhere. You've never heard of it?"

With a scowl, he turns off the TV. "This is boring. Let's play a game instead."

"Sorry, is this too scary for you?" There's a challenge in her words, buried beneath the honey of her tone.

He snorts and stretches out in his own puddle of wine, pretending to humor her, just as she knew he would.

Boys are funny like that.

Dani continues, "'He was born with two souls as well,' the sister explains. 'When he dies, one soul will pass into the next life, while the other lingers as a demon. Sleeping in some dark, grave-like place during the day, coming out at night to drink the blood and devour the innards of any human who crosses its path. In another home, he'd have been killed or driven out at a young age, left to the mercies of the world. Not in mine. My father wouldn't cast him out; not for love of his son but for love of himself. *His* reputation, *his* fortune, *his* legacy. He needs a son to manage these things, to run the taverns and maintain what my father has fought so hard to build, despite all obstacles. Mama could have no children after me, and I—I asked at a young age that I should never have to marry, in exchange for my own silence. But my father needs an heir, and so my brother needs . . .'

"'A wife,' Aniela guesses. She feels colder in the mill than she did in the woods, though there's a fire in the small woodstove in the corner, to keep the sister from freezing in her cage. 'Why *me*?'

"'Those born to become strzyga never live much past their youth. He was running out of time, and the shadchan could find few eligible girls in Kovel whose families were willing, despite his looks and his money. There are . . . rumors, you see. Not of his demonic nature, exactly—my family has been careful to keep the secret, at great cost—but of his human nature. He's already a monster, Aniela. He isn't kind. He isn't good. And there have been girls, poor girls.' The sister stares into the fire, dark eyes distant. 'A boy is all they need from my brother's wife. Then they'll leave her to her fate. A young woman from a fine family would bring too much attention, should she flee or go missing. A girl from Kovel might turn the city against us. But you . . .' Aniela doesn't need her to finish, of course. Nobody will cry for the daughter of a grocer from

Voloshky, just like nobody cries for most of the girls who go missing. Not Jewish girls in the Pale, not Black girls or trans girls or poor girls in America."

Aleks practically snarls, "Can we wrap this shit up already? I don't care about this bitch. I'm getting hungry, and I want to *play*."

"But I'm not done," Dani snaps, then takes a breath and smiles. "I mean, I'm *almost* done. But I'll skip ahead, okay? I'll finish quick. The sister explains that her father locked her in the mill at the start of the Golden Week, lest she try to warn Aniela off, as she'd done the last time they met. She begs Aniela to run. She has family in Łódź on her mother's side, she says, who will take Aniela in as well. But Aniela only kisses her again—goodbye, this time, and perhaps something more—then gives the sister her own traveling coat and rides back to Voloshky in the cold.

"The next day, her wedding day, Aniela is taken to the mikveh for the ritual bath, then seated and veiled. Her braids are loosened and her hair covered with a kerchief, to be replaced by Mama's shterntikhl once she's married. Accompanied by her aunts and cousins, she meets the bridegroom under the chuppah. He lifts her veil to see her face in the lamplight, and somehow, Aniela keeps a pleasant, joyful smile on her face. They share a drink from a wine goblet, the rabbi gives his blessings, and the bridegroom breaks a glass under his fine leather shoe. The crowd cries 'Mazel tov!' Just like that, she's married to a monster."

"That's so weak," Aleks dares to interrupt again.

But Dani really is nearing the end now, and charges ahead. "At the feast, after the badeken and the klezmorim and the guests have taken their turn to entertain, Aniela stands up and asks to take hers. With every pair of eyes trained on her, she tells a story. It's about a girl who goes riding in the woods the day before her wedding and comes across an abandoned watermill on the banks of a dried riverbed. She finds the sister of her beloved tied up inside the mill, wrists bloodied, and learns the truth: that her beloved-to-be is a strzyga, destined to return from death as a demon and devour her. Now, the guests don't know what's happening, but the bridegroom clearly does— still, even as he glares at her with eyes like murder, what can he do in front of their families and the whole of Voloshky?

"And then, fucking *then*—this is so badass, Aleks, I can't even—she reaches inside the bodice of her wedding gown and pulls out the rope she pocketed at the mill the day before, the one stained with the sister's blood, and just *flings* it down on the banquet table for everyone to see. So the people are standing to look now, muttering among themselves, starting to figure things out, when the bridegroom bolts up from his seat"—Dani leaps off the couch to demonstrate—"and comes roaring toward Aniela. But she's prepared for this. Reaching under the tablecloth, she grabs the chalaf she'd hidden that morning before the mikveh. Her papa's knife gleams in the lamplight as she gives a great swing, as swift and strong as any of Papa's, and knife meets neck before the bridegroom can bring her down. His body drops, and his head rolls to face the screaming guests, still frozen in its snarl of monstrous rage. Two sets of teeth are clearly bared to the crowd."

Aleks blinks up at her for a long moment, his face blank of any expression, before he seems to realize and forces a dull laugh. "This story makes no fucking sense. Why would she bother? What was the point of going home or getting married or monologuing? Nobody would do that in real life. If she actually knew what he was, she'd never go near him."

"You're wrong," Dani insists. "She needed everyone to see who he was for themselves. And even more than that, she needed everyone to see who *she* was. Afterward, there was fear in their eyes when they looked at Aniela, and she knew nobody would make her marry again. Nobody would want her. She was free."

"Whatever. So that's the end, right? We can stop talking? 'Cause I *really* want to play now . . ." He reaches up from the couch to drag her down, breaking into his first full grin, verging on a snarl.

She skips backward to the far side of the coffee table, as if this *is* a fun game. "Actually, there's a scene post-credits. A quick one. Aniela leaves town and goes to find the sister in Łódź, after all. They fall in love and make their way to America, pretending to be sisters and widows, then take in orphaned children. They teach their kids what they know about monsters, of course—how to recognize them, and how to fight them. Not just strzyga, but the północnica and shedim and— well, not Baba Yaga, she's kind of niche—but hags in general. Every monster their grandmothers warned them about in bedtime stories and more. The family secrets pass down from their children to their grandchildren, for generations. Aniela's great-great-grandson teaches his child. They teach their daughter, who teaches their son. Who taught me."

Though Aleks doesn't move perceptibly, he's heard her. She can tell by the squeak of leather as every muscle in his body tenses against the couch cushions. Sure enough, he growls, "What the fuck are you talking about?"

"You've never met my dad, obviously—I doubt yours remembers meeting him—but trust me when I say he's gonna be the smuggest human possible tonight. Like, shit, the *last* thing I wanted to do was go home and tell him he was right." Calmly, as though she's going for her keys to the car she didn't drive to

Greenwich (and risk a security recording of her license plate number in the area? No way) Dani swings her backpack around to unbuckle the flap. "Like, an obscenely rich boy invites a young girl over while his parents are in Saint Moritz but doesn't tell her they're away before she arrives? Yeah, loved those pictures they posted on Facebook yesterday of them kitesurfing in Lake Silvaplana." She slips a hand inside, knocking against her wallet and Hydro Flask, fishing deeper. "Who hasn't heard that story one million times? This all just seemed too predictable. But Dad kept pushing. He wouldn't shut up about you after your dad showed him your Instagram at the barbecue. You never smile with your mouth open—you know that—but he swore he saw two sets of teeth in one of your Throwback Thursday toddler pics. *I* didn't see it, not in the post, but I should've known better. Dad beheaded his first strzyga when he was fourteen, you know? He can spot one from a mile away. Me, I guess I need to get a little closer."

"Shut the fuck up, you weird little b—"

"And all those missing girls?" She cuts him off with pleasure. "The ones from lower-income families, who went to the public high school down the street from your private high school? Who showed up in the background of your snaps right before they were never seen again? I knew what you were before I came here, even before I saw—" Dani grins down at him now, a pantomime of his own awful smile, clicking her teeth together. "The truth is it doesn't really matter what you might turn into once you die. You're already a monster."

At last, she touches the familiar hilt, the always-cold steel as much a part of her as any other, and wraps her fingers around it.

Then she lets herself smile for real. "Why do you look so scared, Aleksandr? It's just a story."

ABOUT
THE AUTHORS

DAHLIA ADLER (she/her) is an editor of mathematics by day, a BuzzFeed Books blogger and the LGBTQ Reads overlord by night, and an author and anthologist at every spare moment in between. Her novels include Indie Next List pick *Cool for the Summer* and Junior Library Guild selection *Home Field Advantage*, and she's the editor of the anthologies *His Hideous Heart, That Way Madness Lies, At Midnight,* and, with Jennifer Iacopelli, the upcoming *Out of Our League*. Dahlia lives in New York with her family and an obscene number of books and can be found on Twitter and Instagram @MissDahlELama.

MELISSA ALBERT is the *New York Times* and indie bestselling author of the Hazel Wood series and *Our Crooked Hearts* and a former bookseller and YA lit blogger. Her work has been translated into more than twenty languages and included in the *New York Times Book Review*'s list of Notable Children's Books. She enjoys swimming-pool tourism, genre mash-ups, and living in Brooklyn with her hilarious husband and magnificently goofy son. She has mostly recovered from being too old for Neverland.

TRACY DEONN is the *New York Times* bestselling and award-winning author of *Legendborn* and its sequel, *Bloodmarked*. A second-generation fangirl, Tracy grew up in central North Carolina, where she devoured fantasy books and Southern food in equal measure. After earning her bachelor's and master's degrees in communication and performance studies from the University of North Carolina at Chapel Hill, Tracy worked in live theater, video game production, and K–12 education. When she's not writing, Tracy reads fanfic, arranges puppy playdates, and keeps an eye out for ginger-flavored everything.

H. E. EDGMON (he/they) is a questionable influence, a dog person, and an author of books both irreverent and radical-izing. Born and raised in the rural South, he currently lives in the Pacific Northwest with his eccentric little family. His stories imagine Indigenous worlds and center queer kids saving each other. H. E. has never once gotten enough sleep and probably isn't going to anytime soon. His highly acclaimed debut, *The Witch King*, is out now.

HAFSAH FAIZAL is the *New York Times* bestselling, award-winning author of the Sands of Arawiya duology and *A Tempest of Tea* and the founder of IceyDesigns, where she creates websites for authors and beauteous goodies for everyone else. A *Forbes* 30 Under 30 honoree, when she's not writing, she can be found designing, playing *Assassin's Creed*, or traversing the world. Born in Florida and raised in California, she now resides in Texas with a library of books waiting to be devoured.

STACEY LEE is the *New York Times* and indie bestselling author of historical and contemporary young adult fiction, including

The Downstairs Girl, a Reese's Book Club late summer 2021 YA pick, and her most recent novel, *Luck of the Titanic*, which received five-starred reviews. A native of Southern California and fourth-generation Chinese American, she is a founder of the We Need Diverse Books movement and writes stories for all kids (even the ones who look like adults). Stacey loves board games, has perfect pitch, and, through some mutant gene, can smell musical notes through her nose. Instagram and Twitter: @staceyleeauthor.

ROSELLE LIM is the critically acclaimed author of *Natalie Tan's Book of Luck and Fortune*, *Vanessa Yu's Magical Paris Tea Shop*, and *Sophie Go's Lonely Hearts Club*. She lives on the north shore of Lake Erie and always has an artistic project on the go. You can find her as @rosellewriter on Instagram and Twitter.

DARCIE LITTLE BADGER is a Lipan Apache writer with a PhD in oceanography. Her critically acclaimed debut novel, *Elatsoe*, was featured in *Time* magazine as one of the 100 Best Fantasy Books of All Time. *Elatsoe* also won the Locus Award for Best First Novel and was a Nebula, Ignyte, and Lodestar finalist. Her second fantasy novel, *A Snake Falls to Earth*, was on the National Book Award for Young People's Literature longlist. Darcie is married to a veterinarian named T.

MALINDA LO is the *New York Times* bestselling author of *Last Night at the Telegraph Club*, winner of the National Book Award, and its companion novel, *A Scatter of Light*. Her debut novel, *Ash*, a Sapphic retelling of "Cinderella," was a finalist for the William C. Morris YA Debut Award, the Andre Norton Nebula Award for Middle Grade and Young Adult Fiction, and the Lambda Literary Award. She can be found on social media @malindalo or at malindalo.com.

ALEX LONDON is the author of more than twenty-five books for children, teens, and adults. He's the author of the middle grade sci-fi fantasy series Battle Dragons, as well as Dog Tags, Tides of War, the Wild Ones, Accidental Adventures, and two titles in the 39 Clues series. For young adults, he's the author of the acclaimed cyberpunk duology Proxy and the epic fantasy trilogy Skybound Saga. A former librarian, journalist covering refugee camps and conflict zones, and snorkel salesman, he can now be found in Philadelphia, where he lives with his husband and daughter.

ANNA-MARIE MCLEMORE (they/them) grew up hearing la llorona in the Santa Ana winds and now writes books as queer, Latine, and nonbinary as they are. They are the author of William C. Morris YA Debut Award finalist *The Weight of Feathers*; Stonewall Honor Book *When the Moon Was Ours*; *Wild Beauty*, a *Kirkus Reviews*, *School Library Journal*, and *Booklist* best book of 2017; *Blanca & Roja*, one of *Time* magazine's 100 Best Fantasy Books of All Time; *Dark and Deepest Red*, a Winter 2020 Indie Next List pick; *The Mirror Season*, which was long-listed for the National Book Awards for Young People's Literature; *Lakelore*; and *Self-Made Boys: A Great Gatsby Remix*. Find them online at annamariemclemore.com and on Twitter @LaAnnaMarie.

REBECCA PODOS's debut novel, *The Mystery of Hollow Places*, was a Junior Library Guild selection and a Barnes & Noble Best Young Adult Book of 2016. Her second book, *Like Water*, won the Lambda Literary Award for LGBTQ Children's/

Young Adult. Her latest books include *Fools in Love*, a YA romance anthology coedited with Ashley Herring Blake, and *From Dust, a Flame*. An agent at the Rees Literary Agency in Boston, she can be found on her website, rebeccapodos.com.

RORY POWER lives in Rhode Island. She has an MA in prose fiction from the University of East Anglia and is the *New York Times* bestselling author of *Wilder Girls*, *Burn Our Bodies Down*, and *In a Garden Burning Gold*.

MEREDITH RUSSO was born in Chattanooga, Tennessee, but now lives in Brooklyn with her awful cat. Her debut novel, *If I Was Your Girl*, won the Stonewall Book Award and was a finalist for the Walter Dean Myers Award and the Lambda Literary Award. She has been featured in multiple short fiction and essay anthologies. Her second novel, *Birthday*, tells the story of a boy and a girl who were born for each other, told over the six years it takes them to realize it.

GITA TRELEASE is the author of *All That Glitters*, an NPR Best Book of the Year, and its sequel, *Everything That Burns*. Born in Sweden to Indian and Swedish parents, Gita divides her time between a village in Massachusetts and the wild coast of Maine. Before she became a novelist, she taught classes on monsters and fairy tales, many of which have crept into her stories.

ACKNOWLEDGMENTS

I still cannot believe I have gotten to do *three* of these beautiful collections with the incredible team at Flatiron Books. Sarah Barley, working with you has been such a career highlight, I still want to pinch myself about it sometimes. (And then contemplate how one could retell the story of that pinching and then go running into your inbox with a list of names I think would be *amazing* at retelling the story of pinchings throughout history.) Thank you for everything, and thank you to the wonderful Sydney Jeon (who stepped up *tremendously* here) and all the other indispensable people behind this book, including the publicity and marketing teams of Cat Kenney, Christopher Smith, Katherine Turro, and Nancy Trypuc; the production team of copy editor Bethany Reis, production manager Eva Diaz, and production editor Morgan Mitchell; audiobook producer Ally Demeter; and the library marketing team of Amanda Crimarco, Emily Day, and Samantha Slavin.

Jon Contino and Keith Hayes, at this point I really have to give you your own paragraph in thanks for these museum-worthy covers. I am so in awe of your talent and grateful for the faces you've given all three of these anthologies. And Devan Norman, thank you for the stunningly beautiful pages you've designed for each of these collections. I couldn't possibly love them more.

To my dream of an agent, Patricia Nelson: thank you for letting me drag you into the chaotic world of anthologies, and for all your help, support, patience, and expertise along the way.

Of course, this literally would not be a book without the authors whose phenomenal stories fill it up. Thank you so much to Melissa, Tracy, H. E., Hafsah, Stacey, Rosey, Darcie, Malinda, Alex, Becca, Rory, A-M (especially for suggesting the idea and then shoving it into my hands), Meredith, and Gita for filling these pages with magic both figurative and literal.

I also must acknowledge the brilliant scholarship that helped shape this volume, most notably that of D. L. Ashliman and Maria Tatar.

Big thanks and love to Emily Lloyd-Jones for being the first to read "Say My Name" and convincing me it wasn't too bonkers to submit, and all the other friends who shared wisdom, patience (ahem, Jennifer Iacopelli), and enthusiasm with me over the course of the process. Thank you to all the bloggers, bookstagrammers, and the rest of the book lovers (especially Bethany Robison) who keep showing up for these collections, and all of the teachers and librarians who've brought these stories to their students.

And to my family, for everything from Once Upon a Time to Happily Ever After: I love you.

THE
ORIGINAL
TALES

Please note that some of the original tales contain outdated, offensive language. Proceed with caution.

THE NUTCRACKER
AND MOUSE-KING

Text by E. T. A. Hoffman,
translated by Mrs. St. Simon, retrieved from
Wikisource

CHRISTMAS EVE

During the long, long day of the twenty-fourth of December, the children of Doctor Stahlbaum were not permitted to enter the parlor, much less the adjoining drawing-room. Frederic and Maria sat nestled together in a corner of the back chamber; dusky twilight had come on, and they felt quite gloomy and fearful, for, as was commonly the case on this day, no light was brought in to them. Fred, in great secrecy, and in a whisper, informed his little sister (she was only just seven years old) that ever since morning he had heard a rustling and a rattling, and now and then a gentle knocking, in the forbidden chambers. Not long ago also he had seen a little dark man, with a large chest under his arm, gliding softly through the entry, but he knew very well that it was nobody but Godfather Drosselmeier. Upon this Maria clapped her little hands together for joy, and exclaimed, "Ah, what beautiful things has Godfather Drosselmeier made for us this time!"

Counsellor Drosselmeïer was not a very handsome man; he was small and thin and had many wrinkles in his face, over his right eye he had a large black patch, and he was without hair, for which reason he wore a very nice white wig; this was made of glass, however, and was a very ingenious piece of work. The godfather himself was very ingenious also, he understood all about clocks and watches, and could even make them. Accordingly, when any one of the beautiful clocks in Doctor Stahlbaum's house was sick, and could not sing, Godfather Drosselmeier would have to attend it. He would then take off his glass wig, pull off his brown coat, put on a blue apron, and pierce the clock with sharp-pointed instruments, which usually caused little Maria a great deal of anxiety. But it did the clock no harm; on the contrary, it became quite lively again, and began at once right merrily to rattle, and to strike, and to sing, so that it was a pleasure to all who heard it. Whenever he came, he always brought something pretty in his pocket for the children, sometimes a little man who moved his eyes and made a bow, at others, a box, from which a little bird hopped out when it was opened—sometimes one thing, sometimes another.

When Christmas Eve came, he had always a beautiful piece of work prepared for them, which had cost him a great deal of trouble, and on this account it was always carefully preserved by their parents, after he had given it to them. "Ah, what beautiful present has Godfather Drosselmeier made for us this time!" exclaimed Maria. It was Fred's opinion that this time it could be nothing else than a castle, in which all kinds of fine soldiers marched up and down and went through their exercises; then other soldiers would come, and try to break into the castle, but the soldiers within would fire off their cannon very bravely, until all roared and cracked again. "No, no," cried Maria, interrupting him, "Godfather Drosselmeier has told me of a lovely garden where there is a great lake, upon which beautiful swans swim about, with golden collars around their necks, and sing their sweetest songs. Then there comes a little girl out of the garden down along the lake, and coaxes the swans to the shore, and feeds them with sweet cake."

"Swans never eat cake," interrupted Fred, somewhat roughly, "and even Godfather Drosselmeier himself can't make a whole garden. After all, we have little good of his playthings; they are all taken right away from us again. I like what Papa and Mamma give us much better, for we can keep their presents for ourselves, and do as we please with them." The children now began once more to guess what it could be this time. Maria thought that Miss Trutchen (her great doll) was growing very old, for she fell almost every moment upon the floor, and more awkwardly than ever, which could not happen without leaving sad marks upon her face, and as to neatness in dress, this was now altogether out of the question with her. Scolding did not help the matter in the least. Frederic declared, on the other hand, that a bay horse was wanting in his stable, and his troops were very deficient in cavalry, as his papa very well knew.

By this time it had become quite dark. Frederic and Maria sat close together and did not venture again to speak a word. It seemed now as if soft wings rustled around them, and very distant, but sweet music was heard at intervals. At this moment a shrill sound broke upon their ears—*kling, ling—kling, ling*—the doors flew wide open, and such a dazzling light broke out from the great chamber that with the loud exclamation, "Ah! Ah!" the children stood fixed at the threshold. But Papa and Mamma stepped to the door, took them by the hand, and said, "Come, come, dear children, and see what Christmas has brought you this year."

THE GIFTS

Kind reader, or listener, whatever may be your name, whether Frank, Robert, Henry, Anna, or Maria, I beg you to call to mind the table covered with your last Christmas gifts, as in their newest gloss they first appeared to your delighted vision. You will then be able to imagine the astonishment of the children, as they stood with sparkling eyes, unable to utter a word, for joy at the sight before them. At last Maria called out with a deep sigh, "Ah, how beautiful! Ah, how beautiful!" and Frederic gave two or three leaps in the air higher than he had ever done before. The children must have been very obedient and good children during the past year, for never on any Christmas Eve before had so many beautiful things been given to them. A tall fir tree stood in the middle of the room, covered with gold and silver apples, while sugar almonds, comfits, lemon drops, and every kind of confectionery hung like buds and blossoms upon all its branches. But the greatest beauty about this wonderful tree was the many little lights that sparkled amid its dark boughs, which like stars illuminated its treasures, or like friendly eyes seemed to invite the children to partake of its blossoms and fruit.

The table under the tree shone and flushed with a thousand different colors—ah, what beautiful things were there! Who can describe them? Maria spied the prettiest dolls, a tea set, all kinds of nice little furniture, and what eclipsed all the rest, a silk dress tastefully ornamented with gay ribbons, which hung upon a frame before her eyes, so that she could view it on every side. This she did too, and exclaimed over and over again, "Ah, the sweet—ah, the dear, dear frock! And may I put it on? Yes, yes—may I really, though, wear it?"

In the meanwhile Fred had been galloping round and round the room, trying his new bay horse, which, true enough, he had found, fastened by its bridle to the table. Dismounting again, he said it was a wild creature, but that was nothing; he would soon break him. He then reviewed his new regiment of hussars, who were very elegantly arrayed in red and gold, and carried silver weapons, and rode upon such bright shining horses that you would almost believe these were of pure silver also. The children had now become somewhat more composed, and turned to the picture books, which lay open on the table, where all kinds of beautiful flowers, and gayly dressed people, and boys and girls at play were painted as natural as if they were alive. Yes, the children had just turned to these singular books, when—*kling, ling, kling, ling*—the bell was heard again. They knew that Godfather Drosselmeier was now about to display his Christmas gift, and ran toward a table that stood against the wall, covered by a curtain reaching from the ceiling to the floor. The curtain behind which he had remained so long concealed was quickly drawn aside, and what saw the children then?

Upon a green meadow, spangled with flowers, stood a noble castle, with clear glass windows and golden turrets. A musical clock began to play, when the doors and windows flew open, and little men and women, with feathers in their hats, and long flowing trains, were seen sauntering about in the rooms. In the middle hall, which seemed as if it were all on fire, so many little tapers were burning in silver chandeliers, there were children in white frocks and green jackets, dancing to the sound of the music. A man in an emerald-green cloak at intervals put his head out of the window, nodded, and then disappeared; and Godfather Drosselmeier himself, only that he was not much bigger than Papa's thumb, came now and then to the door of the castle, looked about him, and then went in again. Fred, with his arms resting upon the table, gazed at the beautiful castle, and the little walking and dancing figures, and then said, "Godfather Drosselmeier, let me go into your castle."

The counsellor gave him to understand that that could not be done. And he was right, for it was foolish in Fred to wish to go into a castle, which with all its golden turrets was not as high as his head. Fred saw that likewise himself. After a while as the men and women kept walking back and forth, and the children danced, and the emerald man looked out at his window, and Godfather Drosselmeier came to the door, and all without the least change; Fred called out impatiently, "Godfather Drosselmeier, come out this time at the other door."

"That can never be, dear Fred," said the counsellor.

"Well then," continued Frederic, "let the green man who peeps out at the window walk about with the rest."

"And that can never be," rejoined the counsellor.

"Then the children must come down," cried Fred. "I want to see them nearer."

"All that can never be, I say," replied the counsellor, a little out of humor. "As the mechanism is made, so it must remain."

"So————o," cried Fred, in a drawling tone, "all that can never be! Listen, Godfather Drosselmeier. If your little dressed-up figures in the castle there can do nothing else but always the same thing, they are not good for much, and I care very little about them. No, give me my hussars, who can maneuver backward and forward, as I order them, and are not shut up in a house."

With this, he darted toward a large table, drew up his regiment upon their silver horses, and let them trot and gallop, and cut and slash, to his heart's content. Maria also had softly stolen away, for she too was soon tired of the sauntering and dancing puppets in the castle; but as she was very amiable and good, she did not wish it to be observed so plainly in her as it was in her brother, Fred. Counsellor Drosselmeier turned to the parents, and said, somewhat angrily, "An ingenious work like this was not made for stupid children. I will put up my castle again, and carry it home." But their mother now stepped forward, and desired to see the secret mechanism and curious works by which the little figures were set in motion. The counsellor took it all apart, and then put it together again. While he was employed in this manner he became good-natured once more, and gave the children some nice brown men and women, with gilt faces, hands, and feet. They were all made of sweet thorn, and smelled like gingerbread, at which Frederic and Maria were greatly delighted. At her mother's request, the elder sister, Louise, had put on the new dress which had been given to her, and she looked most charmingly in it, but Maria, when it came to her turn, thought she would like to look at hers a while longer as it hung. This was readily permitted.

THE FAVORITE

The truth is, Maria was unwilling to leave the table then, because she had discovered something upon it, which no one had yet remarked. By the marching out of Fred's hussars, who had been drawn up close to the tree, a curious little man came into view, who stood there silent and retired, as if he were waiting quietly for his turn to be noticed. It must be confessed, a great deal could not be said in favor of the beauty of his figure, for not only was his rather broad, stout body out of all proportion to the little, slim legs that carried it, but his head was by far too large for either. A genteel dress went a great way to compensate for these defects, and led to the belief that he must be a man of taste and good breeding. He wore a hussar's jacket of beautiful bright violet, fastened together with white loops and buttons, pantaloons of exactly the same color, and the neatest boots that ever graced the foot of a student or an officer. They fitted as tight to his little legs as if they were painted upon them. It was laughable to see, that in addition to this handsome apparel, he had hung upon his back a narrow clumsy cloak, that looked as if it were made of wood, and upon his head he wore a woodman's cap; but Maria remembered that Godfather Drosselmeier wore an old shabby cloak and an ugly cap, and still he was a dear, dear godfather. Maria could not help thinking also that even if Godfather Drosselmeier were in other respects as well-dressed as this little fellow, yet after all he would not look half so handsome as he. The longer Maria gazed upon the little man whom she had taken a liking to at first sight, the more she was sensible how much good nature and friendliness was expressed in his features. Nothing but kindness and benevolence shone in his clear green, though somewhat too prominent eyes. It was very becoming to the man that he wore about his chin a nicely trimmed beard of white cotton, for by this the sweet smile upon his deep red lips was rendered much more striking. "Ah, dear

father," exclaimed Maria at last, "to whom belongs that charming little man by the tree there?"

"He shall work industriously for you all, dear child," said
her father. "He can crack the hardest nuts with his teeth,
and he belongs as well to Louise as to you and Fred." With
these words her father took him carefully from the table,
and raised up his wooden cloak, whereupon the little man
stretched his mouth wide open, and showed two rows of
very white sharp teeth. At her father's bidding Maria put
in a nut, and—*crack*—the man had bitten it in two, so that
the shell fell off, and Maria caught the sweet kernel in her
hand. Maria and the other two children were now informed
that this dainty little man came of the family of Nutcrack-
ers, and practiced the profession of his forefathers. Maria
was overjoyed at what she heard, and her father said, "Dear
Maria, since friend Nutcracker is so great a favorite with
you, I place him under your particular care and keeping,
although, as I said before, Louise and Fred shall have as
much right to his services as you."

Maria took him immediately in her arms, and set him to
cracking nuts, but she picked out the smallest, that the little
fellow need not stretch his mouth open so wide, which in truth
was not very becoming to him. Louise sat down by her, and
friend Nutcracker must perform the same service for her too,
which he seemed to do quite willingly, for he kept smiling all
the while very pleasantly. In the meantime Fred had become
tired of riding and parading his hussars, and when he heard
the nuts crack so merrily, he ran to his sister, and laughed
very heartily at the droll little man, who now, since Fred must
have a share in the sport, passed from hand to hand, and thus

there was no end to his labor. Fred always chose the biggest and hardest nuts, when all at once—*crack*—*crack*—it went, and three teeth fell out of Nutcracker's mouth, and his whole under jaw became loose and rickety. "Ah, my poor dear Nutcracker!" said Maria, and snatched him out of Fred's hands.

"That's a stupid fellow," said Fred. "He wants to be a nutcracker, and has poor teeth—he don't understand his trade. Give him to me, Maria. He shall crack nuts for me if he loses all his teeth, and his whole chin into the bargain. Why make such a fuss about such a fellow?"

"No, no," exclaimed Maria, weeping; "you shall not have my dear Nutcracker. See how sorrowfully he looks at me, and shows me his poor mouth. But you are a hard-hearted fellow; you beat your horses; yes, and lately you had one of your soldiers shot through the head."

"That's all right," said Fred, "though you don't understand it. But Nutcracker belongs as much to me as to you, so let me have him."

Maria began to cry bitterly, and rolled up the sick Nutcracker as quickly as she could in her little pocket handkerchief. Their parents now came up with Godfather Drosselmeier. The latter, to Maria's great distress, took Fred's part. But their father said, "I have placed Nutcracker expressly under Maria's protection, and as I see that he is now greatly in need of it, I give her full authority over him, and no one must dispute it. Besides, I wonder at Fred, that he should require further duty from one who has been maimed in the service. As a good soldier, he ought to know that the wounded are not expected to take their place in the ranks."

Fred was much ashamed, and without troubling himself further about nuts or Nutcracker, stole around to the opposite end of the table, where his hussars, after stationing suitable outposts, had encamped for the night. Maria collected together Nutcracker's lost teeth, tied up his wounded chin with a nice white ribbon which she had taken from her dress, and then wrapped up the little fellow more carefully than ever in her handkerchief, for he looked very pale and frightened. Thus she held him, rocking him in her arms like a little child, while she looked over the beautiful pictures of the new picture book, which she found among her other Christmas gifts. Contrary to her usual disposition, she showed some ill-temper toward Father Drosselmeier, who kept continually laughing at her, and asked again and again how it was that she liked to caress such an ugly little fellow. That singular comparison with Drosselmeier, which she made when her eyes first fell upon Nutcracker, now came again into her mind, and she said very seriously: "Who knows, dear Godfather, if you were dressed like my sweet Nutcracker, and had on such bright little boots— who knows but you would then be as handsome as he is!" Maria could not tell why her parents laughed so loudly at this, and why the counsellor's face turned so red, and he, for his part, did not laugh half so heartily this time as he had done more than once before. It is likely there was some particular reason for it.

WONDERS UPON WONDERS

In the sitting-room of the doctor's house, just as you enter the room, there stands on the left hand, close against the wall, a high glass case, in which the children preserve all the beautiful things which are given to them every year. Louise was quite a little girl when her father had the case made by a skillful joiner, who set in it such large, clear panes of glass, and arranged all the parts so well together, that every thing looked much brighter and handsomer when on its shelves than when it was held in the hands. On the upper shelf, which Maria and Fred were unable to reach, stood all Godfather Drosselmeier's curious machines. Immediately below this was a shelf for the picture books; the two lower shelves Maria and Fred filled up as they pleased, but it always happened that Maria used the lower one as a house for her dolls, while Fred, on the contrary, cantoned his troops in the one above.

And so it happened today, for while Fred set his hussars in order above, Maria, having laid Miss Trutchen aside, and having installed the new and sweetly dressed doll in her best furnished chamber below, had invited herself to tea with her. I have said that the chamber was well furnished, and it is true; here was a nice chintz sofa and several tiny chairs, there stood a tea-table, but above all, there was a clean, white little bed for her doll to repose upon. All these things were arranged in one corner of the glass case, the sides of which were hung with gay pictures, and it will readily be supposed that in such a chamber the new doll, Miss Clara, must have found herself very comfortable.

It was now late in the evening, and night, indeed, was close at hand, and Godfather Drosselmeier had long since gone home, yet still the children could not leave the glass case, although their mother repeatedly told them that it was high time to go to bed. "It is true," cried Fred at last; "the poor fellows (meaning his hussars) would like to get a little rest, and as long as I am here, not one of them will dare to nod—I know that." With these words he went up to bed, but Maria begged very hard, "Only leave me here a little while, dear Mother. I have two or three things to attend to, and when they are done I will go immediately to bed." Maria was a very good and sensible child, and therefore her mother could leave her alone with her playthings without anxiety. But for fear she might become so much interested in her new doll and other presents as to forget the lights which burned around the glass case, her mother blew them all out, and left only the lamp which hung down from the ceiling in the middle of the chamber, and which diffused a soft, pleasant light. "Come in soon, dear Maria, or you will not be up in time tomorrow morning," called her mother, as she went up to bed. There was something Maria had at heart to do, which she had not told her mother, though she knew not the reason why; and as soon as she found herself alone she went quickly about it. She still carried in her arms the wounded Nutcracker, rolled up in her pocket handkerchief. Now she laid him carefully upon the table, unrolled the handkerchief softly, and examined his wound. Nutcracker was very pale, but still he smiled so kindly and sorrowfully that it went straight to Maria's heart. "Ah! Nutcracker, Nutcracker, do not be angry at brother Fred because he hurt you so, he did not mean to be so rough; it is the wild soldier's life with his hussars that has made him a little hard-hearted, but otherwise he is a good fellow, I can assure you. Now I will tend you very carefully until you are well and merry again; as to fastening in your teeth and setting your shoulders, that Godfather Drosselmeier must do; he understands such things."

But Maria was hardly able to finish the sentence, for as she mentioned the name of Drosselmeier, friend Nutcracker made a terrible wry face, and there darted something out of his eyes like green sparkling flashes. Maria was just going to fall into a dreadful fright, when behold, it was the sad smiling face of the honest Nutcracker again, which she saw before her, and she knew now that it must be the glare of the lamp, which, stirred by the draft, had flared up, and distorted Nutcracker's features so strangely. "Am I not a foolish girl," she said, "to be so easily frightened, and to think that a wooden puppet could make faces at me? But I love Nutcracker too well, because he is so droll and so good tempered; therefore he shall be taken good care of as he deserves." With this Maria took friend Nutcracker in her arms, walked to the glass case, stooped down, and said to her new doll, "Pray, Miss Clara, be so good as to give up your bed to the sick and wounded Nutcracker, and make out as well as you can with the sofa. Remember that you are well and hearty, or you would not have such fat red cheeks, and very few little dolls have such nice sofas."

Miss Clara, in her gay Christmas attire, looked very grand and haughty, and would not even say "Muck." "But why should I stand upon ceremony?" said Maria, and she took out the bed, laid little Nutcracker down upon it softly, and gently rolled a nice ribbon which she wore around her waist about his poor shoulders, and then drew the bedclothes over him snugly, so that there was nothing to be seen of him below the nose. "He shan't stay with the naughty Clara," she said, and raised the bed with Nutcracker in it to the shelf above, and placed it close by the pretty village, where Fred's hussars were quartered. She locked the case, and was about to go up to bed, when—listen, children—when softly, softly it began to rustle, and to whisper, and to rattle round and round, under the hearth, behind the chairs, behind the cupboards and glass case. The great clock whir—red louder and louder, but it could not strike. Maria turned toward it, and there the large gilt owl that sat on the top had dropped down its wings, so that they covered the whole face, and it stretched out its ugly head with the short crooked beak, and looked just like a cat. And the clock whirred louder in plain words. "Dick—ry, dick—ry, dock—whirr, softly clock, Mouse-King has a fine ear—*prr—prr—pum—pum*—the old song let him hear—*prr—prr—pum—pum*—or he might—run away in a fright—now clock strike softly and light." And *pum— pum*, it went with a dull deadened sound twelve times. Maria began now to tremble with fear, and she was upon the point of running out of the room in terror, when she beheld God-father Drosselmeier, who sat in the owl's place on the top of the clock, and had hung down the skirts of his brown coat just like wings. But she took courage, and cried out loudly, with sobs, "Godfather Drosselmeier, Godfather Drosselmeier, what are you doing up there? Come down, and do not frighten me so, you naughty Godfather Drosselmeier!"

Just then a wild squeaking and whimpering broke out on all sides, and then there was a running, trotting and galloping behind the walls, as if a thousand little feet were in motion, and a thousand little lights flashed out of the crevices in the floor. But they were not lights—no—they were sparkling little eyes, and Maria perceived that mice were all around, peeping out and working their way into the room. Presently it went trot— trot—hop—hop about the chamber, and more and more mice, in greater or smaller parties galloped across, and at last placed themselves in line and column, just as Fred was accustomed to place his soldiers when they went to battle. This Maria thought was very droll, and as she had not that aversion to mice which most children have, her terror was gradually leaving her, when all at once there arose a squeaking so terrible and piercing, that it seemed as if ice-cold water was poured down her back. Ah, what now did she see!

I know, my worthy reader Frederic, that thy heart, like that of the wise and brave soldier Frederic Stahlbaum, sits in the right place, but if thou hadst seen what Maria now beheld, thou wouldst certainly have run away; yes, I believe that thou wouldst have jumped as quickly as possible into bed, and then have drawn the covering over thine ears much farther than was necessary to keep thee warm. Alas! Poor Maria could not do that now, for—listen, children—close before her feet, there burst out sand and lime and crumbled wall stones, as if thrown up by some subterranean force, and seven mice heads with seven sparkling crowns rose out of the floor, squeaking and squealing terribly. Presently the mouse's body to which these seven heads belonged worked its way out, and the great mouse crowned with the seven diadems, squeaking loudly, huzzahed in full chorus, as he advanced to meet his army, which at once set itself in motion, and hott—hott—trot—trot it went—alas, straight toward the glass case—straight toward poor Maria, who stood close before it!

Her heart had before beat so terribly from anxiety and fear that she thought it would leap out of her bosom, and then she knew she must die; but now it seemed as if the blood stood still in her veins. Half fainting, she tottered backward, when clatter—clatter—rattle—rattle it went—and a glass pane which she had struck with her elbow fell in pieces at her feet. She felt at the moment a sharp pain in her left arm, but her heart all at once became much lighter, she heard no more squeaking and squealing, all had become still, and although she did not dare to look, yet she believed that the mice, frightened by the clatter of the broken glass, had retreated into their holes. But what was that again! Close behind her in the glass case a strange bustling and rustling began, and little fine voices were heard. "Up, up, awake—arms take—awake—to the fight—this night—up, up—to the fight." And all the while something rang out clear and sweet like little bells. "Ah, that is my dear musical clock!" exclaimed Maria joyfully, and turned quickly to look.

She then saw how it flashed and lightened strangely in the glass case, and there was a great stir and bustle upon the shelves. Many little figures crossed up and down by each other, and worked and stretched out their arms as if they were making ready. And now, Nutcracker raised himself all of a sudden, threw the bedclothes clear off, and leaped with both feet at once out of bed, crying aloud, "Crack—crack—crack—stupid pack—drive mouse back—stupid pack—crack—crack—mouse—back—crick—crack—stupid pack." With these words he drew his little sword, flourished it in the air, and exclaimed, "My loving vassals, friends and brothers, will you stand by me in the hard fight?" Straightway three Scaramouches, a Harlequin, four Chimney-sweepers, two Guitar-players, and a Drummer cried out, "Yes, my lord, we will follow you with fidelity and courage—we will march with you to battle—to victory or death," and then rushed after the fiery Nutcracker, who ventured the dangerous leap down from the upper shelf. Ah, it was easy enough for them to perform this feat, for beside the fine garments of thick cloth and silk which they wore, the inside of their bodies were made of cotton and tow, so that they came down plump, like bags of wool. But poor Nutcracker had certainly broken his arms or his legs, for remember, it was almost two feet from the shelf where he stood to the floor, and his body was as brittle as if it had been cut out of linden wood. Yes, Nutcracker would certainly have broken his arms or his legs, if, at the moment when he leaped, Miss Clara had not sprung quickly from the sofa, and caught the hero with his drawn sword in her soft arms. "Ah, thou dear, good Clara," sobbed Maria, "how I have wronged thee! Thou didst certainly resign thy bed willingly to little Nutcracker."

But Miss Clara now spoke, as she softly pressed the young hero to her silken bosom. "You will not, oh, my lord! sick and wounded as you are, share the dangers of the fight. See how your brave vassals assemble themselves, eager for the affray, and certain of conquest. Scaramouch, Harlequin, Chimney-sweepers, Guitar-players, Drummer are all ready drawn up below, and the china figures on the shelf stir and move strangely! Will you not, oh, my lord! repose upon the sofa, or from my arms look down upon your victory?" Thus spoke Clara, but Nutcracker demeaned himself very ungraciously, for he kicked and struggled so violently with his legs that Clara was obliged to set him quickly down upon the floor. He then, however, dropped gracefully upon one knee, and said, "Fair lady, the recollection of thy favor and condescension will go with me into the battle and the strife."

Clara then stooped so low that she could take him by the arm, raised him gently from his knees, took off her bespangled girdle, and was about to throw it across his neck, but little Nutcracker stepped two paces backward, laid his hand upon his breast, and said very earnestly, "Not so, fair lady, lavish not thy favors thus upon me, for——" He stopped, sighed heavily, tore off the ribbon which Maria had bound about his shoulders, pressed it to his lips, hung it across him like a scarf, and then boldly flourishing his bright little blade, leaped like a bird over the edge of the glass case upon the floor. You understand, my kind and good readers and listeners, that Nutcracker, even before he had thus come to life, had felt very sensibly the kindness and love which Maria had shown toward him, and it was because he had become so partial to her that he would not receive and wear the girdle of Miss Clara, although it shone and sparkled so brightly. The true and faithful Nutcracker preferred to wear Maria's simple ribbon. But what will now happen? As soon as Nutcracker had leaped out, the squeaking and whistling was heard again. Ah, it is under the large table that the hateful mice have concealed their countless bands, and high above them all towers the dreadful mouse with seven heads! What will now happen!

You can find the rest of the story on Wikisource at https://en.wikisource.org/wiki/Nutcracker_and_Mouse-King.

FITCHER'S
BIRD

Text by Jacob and Wilhelm Grimm, from *Grimm's Household Tales*, edited and translated by Margaret Hunt, retrieved from the Project Gutenberg ebook *Household Tales by Brothers Grimm*

There was once a wizard who used to take the form of a poor man, and went to houses and begged, and caught pretty girls. No one knew whither he carried them, for they were never seen more. One day he appeared before the door of a man who had three pretty daughters; he looked like a poor weak beggar, and carried a basket on his back, as if he meant to collect charitable gifts in it. He begged for a little food, and when the eldest daughter came out and was just reaching him a piece of bread, he did but touch her, and she was forced to jump into his basket. Thereupon he hurried away with long strides, and carried her away into a dark forest to his house, which stood in the midst of it. Everything in the house was magnificent; he gave her whatsoever she could possibly desire, and said, "My darling, thou wilt certainly be happy with me, for thou hast everything thy heart can wish for." This lasted a few days, and then he said, "I must journey forth, and leave thee alone for a short time; there are the keys of the house; thou mayst go everywhere and look at everything except into one room, which this little key here opens, and there I forbid thee to go on pain of death." He likewise gave her an egg and said, "Preserve the egg carefully for me, and carry it continually about with thee, for a great misfortune would arise from the loss of it."

She took the keys and the egg, and promised to obey him in everything. When he was gone, she went all round the house from the bottom to the top, and examined everything. The rooms shone with silver and gold, and she thought she had never seen such great splendor. At length she came to the forbidden door; she wished to pass it by, but curiosity let her have no rest. She examined the key, it looked just like any other; she put it in the keyhole and turned it a little, and the door sprang open. But what did she see when she went in? A great bloody basin stood in the middle of the room, and therein lay human beings, dead and hewn to pieces, and hard by was a block of wood, and a gleaming axe lay upon it. She was so terribly alarmed that the egg which she held in her hand fell into the basin. She got it out and washed the blood off, but in vain; it appeared again in a moment. She washed and scrubbed, but she could not get it out.

It was not long before the man came back from his journey, and the first things which he asked for were the key and the egg. She gave them to him, but she trembled as she did so, and he saw at once by the red spots that she had been in the bloody chamber. "Since thou hast gone into the room against my will," said he, "thou shalt go back into it against thine own. Thy life is ended." He threw her down, dragged her thither by her hair, cut her head off on the block, and hewed her in pieces so that her blood ran on the ground. Then he threw her into the basin with the rest.

"Now I will fetch myself the second," said the wizard, and again he went to the house in the shape of a poor man, and begged. Then the second daughter brought him a piece of bread; he caught her like the first, by simply touching her, and carried her away. She did not fare better than her sister. She allowed herself to be led away by her curiosity, opened the door of the bloody chamber, looked in, and had to atone for it with her life on the wizard's return. Then he went and brought the third sister, but she was clever and crafty. When he had given her the keys and the egg, and had left her, she first put the egg away with great care, and then she examined the house, and at last went into the forbidden room. Alas, what did she behold! Both her sisters lay there in the basin, cruelly murdered, and cut in pieces. But she began to gather their limbs together and put them in order, head, body, arms and legs. And when nothing further was wanting the limbs began to move and unite themselves together, and both the maidens opened their eyes and were once more alive. Then they rejoiced and kissed and caressed each other.

On his arrival, the man at once demanded the keys and the egg, and as he could perceive no trace of any blood on it, he said, "Thou hast stood the test, thou shalt be my bride." He now had no longer any power over her, and was forced to do whatsoever she desired. "Oh, very well," said she, "thou shalt first take a basketful of gold to my father and mother, and carry it thyself on thy back; in the meantime I will prepare for the wedding." Then she ran to her sisters, whom she had hidden in a little chamber, and said, "The moment has come when I can save you. The wretch shall himself carry you home again, but as soon as you are at home send help to me." She put both of them in a basket and covered them quite over with gold, so that nothing of them was to be seen, then she called in the wizard and said to him, "Now carry the basket away, but I shall look through my little window and watch to see if thou stoppest on the way to stand or to rest."

The wizard raised the basket on his back and went away with it, but it weighed him down so heavily that the perspiration streamed from his face. Then he sat down and wanted to rest awhile, but immediately one of the girls in the basket cried, "I am looking through my little window, and I see that thou art resting. Wilt thou go on at once?" He thought it was his bride who was calling that to him and got up on his legs again. Once more he was going to sit down, but instantly she cried, "I am looking through my little window, and I see that thou art resting. Wilt thou go on directly?" And whenever he stood still, she cried this, and then he was forced to go onwards, until at last, groaning and out of breath, he took the basket with the gold and the two maidens into their parents' house. At home, however, the bride prepared the marriage-feast, and sent invitations to the friends of the wizard. Then she took a skull with grinning teeth, put some ornaments on it and a wreath of flowers, carried it upstairs to the garret-window, and let it look out from thence. When all was ready, she got into a barrel of honey, and then cut the feather-bed open and rolled herself in it, until she looked like a wondrous bird, and no one could recognize her. Then she went out of the house, and on her way she met some of the wedding-guests, who asked,

"O, Fitcher's bird, how com'st thou here?"

"I come from Fitcher's house quite near."

"And what may the young bride be doing?"

"From cellar to garret she's swept all clean, and now from the window she's peeping, I ween."

At last she met the bridegroom, who was coming slowly back. He, like the others, asked,

"O, Fitcher's bird, how com'st thou here?"

"I come from Fitcher's house quite near."

"And what may the young bride be doing?"

"From cellar to garret she's swept all clean, and now from the window she's peeping, I ween."

The bridegroom looked up, saw the decked-out skull, thought it was his bride, and nodded to her, greeting her kindly. But when he and his guests had all gone into the house, the brothers and kinsmen of the bride, who had been sent to rescue her, arrived. They locked all the doors of the house, that no one might escape, set fire to it, and the wizard and all his crew had to burn.

RUMPELSTILTSKIN

Text by Jacob and Wilhelm Grimm, from *Kinder-und Hausmärchen*, translated by Edgar Taylor and Marian Edwardes, retrieved from the Project Gutenberg ebook *Grimms' Fairy Tales*

By the side of a wood, in a country a long way off, ran a fine stream of water; and upon the stream there stood a mill. The miller's house was close by, and the miller, you must know, had a very beautiful daughter. She was, moreover, very shrewd and clever; and the miller was so proud of her that he one day told the king of the land, who used to come and hunt in the wood, that his daughter could spin gold out of straw. Now, this king was very fond of money; and when he heard the miller's boast his greediness was raised, and he sent for the girl to be brought before him. Then he led her to a chamber in his palace where there was a great heap of straw, and gave her a spinning wheel, and said, "All this must be spun into gold before morning, as you love your life." It was in vain that the poor maiden said that it was only a silly boast of her father, for that she could do no such thing as spin straw into gold: the chamber door was locked, and she was left alone.

She sat down in one corner of the room, and began to bewail her hard fate; when on a sudden the door opened, and a droll-looking little man hobbled in, and said, "Good morrow to you, my good lass; what are you weeping for?" "Alas!" said

she. "I must spin this straw into gold, and I know not how."
"What will you give me," said the hobgoblin, "to do it for
you?" "My necklace," replied the maiden. He took her at her
word, and sat himself down to the wheel, and whistled and
sang:

"Round about, round about,
   Lo and behold!
Reel away, reel away,
Straw into gold!"

And round about the wheel went merrily; the work was
quickly done, and the straw was all spun into gold.

When the king came and saw this, he was greatly astonished and pleased; but his heart grew still more greedy of gain,
and he shut up the poor miller's daughter again with a fresh
task. Then she knew not what to do, and sat down once more
to weep; but the dwarf soon opened the door, and said, "What
will you give me to do your task?" "The ring on my finger,"
said she. So her little friend took the ring, and began to work
at the wheel again, and whistled and sang:

"Round about, round about,
   Lo and behold!
Reel away, reel away,
   Straw into gold!"

till, long before morning, all was done again.

The king was greatly delighted to see all this glittering
treasure; but still he had not enough: so he took the miller's

daughter to a yet larger heap, and said, "All this must be spun tonight; and if it is, you shall be my queen." As soon as she was alone that dwarf came in, and said, "What will you give me to spin gold for you this third time?" "I have nothing left," said she. "Then say you will give me," said the little man, "the first little child that you may have when you are queen." "That may never be," thought the miller's daughter: and as she knew no other way to get her task done, she said she would do what he asked. Round went the wheel again to the old song, and the manikin once more spun the heap into gold. The king came in the morning, and, finding all he wanted, was forced to keep his word; so he married the miller's daughter, and she really became queen.

At the birth of her first little child she was very glad, and forgot the dwarf, and what she had said. But one day he came into her room, where she was sitting playing with her baby, and put her in mind of it. Then she grieved sorely at her misfortune, and said she would give him all the wealth of the kingdom if he would let her off, but in vain; till at last her tears softened him, and he said, "I will give you three days' grace, and if during that time you tell me my name, you shall keep your child."

Now the queen lay awake all night, thinking of all the odd names that she had ever heard; and she sent messengers all over the land to find out new ones. The next day the little man came, and she began with TIMOTHY, ICHABOD, BENJAMIN, JEREMIAH, and all the names she could remember; but to all and each of them he said, "Madam, that is not my name."

The second day she began with all the comical names she

could hear of, BANDY-LEGS, HUNCHBACK, CROOK-SHANKS, and so on; but the little gentleman still said to every one of them, "Madam, that is not my name."

The third day one of the messengers came back, and said, "I have traveled two days without hearing of any other names; but yesterday, as I was climbing a high hill, among the trees of the forest where the fox and the hare bid each other good night, I saw a little hut; and before the hut burnt a fire; and round about the fire a funny little dwarf was dancing upon one leg, and singing:

"Merrily the feast I'll make.
Today I'll brew, tomorrow bake;
Merrily I'll dance and sing,
For next day will a stranger bring.
Little does my lady dream
Rumpelstiltskin is my name!"

When the queen heard this she jumped for joy, and as soon as her little friend came she sat down upon her throne, and called all her court round to enjoy the fun; and the nurse stood by her side with the baby in her arms, as if it was quite ready to be given up. Then the little man began to chuckle at the thought of having the poor child, to take home with him to his hut in the woods; and he cried out, "Now, lady, what is my name?" "Is it JOHN?" asked she. "No, madam!" "Is it TOM?" "No, madam!" "Is it JEMMY?" "It is not." "Can your name be RUMPELSTILTSKIN?" said the lady slyly. "Some witch told you that!—Some witch told you that!" cried the little man, and dashed his right foot in a rage so deep into the floor that he was forced to lay hold of it with both hands to pull it out.

Then he made the best of his way off, while the nurse laughed and the baby crowed; and all the court jeered at him for having had so much trouble for nothing, and said, "We wish you a very good morning, and a merry feast, Mr. RUMPELSTILTSKIN!"

THE LITTLE MATCH GIRL
(THE LITTLE MATCHSTICK GIRL)

Text by Hans Christian Andersen, retrieved from the Project Gutenberg ebook *Hans Andersen's Fairy Tales*

Most terribly cold it was; it snowed, and was nearly quite dark, and evening—the last evening of the year. In this cold and darkness there went along the street a poor little girl, bareheaded and with naked feet. When she left home she had slippers on, it is true; but what was the good of that? They were very large slippers, which her mother had hitherto worn; so large were they; and the poor little thing lost them as she scuffled away across the street, because of two carriages that rolled by dreadfully fast.

One slipper was nowhere to be found; the other had been laid hold of by an urchin, and off he ran with it; he thought it would do capitally for a cradle when he some day or other should have children himself. So the little maiden walked on with her tiny naked feet that were quite red and blue from cold. She carried a quantity of matches in an old apron, and she held a bundle of them in her hand. Nobody had bought anything of her the whole livelong day; no one had given her a single farthing.

She crept along trembling with cold and hunger—a very picture of sorrow, the poor little thing! The flakes of snow covered her long fair hair, which fell in beautiful curls around her neck; but of that, of course, she never once now thought.

From all the windows the candles were gleaming, and it smelt so deliciously of roast goose, for you know it was New Year's Eve; yes, of that she thought. In a corner formed by two houses, of which one advanced more than the other, she seated herself down and cowered together. Her little feet she had drawn close up to her, but she grew colder and colder, and to go home she did not venture, for she had not sold any matches and could not bring a farthing of money: from her father she would certainly get blows, and at home it was cold too, for above her she had only the roof, through which the wind whistled, even though the largest cracks were stopped up with straw and rags. Her little hands were almost numbed with cold. Oh! A match might afford her a world of comfort, if she only dared take a single one out of the bundle, draw it against the wall, and warm her fingers by it. She drew one out. "Rischt!" How it blazed, how it burnt! It was a warm, bright flame, like a candle, as she held her hands over it: it was a wonderful light. It seemed really to the little maiden as though she were sitting before a large iron stove, with burnished brass feet and a brass ornament at top. The fire burned with such blessed influence; it warmed so delightfully. The little girl had already stretched out her feet to warm them too; but—the small flame went out, the stove vanished: she had only the remains of the burnt-out match in her hand.

She rubbed another against the wall: it burned brightly, and where the light fell on the wall, there the wall became transparent like a veil, so that she could see into the room. On the table was spread a snow-white tablecloth; upon it was a splendid porcelain service, and the roast goose was steaming famously with its stuffing of apple and dried plums. And what was still more capital to behold was, the goose hopped down from the dish, reeled about on the floor with knife and fork in its breast, till it came up to the poor little girl; when—the match went out and nothing but the thick, cold, damp wall was left behind.

She lit another match. Now there she was sitting under the most magnificent Christmas tree: it was still larger and more decorated than the one that she had seen through the glass door in the rich merchant's house. Thousands of lights were burning on the green branches, and gaily-colored pictures, such as she had seen in the shop windows, looked down upon her.

The little maiden stretched out her hands toward them when—the match went out. The lights of the Christmas tree rose higher and higher, she saw them now as stars in heaven; one fell down and formed a long trail of fire.

"Someone is just dead!" said the little girl; for her old grandmother, the only person who had loved her, and who was now no more, had told her that when a star falls, a soul ascends to God.

She drew another match against the wall: it was again light, and in the luster there stood the old grandmother, so bright and radiant, so mild, and with such an expression of love.

"Grandmother!" cried the little one. "Oh, take me with you! You go away when the match burns out; you vanish like the warm stove, like the delicious roast goose, and like the magnificent Christmas tree!" And she rubbed the whole bundle of matches quickly against the wall, for she wanted to be quite sure of keeping her grandmother near her. And the matches gave such a brilliant light that it was brighter than at noonday: never formerly had the grandmother been so beautiful and so tall. She took the little maiden on her arm, and both flew in brightness and in joy so high, so very high, and then above was neither cold, nor hunger, nor anxiety—they were with God.

But in the corner, at the cold hour of dawn, sat the poor girl, with rosy cheeks and with a smiling mouth, leaning against the wall—frozen to death on the last evening of the old year. Stiff and stark sat the child there with her matches, of which one bundle had been burnt. "She wanted to warm herself," people said. No one had the slightest suspicion of what beautiful things she had seen; no one even dreamed of the splendor in which, with her grandmother, she had entered on the joys of a new year.

LITTLE SNOW-WHITE (SNOW WHITE)

Text by Jacob and Wilhelm Grimm, from
Kinder-und Hausmärchen, retrieved from the
website of D. L. Ashliman

Once upon a time in midwinter, when the snowflakes were falling like feathers from heaven, a beautiful queen sat sewing at her window, which had a frame of black ebony wood. As she sewed, she looked up at the snow and pricked her finger with her needle. Three drops of blood fell into the snow. The red on the white looked so beautiful, that she thought, "If only I had a child as white as snow, as red as blood, and as black as this frame." Soon afterward she had a little daughter that was as white as snow, as red as blood, and as black as ebony wood, and therefore they called her Little Snow-White.

Now the queen was the most beautiful woman in all the land, and very proud of her beauty. She had a mirror, which she stood in front of every morning, and asked:

"MIRROR, MIRROR, ON THE WALL,

Who in this land is fairest of all?"

And the mirror always said:

"You, my queen, are fairest of all."

And then she knew for certain that no one in the world was more beautiful than she.

Now, Snow-White grew up, and when she was seven years old, she was so beautiful that she surpassed even the queen herself. Now when the queen asked her mirror:

"MIRROR, MIRROR, ON THE WALL,

Who in this land is fairest of all?"

The mirror said:

"YOU, MY QUEEN, ARE FAIR; IT IS TRUE.

But Little Snow-White is still
A thousand times fairer than you."

When the queen heard the mirror say this, she became pale with envy, and from that hour on, she hated Snow-White. Whenever she looked at her, she thought that Snow-White was to blame that she was no longer the most beautiful woman in the world. This turned her heart around. Her jealousy gave her no peace. Finally she summoned a huntsman and said to him, "Take Snow-White out into the woods to a remote spot, and stab her to death. As proof that she is dead bring her lungs and her liver back to me. I shall cook them with salt and eat them."

The huntsman took Snow-White into the woods. When he took out his hunting knife to stab her, she began to cry, and begged fervently that he might spare her life, promising to run away into the woods and never return. The huntsman took pity on her because she was so beautiful, and he thought, "The wild animals will soon devour her anyway. I'm glad that I don't have to kill her." Just then a young boar came running by. He killed it, cut out its lungs and liver, and took them back to the queen as proof of Snow-White's death. She cooked them with salt and ate them, supposing that she had eaten Snow-White's lungs and liver.

Snow-White was now all alone in the great forest. She was terribly afraid, and began to run. She ran over sharp stones and through thorns the entire day. Finally, just as the sun was about to set, she came to a little house. The house belonged to seven dwarfs. They were working in a mine, and not at home. Snow-White went inside and found everything to be small, but neat and orderly. There was a little table with seven little plates, seven little spoons, seven little knives and forks, seven little mugs, and against the wall there were seven little beds, all freshly made.

Snow-White was hungry and thirsty, so she ate a few vegetables and a little bread from each little plate, and from each little glass she drank a drop of wine. Because she was so tired, she wanted to lie down and go to sleep. She tried each of the seven little beds, one after the other, but none felt right until she came to the seventh one, and she lay down in it and fell asleep.

When night came, the seven dwarfs returned home from the work. They lit their seven little candles, and saw that someone had been in their house.

The first one said, "Who has been sitting in my chair?"

The second one, "Who has been eating from my plate?"

The third one, "Who has been eating my bread?"

The fourth one, "Who has been eating my vegetables?"

The fifth one, "Who has been sticking with my fork?"

The sixth one, "Who has been cutting with my knife?"

The seventh one, "Who has been drinking from my mug?"

Then the first one said, "Who stepped on my bed?"

The second one, "And someone has been lying in my bed."

And so forth until the seventh one, and when he looked at his bed, he found Snow-White lying there, fast asleep. The seven dwarfs all came running, and they cried out with amazement. They fetched their seven candles and looked at Snow-White. "Good heaven! Good heaven!" they cried. "She is so beautiful!" They liked her very much. They did not wake her up, but let her lie there in the bed. The seventh dwarf had to sleep with his companions, one hour with each one, and then the night was done.

When Snow-White woke up, they asked her who she was and how she had found her way to their house. She told them how her mother had tried to kill her, how the huntsman had spared her life, how she had run the entire day, finally coming to their house. The dwarfs pitied her and said, "If you will keep house for us, and cook, sew, make beds, wash, and knit, and keep everything clean and orderly, then you can stay here, and you'll have everything that you want. We come home in the evening, and supper must be ready by then, but we spend the days digging for gold in the mine. You will be alone then. Watch out for the queen, and do not let anyone in."

The queen thought that she was again the most beautiful woman in the land, and the next morning she stepped before the mirror and asked:

"MIRROR, MIRROR, ON THE WALL,

Who in this land is fairest of all?"

The mirror answered once again:

"YOU, MY QUEEN, ARE FAIR; IT IS TRUE.

But Little Snow-White beyond the seven
mountains
Is a thousand times fairer than you."

It startled the queen to hear this, and she knew that she had
been deceived, that the huntsman had not killed Snow-White.
Because only the seven dwarfs lived in the seven mountains,
she knew at once that they must have rescued her. She began
to plan immediately how she might kill her, because she would
have no peace until the mirror once again said that she was
the most beautiful woman in the land. At last she thought of
something to do. She disguised herself as an old peddler woman
and colored her face, so that no one would recognize her, and
went to the dwarfs' house. Knocking on the door she called out,
"Open up. Open up. I'm the old peddler woman with good
wares for sale."

Snow-White peered out the window. "What do you have?"

"Bodice laces, dear child," said the old woman, and held one
up. It was braided from yellow, red, and blue silk. "Would you
like this one?"

"Oh, yes," said Snow-White, thinking, "I can let the old
woman come in. She means well." She unbolted the door and
bargained for the bodice laces.

"You are not laced up properly," said the old woman.
"Come here, I'll do it better." Snow-White stood before her,

and she took hold of the laces and pulled them so tight that Snow-White could not breathe, and she fell down as if she were dead. Then the old woman was satisfied, and she went away.

Nightfall soon came, and the seven dwarfs returned home. They were horrified to find their dear Snow-White lying on the ground as if she were dead. They lifted her up and saw that she was laced up too tightly. They cut the bodice laces in two, and then she could breathe, and she came back to life. "It must have been the queen who tried to kill you," they said. "Take care and do not let anyone in again."

The queen asked her mirror:

"MIRROR, MIRROR, ON THE WALL,

Who in this land is fairest of all?"

The mirror answered once again:

"YOU, MY QUEEN, ARE FAIR; IT IS TRUE.

But Little Snow-White with the seven dwarfs
Is a thousand times fairer than you."

She was so horrified that the blood all ran to her heart, because she knew that Snow-White had come back to life. Then for an entire day and a night she planned how she might catch her. She made a poisoned comb, disguised herself differently, and went out again. She knocked on the door, but Snow-White called out, "I am not allowed to let anyone in."

Then she pulled out the comb, and when Snow-White saw how it glistened, and noted that the woman was a complete stranger, she opened the door, and bought the comb from her. "Come, let me comb your hair," said the peddler woman. She had barely stuck the comb into Snow-White's hair, before the girl fell down and was dead. "That will keep you lying there," said the queen. And she went home with a light heart.

The dwarfs came home just in time. They saw what had happened and pulled the poisoned comb from her hair. Snow-White opened her eyes and came back to life. She promised the dwarfs not to let anyone in again.

The queen stepped before her mirror:

"MIRROR, MIRROR, ON THE WALL,

Who in this land is fairest of all?"

The mirror answered:

"YOU, MY QUEEN, ARE FAIR; IT IS TRUE.

But Little Snow-White with the seven dwarfs
Is a thousand times fairer than you."

When the queen heard this, she shook and trembled with anger. "Snow-White will die, if it costs me my life!" Then she went into her most secret room—no one else was allowed inside—and she made a poisoned, poisoned apple. From the outside it was red and beautiful, and anyone who saw it would want it. Then she disguised herself as a peasant woman, went to the dwarfs' house, and knocked on the door.

Snow-White peeped out and said, "I'm not allowed to let anyone in. The dwarfs have forbidden it most severely."

"If you don't want to, I can't force you," said the peasant woman. "I am selling these apples, and I will give you one to taste."

"No, I can't accept anything. The dwarfs don't want me to."

"If you are afraid, then I will cut the apple in two and eat half of it. Here, you eat the half with the beautiful red cheek!" Now, the apple had been so artfully made that only the red half was poisoned. When Snow-White saw that the peasant woman was eating part of the apple, her desire for it grew stronger, so she finally let the woman hand her the other half through the window. She bit into it, but she barely had the bite in her mouth when she fell to the ground dead.

The queen was happy, went home, and asked her mirror:

"MIRROR, MIRROR, ON THE WALL,

Who in this land is fairest of all?"

And it answered:

"You, my queen, are fairest of all."

"Now I'll have some peace," she said, "because once again I'm the most beautiful woman in the land. Snow-White will remain dead this time."

That evening the dwarfs returned home from the mines. Snow-White was lying on the floor, and she was dead. They loosened her laces and looked in her hair for something poisonous, but nothing helped. They could not bring her back to life. They laid her on a bier, and all seven sat next to her and cried and cried for three days. They were going to bury her, but they saw that she remained fresh. She did not look at all like a dead person, and she still had beautiful red cheeks. They had a glass coffin made for her, and laid her inside, so that she could be seen easily. They wrote her name and her ancestry on it in gold letters, and one of them always stayed at home and kept watch over her.

Snow-White lay there in the coffin a long, long time, and she did not decay. She was still as white as snow and as red as blood, and if she had been able to open her eyes, they still would have been as black as ebony wood. She lay there as if she were asleep.

One day a young prince came to the dwarfs' house and wanted shelter for the night. When he came into their parlor and saw Snow-White lying there in a glass coffin, illuminated so beautifully by seven little candles, he could not get enough of her beauty. He read the golden inscription and saw that she was the daughter of a king. He asked the dwarfs to sell him the coffin with the dead Snow-White, but they would not do this for any amount of gold. Then he asked them to give her to him, for he could not live without being able to see her, and he would keep her, and honor her as his most cherished thing on earth. Then the dwarfs took pity on him and gave him the coffin.

The prince had it carried to his castle, and had it placed in a room where he sat by it the whole day, never taking his eyes from it. Whenever he had to go out and was unable to see Snow-White, he became sad. And he could not eat a bite, unless the coffin was standing next to him. Now, the servants who always had to carry the coffin to and fro became angry about this. One time one of them opened the coffin, lifted Snow-White upright, and said, "We are plagued the whole day long, just because of such a dead girl," and he hit her in the back with his hand. Then the terrible piece of apple that she had bitten off came out of her throat, and Snow-White came back to life.

She walked up to the prince, who was beside himself with joy to see his beloved Snow-White alive. They sat down together at the table and ate with joy.

Their wedding was set for the next day, and Snow-White's godless mother was invited as well. That morning she stepped before the mirror and said:

"MIRROR, MIRROR, ON THE WALL,

Who in this land is fairest of all?"

The mirror answered:

"YOU, MY QUEEN, ARE FAIR; IT IS TRUE.

But the young queen
Is a thousand times fairer than you."

She was horrified to hear this, and so overtaken with fear that she could not say anything. Still, her jealousy drove her to go to the wedding and see the young queen. When she arrived she saw that it was Snow-White. Then they put a pair of iron shoes into the fire until they glowed, and she had to put them on and dance in them. Her feet were terribly burned, and she could not stop until she had danced herself to death.

LITTLE BRIER-ROSE
(SLEEPING BEAUTY)

Text by Jacob and Wilhelm Grimm, from
Kinder-und Hausmärchen, retrieved from
the website of D. L. Ashliman

A king and queen had no children, although they wanted one very much. Then one day while the queen was sitting in her bath, a crab crept out of the water onto the ground and said, "Your wish will soon be fulfilled, and you will bring a daughter into the world." And that is what happened.

The king was so happy about the birth of the princess that he held a great celebration. He also invited the fairies who lived in his kingdom, but because he had only twelve golden plates, one had to be left out, for there were thirteen of them.

The fairies came to the celebration, and as it was ending they presented the child with gifts. The first one promised her virtue, the second one gave beauty, and so on, each one offering something desirable and magnificent. The eleventh fairy had just presented her gift when the thirteenth fairy walked in. She was very angry that she had not been invited and cried out, "Because you did not invite me, I tell you that in her fifteenth year, your daughter will prick herself with a spindle and fall over dead."

The parents were horrified, but the twelfth fairy, who had not yet offered her wish, said, "It shall not be her death. She will only fall into a hundred-year sleep." The king, hoping to rescue his dear child, issued an order that all spindles in the entire kingdom should be destroyed.

The princess grew and became a miracle of beauty. One day, when she had just reached her fifteenth year, the king and queen went away, leaving her all alone in the castle. She walked from room to room, following her heart's desire. Finally she came to an old tower. A narrow stairway led up to it. Being curious, she climbed up until she came to a small door. There was a small yellow key in the door. She turned it, and the door sprang open. She found herself in a small room where an old woman sat spinning flax. She was attracted to the old woman, and joked with her, and said that she too would like to try her hand at spinning. She picked up the spindle, but no sooner did she touch it than she pricked herself with it and then fell down into a deep sleep.

At that same moment the king and his attendants returned, and everyone began to fall asleep: the horses in the stalls, the pigeons on the roof, the dogs in the courtyard, the flies on the walls. Even the fire on the hearth flickered, stopped moving, and fell asleep. The roast stopped sizzling. The cook let go of the kitchen boy, whose hair he was about to pull. The maid dropped the chicken that she was plucking. They all slept. And a thorn hedge grew up around the entire castle, growing higher and higher, until nothing at all could be seen of it.

Princes, who had heard about the beautiful Brier-Rose, came and tried to free her, but they could not penetrate the hedge. It was as if the thorns were firmly attached to hands.

The princes became stuck in them, and they died miserably. And thus it continued for many long years.

Then one day a prince was traveling through the land. An old man told him about the belief that there was a castle behind the thorn hedge, with a wonderfully beautiful princess asleep inside with all of her attendants. His grandfather had told him that many princes had tried to penetrate the hedge, but that they had gotten stuck in the thorns and had been pricked to death.

"I'm not afraid of that," said the prince. "I shall penetrate the hedge and free the beautiful Brier-Rose."

He went forth, but when he came to the thorn hedge, it turned into flowers. They separated, and he walked through, but after he passed, they turned back into thorns. He went into the castle. Horses and colorful hunting dogs were asleep in the courtyard. Pigeons, with their little heads stuck under their wings, were sitting on the roof. As he walked inside, the flies on the wall, the fire in the kitchen, the cook and the maid were all asleep. He walked further. All the attendants were asleep; and still further, the king and the queen. It was so quiet that he could hear his own breath.

Finally he came to the old tower where Brier-Rose was lying asleep. The prince was so amazed at her beauty that he bent over and kissed her. At that moment she awoke, and with her the king and the queen, and all the attendants, and the horses and the dogs, and the pigeons on the roof, and the flies on the walls. The fire stood up and flickered, and then finished cooking the food. The roast sizzled away. The cook boxed the kitchen boy's ears. And the maid finished plucking the chicken. Then the prince and Brier-Rose got married, and they lived long and happily until they died.

THE MASTER CAT, OR PUSS IN BOOTS

Text by Charles Perrault,
translated by Robert Samber and J. E. Mansion,
retrieved from the Project Gutenberg ebook
The Fairy Tales of Charles Perrault

There was a miller, who left no more estate to the three sons he had, than his Mill, his Ass, and his Cat. The partition was soon made. Neither the scrivener nor attorney were sent for. They would soon have eaten up all the poor patrimony. The eldest had the Mill, the second the Ass, and the youngest nothing but the Cat.

The poor young fellow was quite comfortless at having so poor a lot.

"My brothers," said he, "may get their living handsomely enough, by joining their stocks together; but for my part, when I have eaten up my Cat, and made me a muff of his skin, I must die with hunger."

The Cat, who heard all this, but made as if he did not, said to him with a grave and serious air:

"Do not thus afflict yourself, my good master; you have only to give me a bag, and get a pair of boots made for me, that I may scamper through the dirt and the brambles, and you shall see that you have not so bad a portion of me as you imagine."

Though the Cat's master did not build very much upon what he said, he had however often seen him play a great many cunning tricks to catch rats and mice; as when he used to hang by the heels, or hide himself in the meal, and make as if he were dead; so that he did not altogether despair of his affording him some help in his miserable condition.

When the Cat had what he asked for, he booted himself very gallantly; and putting his bag about his neck, he held the strings of it in his two forepaws, and went into a warren where was great abundance of rabbits. He put bran and sow thistle into his bag, and stretching himself out at length, as if he had been dead, he waited for some young rabbit, not yet acquainted with the deceits of the world, to come and rummage his bag for what he had put into it.

Scarce was he lain down, but he had what he wanted; a rash and foolish young rabbit jumped into his bag, and Monsieur Puss, immediately drawing closed the strings, took and killed him without pity. Proud of his prey, he went with it to the palace, and asked to speak with His Majesty. He was shown upstairs into the King's apartment, and, making a low reverence, said to him:

"I have brought you, sir, a rabbit of the warren which my noble lord the Marquis of Carabas"—for that was the title which Puss was pleased to give his master—"has commanded me to present to Your Majesty from him."

"Tell thy master," said the King, "that I thank him, and that he does me a great deal of pleasure."

Another time he went and hid himself among some standing corn, holding still his bag open; and when a brace of partridges ran into it, he drew the strings, and so caught them both. He went and made a present of these to the King, as he had done before of the rabbit which he took in the warren. The King in like manner received the partridges with great pleasure, and ordered him some money to drink.

The Cat continued for two or three months, thus to carry His Majesty, from time to time, game of his master's taking. One day in particular, when he knew for certain that the King was to take the air, along the riverside, with his daughter, the most beautiful princess in the world, he said to his master:

"If you will follow my advice, your fortune is made; you have nothing else to do, but go and wash yourself in the river, in that part I shall show you, and leave the rest to me."

The Marquis of Carabas did what the Cat advised him to, without knowing why or wherefore.

While he was washing, the King passed by, and the Cat began to cry out, as loud as he could:

"Help, help, my lord Marquis of Carabas is drowning."

At this noise the King put his head out of his coach window, and finding it was the Cat who had so often brought him such good game, he commanded his guards to run immediately to the assistance of his lordship the Marquis of Carabas.

While they were drawing the poor Marquis out of the river, the Cat came up to the coach, and told the King that while his master was washing, there came by some rogues, who went off with his clothes, though he had cried out "Thieves, thieves," several times, as loud as he could. This cunning Cat had hidden them under a great stone. The King immediately commanded the officers of his wardrobe to run and fetch one of his best suits for the lord Marquis of Carabas.

The King received him with great kindness, and as the fine clothes he had given him extremely set off his good mien (for he was well made, and very handsome in his person), the King's daughter took a secret inclination to him, and the Marquis of Carabas had no sooner cast two or three respectful and somewhat tender glances, but she fell in love with him to distraction. The King would needs have him come into his coach, and take part of the airing. The Cat, quite overjoyed to see his project begin to succeed, marched on before, and meeting with some countrymen, who were mowing a meadow, he said to them:

"Good people, you who are mowing, if you do not tell the King that the meadow you mow belongs to my lord Marquis of Carabas, you shall be chopped as small as mincemeat."

The King did not fail asking of the mowers to whom the meadow they were mowing belonged.

"To my lord Marquis of Carabas," answered they all together; for the Cat's threats had made them terribly afraid.

"Truly a fine estate," said the King to the Marquis of Carabas.

"You see, sir," said the Marquis, "this is a meadow which never fails to yield a plentiful harvest every year."

The Master Cat, who still went on before, met with some reapers, and said to them:

"Good people, you who are reaping, if you do not tell the King that all this corn belongs to the Marquis of Carabas, you shall be chopped as small as mincemeat."

The King, who passed by a moment after, would needs know to whom all that corn, which he then saw, did belong. "To my lord Marquis of Carabas," replied the reapers; and the King again congratulated the Marquis.

The Master Cat, who went always before, said the same words to all he met; and the King was astonished at the vast estates of my lord Marquis of Carabas.

Monsieur Puss came at last to a stately castle, the master of which was an Ogre, the richest had ever been known; for all the lands which the King had then gone over belonged to this castle. The Cat, who had taken care to inform himself who this Ogre was, and what he could do, asked to speak with him, saying he could not pass so near his castle, without having the honor of paying his respects to him.

The Ogre received him as civilly as an Ogre could do, and made him sit down.

"I have been assured," said the Cat, "that you have the gift of being able to change yourself into all sorts of creatures you have a mind to; you can, for example, transform yourself into a lion, or elephant, and the like."

"This is true," answered the Ogre very briskly, "and to convince you, you shall see me now become a lion."

Puss was so sadly terrified at the sight of a lion so near him that he immediately got into the gutter, not without abundance of trouble and danger, because of his boots, which were ill-suited for walking upon the tiles. A little while after, when Puss saw that the Ogre had resumed his natural form, he came down, and owned he had been very much frightened.

"I have been moreover informed," said the Cat, "but I know not how to believe it, that you have also the power to take on you the shape of the smallest animals; for example, to change yourself into a rat or a mouse; but I must own to you, I take this to be impossible."

"Impossible?" cried the Ogre, "you shall see that presently," and at the same time changed into a mouse, and began to run about the floor.

Puss no sooner perceived this, but he fell upon him, and ate him up.

Meanwhile the King, who saw, as he passed, this fine castle

of the Ogre's, had a mind to go into it. Puss, who heard the noise of His Majesty's coach running over the drawbridge, ran out and said to the King:

"Your Majesty is welcome to this castle of my lord Marquis of Carabas."

"What! My lord Marquis?" cried the King. "And does this castle also belong to you? There can be nothing finer than this court, and all the stately buildings which surround it; let us go into it, if you please."

The Marquis gave his hand to the Princess, and followed the King, who went up first. They passed into a spacious hall, where they found a magnificent collation which the Ogre had prepared for his friends, who were that very day to visit him, but dared not to enter knowing the King was there. His Majesty was perfectly charmed with the good qualities of my lord Marquis of Carabas, as was his daughter, who was fallen violently in love with him; and seeing the vast estate he possessed, said to him, after having drank five or six glasses:

"It will be owing to yourself only, my lord Marquis, if you are not my son-in-law."

The Marquis, making several low bows, accepted the honor which His Majesty conferred upon him, and forthwith, that very same day, married the Princess.

Puss became a great lord, and never ran after mice anymore, but only for his diversion.

THE MORAL

How advantageous it may be, by long descent of pedigree, to enjoy a great estate, yet knowledge how to act, we see, joined with consummate industry (nor wonder ye thereat), doth often prove a greater boon, as should be to young people known.

ANOTHER

If the son of a miller so soon gains the heart of a beautiful princess, and makes her impart sweet languishing glances, eyes melting for love, it must be remarked of fine clothes how they move, and that youth, a good face, a good air, with good mien, are not always indifferent mediums to win the love of the fair, and gently inspire the flames of sweet passion, and tender desire.

LITTLE RED-CAP
(LITTLE RED RIDING HOOD)

Text by Jacob and Wilhelm Grimm, from *Kinder-und Hausmärchen*, translated by Edgar Taylor and Marian Edwardes, retrieved from the Project Gutenberg ebook *Grimms' Fairy Tales*

Once upon a time there was a dear little girl who was loved by everyone who looked at her, but most of all by her grandmother, and there was nothing that she would not have given to the child. Once she gave her a little cap of red velvet, which suited her so well that she would never wear anything else; so she was always called "Little Red-Cap."

One day her mother said to her: "Come, Little Red-Cap, here is a piece of cake and a bottle of wine; take them to your grandmother, she is ill and weak, and they will do her good. Set out before it gets hot, and when you are going, walk nicely and quietly and do not run off the path, or you may fall and break the bottle, and then your grandmother will get nothing; and when you go into her room, don't forget to say, 'Good morning,' and don't peep into every corner before you do it."

"I will take great care," said Little Red-Cap to her mother, and gave her hand on it.

The grandmother lived out in the wood, half a league from the village, and just as Little Red-Cap entered the wood, a wolf met her. Red-Cap did not know what a wicked creature he was, and was not at all afraid of him.

"Good day, Little Red-Cap," said he.

"Thank you kindly, wolf."

"Whither away so early, Little Red-Cap?"

"To my grandmother's."

"What have you got in your apron?"

"Cake and wine; yesterday was baking day, so poor sick grandmother is to have something good, to make her stronger."

"Where does your grandmother live, Little Red-Cap?"

"A good quarter of a league farther on in the wood; her house stands under the three large oak trees, the nut trees are just below; you surely must know it," replied Little Red-Cap.

The wolf thought to himself: "What a tender young creature! What a nice plump mouthful—she will be better to eat than the old woman. I must act craftily, so as to catch both." So he walked for a short time by the side of Little Red-Cap, and then he said: "See, Little Red-Cap, how pretty the flowers are about here— why do you not look round? I believe, too, that you do not hear how sweetly the little birds are singing; you walk gravely along as if you were going to school, while everything else out here in the wood is merry."

Little Red-Cap raised her eyes, and when she saw the sun-beams dancing here and there through the trees, and pretty flowers growing everywhere, she thought: "Suppose I take Grandmother a fresh nosegay; that would please her too. It is so early in the day that I shall still get there in good time"; and so she ran from the path into the wood to look for flowers. And whenever she had picked one, she fancied that she saw a still prettier one farther on, and ran after it, and so got deeper and deeper into the wood.

Meanwhile the wolf ran straight to the grandmother's house and knocked at the door.

"Who is there?"

"Little Red-Cap," replied the wolf. "She is bringing cake and wine; open the door."

"Lift the latch," called out the grandmother. "I am too weak, and cannot get up."

The wolf lifted the latch, the door sprang open, and without saying a word he went straight to the grandmother's bed, and devoured her. Then he put on her clothes, dressed himself in her cap, laid himself in bed, and drew the curtains.

Little Red-Cap, however, had been running about picking flowers, and when she had gathered so many that she could carry no more, she remembered her grandmother, and set out on the way to her.

She was surprised to find the cottage door standing open, and when she went into the room, she had such a strange feeling that she said to herself: "Oh dear! How uneasy I feel today, and at other times I like being with Grandmother so much." She called out: "Good morning," but received no answer; so she went to the bed and drew back the curtains. There lay her grandmother with her cap pulled far over her face, and looking very strange.

"Oh! Grandmother," she said, "what big ears you have!"

"The better to hear you with, my child," was the reply.

"But, Grandmother, what big eyes you have!" she said.

"The better to see you with, my dear."

"But, Grandmother, what large hands you have!"

"The better to hug you with."

"Oh! But, Grandmother, what a terrible big mouth you have!"

"The better to eat you with!"

And scarcely had the wolf said this, than with one bound he was out of bed and swallowed up Red-Cap.

When the wolf had appeased his appetite, he lay down again in the bed, fell asleep, and began to snore very loud. The huntsman was just passing the house, and thought to himself: "How the old woman is snoring! I must just see if she wants anything." So he went into the room, and when he came to the bed, he saw that the wolf was lying in it. "Do I find you here, you old sinner!" said he. "I have long sought you!" Then just as he was going to fire at him, it occurred to him that the wolf might have devoured the grandmother, and that she might still be saved, so he did not fire, but took a pair of scissors, and began to cut open the stomach of the sleeping wolf. When he had made two snips, he saw the Little Red-Cap shining, and then he made two snips more, and the little girl sprang out, crying: "Ah, how frightened I have been! How dark it was inside the wolf"; and after that the aged grandmother came out alive also, but scarcely able to breathe. Red-Cap, however, quickly fetched great stones with which they filled the wolf's belly, and when he awoke, he wanted to run away, but the stones were so heavy that he collapsed at once, and fell dead.

Then all three were delighted. The huntsman drew off the wolf's skin and went home with it; the grandmother ate the cake and drank the wine which Red-Cap had brought, and revived, but Red-Cap thought to herself: "As long as I live, I will never by myself leave the path, to run into the wood, when my mother has forbidden me to do so."

It also related that once when Red-Cap was again taking cakes to the old grandmother, another wolf spoke to her, and tried to entice her from the path. Red-Cap, however, was on her guard, and went straight forward on her way, and told her grandmother that she had met the wolf, and that he had said "good morning" to her, but with such a wicked look in his eyes, that if they had not been on the public road she was certain he would have eaten her up. "Well," said the grandmother, "we will shut the door, that he may not come in." Soon afterward the wolf knocked, and cried: "Open the door, Grandmother, I am Little Red-Cap, and am bringing you some cakes." But they did not speak, or open the door, so the graybeard stole twice or thrice round the house, and at last jumped on the roof, intending to wait until Red-Cap went home in the evening, and then to steal after her and devour her in the darkness. But the grandmother saw what was in his thoughts. In front of the house was a great stone trough, so she said to the child: "Take the pail, Red-Cap; I made some sausages yesterday, so carry the water in which I boiled them to the trough." Red-Cap carried until the great trough was quite full. Then the smell of the sausages reached the wolf, and he sniffed and peeped down, and at last stretched out his neck so far that he could no longer keep his footing and began to slip, and slipped down from the roof straight into the great trough, and was drowned. But Red-Cap went joyously home, and no one ever did anything to harm her again.

FRAU TRUDE

Text by Jacob and Wilhelm Grimm, from *Grimm's Household Tales*, translated by Margaret Hunt, retrieved from the Project Gutenberg ebook *Household Tales by Brothers Grimm*

There was once a little girl who was obstinate and inquisitive, and when her parents told her to do anything, she did not obey them, so how could she fare well? One day she said to her parents, "I have heard so much of Frau Trude, I will go to her some day. People say that everything about her does look so strange, and that there are such odd things in her house, that I have become quite curious!"

Her parents absolutely forbade her, and said, "Frau Trude is a bad woman, who does wicked things, and if thou goest to her, thou art no longer our child."

But the maiden did not let herself be turned aside by her parents' prohibition, and still went to Frau Trude. And when she got to her, Frau Trude said, "Why art thou so pale?"

"Ah," she replied, and her whole body trembled, "I have been so terrified at what I have seen."

"What hast thou seen?"

"I saw a black man on your steps."

"That was a collier."

"Then I saw a green man."

"That was a huntsman."

"After that I saw a blood-red man."

"That was a butcher."

"Ah, Frau Trude, I was terrified; I looked through the window and saw not you, but, as I verily believe, the devil himself with a head of fire."

"Oho!" said she. "Then thou hast seen the witch in her proper costume. I have been waiting for thee, and wanting thee a long time already; thou shalt give me some light." Then she changed the girl into a block of wood, and threw it into the fire. And when it was in full blaze she sat down close to it, and warmed herself by it, and said, "That shines bright for once in a way."

THE NIGHTINGALE

Text by Hans Christian Andersen, retrieved from the Project Gutenberg ebook *Fairy Tales of Hans Christian Andersen*

In China, you know, the emperor is a Chinese, and all those about him are Chinamen also. The story I am going to tell you happened a great many years ago, so it is well to hear it now before it is forgotten. The emperor's palace was the most beautiful in the world. It was built entirely of porcelain, and very costly, but so delicate and brittle that whoever touched it was obliged to be careful. In the garden could be seen the most singular flowers, with pretty silver bells tied to them, which tinkled so that everyone who passed could not help noticing the flowers. Indeed, everything in the emperor's garden was remarkable, and it extended so far that the gardener himself did not know where it ended. Those who traveled beyond its limits knew that there was a noble forest, with lofty trees, sloping down to the deep blue sea, and the great ships sailed under the shadow of its branches. In one of these trees lived a nightingale, who sang so beautifully that even the poor fishermen, who had so many other things to do, would stop and listen. Sometimes, when they went at night to spread their nets, they would hear her sing, and say, "Oh, is not that beautiful?" But when they returned to their fishing, they forgot the bird until the next night. Then they would hear it again, and exclaim, "Oh, how beautiful is the nightingale's song!"

Travelers from every country in the world came to the city of the emperor, which they admired very much, as well as the palace and gardens; but when they heard the nightingale, they all declared it to be the best of all. And the travelers, on their return home, related what they had seen; and learned men wrote books, containing descriptions of the town, the palace, and the gardens; but they did not forget the nightingale, which was really the greatest wonder. And those who could write poetry composed beautiful verses about the nightingale, who lived in a forest near the deep sea. The books traveled all over the world, and some of them came into the hands of the emperor; and he sat in his golden chair, and, as he read, he nodded his approval every moment, for it pleased him to find such a beautiful description of his city, his palace, and his gardens. But when he came to the words "the nightingale is the most beautiful of all," he exclaimed, "What is this? I know nothing of any nightingale. Is there such a bird in my empire? And even in my garden? I have never heard of it. Something, it appears, may be learned from books."

Then he called one of his lords-in-waiting, who was so high-bred that when any in an inferior rank to himself spoke to him, or asked him a question, he would answer, "Pooh," which means nothing.

"There is a very wonderful bird mentioned here, called a nightingale," said the emperor; "they say it is the best thing in my large kingdom. Why have I not been told of it?"

"I have never heard the name," replied the cavalier; "she has not been presented at court."

"It is my pleasure that she shall appear this evening," said the emperor; "the whole world knows what I possess better than I do myself."

"I have never heard of her," said the cavalier; "yet I will endeavor to find her."

But where was the nightingale to be found? The nobleman went upstairs and down, through halls and passages; yet none of those whom he met had heard of the bird. So he returned to the emperor, and said that it must be a fable, invented by those who had written the book. "Your Imperial Majesty," said he, "cannot believe everything contained in books; sometimes they are only fiction, or what is called the black art."

"But the book in which I have read this account," said the emperor, "was sent to me by the great and mighty emperor of Japan, and therefore it cannot contain a falsehood. I will hear the nightingale, she must be here this evening; she has my highest favor; and if she does not come, the whole court shall be trampled upon after supper is ended."

"Tsing-pe!" cried the lord-in-waiting, and again he ran up and down stairs, through all the halls and corridors; and half the court ran with him, for they did not like the idea of being trampled upon. There was a great inquiry about this wonderful nightingale, whom all the world knew, but who was unknown to the court.

At last they met with a poor little girl in the kitchen, who said, "Oh, yes, I know the nightingale quite well; indeed, she can sing. Every evening I have permission to take home to my poor sick mother the scraps from the table; she lives down by the seashore, and as I come back I feel tired, and I sit down in the wood to rest, and listen to the nightingale's song. Then the tears come into my eyes, and it is just as if my mother kissed me."

"Little maiden," said the lord-in-waiting, "I will obtain for you constant employment in the kitchen, and you shall have permission to see the emperor dine, if you will lead us to the nightingale; for she is invited for this evening to the palace." So she went into the wood where the nightingale sang, and half the court followed her. As they went along, a cow began lowing.

"Oh," said a young courtier, "now we have found her; what wonderful power for such a small creature; I have certainly heard it before."

"No, that is only a cow lowing," said the little girl; "we are a long way from the place yet."

Then some frogs began to croak in the marsh.

"Beautiful," said the young courtier again. "Now I hear it, tinkling like little church bells."

"No, those are frogs," said the little maiden; "but I think we shall soon hear her now," and presently the nightingale began to sing.

"Hark, hark! There she is," said the girl, "and there she sits," she added, pointing to a little gray bird who was perched on a bough.

"Is it possible?" said the lord-in-waiting. "I never imagined it would be a little, plain, simple thing like that. She has certainly changed color at seeing so many grand people around her."

"Little nightingale," cried the girl, raising her voice, "our most gracious emperor wishes you to sing before him."

"With the greatest pleasure," said the nightingale, and began to sing most delightfully.

"It sounds like tiny glass bells," said the lord-in-waiting, "and see how her little throat works. It is surprising that we have never heard this before; she will be a great success at court."

"Shall I sing once more before the emperor?" asked the nightingale, who thought he was present.

"My excellent little nightingale," said the courtier, "I have the great pleasure of inviting you to a court festival this evening, where you will gain imperial favor by your charming song."

"My song sounds best in the green wood," said the bird; but still she came willingly when she heard the emperor's wish.

The palace was elegantly decorated for the occasion. The walls and floors of porcelain glittered in the light of a thousand lamps. Beautiful flowers, round which little bells were tied, stood in the corridors: what with the running to and fro and the draft, these bells tinkled so loudly that no one could speak to be heard. In the center of the great hall, a golden perch had been fixed for the nightingale to sit on. The whole court was present, and the little kitchen maid had received permission to stand by the door. She was not installed as a real court cook. All were in full dress, and every eye was turned to the little gray bird when the emperor nodded to her to begin. The nightingale sang so sweetly that the tears came into the emperor's eyes, and then rolled down his cheeks, as her song became still more touching and went to everyone's heart. The emperor was so delighted that he declared the nightingale should have his gold slipper to wear round her neck, but she declined the honor with thanks: she had been sufficiently rewarded already. "I have seen tears in an emperor's eyes," she said; "that is my richest reward. An emperor's tears have wonderful power, and are quite sufficient honor for me;" and then she sang again more enchantingly than ever.

"That singing is a lovely gift;" said the ladies of the court to each other; and then they took water in their mouths to make them utter the gurgling sounds of the nightingale when they spoke to anyone, so that they might fancy themselves nightingales. And the footmen and chambermaids also expressed their satisfaction, which is saying a great deal, for they are very difficult to please. In fact the nightingale's visit was most successful. She was now to remain at court, to have her own cage, with liberty to go out twice a day, and once during the night. Twelve servants were appointed to attend her on these occasions, who each held her by a silken string fastened to her leg. There was certainly not much pleasure in this kind of flying.

The whole city spoke of the wonderful bird, and when two people met, one said "nightin," and the other said "gale," and they understood what was meant, for nothing else was talked of. Eleven peddlers' children were named after her, but none of them could sing a note.

One day the emperor received a large packet on which was written "The Nightingale." "Here is no doubt a new book about our celebrated bird," said the emperor. But instead of a book, it was a work of art contained in a casket, an artificial nightingale made to look like a living one, and covered all over with diamonds, rubies, and sapphires. As soon as the artificial bird was wound up, it could sing like the real one, and could move its tail up and down, which sparkled with silver and gold. Round its neck hung a piece of ribbon, on which was written "The Emperor of China's nightingale is poor compared with that of the Emperor of Japan's."

"This is very beautiful," exclaimed all who saw it, and he who had brought the artificial bird received the title of "Imperial Nightingale-bringer-in-chief."

"Now they must sing together," said the court, "and what a duet it will be." But they did not get on well, for the real nightingale sang in its own natural way, but the artificial bird sang only waltzes.

"That is not a fault," said the music master, "it is quite perfect to my taste," so then it had to sing alone, and was as successful as the real bird; besides, it was so much prettier to look at, for it sparkled like bracelets and breastpins. Three and thirty times did it sing the same tunes without being tired; the people would gladly have heard it again, but the emperor said the living nightingale ought to sing something. But where was she? No one had noticed her when she flew out at the open window, back to her own green woods.

"What strange conduct," said the emperor, when her flight had been discovered; and all the courtiers blamed her, and said she was a very ungrateful creature.

"But we have the best bird after all," said one, and then they would have the bird sing again, although it was the thirty-fourth time they had listened to the same piece, and even then they had not learned it, for it was rather difficult. But the music master praised the bird in the highest degree, and even asserted that it was better than a real nightingale, not only in its dress and the beautiful diamonds, but also in its musical power. "For you must perceive, my chief lord and emperor, that with a real nightingale we can never tell what is going to be sung, but with this bird everything is settled. It can be opened and explained, so that people may understand how the waltzes are formed, and why one note follows upon another."

"This is exactly what we think," they all replied, and then the music master received permission to exhibit the bird to the people on the following Sunday, and the emperor commanded that they should be present to hear it sing. When they heard it they were like people intoxicated; however it must have been with drinking tea, which is quite a Chinese custom. They all said "Oh!" and held up their forefingers and nodded, but a poor fisherman, who had heard the real night-ingale, said, "It sounds prettily enough, and the melodies are all alike; yet there seems something wanting, I cannot exactly tell what."

And after this the real nightingale was banished from the empire, and the artificial bird placed on a silk cushion close to the emperor's bed. The presents of gold and precious stones which had been received with it were round the bird, and it was now advanced to the title of "Little Imperial Toilet Singer," and to the rank of No. 1 on the left hand; for the emperor considered the left side, on which the heart lies, as the most noble, and the heart of an emperor is in the same place as that of other people.

The music master wrote a work, in twenty-five volumes, about the artificial bird, which was very learned and very long, and full of the most difficult Chinese words; yet all the people said they had read it, and understood it, for fear of being thought stupid and having their bodies trampled upon.

So a year passed, and the emperor, the court, and all the other Chinese knew every little turn in the artificial bird's song; and for that same reason it pleased them better. They could sing with the bird, which they often did. The street-boys sang, "Zi-zi-zi, cluck, cluck, cluck," and the emperor himself could sing it also. It was really most amusing.

One evening, when the artificial bird was singing its best, and the emperor lay in bed listening to it, something inside the bird sounded "*whizz*." Then a spring cracked. "*Whir-r-r-r*" went all the wheels, running round, and then the music stopped. The emperor immediately sprang out of bed, and called for his physician; but what could he do? Then they sent for a watchmaker; and, after a great deal of talking and examination, the bird was put into something like order; but he said that it must be used very carefully, as the barrels were worn, and it would be impossible to put in new ones without injuring the music. Now there was great sorrow, as the bird could only be allowed to play once a year; and even that was dangerous for the works inside it. Then the music master made a little speech, full of hard words, and declared that the bird was as good as ever; and of course no one contradicted him.

Five years passed, and then a real grief came upon the land. The Chinese really were fond of their emperor, and he now lay so ill that he was not expected to live. Already a new emperor had been chosen and the people who stood in the street asked the lord-in-waiting how the old emperor was; but he only said, "Pooh!" and shook his head.

Cold and pale lay the emperor in his royal bed; the whole court thought he was dead, and everyone ran away to pay homage to his successor. The chamberlains went out to have a talk on the matter, and the ladies' maids invited company to take coffee. Cloth had been laid down on the halls and passages, so that not a footstep should be heard, and all was silent and still. But the emperor was not yet dead, although he lay white and stiff on his gorgeous bed, with the long velvet curtains and heavy gold tassels. A window stood open, and the moon shone in upon the emperor and the artificial bird. The poor emperor, finding he could scarcely breathe with a strange weight on his chest, opened his eyes, and saw Death sitting there. He had put on the emperor's golden crown, and held in one hand his sword of state, and in the other his beautiful banner. All around the bed and peeping through the long velvet curtains were a number of strange heads, some very ugly, and others lovely and gentle-looking. These were the emperor's good and bad deeds, which stared him in the face now Death sat at his heart.

"Do you remember this?" "Do you recollect that?" they asked one after another, thus bringing to his remembrance circumstances that made the perspiration stand on his brow.

"I know nothing about it," said the emperor. "Music! Music!" he cried. "The large Chinese drum! That I may not hear what they say." But they still went on, and Death nodded like a Chinaman to all they said. "Music! Music!" shouted the emperor. "You little precious golden bird, sing, pray sing! I have given you gold and costly presents; I have even hung my golden slipper round your neck. Sing! Sing!" But the bird remained silent. There was no one to wind it up, and therefore it could not sing a note.

Death continued to stare at the emperor with his cold, hollow eyes, and the room was fearfully still. Suddenly there came through the open window the sound of sweet music. Outside, on the bough of a tree, sat the living nightingale. She had heard of the emperor's illness, and was therefore come to sing to him of hope and trust. And as she sung, the shadows grew paler and paler; the blood in the emperor's veins flowed more rapidly, and gave life to his weak limbs; and even Death himself listened, and said, "Go on, little nightingale, go on."

"Then will you give me the beautiful golden sword and that rich banner? And will you give me the emperor's crown?" said the bird.

So Death gave up each of these treasures for a song; and the nightingale continued her singing. She sang of the quiet churchyard, where the white roses grow, where the elder tree wafts its perfume on the breeze, and the fresh, sweet grass is moistened by the mourners' tears. Then Death longed to go and see his garden, and floated out through the window in the form of a cold, white mist.

"Thanks, thanks, you heavenly little bird. I know you well. I banished you from my kingdom once, and yet you have charmed away the evil faces from my bed, and banished Death from my heart, with your sweet song. How can I reward you?"

"You have already rewarded me," said the nightingale. "I shall never forget that I drew tears from your eyes the first time I sang to you. These are the jewels that rejoice a singer's heart. But now sleep, and grow strong and well again. I will sing to you again."

And as she sang, the emperor fell into a sweet sleep; and how mild and refreshing that slumber was! When he awoke, strengthened and restored, the sun shone brightly through the window; but not one of his servants had returned—they all believed he was dead; only the nightingale still sat beside him, and sang.

"You must always remain with me," said the emperor. "You shall sing only when it pleases you; and I will break the artificial bird into a thousand pieces."

"No; do not do that," replied the nightingale; "the bird did very well as long as it could. Keep it here still. I cannot live in the palace, and build my nest; but let me come when I like. I will sit on a bough outside your window, in the evening, and sing to you, so that you may be happy, and have thoughts full of joy. I will sing to you of those who are happy, and those who suffer; of the good and the evil, who are hidden around you. The little singing bird flies far from you and your court to the home of the fisherman and the peasant's cot. I love your heart better than your crown; and yet something holy lingers round that also. I will come, I will sing to you; but you must promise me one thing."

"Everything," said the emperor, who, having dressed himself in his imperial robes, stood with the hand that held the heavy golden sword pressed to his heart.

"I only ask one thing," she replied; "let no one know that you have a little bird who tells you everything. It will be best to conceal it." So saying, the nightingale flew away.

The servants now came in to look after the dead emperor; when, lo! There he stood, and, to their astonishment, said, "Good morning."

CINDERELLA,

OR THE LITTLE GLASS SLIPPER

Text by Charles Perrault, translated
by Robert Samber and J. E. Mansion,
retrieved from the Project Gutenberg ebook
The Fairy Tales of Charles Perrault

Once there was a gentleman who married, for his second wife, the proudest and most haughty woman that was ever seen. She had, by a former husband, two daughters of her own, who were, indeed, exactly like her in all things. He had likewise, by another wife, a young daughter, but of unparalleled goodness and sweetness of temper, which she took from her mother, who was the best creature in the world.

No sooner were the ceremonies of the wedding over but the stepmother began to show herself in her true colors. She could not bear the good qualities of this pretty girl, and the less because they made her own daughters appear the more odious. She employed her in the meanest work of the house. She scoured the dishes, tables, etc., and cleaned madam's chamber, and those of misses, her daughters. She slept in a sorry garret, on a wretched straw bed, while her sisters slept in fine rooms, with floors all inlaid, on beds of the very newest fashion, and where they had looking glasses so large that they could see themselves at their full length from head to foot.

The poor girl bore it all patiently, and dared not tell her father, who would have scolded her; for his wife governed him entirely. When she had done her work, she used to go to the chimney corner, and sit down there in the cinders and ashes, which caused her to be called Cinderwench. Only the younger sister, who was not so rude and uncivil as the older one, called her Cinderella. However, Cinderella, notwithstanding her coarse apparel, was a hundred times more beautiful than her sisters, although they were always dressed very richly.

It happened that the king's son gave a ball, and invited all persons of fashion to it. Our young misses were also invited, for they cut a very grand figure among those of quality. They were mightily delighted at this invitation, and wonderfully busy in selecting the gowns, petticoats, and hair dressing that would best become them. This was a new difficulty for Cinderella; for it was she who ironed her sisters' linen and pleated their ruffles. They talked all day long of nothing but how they should be dressed.

"For my part," said the eldest, "I will wear my red velvet suit with French trimming."

"And I," said the youngest, "shall have my usual petticoat; but then, to make amends for that, I will put on my gold-flowered cloak, and my diamond stomacher, which is far from being the most ordinary one in the world."

They sent for the best hairdresser they could get to make up their headpieces and adjust their hairdos, and they had their red brushes and patches from Mademoiselle de la Poche.

They also consulted Cinderella in all these matters, for she had excellent ideas, and her advice was always good. Indeed, she even offered her services to fix their hair, which they very willingly accepted. As she was doing this, they said to her, "Cinderella, would you not like to go to the ball?"

"Alas!" said she. "You only jeer me; it is not for such as I am to go to such a place."

"You are quite right," they replied. "It would make the people laugh to see a Cinderwench at a ball."

Anyone but Cinderella would have fixed their hair awry, but she was very good, and dressed them perfectly well. They were so excited that they hadn't eaten a thing for almost two days. Then they broke more than a dozen laces trying to have themselves laced up tightly enough to give them a fine slender shape. They were continually in front of their looking glass. At last the happy day came. They went to court, and Cinderella followed them with her eyes as long as she could. When she lost sight of them, she started to cry.

Her godmother, who saw her all in tears, asked her what was the matter.

"I wish I could. I wish I could." She was not able to speak the rest, being interrupted by her tears and sobbing.

This godmother of hers, who was a fairy, said to her, "You wish that you could go to the ball; is it not so?"

"Yes," cried Cinderella, with a great sigh.

"Well," said her godmother, "be but a good girl, and I will contrive that you shall go." Then she took her into her chamber, and said to her, "Run into the garden, and bring me a pumpkin."

Cinderella went immediately to gather the finest she could get, and brought it to her godmother, not being able to imagine how this pumpkin could help her go to the ball. Her godmother scooped out all the inside of it, leaving nothing but the rind. Having done this, she struck the pumpkin with her wand, and it was instantly turned into a fine coach, gilded all over with gold.

She then went to look into her mousetrap, where she found six mice, all alive, and ordered Cinderella to lift up a little the trapdoor. She gave each mouse, as it went out, a little tap with her wand, and the mouse was that moment turned into a fine horse, which altogether made a very fine set of six horses of a beautiful mouse-colored dapple gray.

Being at a loss for a coachman, Cinderella said, "I will go and see if there is not a rat in the rat trap that we can turn into a coachman."

"You are right," replied her godmother. "Go and look."

Cinderella brought the trap to her, and in it there were three huge rats. The fairy chose the one which had the largest beard, touched him with her wand, and turned him into a fat, jolly coachman, who had the smartest whiskers that eyes ever beheld.

After that, she said to her, "Go again into the garden, and you will find six lizards behind the watering pot. Bring them to me."

She had no sooner done so but her godmother turned them into six footmen, who skipped up immediately behind the coach, with their liveries all bedaubed with gold and silver, and clung as close behind each other as if they had done nothing else their whole lives. The fairy then said to Cinderella, "Well, you see here an equipage fit to go to the ball with; are you not pleased with it?"

"Oh, yes," she cried; "but must I go in these nasty rags?"

Her godmother then touched her with her wand, and, at the same instant, her clothes turned into cloth of gold and silver, all beset with jewels. This done, she gave her a pair of glass slippers, the prettiest in the whole world. Being thus decked out, she got up into her coach; but her godmother, above all things, commanded her not to stay past midnight, telling her, at the same time, that if she stayed one moment longer, the coach would be a pumpkin again, her horses mice, her coachman a rat, her footmen lizards, and that her clothes would become just as they were before.

She promised her godmother to leave the ball before midnight; and then drove away, scarcely able to contain herself for joy. The king's son, who was told that a great princess, whom nobody knew, had arrived, ran out to receive her. He gave her his hand as she alighted from the coach, and led her into the hall, among all the company. There was immediately a profound silence. Everyone stopped dancing, and the violins ceased to play, so entranced was everyone with the singular beauties of the unknown newcomer.

Nothing was then heard but a confused noise of, "How beautiful she is! How beautiful she is!"

The king himself, old as he was, could not help watching her, and telling the queen softly that it was a long time since he had seen so beautiful and lovely a creature.

All the ladies were busied in considering her clothes and headdress, hoping to have some made next day after the same pattern, provided they could find such fine materials and as able hands to make them.

The king's son led her to the most honorable seat, and afterwards took her out to dance with him. She danced so very gracefully that they all more and more admired her. A fine meal was served up, but the young prince ate not a morsel, so intently was he busied in gazing on her.

She went and sat down by her sisters, showing them a thousand civilities, giving them part of the oranges and citrons which the prince had presented her with, which very much surprised them, for they did not know her. While Cinderella was thus amusing her sisters, she heard the clock strike eleven and three-quarters, whereupon she immediately made a courtesy to the company and hurried away as fast as she could.

Arriving home, she ran to seek out her godmother, and, after having thanked her, she said she could not but heartily wish she might go to the ball the next day as well, because the king's son had invited her.

As she was eagerly telling her godmother everything that had happened at the ball, her two sisters knocked at the door, which Cinderella ran and opened.

"You stayed such a long time!" she cried, gaping, rubbing her eyes and stretching herself as if she had been sleeping; she had not, however, had any manner of inclination to sleep while they were away from home.

"If you had been at the ball," said one of her sisters, "you would not have been tired with it. The finest princess was there, the most beautiful that mortal eyes have ever seen. She showed us a thousand civilities, and gave us oranges and citrons."

Cinderella seemed very indifferent in the matter. Indeed, she asked them the name of that princess; but they told her they did not know it, and that the king's son was very uneasy on her account and would give all the world to know who she was. At this Cinderella, smiling, replied, "She must, then, be very beautiful indeed; how happy you have been! Could not I see her? Ah, dear Charlotte, do lend me your yellow dress which you wear every day."

"Yes, to be sure!" cried Charlotte. "Lend my clothes to such a dirty Cinderwench as you are! I should be such a fool."

Cinderella, indeed, well expected such an answer, and was very glad of the refusal; for she would have been sadly put to it, if her sister had lent her what she asked for jestingly.

The next day the two sisters were at the ball, and so was Cinderella, but dressed even more magnificently than before. The king's son was always by her, and never ceased his compliments and kind speeches to her. All this was so far from being tiresome to her, and, indeed, she quite forgot what her godmother had told her. She thought that it was no later than eleven when she counted the clock striking twelve. She jumped up and fled, as nimble as a deer. The prince followed, but could not overtake her. She left behind one of her glass slippers, which the prince picked up most carefully. She reached home, but quite out of breath, and in her nasty old clothes, having nothing left of all her finery but one of the little slippers, the mate to the one that she had dropped.

The guards at the palace gate were asked if they had not seen a princess go out. They replied that they had seen nobody leave but a young girl, very shabbily dressed, and who had more the air of a poor country wench than a gentlewoman.

When the two sisters returned from the ball Cinderella asked them if they had been well entertained, and if the fine lady had been there.

They told her, yes, but that she hurried away immediately when it struck twelve, and with so much haste that she dropped one of her little glass slippers, the prettiest in the world, which the king's son had picked up; that he had done nothing but look at her all the time at the ball, and that most certainly he was very much in love with the beautiful person who owned the glass slipper.

What they said was very true; for a few days later, the king's son had it proclaimed, by sound of trumpet, that he would marry her whose foot this slipper would just fit. They began to try it on the princesses, then the duchesses and all the court, but in vain; it was brought to the two sisters, who did all they possibly could to force their foot into the slipper, but they did not succeed.

Cinderella, who saw all this, and knew that it was her slipper, said to them, laughing, "Let me see if it will not fit me."

Her sisters burst out laughing, and began to banter with her. The gentleman who was sent to try the slipper looked earnestly at Cinderella, and, finding her very handsome, said that it was only just that she should try as well, and that he had orders to let everyone try.

He had Cinderella sit down, and, putting the slipper to her foot, he found that it went on very easily, fitting her as if it had been made of wax. Her two sisters were greatly astonished, but then even more so, when Cinderella pulled out of her pocket the other slipper, and put it on her other foot. Then in came her godmother and touched her wand to Cinderella's clothes, making them richer and more magnificent than any of those she had worn before.

And now her two sisters found her to be that fine, beautiful lady whom they had seen at the ball. They threw themselves at her feet to beg pardon for all the ill treatment they had made her undergo. Cinderella took them up, and, as she embraced them, said that she forgave them with all her heart, and wanted them always to love her.

She was taken to the young prince, dressed as she was. He thought she was more charming than before, and, a few days after, married her. Cinderella, who was no less good than beautiful, gave her two sisters lodgings in the palace, and that very same day matched them with two great lords of the court.

MORAL

Beauty in a woman is a rare treasure that will always be admired. Graciousness, however, is priceless and of even greater value. This is what Cinderella's godmother gave to her when she taught her to behave like a queen. Young women, in the winning of a heart, graciousness is more important than a beautiful hairdo. It is a true gift of the fairies. Without it, nothing is possible; with it, one can do anything.

ANOTHER MORAL

Without doubt it is a great advantage to have intelligence, courage, good breeding, and common sense. These and similar talents come only from heaven, and it is good to have them. However, even these may fail to bring you success, without the blessing of a godfather or a godmother.

THE LITTLE MERMAID

Text by Hans Christian Andersen, retrieved
from the Project Gutenberg ebook
Hans Andersen's Fairy Tales

*f*ar out in the ocean, where the water is as blue as the prettiest cornflower and as clear as crystal, it is very, very deep; so deep, indeed, that no cable could sound it, and many church steeples, piled one upon another, would not reach from the ground beneath to the surface of the water above. There dwell the Sea King and his subjects.

We must not imagine that there is nothing at the bottom of the sea but bare yellow sand. No, indeed, for on this sand grow the strangest flowers and plants, the leaves and stems of which are so pliant that the slightest agitation of the water causes them to stir as if they had life. Fishes, both large and small, glide between the branches as birds fly among the trees here upon land.

In the deepest spot of all stands the castle of the Sea King. Its walls are built of coral, and the long Gothic windows are of the clearest amber. The roof is formed of shells that open and close as the water flows over them. Their appearance is very beautiful, for in each lies a glittering pearl which would be fit for the diadem of a queen.

The Sea King had been a widower for many years, and his aged mother kept house for him. She was a very sensible woman, but exceedingly proud of her high birth, and on that account wore twelve oysters on her tail, while others of high rank were only allowed to wear six.

She was, however, deserving of very great praise, especially for her care of the little sea princesses, her six granddaughters. They were beautiful children, but the youngest was the prettiest of them all. Her skin was as clear and delicate as a rose leaf, and her eyes as blue as the deepest sea; but, like all the others, she had no feet and her body ended in a fish's tail. All day long they played in the great halls of the castle or among the living flowers that grew out of the walls. The large amber windows were open, and the fish swam in, just as the swallows fly into our houses when we open the windows; only the fishes swam up to the princesses, ate out of their hands, and allowed themselves to be stroked.

Outside the castle there was a beautiful garden, in which grew bright red and dark blue flowers, and blossoms like flames of fire; the fruit glittered like gold, and the leaves and stems waved to and fro continually. The earth itself was the finest sand, but blue as the flame of burning sulfur. Over everything lay a peculiar blue radiance, as if the blue sky were everywhere, above and below, instead of the dark depths of the sea. In calm weather the sun could be seen, looking like a reddish-purple flower with light streaming from the calyx.

Each of the young princesses had a little plot of ground in the garden, where she might dig and plant as she pleased. One arranged her flower bed in the form of a whale; another preferred to make hers like the figure of a little mermaid; while the youngest child made hers round, like the sun, and in it grew flowers as red as his rays at sunset.

She was a strange child, quiet and thoughtful. While her

sisters showed delight at the wonderful things which they obtained from the wrecks of vessels, she cared only for her pretty flowers, red like the sun, and a beautiful marble statue. It was the representation of a handsome boy, carved out of pure white stone, which had fallen to the bottom of the sea from a wreck.

She planted by the statue a rose-colored weeping willow. It grew rapidly and soon hung its fresh branches over the statue, almost down to the blue sands. The shadows had the color of violet and waved to and fro like the branches, so that it seemed as if the crown of the tree and the root were at play, trying to kiss each other.

Nothing gave her so much pleasure as to hear about the world above the sea. She made her old grandmother tell her all she knew of the ships and of the towns, the people and the animals. To her it seemed most wonderful and beautiful to hear that the flowers of the land had fragrance, while those below the sea had none; that the trees of the forest were green; and that the fishes among the trees could sing so sweetly that it was a pleasure to listen to them. Her grandmother called the birds fishes, or the little mermaid would not have understood what was meant, for she had never seen birds.

"When you have reached your fifteenth year," said the grandmother, "you will have permission to rise up out of the sea and sit on the rocks in the moonlight, while the great ships go sailing by. Then you will see both forests and towns."

In the following year, one of the sisters would be fifteen, but as each was a year younger than the other, the youngest would have to wait five years before her turn came to rise up from the bottom of the ocean to see the earth as we do. However, each promised to tell the others what she saw on her first visit and what she thought was most beautiful. Their grandmother could not tell them enough—there were so many things about which they wanted to know.

None of them longed so much for her turn to come as the youngest—she who had the longest time to wait and who was so quiet and thoughtful. Many nights she stood by the open window, looking up through the dark blue water and watching the fish as they splashed about with their fins and tails. She could see the moon and stars shining faintly, but through the water they looked larger than they do to our eyes. When something like a black cloud passed between her and them, she knew that it was either a whale swimming over her head, or a ship full of human beings who never imagined that a pretty little mermaid was standing beneath them, holding out her white hands toward the keel of their ship.

At length the eldest was fifteen and was allowed to rise to the surface of the ocean.

When she returned she had hundreds of things to talk about. But the finest thing, she said, was to lie on a sand bank in the quiet moonlit sea, near the shore, gazing at the lights of the nearby town, which twinkled like hundreds of stars, and listening to the sounds of music, the noise of carriages, the voices of human beings, and the merry pealing of the bells in the church steeples. Because she could not go near all these wonderful things, she longed for them all the more.

Oh, how eagerly did the youngest sister listen to all these descriptions! And afterward, when she stood at the open window looking up through the dark blue water, she thought of the great city, with all its bustle and noise, and even fancied she could hear the sound of the church bells down in the depths of the sea.

In another year the second sister received permission to

rise to the surface of the water and to swim about where she pleased. She rose just as the sun was setting, and this, she said, was the most beautiful sight of all. The whole sky looked like gold, and violet and rose-colored clouds, which she could not describe, drifted across it. And more swiftly than the clouds flew a large flock of wild swans toward the setting sun, like a long white veil across the sea. She also swam toward the sun, but it sank into the waves, and the rosy tints faded from the clouds and from the sea.

The third sister's turn followed, and she was the boldest of them all, for she swam up a broad river that emptied into the sea. On the banks she saw green hills covered with beautiful vines, and palaces and castles peeping out from amid the proud trees of the forest. She heard birds singing and felt the rays of the sun so strongly that she was obliged often to dive under the water to cool her burning face. In a narrow creek she found a large group of little human children, almost naked, sporting about in the water. She wanted to play with them, but they fled in a great fright; and then a little black animal—it was a dog, but she did not know it, for she had never seen one before— came to the water and barked at her so furiously that she became frightened and rushed back to the open sea. But she said she should never forget the beautiful forest, the green hills, and the pretty children who could swim in the water although they had no tails.

The fourth sister was more timid. She remained in the midst of the sea, but said it was quite as beautiful there as nearer the land. She could see many miles around her, and the sky above looked like a bell of glass. She had seen the ships, but at such a great distance that they looked like seagulls. The dolphins sported in the waves, and the great whales spouted water from their nostrils till it seemed as if a hundred fountains were playing in every direction.

The fifth sister's birthday occurred in the winter, so when her turn came she saw what the others had not seen the first time they went up. The sea looked quite green, and large icebergs were floating about, each like a pearl, she said, but larger and loftier than the churches built by men. They were of the most singular shapes and glittered like diamonds. She had seated herself on one of the largest and let the wind play with her long hair. She noticed that all the ships sailed past very rapidly, steering as far away as they could, as if they were afraid of the iceberg. Toward evening, as the sun went down, dark clouds covered the sky, the thunder rolled, and the flashes of lightning glowed red on the icebergs as they were tossed about by the heaving sea. On all the ships the sails were reefed with fear and trembling, while she sat on the floating iceberg, calmly watching the lightning as it darted its forked flashes into the sea.

Each of the sisters, when first she had permission to rise to the surface, was delighted with the new and beautiful sights. Now that they were grown-up girls and could go when they pleased, they had become quite indifferent about it. They soon wished themselves back again, and after a month had passed they said it was much more beautiful down below and pleasanter to be at home.

Yet often, in the evening hours, the five sisters would twine their arms about each other and rise to the surface together. Their voices were more charming than that of any human being, and before the approach of a storm, when they feared that a ship might be lost, they swam before the vessel, singing enchanting songs of the delights to be found in the depths of the sea and begging the voyagers not to fear if they sank to the bottom. But the sailors could not understand the song and thought it was the sighing of the storm. These things were never beautiful to them, for if the ship sank, the men were drowned and their dead bodies alone reached the palace of the Sea King.

When the sisters rose, arm in arm, through the water, their youngest sister would stand quite alone, looking after them, ready to cry—only, since mermaids have no tears, she suffered more acutely.

"Oh, were I but fifteen years old!" said she. "I know that I shall love the world up there, and all the people who live in it."

At last she reached her fifteenth year.

"Well, now you are grown up," said the old dowager, her grandmother. "Come, and let me adorn you like your sisters." And she placed in her hair a wreath of white lilies, of which every flower leaf was half a pearl. Then the old lady ordered eight great oysters to attach themselves to the tail of the princess to show her high rank.

"But they hurt me so," said the little mermaid.

"Yes, I know; pride must suffer pain," replied the old lady.

Oh, how gladly she would have shaken off all this grandeur and laid aside the heavy wreath! The red flowers in her own garden would have suited her much better. But she could not change herself, so she said farewell and rose as lightly as a bubble to the surface of the water.

The sun had just set when she raised her head above the waves. The clouds were tinted with crimson and gold, and through the glimmering twilight beamed the evening star in all its beauty. The sea was calm, and the air mild and fresh. A large ship with three masts lay becalmed on the water; only one sail was set, for not a breeze stirred, and the sailors sat idle on deck or amidst the rigging. There was music and song on board, and as darkness came on, a hundred colored lanterns were lighted, as if the flags of all nations waved in the air.

The little mermaid swam close to the cabin windows, and now and then, as the waves lifted her up, she could look in through glass windowpanes and see a number of gayly dressed people.

Among them, and the most beautiful of all, was a young prince with large, black eyes. He was sixteen years of age, and his birthday was being celebrated with great display. The sailors were dancing on deck, and when the prince came out of the cabin, more than a hundred rockets rose in the air, making it as bright as day. The little mermaid was so startled that she dived under water, and when she again stretched out her head, it looked as if all the stars of heaven were falling around her.

She had never seen such fireworks before. Great suns spurted fire about, splendid fireflies flew into the blue air, and everything was reflected in the clear, calm sea beneath. The ship itself was so brightly illuminated that all the people, and even the smallest rope, could be distinctly seen. How handsome the young prince looked, as he pressed the hands of all his guests and smiled at them, while the music resounded through the clear night air!

It was very late, yet the little mermaid could not take her eyes from the ship or from the beautiful prince. The colored lanterns had been extinguished, no more rockets rose in the air, and the cannon had ceased firing; but the sea became restless, and a moaning, grumbling sound could be heard beneath the waves. Still the little mermaid remained by the cabin window, rocking up and down on the water, so that she could look within. After a while the sails were quickly set, and the ship went on her way. But soon the waves rose higher, heavy clouds darkened the sky, and lightning appeared in the distance. A dreadful storm was approaching. Once more the sails were furled, and the great ship pursued her flying course over the raging sea. The waves rose mountain high, as if they would overtop the mast, but the ship dived like a swan between them, then rose again on their lofty, foaming crests. To the little mermaid this was pleasant sport; but not so to the sailors. At length the ship groaned and creaked; the thick planks gave way under the lashing of the sea, as the waves broke over the deck; the mainmast snapped asunder like a reed, and as the ship lay over on her side, the water rushed in.

The little mermaid now perceived that the crew were in danger; even she was obliged to be careful, to avoid the beams and planks of the wreck that lay scattered on the water. At one moment it was pitch-dark so that she could not see a single object, but when a flash of lightning came it revealed the whole scene; she could see everyone who had been on board except the prince. When the ship parted, she had seen him sink into the deep waves, and she was glad, for she thought he would now be with her. Then she remembered that human beings could not live in the water, so that when he got down to her father's palace he would certainly be quite dead.

No, he must not die! So she swam about among the beams and planks that strewed the surface of the sea, forgetting that they could crush her to pieces. Diving deep under the dark waters, rising and falling with the waves, she at length managed to reach the young prince, who was fast losing the power to swim in that stormy sea. His limbs were failing him, his beautiful eyes were closed, and he would have died had not the little mermaid come to his assistance. She held his head above the water and let the waves carry them where they would.

In the morning the storm had ceased, but of the ship not a single fragment could be seen. The sun came up red and shining out of the water, and its beams brought back the hue of health to the prince's cheeks, but his eyes remained closed. The mermaid kissed his high, smooth forehead and stroked back his wet hair. He seemed to her like the marble statue in her little garden, so she kissed him again and wished that he might live.

Presently they came in sight of land, and she saw lofty blue mountains on which the white snow rested as if a flock of swans were lying upon them. Beautiful green forests were near the shore, and close by stood a large building, whether a church or a convent she could not tell. Orange and citron trees grew in the garden, and before the door stood lofty palms. The sea here formed a little bay, in which the water lay quiet and still, but very deep. She swam with the handsome prince to the beach, which was covered with fine white sand, and there she laid him in the warm sunshine, taking care to raise his head higher than his body. Then bells sounded in the large white building, and some young girls came into the garden. The little mermaid swam out farther from the shore and hid herself among some high rocks that rose out of the water. Covering her head and neck with the foam of the sea, she watched there to see what would become of the poor prince.

It was not long before she saw a young girl approach the spot where the prince lay. She seemed frightened at first, but only for a moment; then she brought a number of people, and the mermaid saw that the prince came to life again and smiled upon those who stood about him. But to her he sent no smile; he knew not that she had saved him. This made her very sorrowful, and when he was led away into the great building, she dived down into the water and returned to her father's castle.

She had always been silent and thoughtful, and now she was more so than ever. Her sisters asked her what she had seen during her first visit to the surface of the water, but she could tell them nothing. Many an evening and morning did she rise to the place where she had left the prince. She saw the fruits in the garden ripen and watched them gathered; she watched the snow on the mountaintops melt away; but never did she see the prince, and therefore she always returned home more sorrowful than before.

It was her only comfort to sit in her own little garden and fling her arm around the beautiful marble statue, which was like the prince. She gave up tending her flowers, and they grew in wild confusion over the paths, twining their long leaves and stems round the branches of the trees so that the whole place became dark and gloomy.

At length she could bear it no longer and told one of her sisters all about it. Then the others heard the secret, and very soon it became known to several mermaids, one of whom had an intimate friend who happened to know about the prince. She had also seen the festival on board ship, and she told them where the prince came from and where his palace stood.

"Come, little sister," said the other princesses. Then they entwined their arms and rose together to the surface of the water, near the spot where they knew the prince's palace stood. It was built of bright-yellow, shining stone and had long flights of marble steps, one of which reached quite down to the sea. Splendid gilded cupolas rose over the roof, and between the pillars that surrounded the whole building stood lifelike statues of marble. Through the clear crystal of the lofty windows could be seen noble rooms, with costly silk curtains and hang-ings of tapestry and walls covered with beautiful paintings. In the center of the largest salon a fountain threw its sparkling jets high up into the glass cupola of the ceiling, through which the sun shone in upon the water and upon the beautiful plants that grew in the basin of the fountain.

Now that the little mermaid knew where the prince lived, she spent many an evening and many a night on the water near the palace. She would swim much nearer the shore than any of the others had ventured, and once she went up the nar-row channel under the marble balcony, which threw a broad shadow on the water. Here she sat and watched the young prince, who thought himself alone in the bright moonlight.

She often saw him evenings, sailing in a beautiful boat on which music sounded and flags waved. She peeped out from among the green rushes, and if the wind caught her long silvery-white veil, those who saw it believed it to be a swan, spreading out its wings.

Many a night, too, when the fishermen set their nets by the light of their torches, she heard them relate many good things about the young prince. And this made her glad that she had saved his life when he was tossed about half-dead on the waves. She remembered how his head had rested on her bosom and how heartily she had kissed him, but he knew nothing of all this and could not even dream of her.

She grew more and more to like human beings and wished more and more to be able to wander about with those whose world seemed to be so much larger than her own. They could fly over the sea in ships and mount the high hills which were far above the clouds; and the lands they possessed, their woods and their fields, stretched far away beyond the reach of her sight. There was so much that she wished to know! But her sisters were unable to answer all her questions. She then went to her old grandmother, who knew all about the upper world, which she rightly called "the lands above the sea."

"If human beings are not drowned," asked the little mermaid, "can they live forever? Do they never die, as we do here in the sea?"

"Yes," replied the old lady, "they must also die, and their term of life is even shorter than ours. We sometimes live for three hundred years, but when we cease to exist here, we become only foam on the surface of the water and have not even a grave among those we love. We have not immortal souls, we shall never live again; like the green seaweed when once it has been cut off, we can never flourish more. Human beings, on the contrary, have souls which live forever, even after the body has been turned to dust. They rise up through the clear, pure air, beyond the glittering stars. As we rise out of the water and behold all the land of the earth, so do they rise to unknown and glorious regions which we shall never see."

"Why have not we immortal souls?" asked the little mermaid, mournfully. "I would gladly give all the hundreds of years that I have to live, to be a human being only for one day and to have the hope of knowing the happiness of that glorious world above the stars."

"You must not think that," said the old woman. "We believe that we are much happier and much better off than human beings."

"So I shall die," said the little mermaid, "and as the foam of the sea I shall be driven about, never again to hear the music of the waves or to see the pretty flowers or the red sun? Is there anything I can do to win an immortal soul?"

"No," said the old woman; "unless a man should love you so much that you were more to him than his father or his mother, and if all his thoughts and all his love were fixed upon you, and the priest placed his right hand in yours, and he promised to be true to you here and hereafter—then his soul would glide into your body, and you would obtain a share in the future happiness of mankind. He would give to you a soul and retain his own as well; but this can never happen. Your fish's tail, which among us is considered so beautiful, on earth is thought to be quite ugly. They do not know any better, and they think it necessary, in order to be handsome, to have two stout props, which they call legs."

Then the little mermaid sighed and looked sorrowfully at her fish's tail. "Let us be happy," said the old lady, "and dart and spring about during the three hundred years that we have to live, which is really quite long enough. After that we can rest ourselves all the better. This evening we are going to have a court ball."

It was one of those splendid sights which we can never see on earth. The walls and the ceiling of the large ballroom were of thick but transparent crystal. Many hundreds of colossal shells—some of a deep red, others of a grass green—with blue fire in them, stood in rows on each side. These lighted up the whole salon, and shone through the walls so that the sea was also illuminated. Innumerable fishes, great and small, swam past the crystal walls; on some of them the scales glowed with a purple brilliance, and on others shone like silver and gold. Through the halls flowed a broad stream, and in it danced the mermen and the mermaids to the music of their own sweet singing.

No one on earth has such lovely voices as they, but the little mermaid sang more sweetly than all. The whole court applauded her with hands and tails, and for a moment her heart felt quite gay, for she knew she had the sweetest voice either on earth or in the sea. But soon she thought again of the world above her; she could not forget the charming prince, nor her sorrow that she had not an immortal soul like his. She crept away silently out of her father's palace, and while everything within was gladness and song, she sat in her own little garden, sorrowful and alone. Then she heard the bugle sounding through the water and thought: "He is certainly sailing above, he in whom my wishes center and in whose hands I should like to place the happiness of my life. I will venture all for him and to win an immortal soul. While my sisters are dancing in my father's palace I will go to the sea witch, of whom I have always been so much afraid; she can give me counsel and help."

Then the little mermaid went out from her garden and took the road to the foaming whirlpools, behind which the sorceress lived. She had never been that way before. Neither flowers nor grass grew there; nothing but bare, gray, sandy ground stretched out to the whirlpool, where the water, like foaming mill wheels, seized everything that came within its reach and cast it into the fathomless deep. Through the midst of these crushing whirlpools the little mermaid was obliged to pass before she could reach the dominions of the sea witch. Then, for a long distance, the road lay across a stretch of warm, bubbling mire, called by the witch her turf moor.

Beyond this was the witch's house, which stood in the center of a strange forest, where all the trees and flowers were polypi, half animals and half plants. They looked like serpents with a hundred heads, growing out of the ground. The branches were long, slimy arms, with fingers like flexible worms, moving limb after limb from the root to the top. All that could be reached in the sea they seized upon and held fast, so that it never escaped from their clutches.

The little mermaid was so alarmed at what she saw that she stood still and her heart beat with fear. She came very near turning back, but she thought of the prince and of the human soul for which she longed, and her courage returned. She fastened her long, flowing hair round her head, so that the polypi should not lay hold of it. She crossed her hands on her bosom, and then darted forward as a fish shoots through the water, between the supple arms and fingers of the ugly polypi, which were stretched out on each side of her. She saw that they all held in their grasp something they had seized with their numerous little arms, which were as strong as iron bands. Tightly grasped in their clinging arms were white skeletons of human beings who had perished at sea and had sunk down into the deep waters; skeletons of land animals; and oars, rudders, and chests, of ships. There was even a little mermaid whom they had caught and strangled, and this seemed the most shocking of all to the little princess.

She now came to a space of marshy ground in the wood, where large, fat water snakes were rolling in the mire and showing their ugly, drab-colored bodies. In the midst of this spot stood a house, built of the bones of shipwrecked human beings. There sat the sea witch, allowing a toad to eat from her mouth just as people sometimes feed a canary with pieces of sugar. She called the ugly water snakes her little chickens and allowed them to crawl all over her bosom.

"I know what you want," said the sea witch. "It is very stupid of you, but you shall have your way, though it will bring you to sorrow, my pretty princess. You want to get rid of your fish's tail and to have two supports instead, like human beings on earth, so that the young prince may fall in love with you and so that you may have an immortal soul." And then the witch laughed so loud and so disgustingly that the toad and the snakes fell to the ground and lay there wriggling.

"You are but just in time," said the witch, "for after sunrise tomorrow I should not be able to help you till the end of another year. I will prepare a draft for you, with which you must swim to land tomorrow before sunrise; seat yourself there and drink it. Your tail will then disappear, and shrink up into what men call legs.

"You will feel great pain, as if a sword were passing through you. But all who see you will say that you are the prettiest little human being they ever saw. You will still have the same floating gracefulness of movement, and no dancer will ever tread so lightly. Every step you take, however, will be as if you were treading upon sharp knives and as if the blood must flow. If you will bear all this, I will help you."

"Yes, I will," said the little princess in a trembling voice, as she thought of the prince and the immortal soul.

"But think again," said the witch, "for when once your shape has become like a human being, you can no more be a mermaid. You will never return through the water to your sisters or to your father's palace again. And if you do not win the love of the prince, so that he is willing to forget his father and mother for your sake and to love you with his whole soul and allow the priest to join your hands that you may be man and wife, then you will never have an immortal soul. The first morning after he marries another, your heart will break and you will become foam on the crest of the waves."

"I will do it," said the little mermaid, and she became pale as death.

"But I must be paid, also," said the witch, "and it is not a trifle that I ask. You have the sweetest voice of any who dwell here in the depths of the sea, and you believe that you will be able to charm the prince with it. But this voice you must give to me. The best thing you possess will I have as the price of my costly draft, which must be mixed with my own blood so that it may be as sharp as a two-edged sword."

"But if you take away my voice," said the little mermaid, "what is left for me?"

"Your beautiful form, your graceful walk, and your expressive eyes. Surely with these you can enchain a man's heart. Well, have you lost your courage? Put out your little tongue, that I may cut it off as my payment; then you shall have the powerful draft."

"It shall be," said the little mermaid.

Then the witch placed her cauldron on the fire, to prepare the magic draft.

"Cleanliness is a good thing," said she, scouring the vessel with snakes which she had tied together in a large knot. Then she pricked herself in the breast and let the black blood drop into the cauldron. The steam that rose twisted itself into such horrible shapes that no one could look at them without fear. Every moment the witch threw a new ingredient into the vessel, and when it began to boil, the sound was like the weeping of a crocodile. When at last the magic draft was ready, it looked like the clearest water.

"There it is for you," said the witch. Then she cut off the mermaid's tongue, so that she would never again speak or sing. "If the polypi should seize you as you return through the wood," said the witch, "throw over them a few drops of the potion, and their fingers will be torn into a thousand pieces." But the little mermaid had no occasion to do this, for the polypi sprang back in terror when they caught sight of the glittering draft, which shone in her hand like a twinkling star.

So she passed quickly through the wood and the marsh and between the rushing whirlpools. She saw that in her father's palace the torches in the ballroom were extinguished and that all within were asleep. But she did not venture to go in to them, for now that she was dumb and going to leave them forever she felt as if her heart would break. She stole into the garden, took a flower from the flower bed of each of her sisters, kissed her hand toward the palace a thousand times, and then rose up through the dark blue waters.

The sun had not risen when she came in sight of the prince's palace and approached the beautiful marble steps, but the moon shone clear and bright. Then the little mermaid drank the magic draft, and it seemed as if a two-edged sword went through her delicate body. She fell into a swoon and lay like one dead. When the sun rose and shone over the sea, she recovered and felt a sharp pain, but before her stood the handsome young prince.

He fixed his coal-black eyes upon her so earnestly that she cast down her own and then became aware that her fish's tail was gone and that she had as pretty a pair of white legs and tiny feet as any little maiden could have. But she had no clothes, so she wrapped herself in her long, thick hair. The prince asked her who she was and whence she came. She looked at him mildly and sorrowfully with her deep blue eyes, but could not speak. He took her by the hand and led her to the palace.

Every step she took was as the witch had said it would be; she felt as if she were treading upon the points of needles or sharp knives. She bore it willingly, however, and moved at the prince's side as lightly as a bubble, so that he and all who saw her wondered at her graceful, swaying movements. She was very soon arrayed in costly robes of silk and muslin and was the most beautiful creature in the palace; but she was dumb and could neither speak nor sing.

Beautiful female slaves, dressed in silk and gold, stepped forward and sang before the prince and his royal parents. One sang better than all the others, and the prince clapped his hands and smiled at her. This was a great sorrow to the little mermaid, for she knew how much more sweetly she herself once could sing, and she thought, "Oh, if he could only know that I have given away my voice forever, to be with him!"

The slaves next performed some pretty fairy-like dances, to the sound of beautiful music. Then the little mermaid raised her lovely white arms, stood on the tips of her toes, glided over the floor, and danced as no one yet had been able to dance. At each moment her beauty was more revealed, and her expressive eyes appealed more directly to the heart than the songs of the slaves. Everyone was enchanted, especially the prince, who called her his little foundling. She danced again quite readily, to please him, though each time her foot touched the floor it seemed as if she trod on sharp knives.

The prince said she should remain with him always, and she was given permission to sleep at his door, on a velvet cushion. He had a page's dress made for her, that she might accompany him on horseback. They rode together through the sweet-scented woods, where the green boughs touched their shoulders, and the little birds sang among the fresh leaves. She climbed with him to the tops of high mountains, and although her tender feet bled so that even her steps were marked, she only smiled, and followed him till they could see the clouds beneath them like a flock of birds flying to distant lands. While at the prince's palace, and when all the household were asleep, she would go and sit on the broad marble steps, for it eased her burning feet to bathe them in the cold seawater. It was then that she thought of all those below in the deep.

Once during the night her sisters came up arm in arm, singing sorrowfully as they floated on the water. She beckoned to them, and they recognized her and told her how she had grieved them; after that, they came to the same place every night. Once she saw in the distance her old grandmother, who had not been to the surface of the sea for many years, and the old Sea King, her father, with his crown on his head. They stretched out their hands toward her, but did not venture so near the land as her sisters had.

As the days passed she loved the prince more dearly, and he loved her as one would love a little child. The thought never came to him to make her his wife. Yet unless he married her, she could not receive an immortal soul, and on the morning after his marriage with another, she would dissolve into the foam of the sea.

"Do you not love me the best of them all?" the eyes of the little mermaid seemed to say when he took her in his arms and kissed her fair forehead.

"Yes, you are dear to me," said the prince, "for you have the best heart and you are the most devoted to me. You are like a young maiden whom I once saw, but whom I shall never meet again. I was in a ship that was wrecked, and the waves cast me ashore near a holy temple where several young maidens performed the service. The youngest of them found me on the shore and saved my life. I saw her but twice, and she is the only one in the world whom I could love. But you are like her, and you have almost driven her image from my mind. She belongs to the holy temple, and good fortune has sent you to me in her stead. We will never part."

"Ah, he knows not that it was I who saved his life," thought the little mermaid. "I carried him over the sea to the wood where the temple stands; I sat beneath the foam and watched till the human beings came to help him. I saw the pretty maiden that he loves better than he loves me." The mermaid sighed deeply, but she could not weep. "He says the maiden belongs to the holy temple, therefore she will never return to the world—they will meet no more. I am by his side and see him every day. I will take care of him, and love him, and give up my life for his sake."

Very soon it was said that the prince was to marry and that the beautiful daughter of a neighboring king would be his wife, for a fine ship was being fitted out. Although the prince gave out that he intended merely to pay a visit to the king, it was generally supposed that he went to court the princess. A great company were to go with him. The little mermaid smiled and shook her head. She knew the prince's thoughts better than any of the others.

"I must travel," he had said to her; "I must see this beautiful princess. My parents desire it, but they will not oblige me to bring her home as my bride. I cannot love her, because she is not like the beautiful maiden in the temple, whom you resemble. If I were forced to choose a bride, I would choose you, my dumb foundling, with those expressive eyes." Then he kissed her rosy mouth, played with her long, waving hair, and laid his head on her heart, while she dreamed of human happiness and an immortal soul.

"You are not afraid of the sea, my dumb child, are you?" he said, as they stood on the deck of the noble ship which was to carry them to the country of the neighboring king. Then he told her of storm and of calm, of strange fishes in the deep beneath them, and of what the divers had seen there. She smiled at his descriptions, for she knew better than anyone what wonders were at the bottom of the sea.

In the moonlit night, when all on board were asleep except the man at the helm, she sat on deck, gazing down through the clear water. She thought she could distinguish her father's castle, and upon it her aged grandmother, with the silver crown on her head, looking through the rushing tide at the keel of the vessel. Then her sisters came up on the waves and gazed at her mournfully, wringing their white hands. She beckoned to them, and smiled, and wanted to tell them how happy and well-off she was. But the cabin boy approached, and when her sisters dived down, he thought what he saw was only the foam of the sea.

The next morning the ship sailed into the harbor of a beautiful town belonging to the king whom the prince was going to visit. The church bells were ringing, and from the high towers sounded a flourish of trumpets. Soldiers, with flying colors and glittering bayonets, lined the roads through which they passed. Every day was a festival, balls and entertainments following one another. But the princess had not yet appeared. People said that she had been brought up and educated in a religious house, where she was learning every royal virtue.

At last she came. Then the little mermaid, who was anxious to see whether she was really beautiful, was obliged to admit that she had never seen a more perfect vision of beauty. Her skin was delicately fair, and beneath her long, dark eyelashes her laughing blue eyes shone with truth and purity.

"It was you," said the prince, "who saved my life when I lay as if dead on the beach," and he folded his blushing bride in his arms.

"Oh, I am too happy!" said he to the little mermaid. "My fondest hopes are now fulfilled. You will rejoice at my happiness, for your devotion to me is great and sincere."

The little mermaid kissed his hand and felt as if her heart were already broken. His wedding morning would bring death to her, and she would change into the foam of the sea.

All the church bells rang, and the heralds rode through the town proclaiming the betrothal. Perfumed oil was burned in costly silver lamps on every altar. The priests waved the censers, while the bride and the bridegroom joined their hands and received the blessing of the bishop. The little mermaid, dressed in silk and gold, held up the bride's train; but her ears heard nothing of the festive music, and her eyes saw not the holy ceremony. She thought of the night of death which was coming to her, and of all she had lost in the world.

On the same evening the bride and bridegroom went on board the ship. Cannons were roaring, flags waving, and in the center of the ship a costly tent of purple and gold had been erected. It contained elegant sleeping couches for the bridal pair during the night. The ship, under a favorable wind, with swelling sails, glided away smoothly and lightly over the calm sea.

When it grew dark, a number of colored lamps were lighted and the sailors danced merrily on the deck. The little mermaid could not help thinking of her first rising out of the sea, when she had seen similar joyful festivities, so she too joined in the dance, poised herself in the air as a swallow when he pursues his prey, and all present cheered her wonderingly. She had never danced so gracefully before. Her tender feet felt as if cut with sharp knives, but she cared not for the pain; a sharper pang had pierced her heart.

She knew this was the last evening she should ever see the

prince for whom she had forsaken her kindred and her home. She had given up her beautiful voice and suffered unheard-of pain daily for him, while he knew nothing of it. This was the last evening that she should breathe the same air with him or gaze on the starry sky and the deep sea. An eternal night, without a thought or a dream, awaited her. She had no soul, and now could never win one.

All was joy and gaiety on the ship until long after midnight. She smiled and danced with the rest, while the thought of death was in her heart. The prince kissed his beautiful bride and she played with his raven hair till they went arm in arm to rest in the sumptuous tent. Then all became still on board the ship, and only the pilot, who stood at the helm, was awake. The little mermaid leaned her white arms on the edge of the vessel and looked toward the east for the first blush of morning—for that first ray of the dawn which was to be her death. She saw her sisters rising out of the flood. They were as pale as she, but their beautiful hair no longer waved in the wind; it had been cut off.

"We have given our hair to the witch," said they, "to obtain help for you, that you may not die tonight. She has given us a knife; see, it is very sharp. Before the sun rises you must plunge it into the heart of the prince. When the warm blood falls upon your feet they will grow together again into a fish's tail, and you will once more be a mermaid and can return to us to live out your three hundred years before you are changed into the salt sea foam. Haste, then; either he or you must die before sunrise. Our old grandmother mourns so for you that her white hair is falling, as ours fell under the witch's scissors. Kill the prince, and come back. Hasten! Do you not see the first red streaks in the sky? In a few minutes the sun will rise, and you must die."

Then they sighed deeply and mournfully, and sank beneath the waves.

The little mermaid drew back the crimson curtain of the tent and beheld the fair bride, whose head was resting on the prince's breast. She bent down and kissed his noble brow, then looked at the sky, on which the rosy dawn grew brighter and brighter. She glanced at the sharp knife and again fixed her eyes on the prince, who whispered the name of his bride in his dreams.

She was in his thoughts, and the knife trembled in the hand of the little mermaid—but she flung it far from her into the waves. The water turned red where it fell, and the drops that spurted up looked like blood. She cast one more lingering, half-fainting glance at the prince, then threw herself from the ship into the sea and felt her body dissolving into foam.

The sun rose above the waves, and his warm rays fell on the cold foam of the little mermaid, who did not feel as if she were dying. She saw the bright sun, and hundreds of transparent, beautiful creatures floating around her—she could see through them the white sails of the ships and the red clouds in the sky. Their speech was melodious, but could not be heard by mortal ears—just as their bodies could not be seen by mortal eyes. The little mermaid perceived that she had a body like theirs and that she continued to rise higher and higher out of the foam. "Where am I?" asked she, and her voice sounded ethereal, like the voices of those who were with her. No earthly music could imitate it.

"Among the daughters of the air," answered one of them. "A mermaid has not an immortal soul, nor can she obtain one unless she wins the love of a human being. On the will of another hangs her eternal destiny. But the daughters of the air, although they do not possess an immortal soul, can, by their good deeds, procure one for themselves. We fly to warm countries and cool the sultry air that destroys mankind with the pestilence. We carry the perfume of the flowers to spread health and restoration.

"After we have striven for three hundred years to do all the good in our power, we receive an immortal soul and take part in the happiness of mankind. You, poor little mermaid, have tried with your whole heart to do as we are doing. You have suffered and endured, and raised yourself to the spirit world by your good deeds, and now, by striving for three hundred years in the same way, you may obtain an immortal soul."

The little mermaid lifted her glorified eyes toward the sun and, for the first time, felt them filling with tears.

On the ship in which she had left the prince there were life and noise, and she saw him and his beautiful bride searching for her. Sorrowfully they gazed at the pearly foam, as if they knew she had thrown herself into the waves. Unseen she kissed the forehead of the bride and fanned the prince, and then mounted with the other children of the air to a rosy cloud that floated above.

"After three hundred years, thus shall we float into the kingdom of heaven," said she. "And we may even get there sooner," whispered one of her companions. "Unseen we can enter the houses of men where there are children, and for every day on which we find a good child that is the joy of his parents and deserves their love, our time of probation is shortened. The child does not know, when we fly through the room, that we smile with joy at his good conduct—for we can count one year less of our three hundred years. But when we see a naughty or a wicked child we shed tears of sorrow, and for every tear a day is added to our time of trial."

HANSEL & GRETEL

Text by Jacob and Wilhelm Grimm, from *Kinder-und Hausmärchen*, translated by Edgar Taylor and Marian Edwardes, retrieved from the Project Gutenberg ebook *Grimms' Fairy Tales*

Hard by a great forest dwelt a poor woodcutter with his wife and his two children. The boy was called Hansel and the girl Gretel. He had little to bite and to break, and once when great dearth fell on the land, he could no longer procure even daily bread. Now when he thought over this by night in his bed, and tossed about in his anxiety, he groaned and said to his wife: "What is to become of us? How are we to feed our poor children, when we no longer have anything even for ourselves?" "I'll tell you what, husband," answered the woman, "early tomorrow morning we will take the children out into the forest to where it is the thickest; there we will light a fire for them, and give each of them one more piece of bread, and then we will go to our work and leave them alone. They will not find the way home again, and we shall be rid of them." "No, wife," said the man, "I will not do that; how can I bear to leave my children alone in the forest?—the wild animals would soon come and tear them to pieces." "Oh, you fool!" said she. "Then we must all four die of hunger, you may as well plane the planks for our coffins," and she left him no peace until he consented. "But I feel very sorry for the poor children, all the same," said the man.

The two children had also not been able to sleep for hunger, and had heard what their stepmother had said to their father. Gretel wept bitter tears, and said to Hansel: "Now all is over with us." "Be quiet, Gretel," said Hansel, "do not distress yourself, I will soon find a way to help us." And when the old folks had fallen asleep, he got up, put on his little coat, opened the door below, and crept outside. The moon shone brightly, and the white pebbles which lay in front of the house glittered like real silver pennies. Hansel stooped and stuffed the little pocket of his coat with as many as he could get in. Then he went back and said to Gretel: "Be comforted, dear little sister, and sleep in peace, God will not forsake us," and he lay down again in his bed. When day dawned, but before the sun had risen, the woman came and awoke the two children, saying: "Get up, you sluggards! We are going into the forest to fetch wood." She gave each a little piece of bread, and said: "There is something for your dinner, but do not eat it up before then, for you will get nothing else." Gretel took the bread under her apron, as Hansel had the pebbles in his pocket. Then they all set out together on the way to the forest. When they had walked a short time, Hansel stood still and peeped back at the house, and did so again and again. His father said: "Hansel, what are you looking at there and staying behind for? Pay attention, and do not forget how to use your legs." "Ah, Father," said Hansel, "I am looking at my little white cat, which is sitting up on the roof, and wants to say goodbye to me." The wife said: "Fool, that is not your little cat, that is the morning sun which is shining on the chimneys." Hansel, however, had not been looking back at the cat, but had been constantly throwing one of the white pebble-stones out of his pocket on the road.

When they had reached the middle of the forest, the father

said: "Now, children, pile up some wood, and I will light a fire that you may not be cold." Hansel and Gretel gathered brushwood together, as high as a little hill. The brushwood was lighted, and when the flames were burning very high, the woman said: "Now, children, lay yourselves down by the fire and rest. We will go into the forest and cut some wood. When we have done, we will come back and fetch you away."

Hansel and Gretel sat by the fire, and when noon came, each ate a little piece of bread, and as they heard the strokes of the wood-axe they believed that their father was near. It was not the axe, however, but a branch which he had fastened to a withered tree which the wind was blowing backwards and forwards. And as they had been sitting such a long time, their eyes closed with fatigue, and they fell fast asleep. When at last they awoke, it was already dark night. Gretel began to cry and said: "How are we to get out of the forest now?" But Hansel comforted her and said: "Just wait a little, until the moon has risen, and then we will soon find the way." And when the full moon had risen, Hansel took his little sister by the hand, and followed the pebbles which shone like newly coined silver pieces, and showed them the way.

They walked the whole night long, and by break of day came once more to their father's house. They knocked at the door, and when the woman opened it and saw that it was Hansel and Gretel, she said: "You naughty children, why have you slept so long in the forest? We thought you were never coming back at all!" The father, however, rejoiced, for it had cut him to the heart to leave them behind alone.

Not long afterwards, there was once more great dearth throughout the land, and the children heard their mother saying at night to their father: "Everything is eaten again, we have one half loaf left, and that is the end. The children must go, we will take them farther into the wood, so that they will not find their way out again; there is no other means of saving ourselves!" The man's heart was heavy, and he thought: "It would be better for you to share the last mouthful with your children." The woman, however, would listen to nothing that he had to say, but scolded and reproached him. He who says A must say B, likewise, and as he had yielded the first time, he had to do so a second time also.

The children, however, were still awake and had heard the conversation. When the old folks were asleep, Hansel again got up, and wanted to go out and pick up pebbles as he had done before, but the woman had locked the door, and Hansel could not get out. Nevertheless he comforted his little sister, and said: "Do not cry, Gretel, go to sleep quietly, the good God will help us."

Early in the morning came the woman, and took the children out of their beds. Their piece of bread was given to them, but it was still smaller than the time before. On the way into the forest Hansel crumbled his in his pocket, and often stood still and threw a morsel on the ground. "Hansel, why do you stop and look round?" said the father. "Go on." "I am looking back at my little pigeon which is sitting on the roof, and wants to say goodbye to me," answered Hansel. "Fool!" said the woman. "That is not your little pigeon, that is the morning sun that is shining on the chimney." Hansel, however, little by little, threw all the crumbs on the path.

The woman led the children still deeper into the forest, where they had never in their lives been before. Then a great fire was again made, and the mother said: "Just sit there, you children, and when you are tired you may sleep a little; we are going into the forest to cut wood, and in the evening when we are done, we will come and fetch you away." When it was noon, Gretel shared her piece of bread with Hansel, who had scattered his by the way. Then they fell asleep and evening passed, but no one came to the poor children. They did not awake until it was dark night, and Hansel comforted his little sister and said: "Just wait, Gretel, until the moon rises, and then we shall see the crumbs of bread which I have strewn about, they will show us our way home again." When the moon came they set out, but they found no crumbs, for the many thousands of birds which fly about in the woods and fields had picked them all up. Hansel said to Gretel: "We shall soon find the way," but they did not find it. They walked the whole night and all the next day too from morning till evening, but they did not get out of the forest, and were very hungry, for they had nothing to eat but two or three berries, which grew on the ground. And as they were so weary that their legs would carry them no longer, they lay down beneath a tree and fell asleep.

It was now three mornings since they had left their father's house. They began to walk again, but they always came deeper into the forest, and if help did not come soon, they must die of hunger and weariness. When it was midday, they saw a beautiful snow-white bird sitting on a bough, which sang so delightfully that they stood still and listened to it. And when its song was over, it spread its wings and flew away before them, and they followed it until they reached a little house, on the roof of which it alighted; and when they approached the little house they saw that it was built of bread and covered with cakes, but that the windows were of clear sugar. "We will set to work on that," said Hansel, "and have a good meal. I will eat a bit of the roof, and you, Gretel, can eat some of the window, it will taste sweet." Hansel reached up above, and broke off a little of the roof to try how it tasted, and Gretel leaned against the window and nibbled at the panes. Then a soft voice cried from the parlor:

"Nibble, nibble, gnaw,
Who is nibbling at my little house?"

The children answered:

"The wind, the wind,
The heaven-born wind,"

and went on eating without disturbing themselves. Hansel, who liked the taste of the roof, tore down a great piece of it, and Gretel pushed out the whole of one round window-pane, sat down, and enjoyed herself with it. Suddenly the door opened, and a woman as old as the hills, who supported herself on crutches, came creeping out. Hansel and Gretel were so terribly frightened that they let fall what they had in their hands. The old woman, however, nodded her head, and said: "Oh, you dear children, who has brought you here? Do come in, and stay with me. No harm shall happen to you." She took them both by the hand, and led them into her little house. Then good food was set before them, milk and pancakes, with sugar, apples, and nuts. Afterward two pretty little beds were covered with clean white linen, and Hansel and Gretel lay down in them, and thought they were in heaven.

The old woman had only pretended to be so kind; she was in reality a wicked witch, who lay in wait for children, and had only built the little house of bread in order to entice them there. When a child fell into her power, she killed it, cooked and ate it, and that was a feast day with her. Witches have red eyes, and cannot see far, but they have a keen scent like the beasts, and are aware when human beings draw near. When Hansel and Gretel came into her neighborhood, she laughed with malice, and said mockingly: "I have them, they shall not escape me again!" Early in the morning before the children were awake, she was already up, and when she saw both of them sleeping and looking so pretty, with their plump and rosy cheeks, she muttered to herself: "That will be a dainty mouthful!" Then she seized Hansel with her shriveled hand, carried him into a little stable, and locked him in behind a grated door. Scream as he might, it would not help him. Then she went to Gretel, shook her till she awoke, and cried: "Get up, lazy thing, fetch some water, and cook something good for your brother, he is in the stable outside, and is to be made fat. When he is fat, I will eat him." Gretel began to weep bitterly, but it was all in vain, for she was forced to do what the wicked witch commanded.

And now the best food was cooked for poor Hansel, but Gretel got nothing but crab-shells. Every morning the woman crept to the little stable, and cried: "Hansel, stretch out your finger that I may feel if you will soon be fat." Hansel, however, stretched out a little bone to her, and the old woman, who had dim eyes, could not see it, and thought it was Hansel's finger, and was astonished that there was no way of fattening him. When four weeks had gone by, and Hansel still remained thin, she was seized with impatience and would not wait any longer. "Now, then, Gretel," she cried to the girl, "stir yourself, and bring some water. Let Hansel be fat or lean, tomorrow I will kill him, and cook him." Ah, how the poor little sister did lament when she had to fetch the water, and how her tears did flow down her cheeks! "Dear God, do help us," she cried. "If the wild beasts in the forest had but devoured us, we should at any rate have died together." "Just keep your noise to yourself," said the old woman, "it won't help you at all."

Early in the morning, Gretel had to go out and hang up the cauldron with the water, and light the fire. "We will bake first," said the old woman. "I have already heated the oven, and kneaded the dough." She pushed poor Gretel out to the oven, from which flames of fire were already darting. "Creep in," said the witch, "and see if it is properly heated, so that we can put the bread in." And once Gretel was inside, she intended to shut the oven and let her bake in it, and then she would eat her, too. But Gretel saw what she had in mind, and said: "I do not know how I am to do it; how do I get in?" "Silly goose," said the old woman. "The door is big enough; just look, I can get in myself!" and she crept up and thrust her head into the oven. Then Gretel gave her a push that drove her far into it, and shut the iron door, and fastened the bolt. Oh! Then she began to howl quite horribly, but Gretel ran away and the godless witch was miserably burned to death.

Gretel, however, ran like lightning to Hansel, opened his little stable, and cried: "Hansel, we are saved! The old witch is dead!" Then Hansel sprang like a bird from its cage when the door is opened. How they did rejoice and embrace each other, and dance about and kiss each other! And as they had no longer any need to fear her, they went into the witch's house, and in every corner there stood chests full of pearls and jewels. "These are far better than pebbles!" said Hansel, and thrust into his pockets whatever could be got in, and Gretel said:

"I, too, will take something home with me," and filled her pinafore full. "But now we must be off," said Hansel, "that we may get out of the witch's forest."

When they had walked for two hours, they came to a great stretch of water. "We cannot cross," said Hansel, "I see no foot-plank, and no bridge." "And there is also no ferry," answered Gretel, "but a white duck is swimming there: if I ask her, she will help us over." Then she cried:

> *"Little duck, little duck, dost thou see,*
> *Hansel and Gretel are waiting for thee?*
> *There's never a plank, or bridge in sight,*
> *Take us across on thy back so white."*

The duck came to them, and Hansel seated himself on its back, and told his sister to sit by him. "No," replied Gretel, "that will be too heavy for the little duck; she shall take us across, one after the other." The good little duck did so, and when they were once safely across and had walked for a short time, the forest seemed to be more and more familiar to them, and at length they saw from afar their father's house. Then they began to run, rushed into the parlor, and threw themselves round their father's neck. The man had not known one happy hour since he had left the children in the forest; the woman, however, was dead. Gretel emptied her pinafore until pearls and precious stones ran about the room, and Hansel threw one handful after another out of his pocket to add to them. Then all anxiety was at an end, and they lived together in perfect happiness. My tale is done, there runs a mouse; whosoever catches it, may make himself a big fur cap out of it.

THE ROBBER BRIDEGROOM

Text by Jacob and Wilhelm Grimm, from *Kinder-und Hausmärchen*, translated by Edgar Taylor and Marian Edwardes, retrieved from the Project Gutenberg ebook *Grimms' Fairy Tales*

There was once a miller who had one beautiful daughter, and as she was grown up, he was anxious that she should be well married and provided for. He said to himself, "I will give her to the first suitable man who comes and asks for her hand." Not long after a suitor appeared, and as he appeared to be very rich and the miller could see nothing in him with which to find fault, he betrothed his daughter to him. But the girl did not care for the man as a girl ought to care for her betrothed husband. She did not feel that she could trust him, and she could not look at him nor think of him without an inward shudder. One day he said to her, "You have not yet paid me a visit, although we have been betrothed for some time." "I do not know where your house is," she answered. "My house is out there in the dark forest," he said. She tried to excuse herself by saying that she would not be able to find the way thither. Her betrothed only replied, "You must come and see me next Sunday; I have already invited guests for that day, and that you may not mistake the way, I will strew ashes along the path."

When Sunday came, and it was time for the girl to start, a feeling of dread came over her which she could not explain, and that she might be able to find her path again, she filled her pockets with peas and lentils to sprinkle on the ground as she went along. On reaching the entrance to the forest she found the path strewed with ashes, and these she followed, throwing down some peas on either side of her at every step she took. She walked the whole day until she came to the deepest, darkest part of the forest. There she saw a lonely house, looking so grim and mysterious, that it did not please her at all. She stepped inside, but not a soul was to be seen, and a great silence reigned throughout. Suddenly a voice cried:

"Turn back, turn back, young maiden fair,
Linger not in this murderers' lair."

The girl looked up and saw that the voice came from a bird hanging in a cage on the wall. Again it cried:

"Turn back, turn back, young maiden fair,
Linger not in this murderers' lair."

The girl passed on, going from room to room of the house, but they were all empty, and still she saw no one. At last she came to the cellar, and there sat a very, very old woman, who could not keep her head from shaking. "Can you tell me," asked the girl, "if my betrothed husband lives here?"

"Ah, you poor child," answered the old woman, "what a place for you to come to! This is a murderers' den. You think yourself a promised bride, and that your marriage will soon take place, but it is with death that you will keep your marriage feast. Look, do you see that large cauldron of water which I am obliged to keep on the fire! As soon as they have you in their power they will kill you without mercy, and cook and eat you, for they are eaters of men. If I did not take pity on you and save you, you would be lost."

Thereupon the old woman led her behind a large cask, which quite hid her from view. "Keep as still as a mouse," she said; "do not move or speak, or it will be all over with you. Tonight, when the robbers are all asleep, we will flee together. I have long been waiting for an opportunity to escape."

The words were hardly out of her mouth when the godless crew returned, dragging another young girl along with them. They were all drunk, and paid no heed to her cries and lamentations. They gave her wine to drink, three glasses full, one of white wine, one of red, and one of yellow, and with that her heart gave way and she died. Then they tore off her dainty clothing, laid her on a table, and cut her beautiful body into pieces, and sprinkled salt upon it.

The poor betrothed girl crouched trembling and shuddering behind the cask, for she saw what a terrible fate had been intended for her by the robbers. One of them now noticed a gold ring still remaining on the little finger of the murdered girl, and as he could not draw it off easily, he took a hatchet and cut off the finger; but the finger sprang into the air, and fell behind the cask into the lap of the girl who was hiding there. The robber took a light and began looking for it, but he could not find it. "Have you looked behind the large cask?" said one of the others. But the old woman called out, "Come and eat your suppers, and let the thing be till tomorrow; the finger won't run away."

"The old woman is right," said the robbers, and they ceased looking for the finger and sat down.

The old woman then mixed a sleeping draft with their wine, and before long they were all lying on the floor of the cellar, fast asleep and snoring. As soon as the girl was assured of this, she came from behind the cask. She was obliged to step over the bodies of the sleepers, who were lying close together, and every moment she was filled with renewed dread lest she should awaken them. But God helped her, so that she passed safely over them, and then she and the old woman went upstairs, opened the door, and hastened as fast as they could from the murderers' den. They found the ashes scattered by the wind, but the peas and lentils had sprouted, and grown sufficiently above the ground, to guide them in the moonlight along the path. All night long they walked, and it was morning before they reached the mill. Then the girl told her father all that had happened.

The day came that had been fixed for the marriage. The bridegroom arrived and also a large company of guests, for the miller had taken care to invite all his friends and relations. As they sat at the feast, each guest in turn was asked to tell a tale; the bride sat still and did not say a word.

"And you, my love," said the bridegroom, turning to her, "is there no tale you know? Tell us something."

"I will tell you a dream, then," said the bride. "I went alone through a forest and came at last to a house; not a soul could I find within, but a bird that was hanging in a cage on the wall cried:

'Turn back, turn back, young maiden fair,
Linger not in this murderers' lair.'

"And again a second time it said these words."

"My darling, this is only a dream."

"I went on through the house from room to room, but they were all empty, and everything was so grim and mysterious. At last I went down to the cellar, and there sat a very, very old woman, who could not keep her head still. I asked her if my betrothed lived here, and she answered, 'Ah, you poor child, you are come to a murderers' den; your betrothed does indeed live here, but he will kill you without mercy and afterwards cook and eat you.'"

"My darling, this is only a dream."

"The old woman hid me behind a large cask, and scarcely had she done this when the robbers returned home, dragging a young girl along with them. They gave her three kinds of wine to drink, white, red, and yellow, and with that she died."

"My darling, this is only a dream."

"Then they tore off her dainty clothing, and cut her beautiful body into pieces and sprinkled salt upon it."

"My darling, this is only a dream."

"And one of the robbers saw that there was a gold ring still left on her finger, and as it was difficult to draw off, he took a hatchet and cut off her finger; but the finger sprang into the air and fell behind the great cask into my lap. And here is the finger with the ring." And with these words the bride drew forth the finger and showed it to the assembled guests.

The bridegroom, who during this recital had grown deadly pale, up and tried to escape, but the guests seized him and held him fast. They delivered him up to justice, and he and all his murderous band were condemned to death for their wicked deeds.

ABOUT
THE ORIGINAL AUTHORS

HANS CHRISTIAN ANDERSEN (B. 1805) was a Danish author best known for his fairy tales, though he did write many other types of work. He was born into a poor family but was uplifted by the director of the Royal Theatre in Copenhagen, who financed his schooling, and in 1828 he was admitted to the University of Copenhagen. Almost immediately, he began producing literary and theatrical work, and published his first book of fairy tales, entitled *Eventyr, fortalte for børn*, in 1835. He continued publishing for decades, even while struggling in his personal relationships, and spent the earlier years of the 1870s traveling around the world. He died in Copenhagen in 1875.

JACOB (B. 1785) AND WILHELM (B. 1786) GRIMM were German scholars of folklore, mythology, and oral tradition who are credited with the popularization of many well-known fairy tales. Though both brothers went to law school at the University of Marburg, various influences and circumstances led them away from civil service and toward an interest in literary research. In 1812, they published the first volume of *Kinder-und Hausmärchen*, or *Children and Household Tales*, though it's been colloquially known as *Grimms' Fairy Tales*. The second volume came two years later, and new editions continued to publish throughout their lifetime. In addition to these books, they published a considerable amount of work in the areas of linguistic, mythology, folklore, and medieval studies. They became librarians and professors, retiring in the mid-nineteenth century to focus on their own work. They died four years apart, Wilhelm in 1859 followed by Jacob in 1863.

CHARLES PERRAULT (B. 1628) was a French author, poet, and leading member of the Académie Française, to which he was elected in 1671. He initially worked as an official in charge of royal buildings but became well known in the literary world and was a controversial figure for his admiration of modern writers over ancient ones. Inspired by his children and newly unemployed, he began writing his famous volume of fairy tales in 1695, which was published two years later as *Contes de ma mère l'oye* (*Tales of Mother Goose*). He died in Paris in 1703.